PRAISE FOR

SUPER SONS

RECEIVED
APR - - 2019
BY

"As the breathtaking action unfolds, the mysteries pile up—and there is danger on every page. My kind of story! I want to see more, more, MORE!"
—**R.L. STINE,** AUTHOR OF *GOOSEBUMPS* AND *FEAR STREET*

"Precocious, poignant, and powerful! I hope you packed a lunch, because you're not gonna want to put this book down."
—**JOEY BRAGG,** STAR OF *LIV AND MADDIE*

"This all-new SUPER SONS is a surefire, fun read as four young strangers meet and band together against the looming backdrop of global doom."
—**DAN JURGENS,** AUTHOR OF THE *ADVENTURES OF SUPERMAN* AND *BATMAN BEYOND*

"A super-fun, super-exciting, and most of all *super*-story!"
—**PETER J. TOMASI,** AUTHOR, *SUPER SONS,* *BATMAN: DETECTIVE COMICS, SUPERMAN*

D0004055

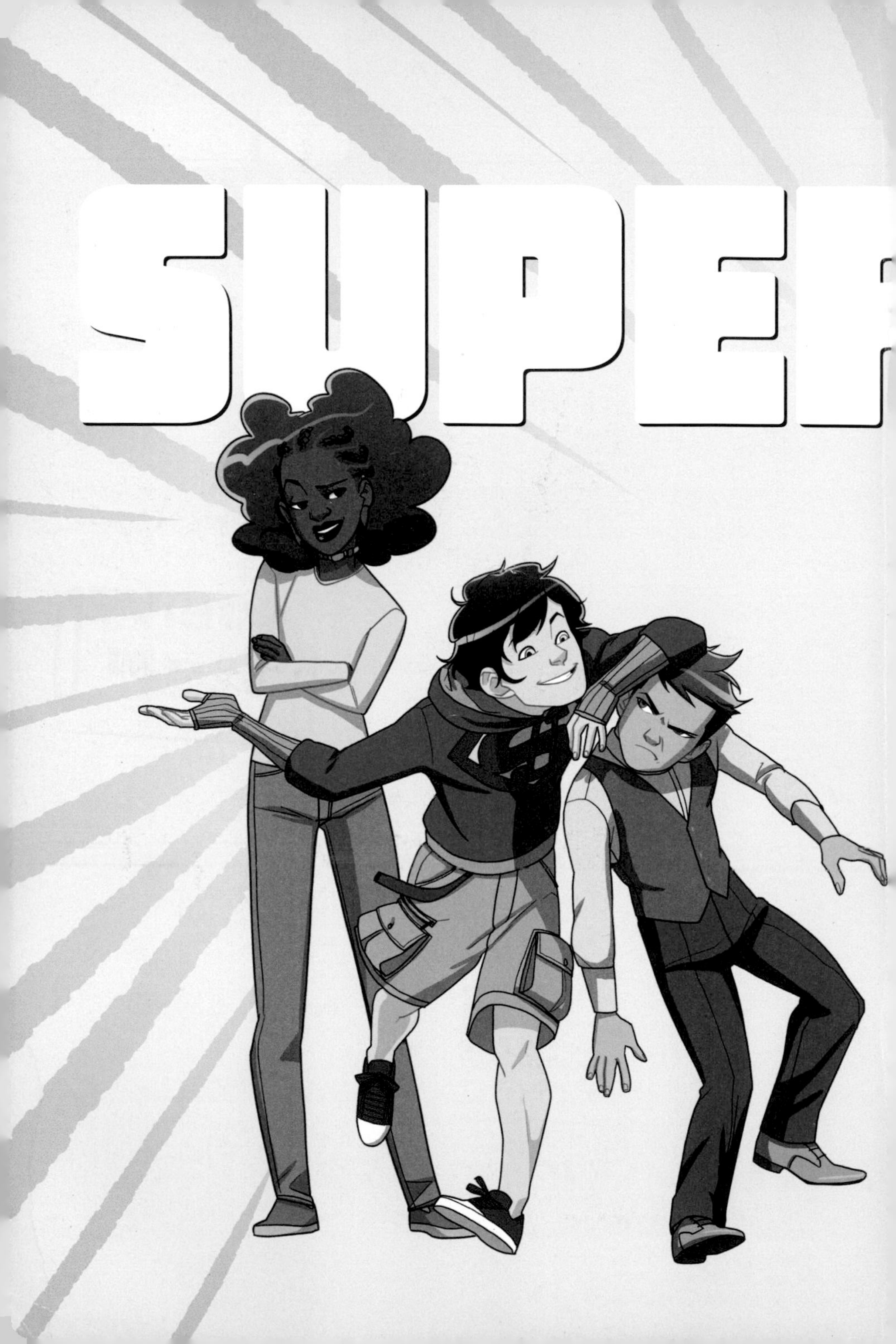
SUPEF

R SONS

BOOK 1
THE POLARSHIELD PROJECT

WRITTEN BY
Ridley Pearson

ART BY
Ile Gonzalez

Letterer: Saida Temofonte

SUPERMAN created by JERRY SIEGEL and JOE SHUSTER
SUPERBOY created by JERRY SIEGEL
By special arrangement with the JERRY SIEGEL family

BEN ABERNATHY &
MICHELE R. WELLS Editors

STEVE COOK Design Director - Books

AMIE BROCKWAY-METCALF Publication Design

BOB HARRAS Senior VP - Editor-in-Chief, DC Comics

BOBBIE CHASE VP & Executive Editor, Young Reader & Talent Development

DAN DiDIO Publisher

JIM LEE Publisher & Chief Creative Officer

AMIT DESAI Executive VP - Business & Marketing Strategy
Direct to Consumer & Global Franchise Management

MARK CHIARELLO Senior VP - Art, Design & Collected Editions

JOHN CUNNINGHAM Senior VP - Sales & Trade Marketing

BRIAR DARDEN VP - Business Affairs

ANNE DePIES Senior VP - Business Strategy, Finance & Administration

DON FALLETTI VP - Manufacturing Operations

LAWRENCE GANEM VP - Editorial Administration & Talent Relations

ALISON GILL Senior VP - Manufacturing & Operations

JASON GREENBERG VP - Business Strategy & Finance

HANK KANALZ Senior VP - Editorial Strategy & Administration

JAY KOGAN Senior VP - Legal Affairs

NICK J. NAPOLITANO VP - Manufacturing Administration

LISETTE OSTERLOH VP - Digital Marketing & Events

EDDIE SCANNELL VP - Consumer Marketing

COURTNEY SIMMONS Senior VP - Publicity & Communications

JIM (SKI) SOKOLOWSKI VP - Comic Book Specialty Sales & Trade Marketing

NANCY SPEARS VP - Mass, Book, Digital Sales & Trade Marketing

Super Sons logo designed by RIAN HUGHES

Super Sons v.1: The Polarshield Project

Published by DC Comics. Copyright © 2019 DC Comics. All Rights Reserved. All Rights Reserved. All characters, their distinctive likenesses and related elements featured in this publication are trademarks of DC Comics. DC ZOOM is a trademark of DC Comics. The stories, characters and incidents featured in this publication are entirely fictional. DC Comics does not read or accept unsolicited submissions of ideas, stories or artwork.

DC Comics, 2900 West Alameda Ave., Burbank, CA 91505

Printed by LSC Communications, Crawfordsville, IN, USA. 2/22/19. First Printing.

ISBN: 978-1-4012-8639-2

PEFC Certified

This product is from sustainably managed forests and controlled sources

PEFC/29-31-337   www.pefc.org

Library of Congress Cataloging-in-Publication Data

Names: Pearson, Ridley, writer. | Gonzales, Ile, artist. | Temofonte, Saida, letterer.
Title: Super Sons : the Polarshield project / written by Ridley Pearson ; art by Ile Gonzales ; lettered by Saida Temofonte.
Other titles: Polarshield project
Description: Burbank, CA : DC Zoom, [2019] | Summary: "The polar ice caps have nearly melted away, causing devastation to coastal cities. Jon Kent and Damian "Ian" Wayne are opposite in every way except one--they are the sons of the World's Greatest Heroes! To uncover a global conspiracy, this unlikely dynamic duo will need to learn to trust each other and work together to save the Earth."-- Provided by publisher.
Identifiers: LCCN 2018043959 | ISBN 9781401286392 (paperback)
Subjects: LCSH: Graphic novels. | CYAC: Graphic novels. | Superheroes--Fiction. | BISAC: JUVENILE FICTION / Comics & Graphic Novels / Superheroes.
Classification: LCC PZ7.7.P36 S87 2019 | DDC 741.5/973--dc23

dear reader,

Like my characters, I come from a different world. The DC Comics Universe was new to me when I was asked to write SUPER SONS. DC Comics was good enough to encourage me to write my version of the sons of Batman and Superman.

For those familiar with these characters, you will meet a different Jonathan Kent and Damian Wayne in these pages. You will also meet a young woman named Candace who is a long way from home. Her past will soon catch up with her.

This is a story about fathers and sons, mothers and daughters. Friends. Enemies. Competitors. School. Adventure. They are in a world of climate change, flooding, and global disaster. In these stories our characters will literally "sink or swim."

Most of all, they will explore themselves, their families, their enemies, and a world I've built for them to live in. Welcome to the country of Coleumbria. The continent of Landis. The destruction of Metropolis. A world of strange powers. The world of the Super Sons. My world. And now one I'm sharing with you. Come along with me for a wild ride!

ridley pearson

SUPER SONS

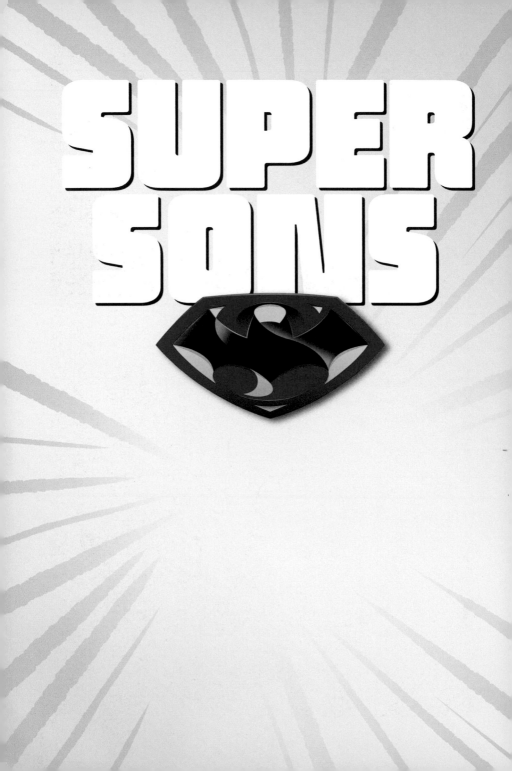

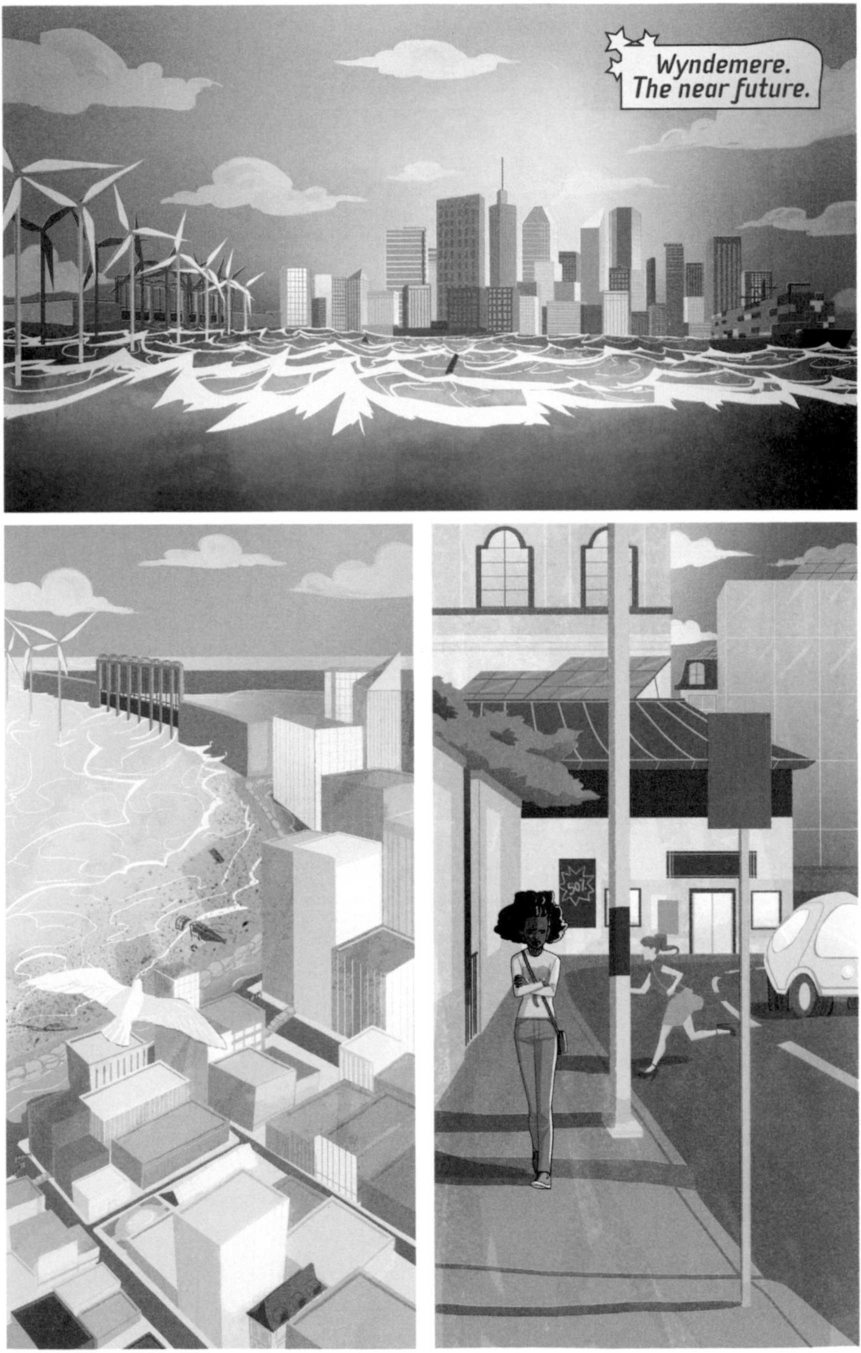
Wyndemere.
The near future.

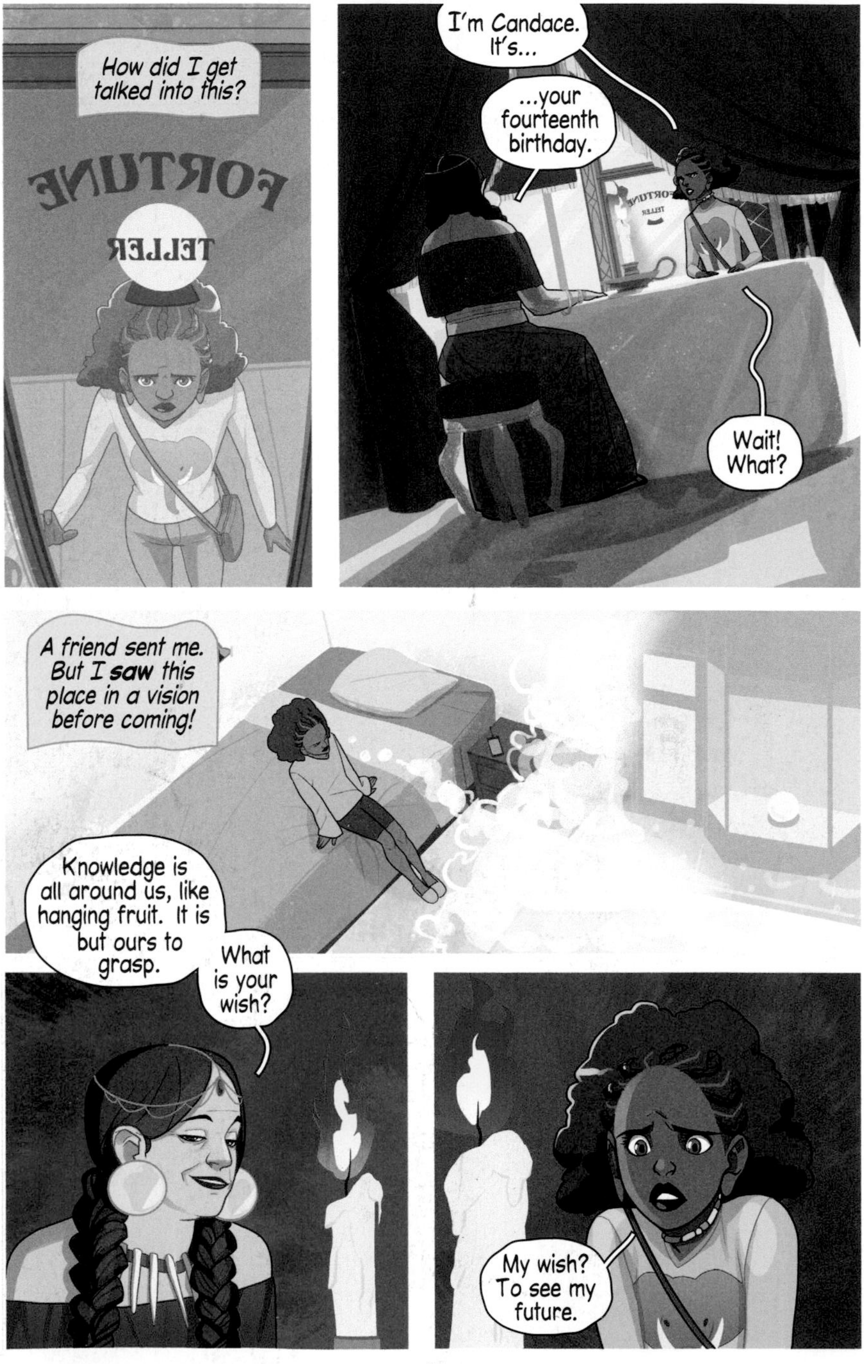
How did I get talked into this?
FORTUNE
TELLER
I'm Candace. It's...
...your fourteenth birthday.
Wait! What?
A friend sent me. But I **saw** this place in a vision before coming!
Knowledge is all around us, like hanging fruit. It is but ours to grasp.
What is your wish?
My wish? To see my future.

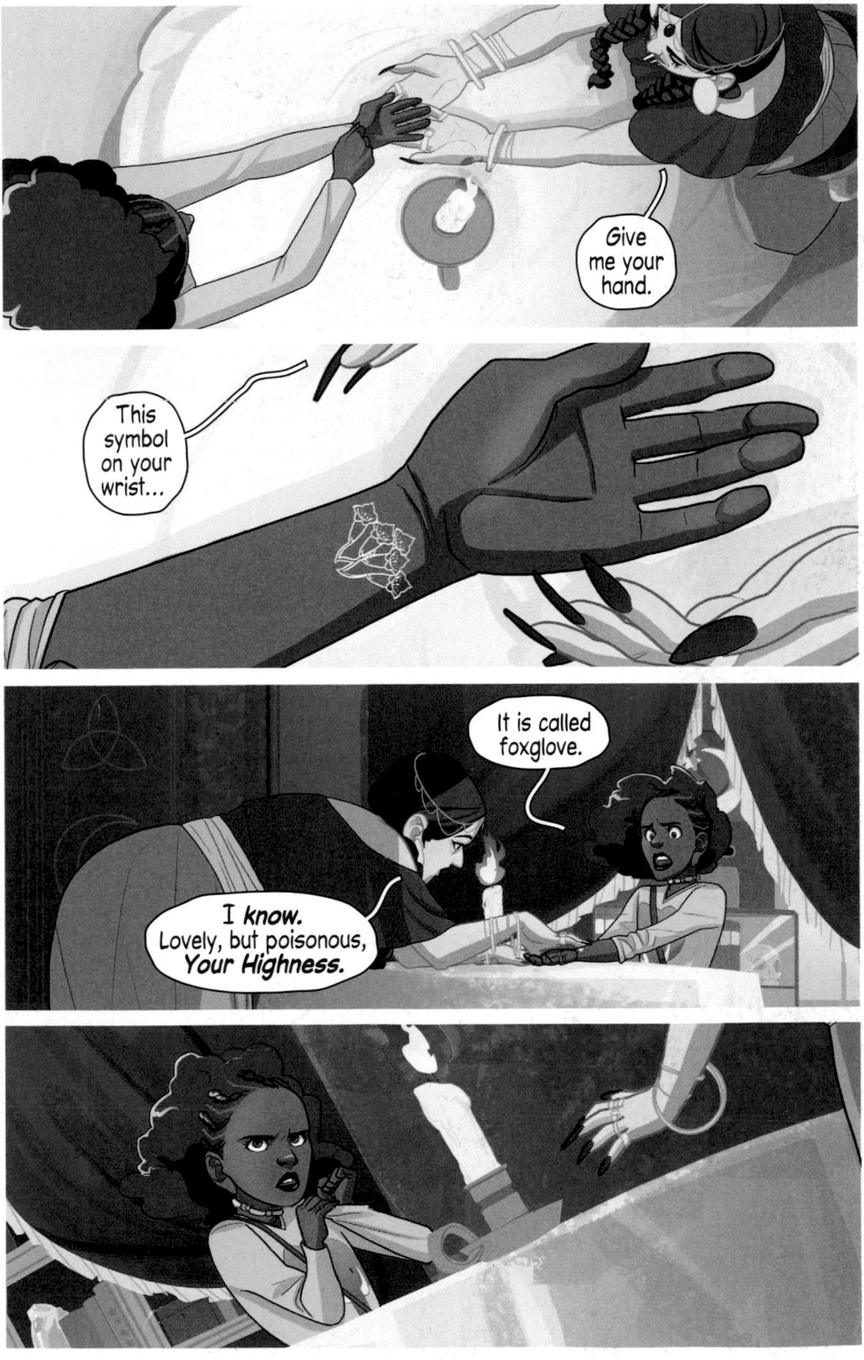
Give me your hand.
This symbol on your wrist...
It is called foxglove.
I *know.* Lovely, but poisonous, ***Your Highness.***

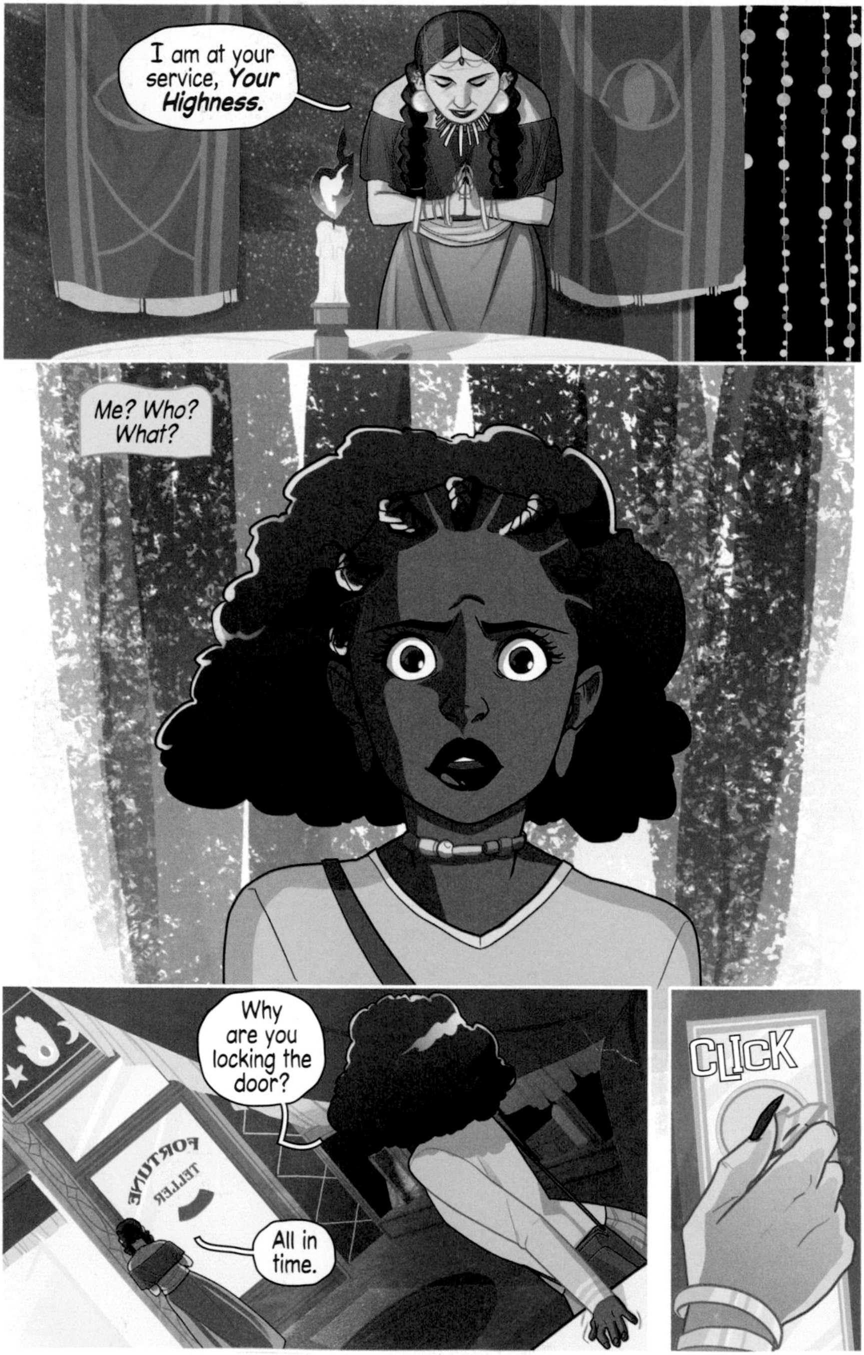

I am at your service, ***Your Highness.***
Me? Who? What?
Why are you locking the door?
FORTUNE TELLER
All in time.
CLICK

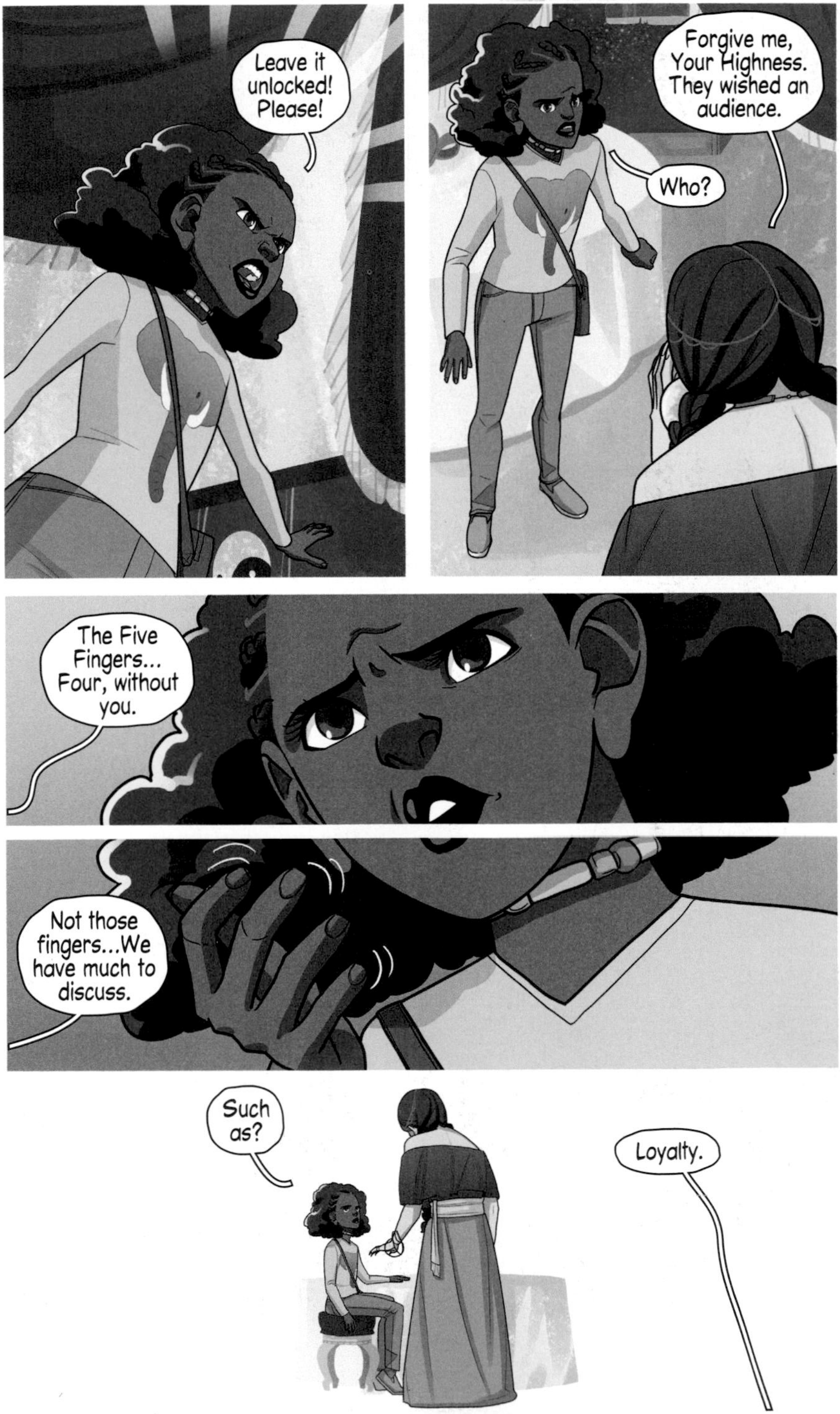
Leave it unlocked! Please!
Forgive me, Your Highness. They wished an audience.
Who?
The Five Fingers... Four, without you.
Not those fingers...We have much to discuss.
Such as?
Loyalty.

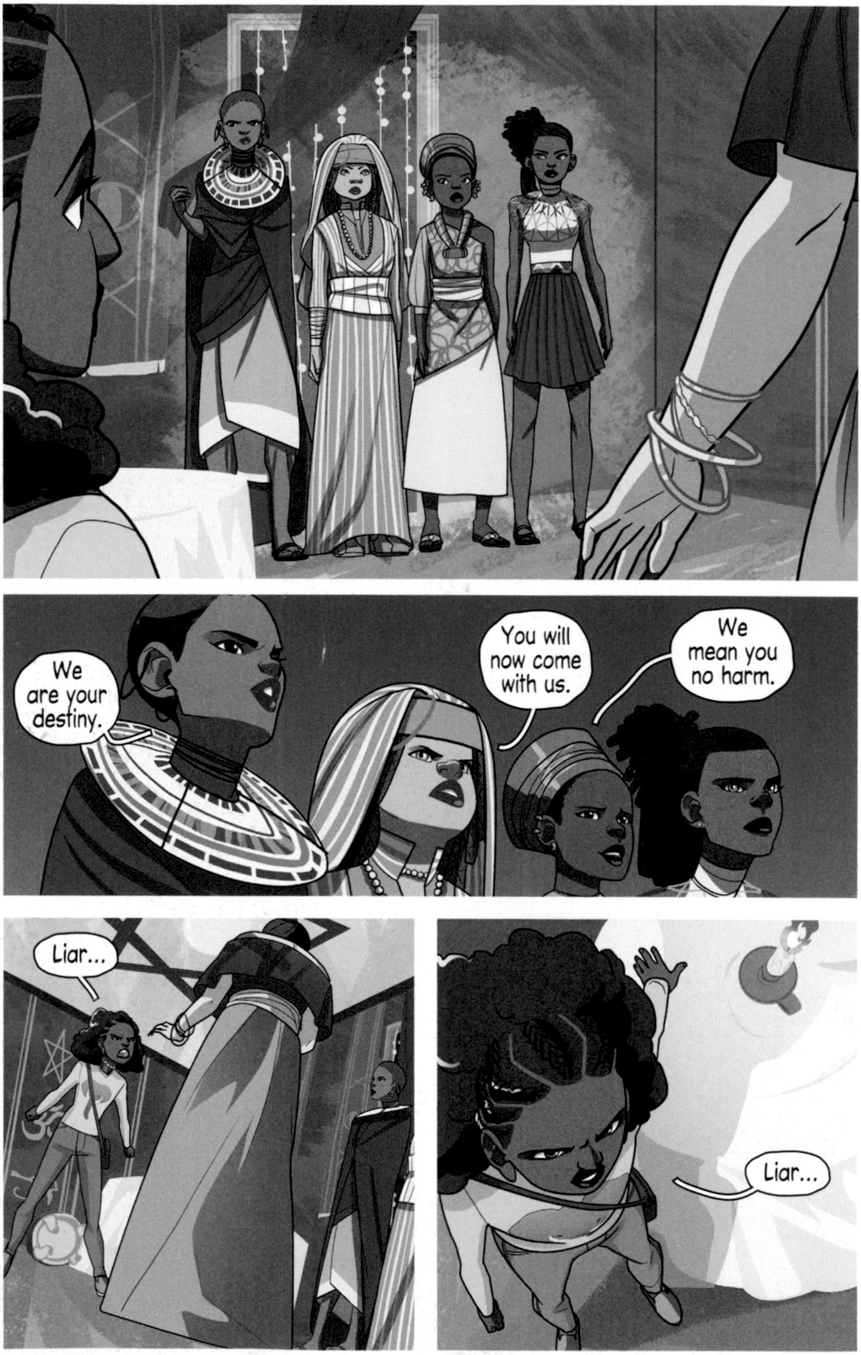

We are your destiny.
You will now come with us.
We mean you no harm.
Liar...
Liar...

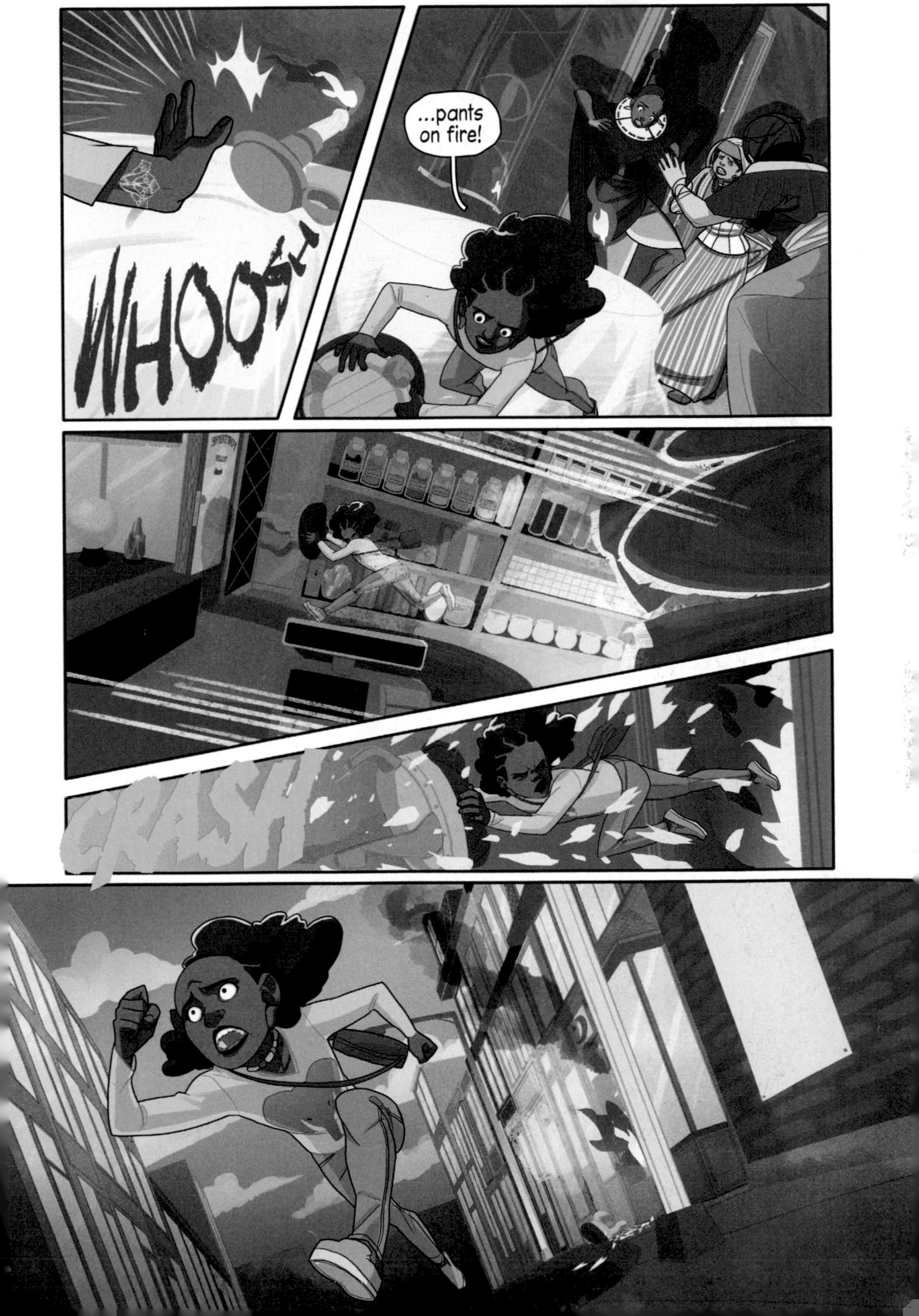
WHOOSH
...pants on fire!
CRASH

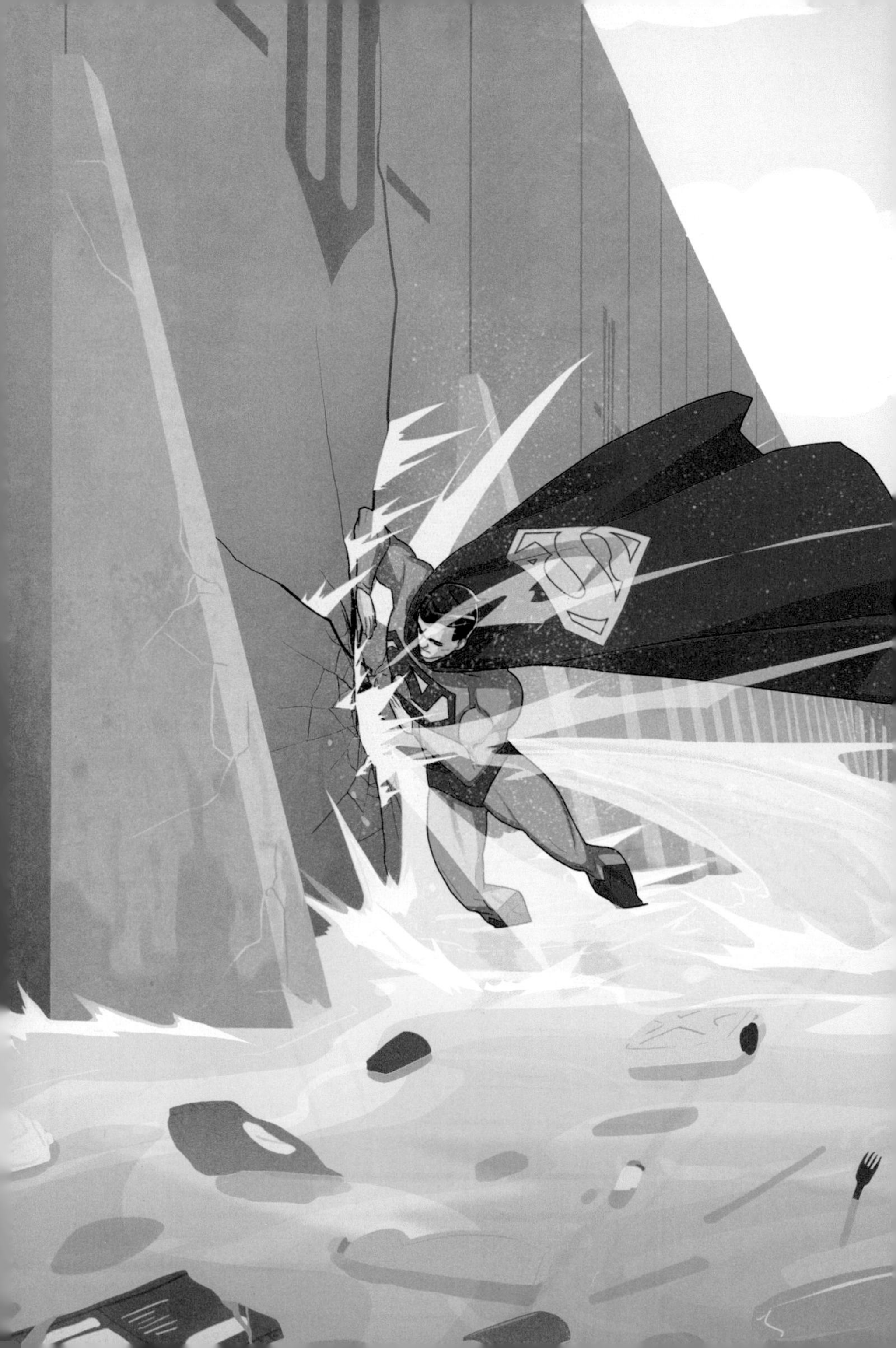

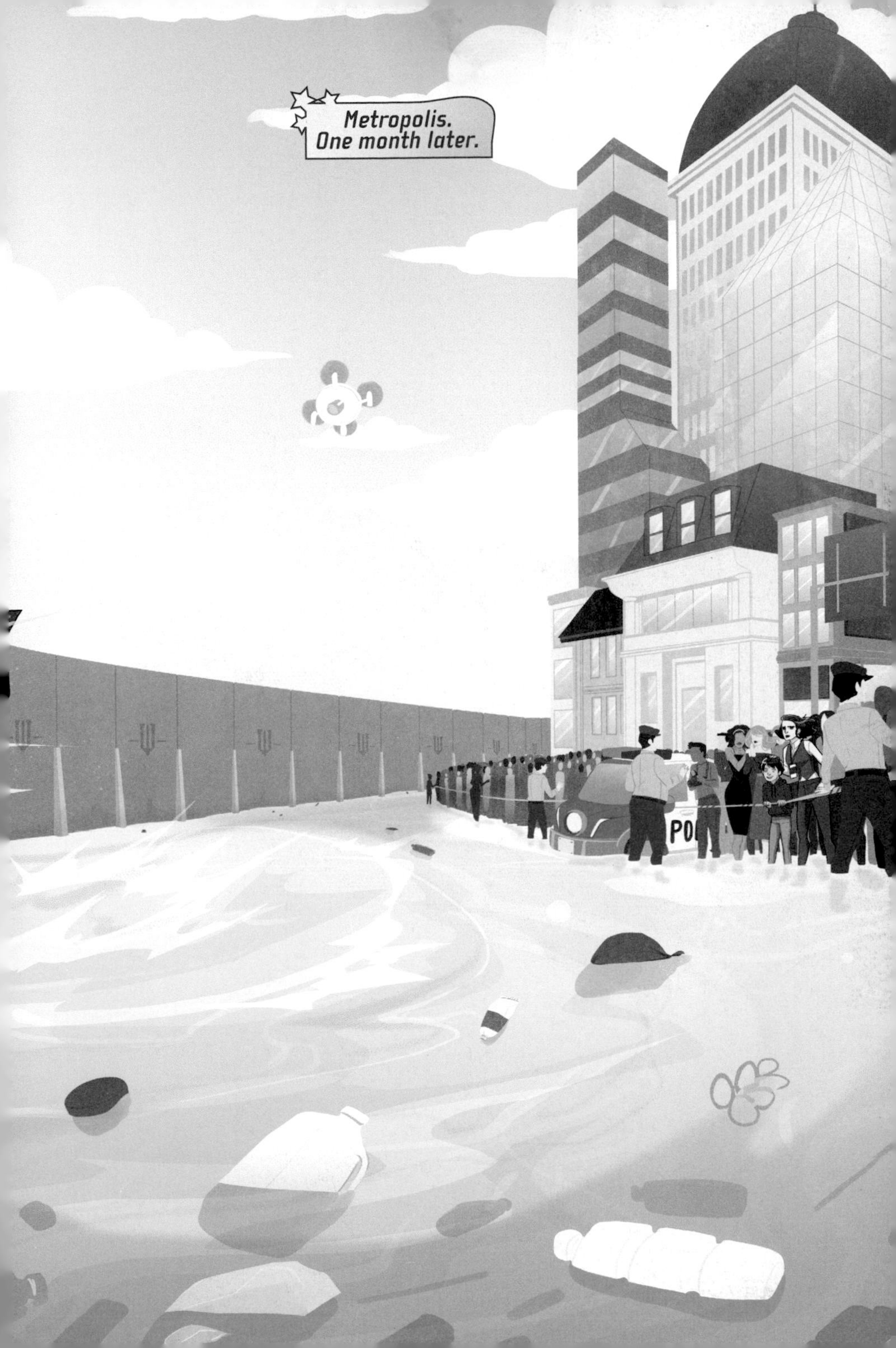
Metropolis.
One month later.
PO

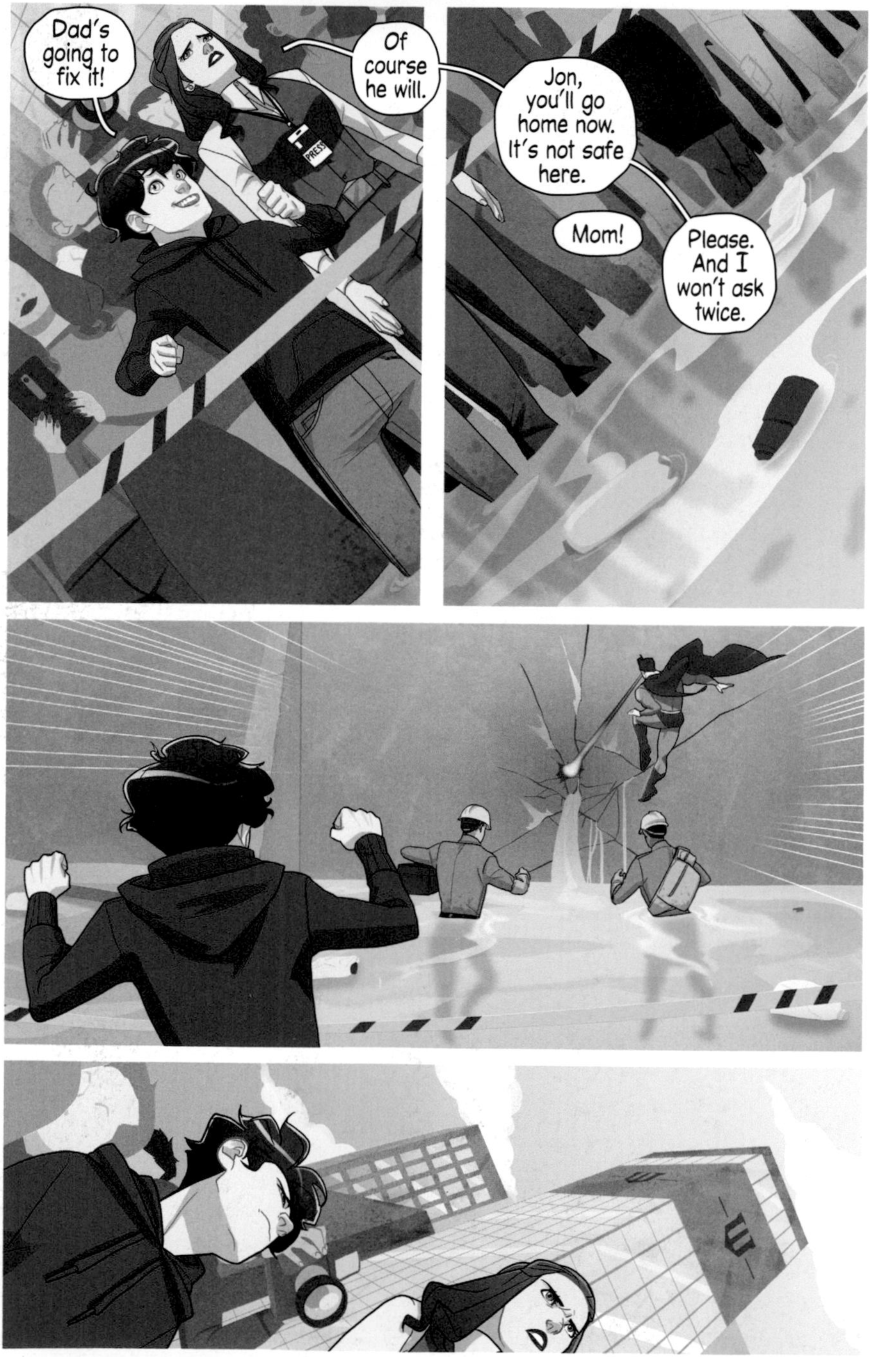

Dad's going to fix it!
Of course he will.
PRESS
Jon, you'll go home now. It's not safe here.
Mom!
Please. And I won't ask twice.

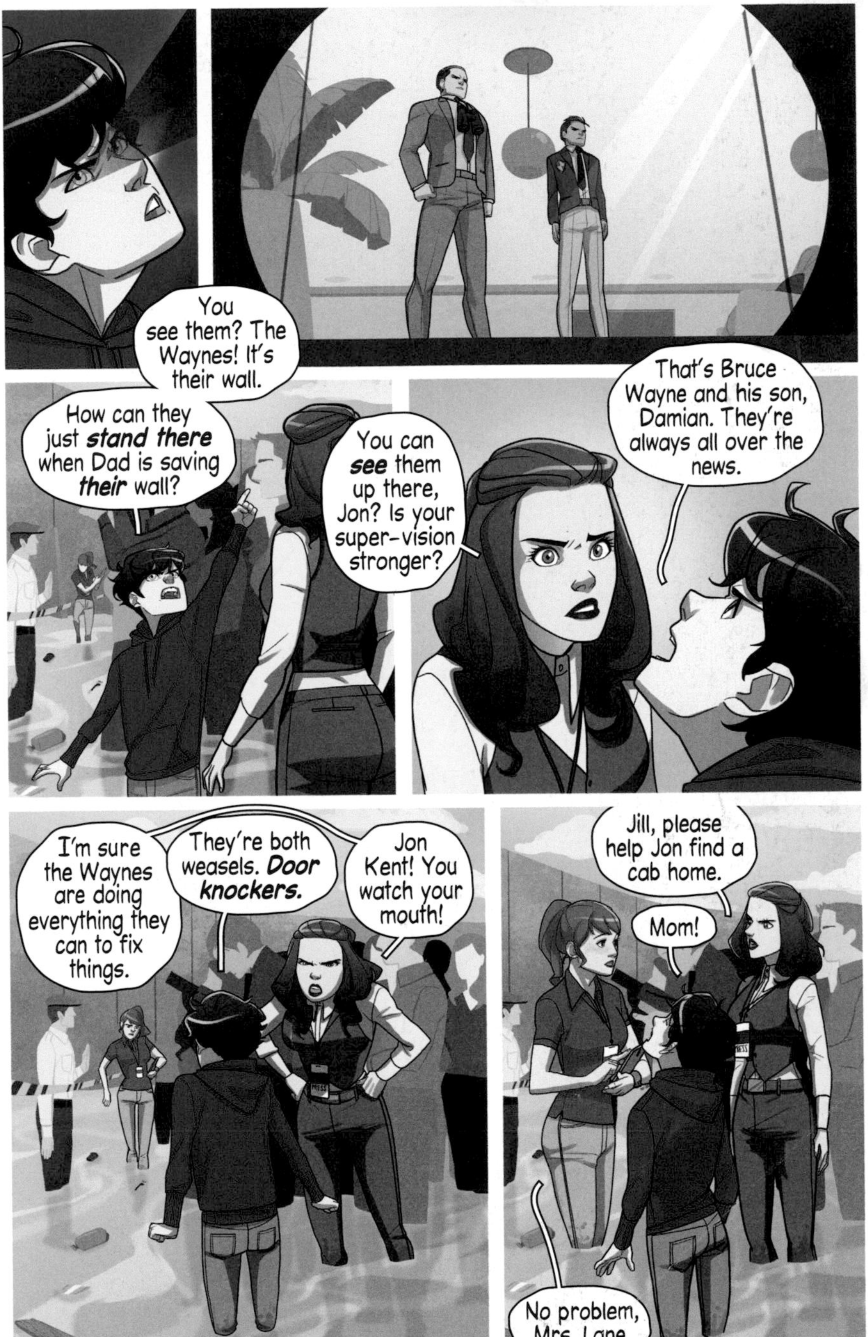
You see them? The Waynes! It's their wall.
How can they just ***stand there*** when Dad is saving ***their*** wall?
You can ***see*** them up there, Jon? Is your super-vision stronger?
That's Bruce Wayne and his son, Damian. They're always all over the news.
I'm sure the Waynes are doing everything they can to fix things.
They're both weasels. ***Door knockers.***
Jon Kent! You watch your mouth!
Jill, please help Jon find a cab home.
Mom!
No problem, Mrs. Lane.

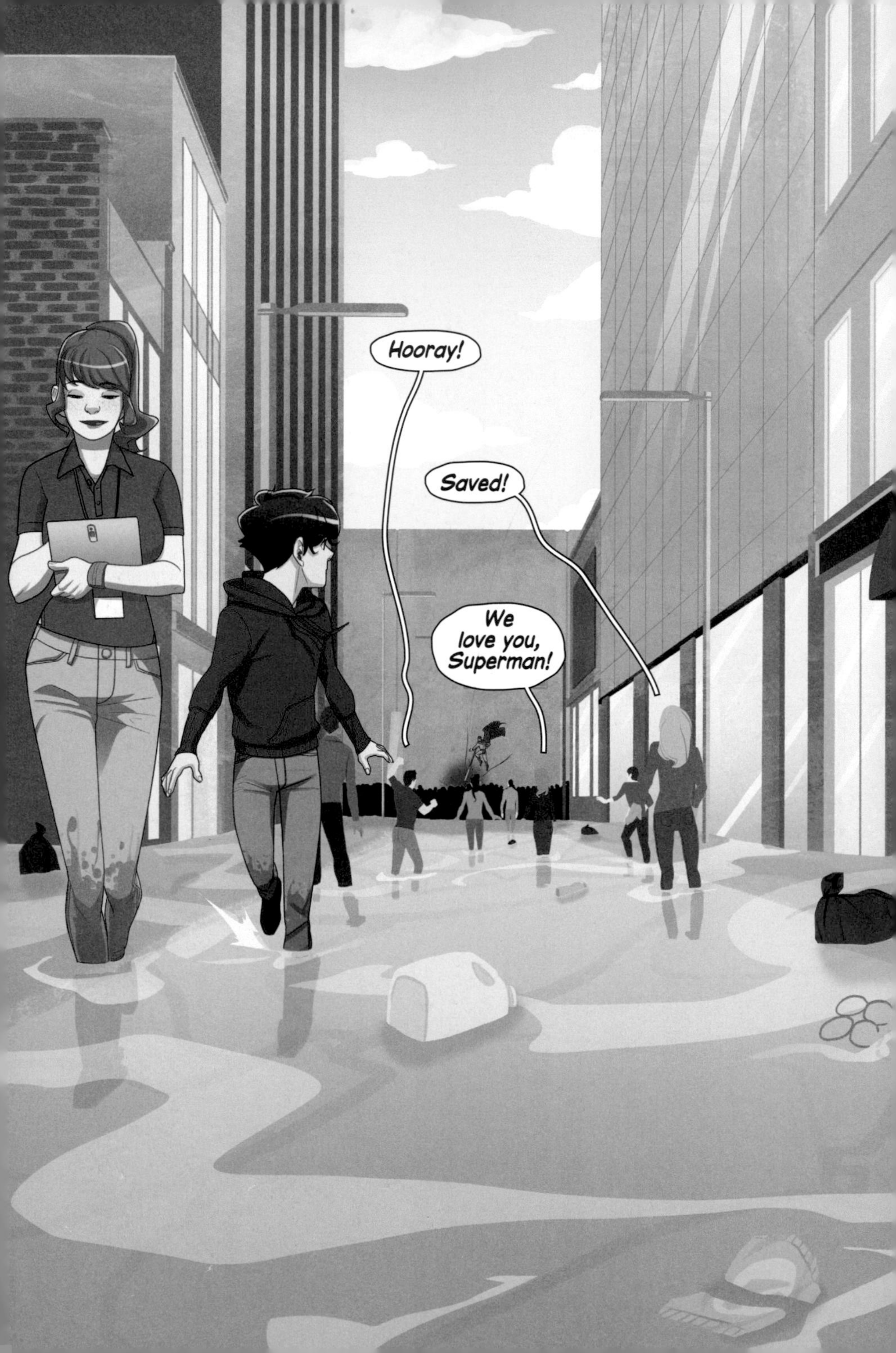
Hooray!
Saved!
We love you, Superman!

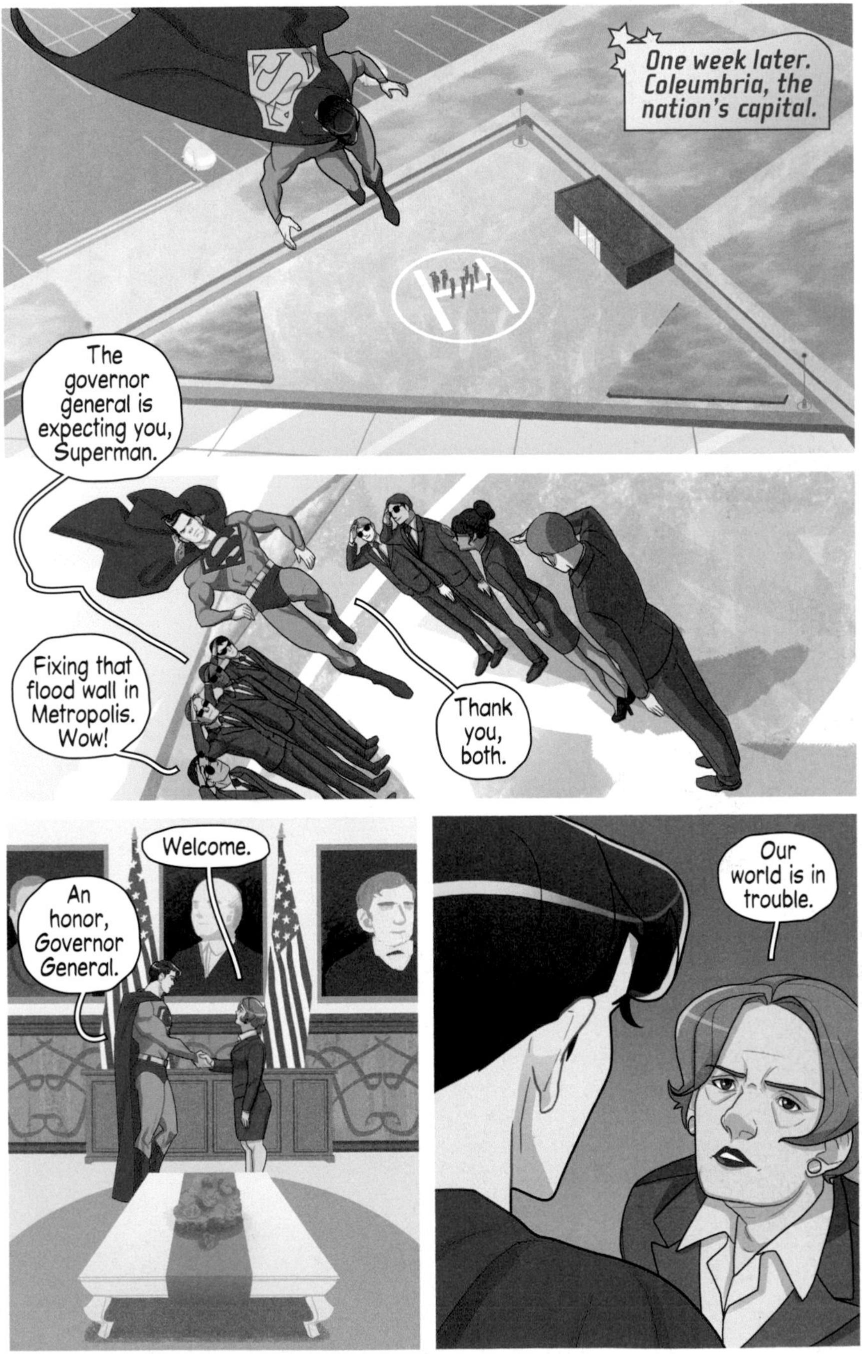
One week later. Coleumbria, the nation's capital.
The governor general is expecting you, Superman.
Fixing that flood wall in Metropolis. Wow!
Thank you, both.
Welcome.
An honor, Governor General.
Our world is in trouble.

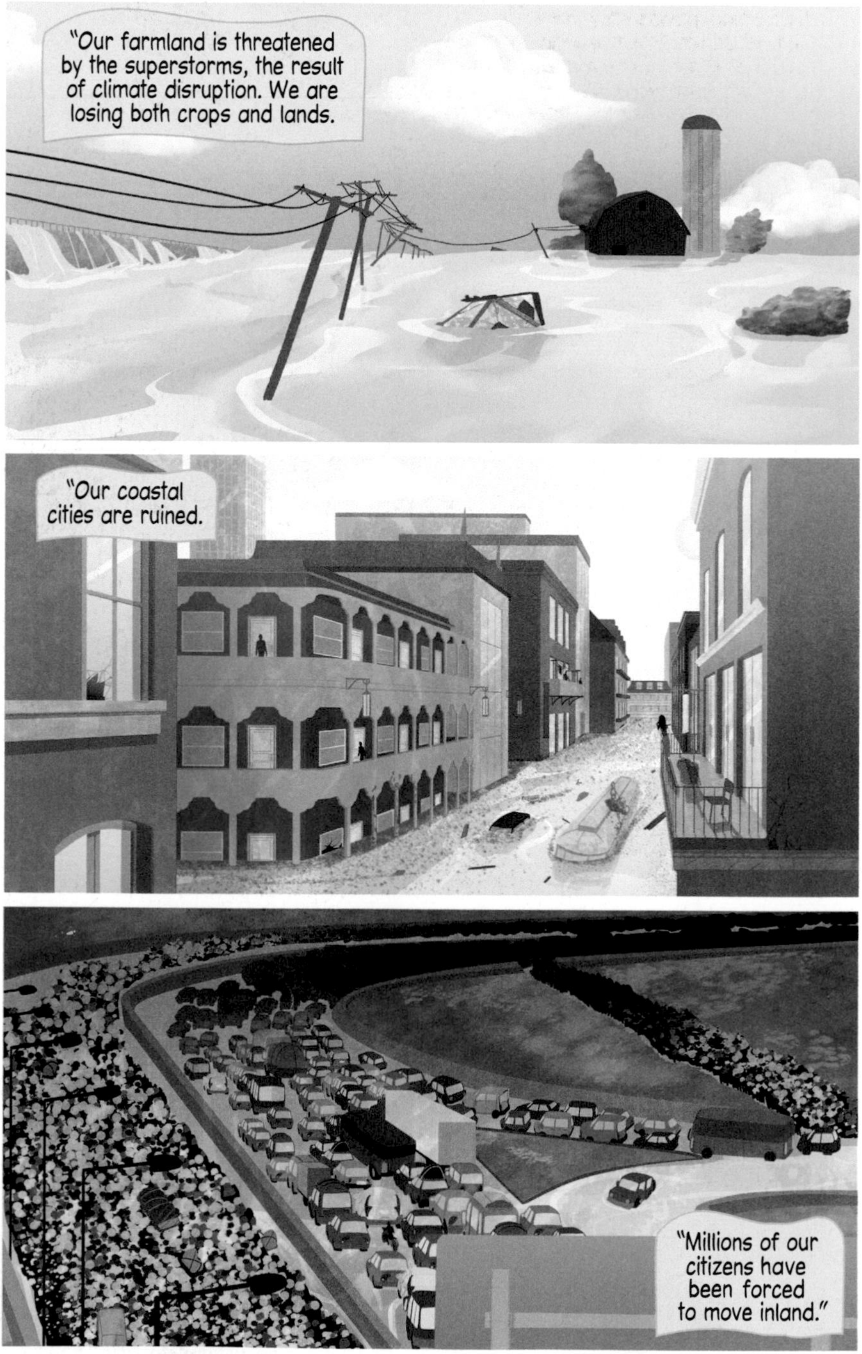
"Our farmland is threatened by the superstorms, the result of climate disruption. We are losing both crops and lands.
"Our coastal cities are ruined.
"Millions of our citizens have been forced to move inland."

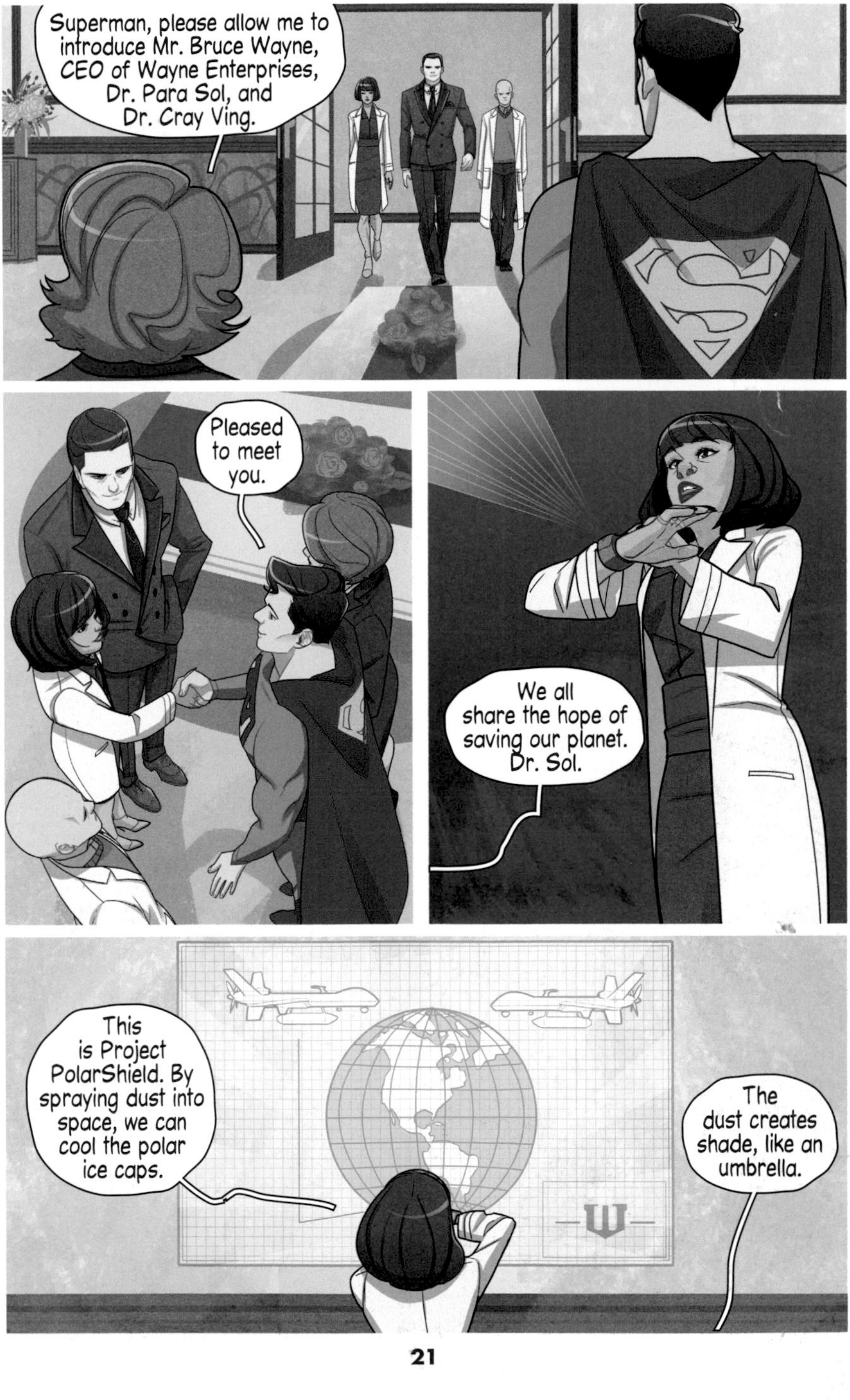
Superman, please allow me to introduce Mr. Bruce Wayne, CEO of Wayne Enterprises, Dr. Para Sol, and Dr. Cray Ving.
Pleased to meet you.
We all share the hope of saving our planet. Dr. Sol.
This is Project PolarShield. By spraying dust into space, we can cool the polar ice caps.
The dust creates shade, like an umbrella.

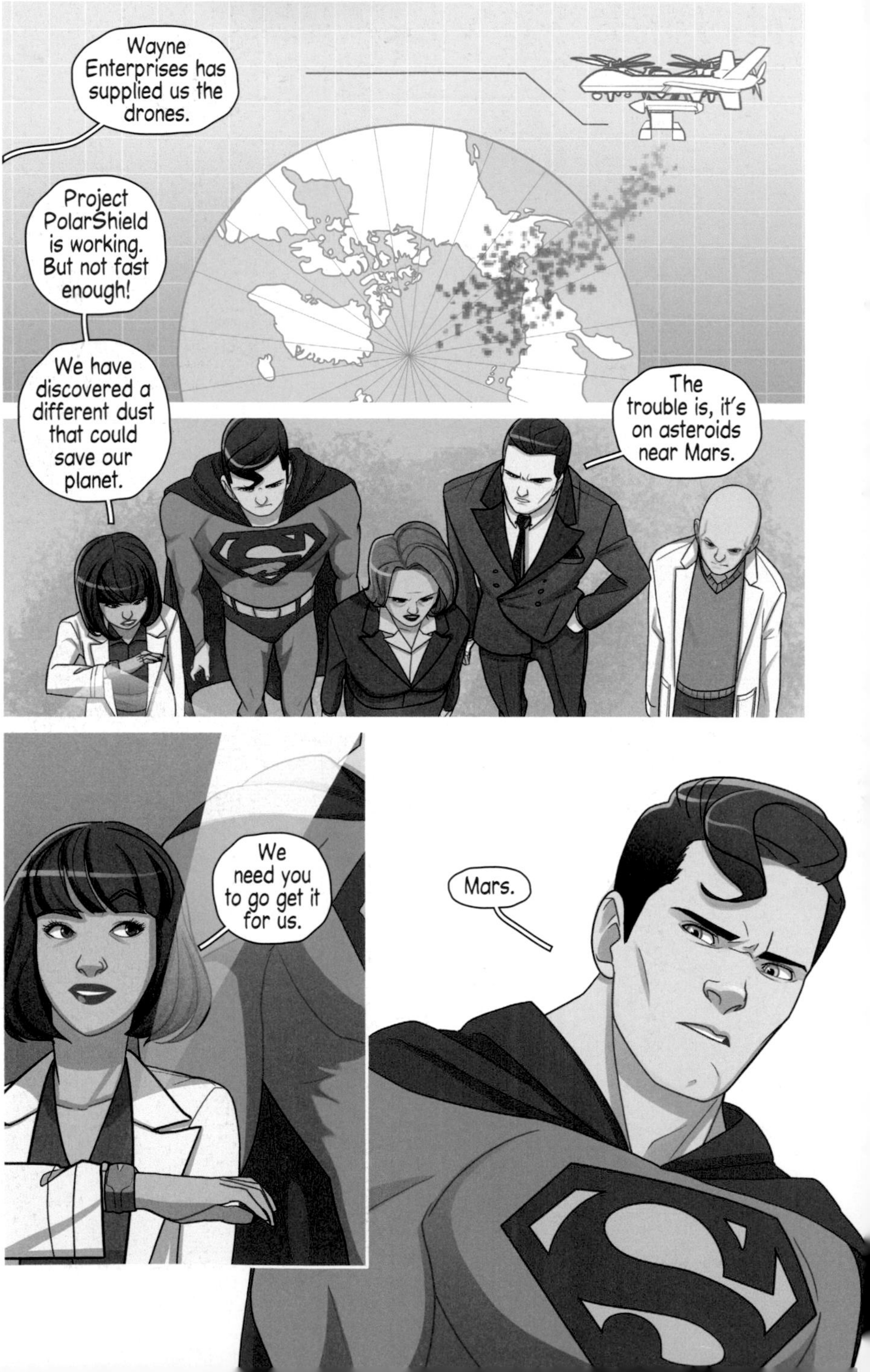
Wayne Enterprises has supplied us the drones.
Project PolarShield is working. But not fast enough!
We have discovered a different dust that could save our planet.
The trouble is, it's on asteroids near Mars.
We need you to go get it for us.
Mars.

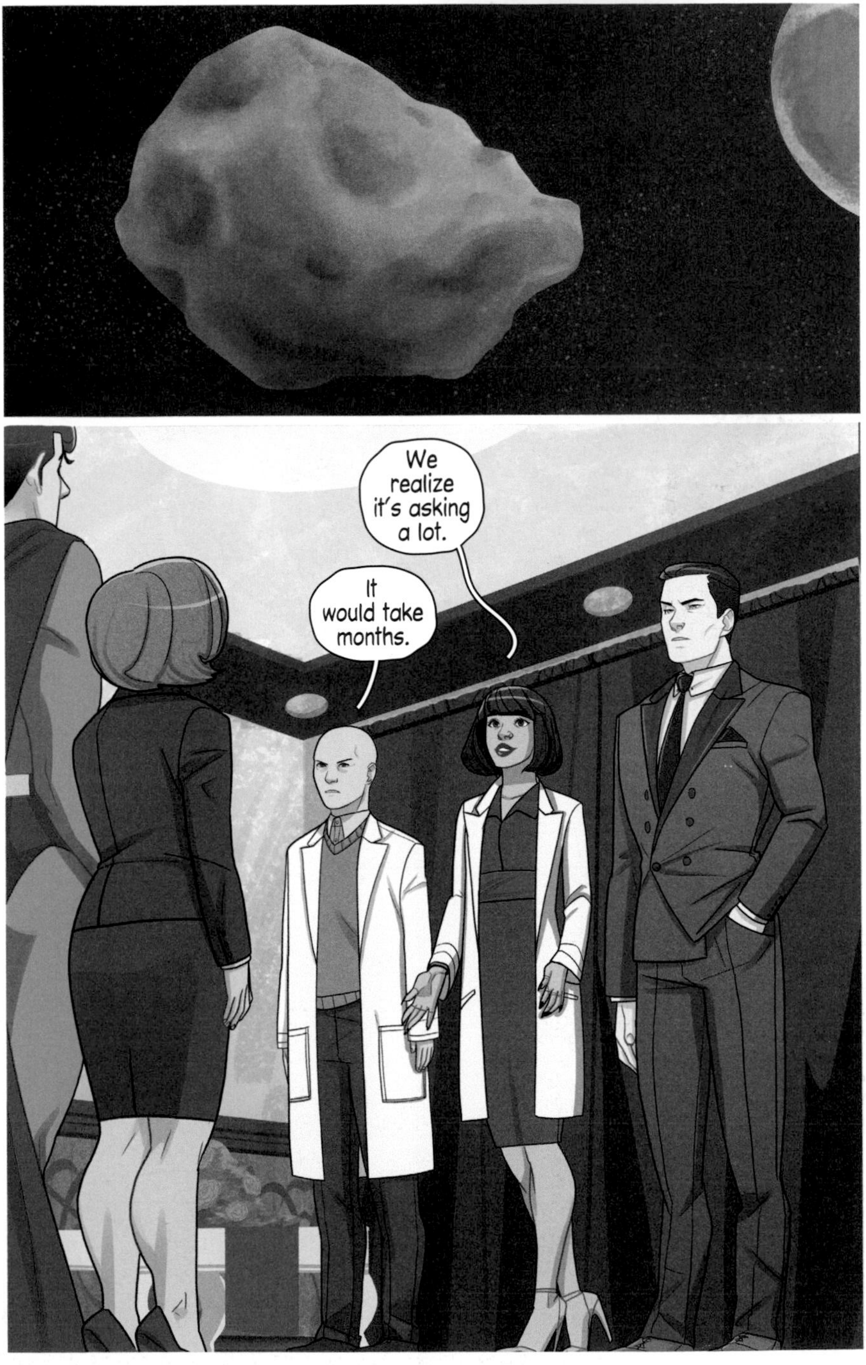
We realize it's asking a lot.
It would take months.

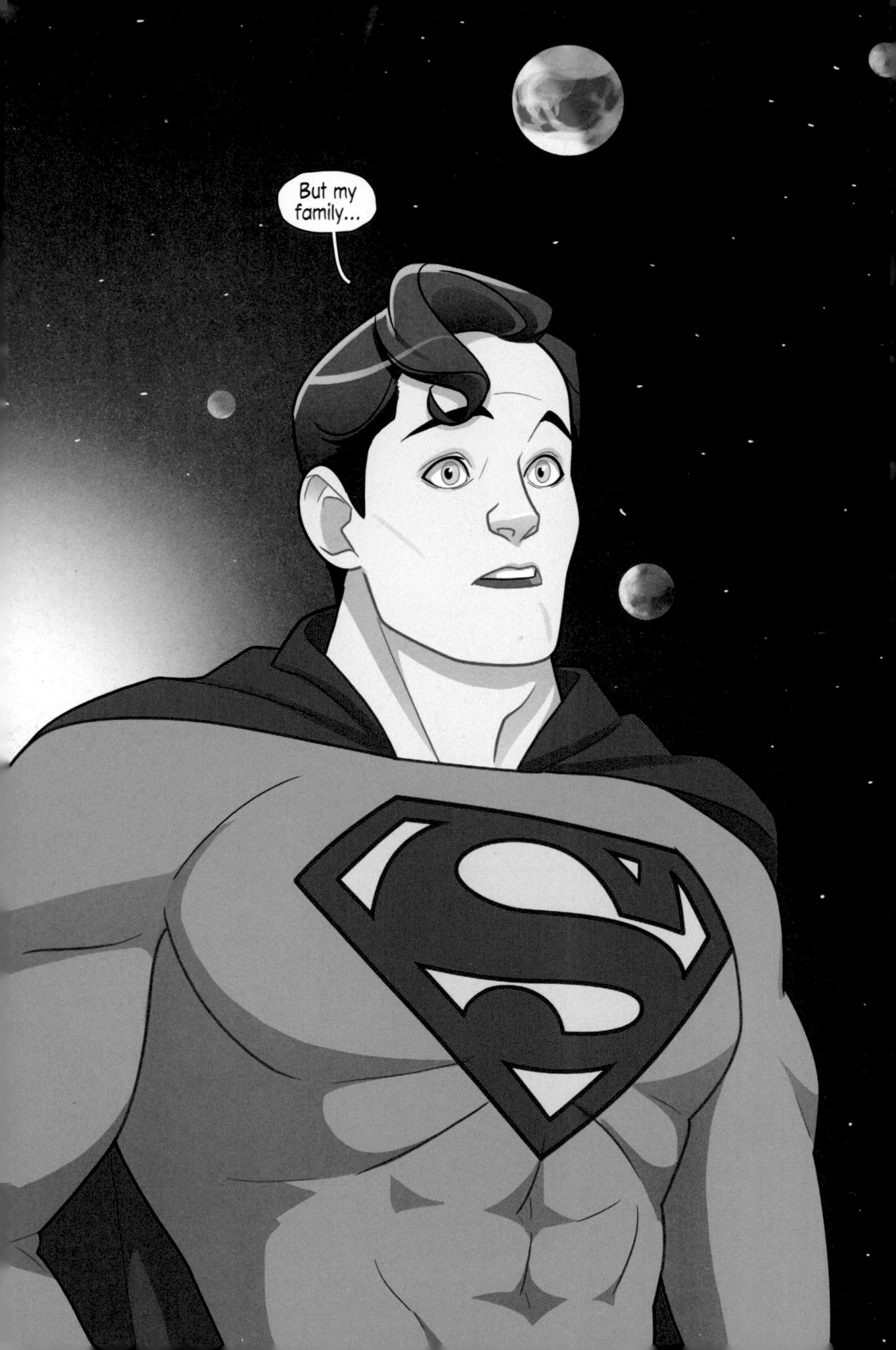
But my family...

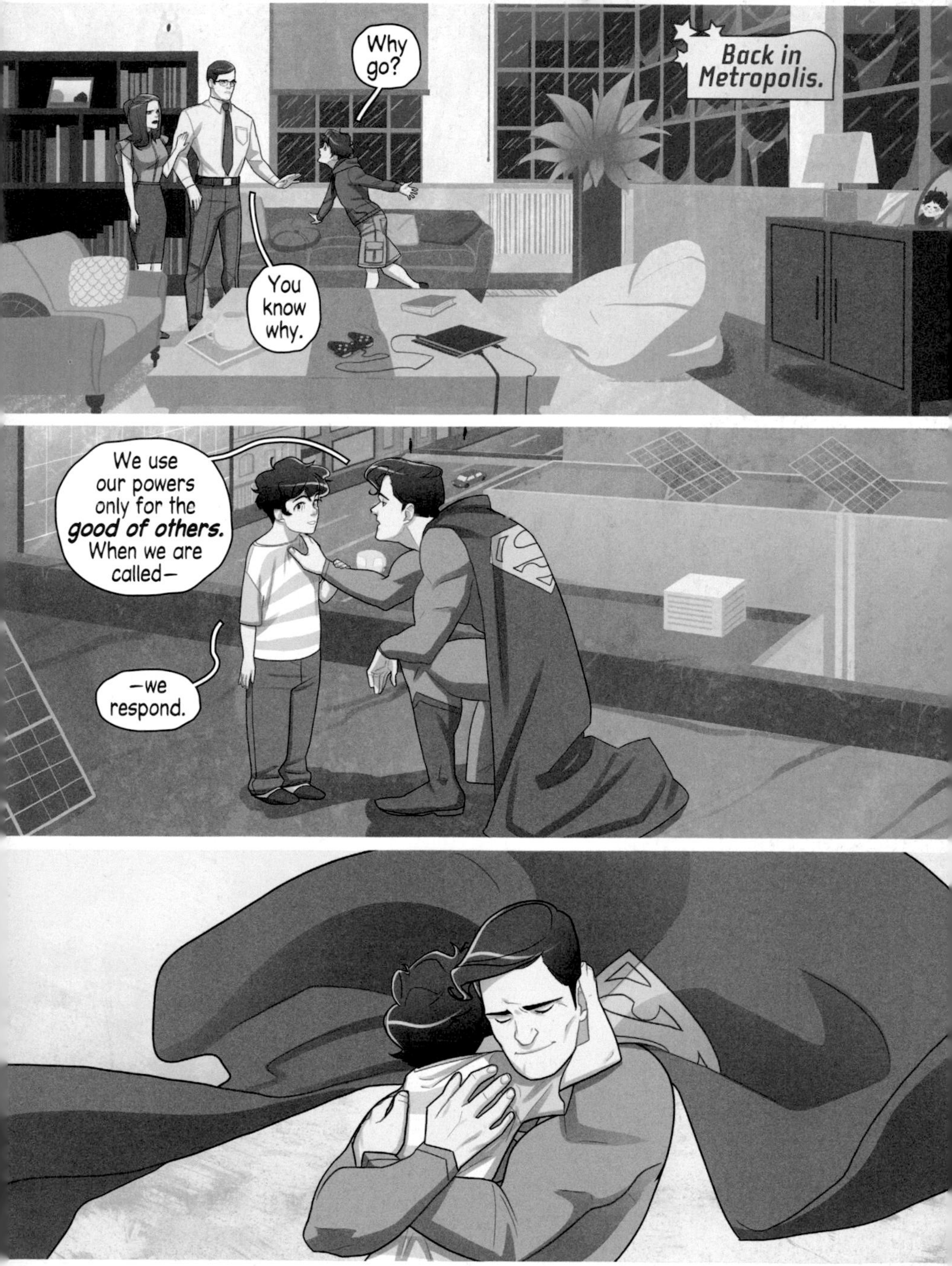
Back in Metropolis.
Why go?
You know why.
We use our powers only for the ***good of others.*** When we are called—
—we respond.

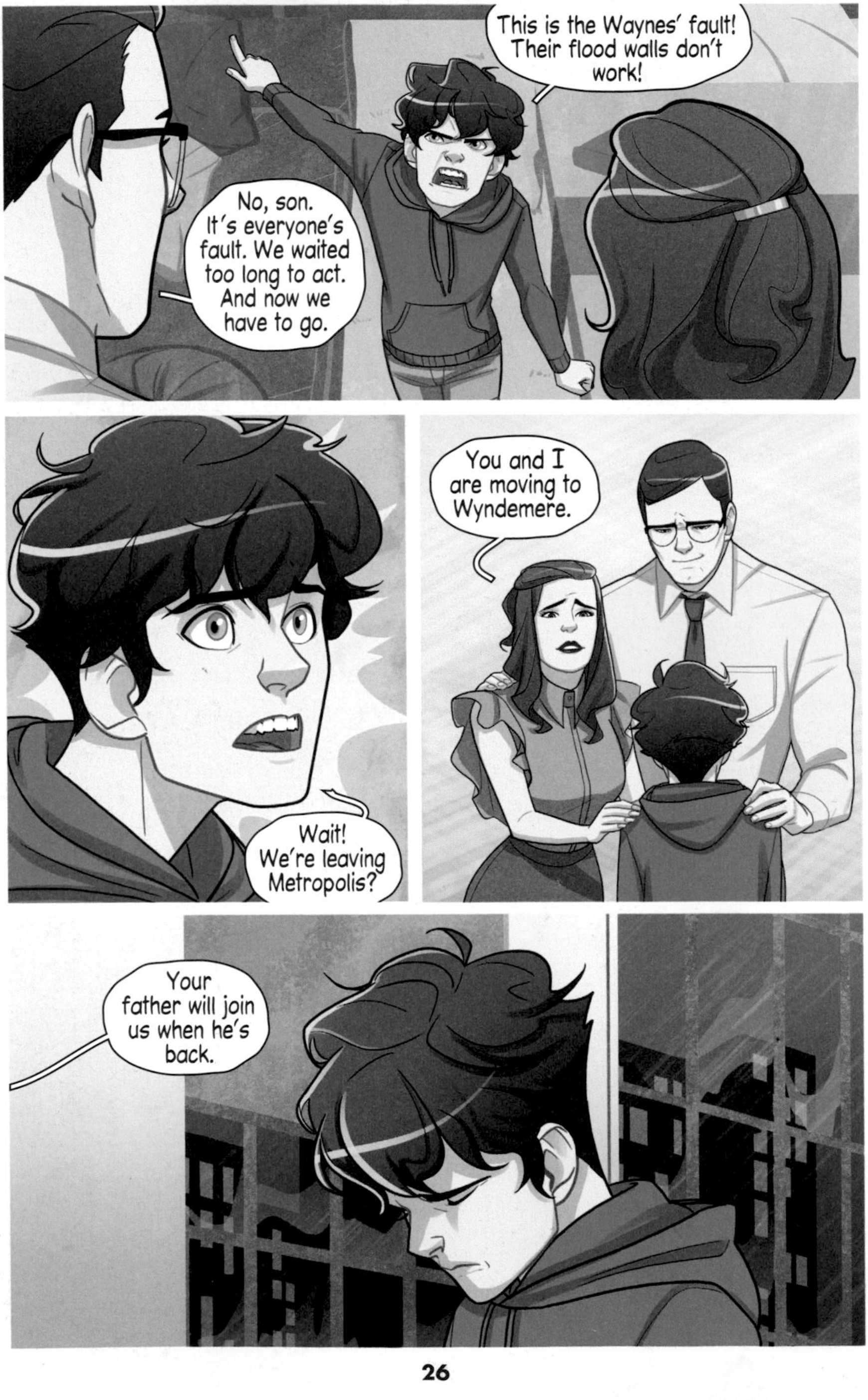
This is the Waynes' fault! Their flood walls don't work!
No, son. It's everyone's fault. We waited too long to act. And now we have to go.
Wait! We're leaving Metropolis?
You and I are moving to Wyndemere.
Your father will join us when he's back.

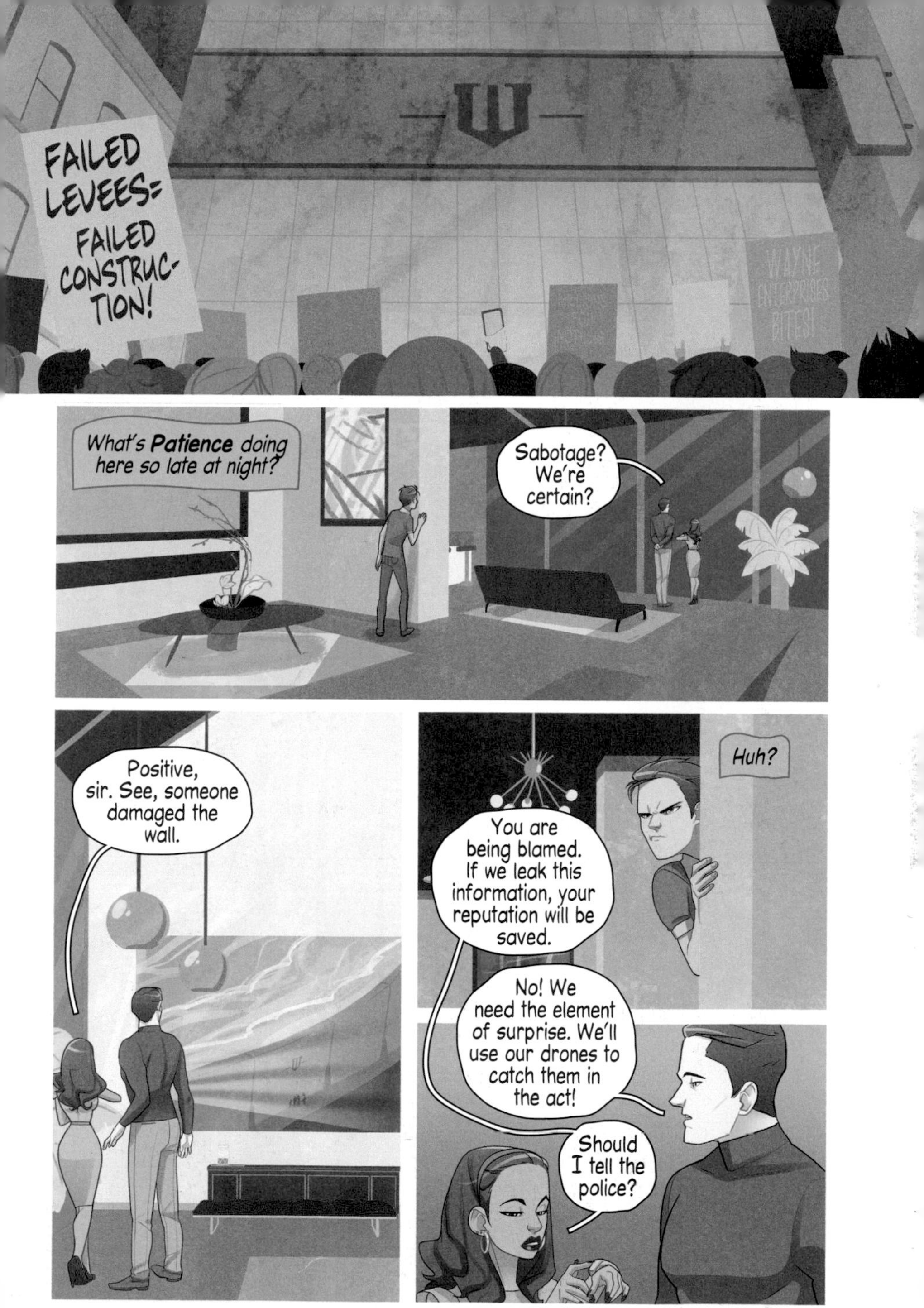
FAILED LEVEES= FAILED CONSTRUC-TION!
WAYNE ENTERPRISES BITES!
What's **Patience** doing here so late at night?
Sabotage? We're certain?
Positive, sir. See, someone damaged the wall.
Huh?
You are being blamed. If we leak this information, your reputation will be saved.
No! We need the element of surprise. We'll use our drones to catch them in the act!
Should I tell the police?

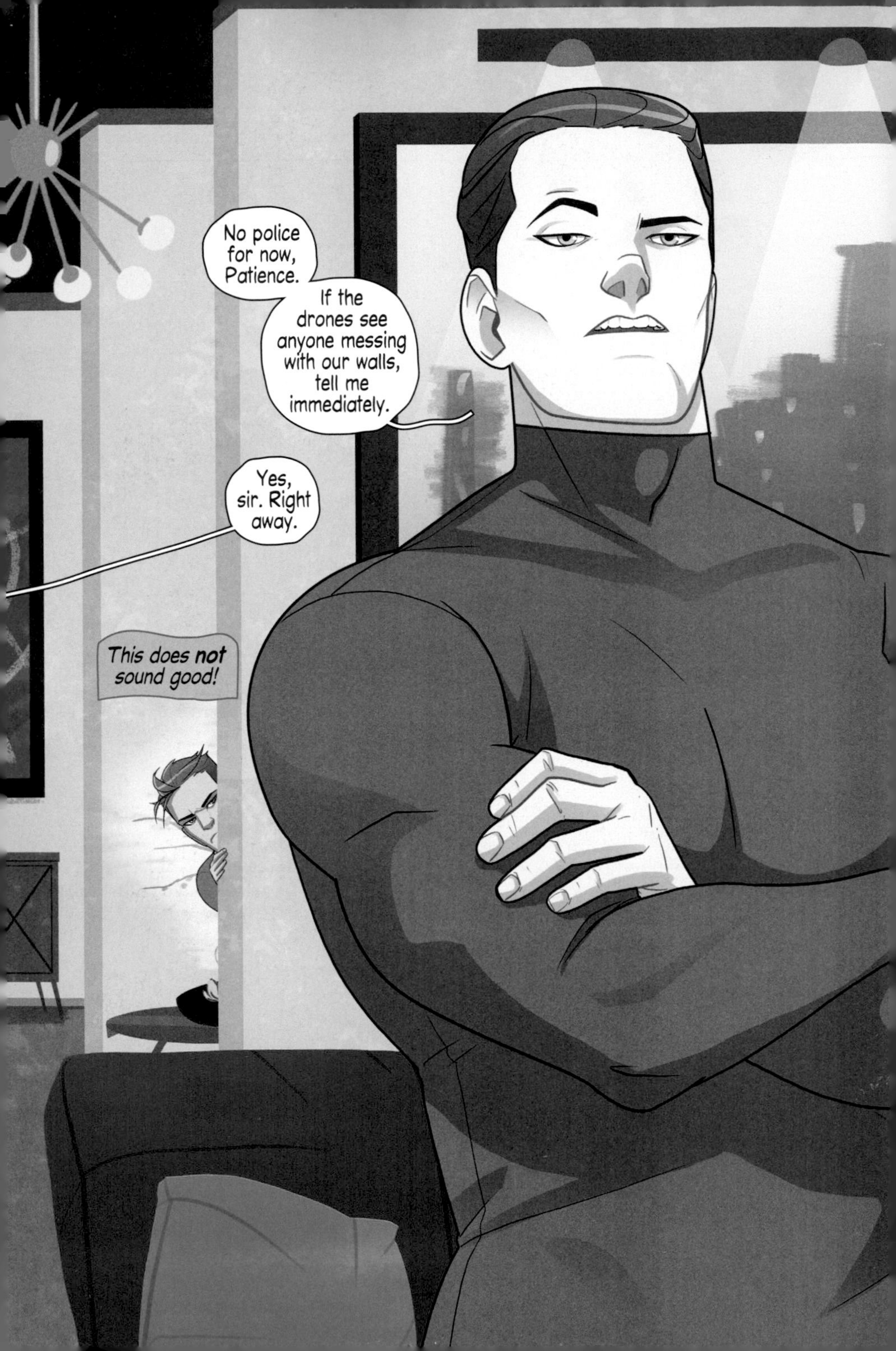
No police for now, Patience.
If the drones see anyone messing with our walls, tell me immediately.
Yes, sir. Right away.
This does **not** sound good!

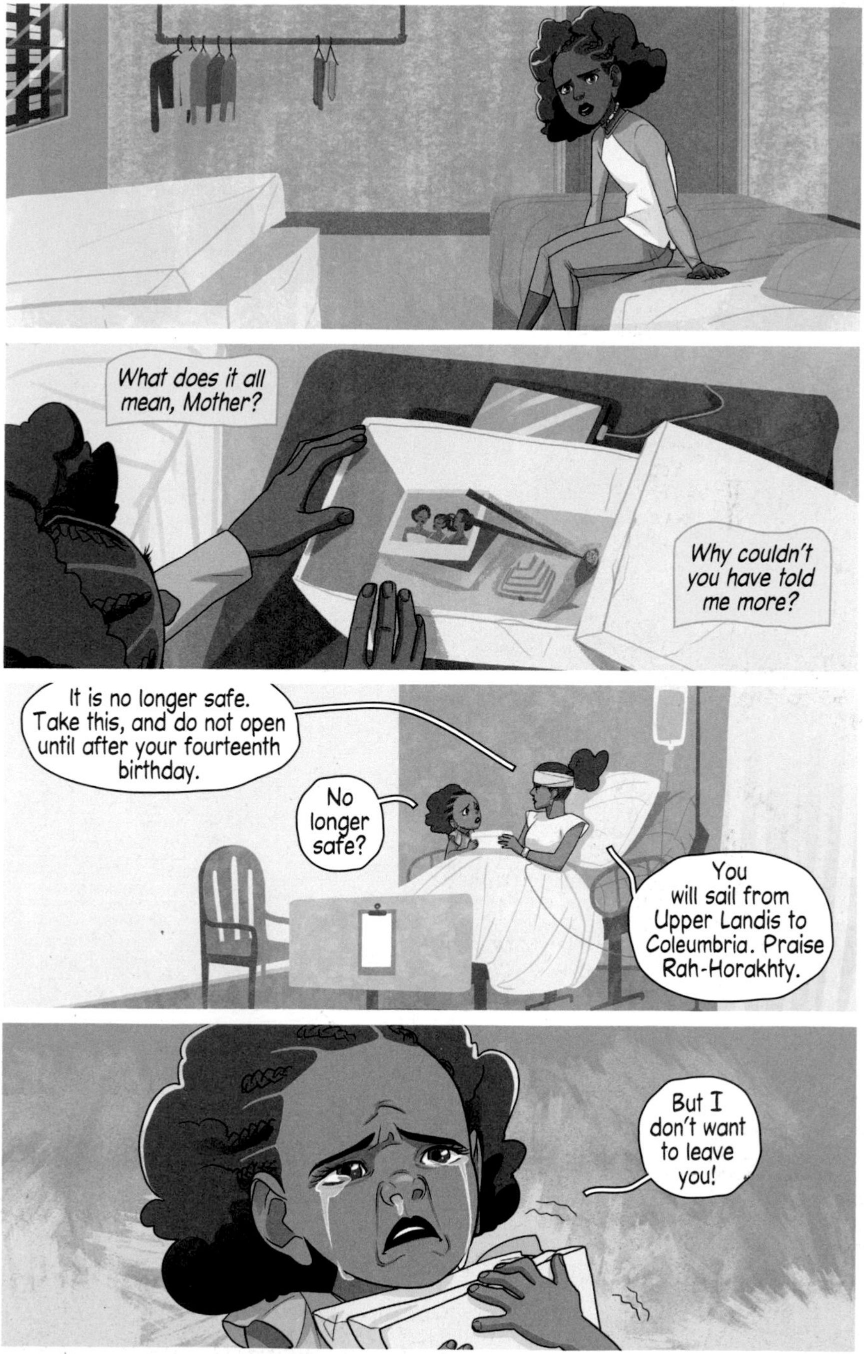
What does it all mean, Mother?
Why couldn't you have told me more?
It is no longer safe. Take this, and do not open until after your fourteenth birthday.
No longer safe?
You will sail from Upper Landis to Coleumbria. Praise Rah-Horakhty.
But I don't want to leave you!

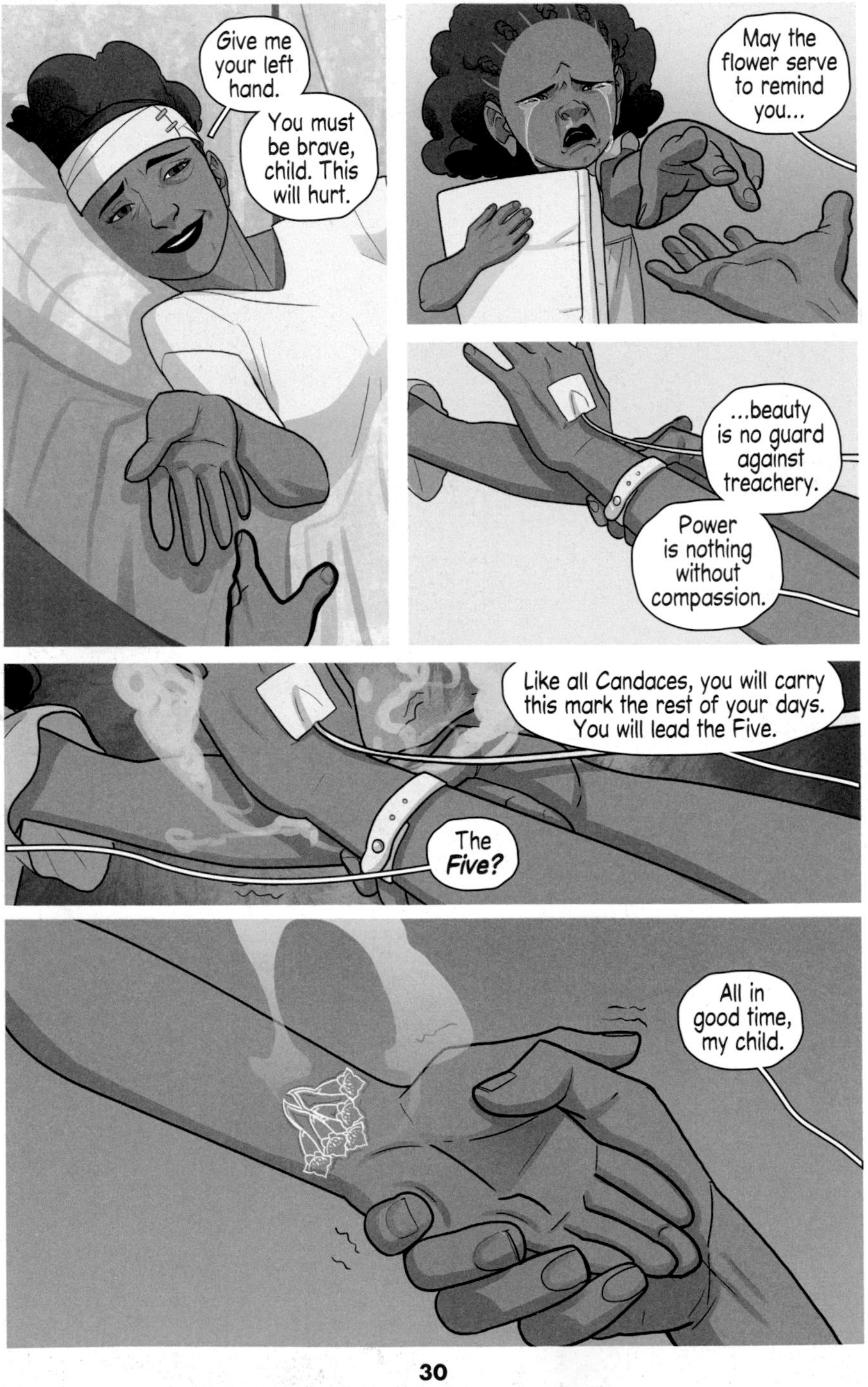

Give me your left hand.
You must be brave, child. This will hurt.
May the flower serve to remind you...
...beauty is no guard against treachery.
Power is nothing without compassion.
Like all Candaces, you will carry this mark the rest of your days. You will lead the Five.
The *Five?*
All in good time, my child.

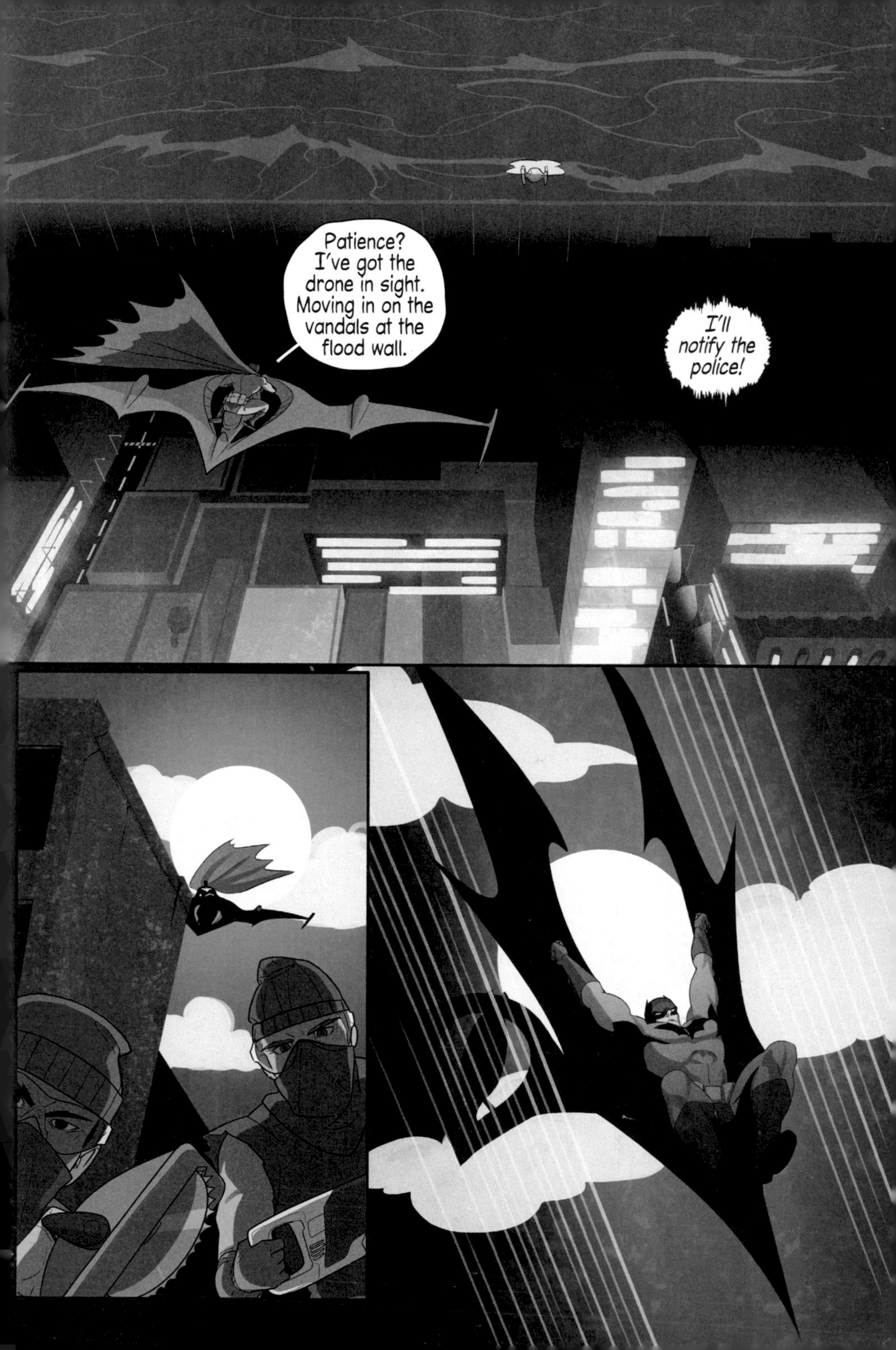
Patience? I've got the drone in sight. Moving in on the vandals at the flood wall.
I'll notify the police!

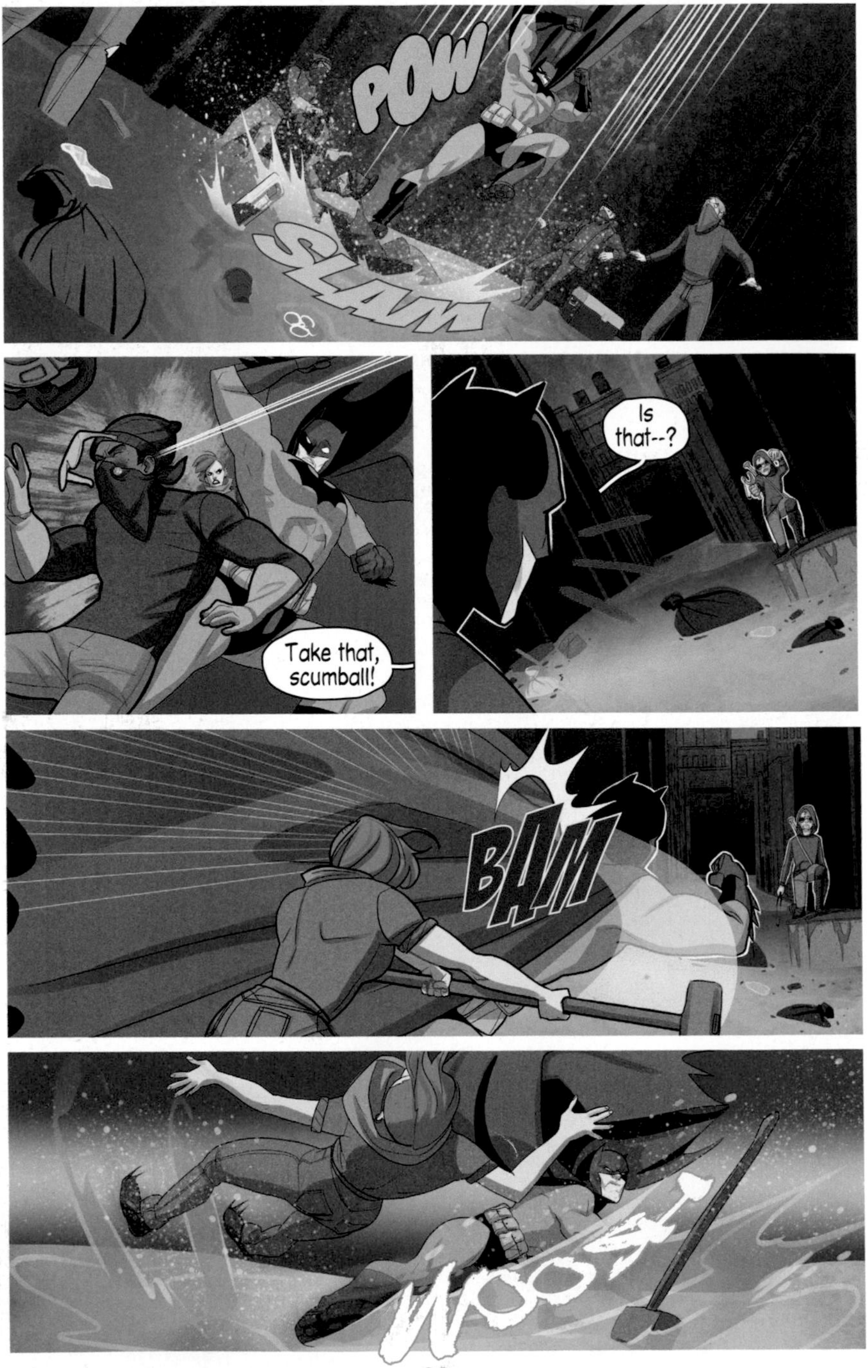
POW
SLAM
Take that, scumball!
Is that--?
BAM
WOOSH

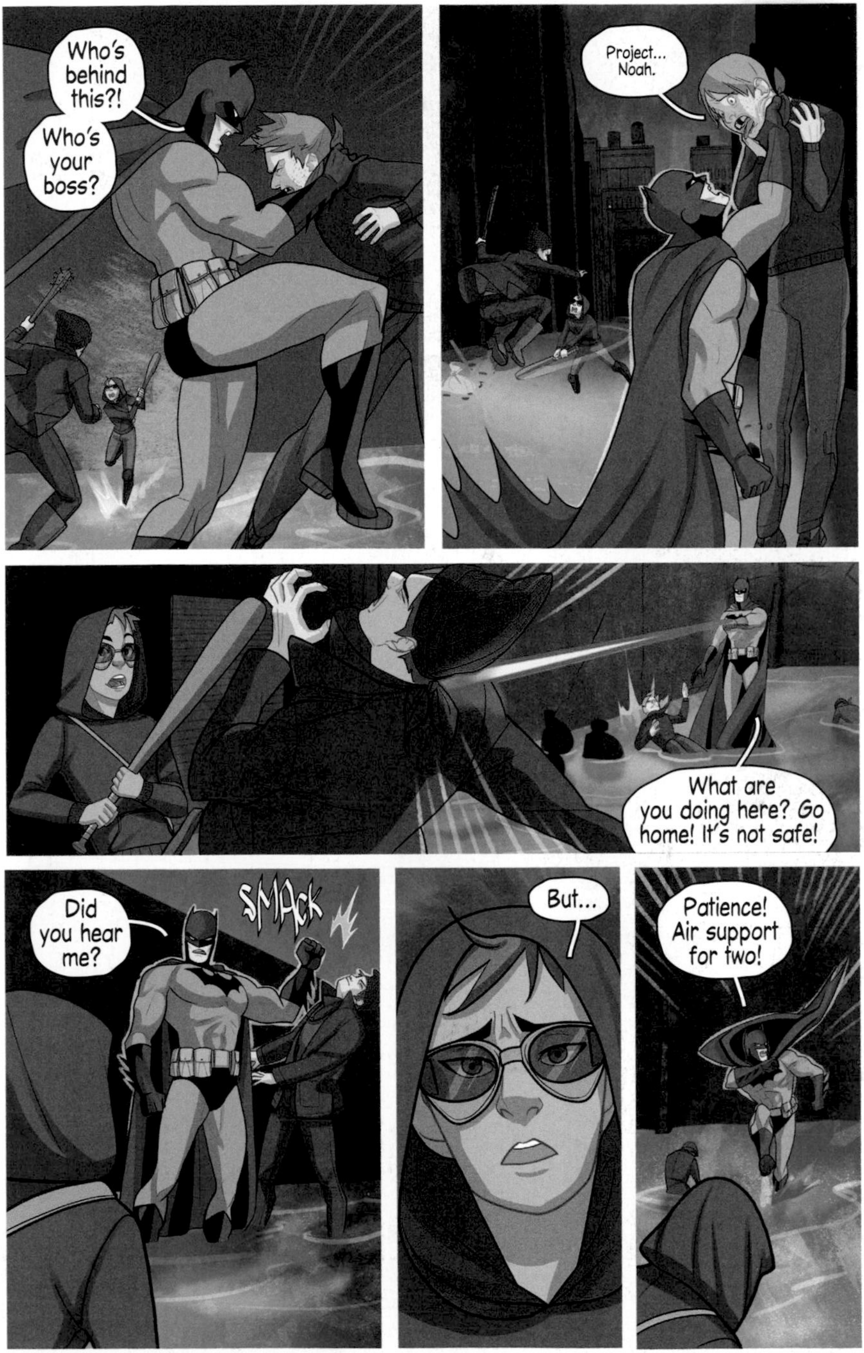
Who's behind this?!
Who's your boss?
Project... Noah.
What are you doing here? Go home! It's not safe!
Did you hear me?
SMACK
But...
Patience! Air support for two!

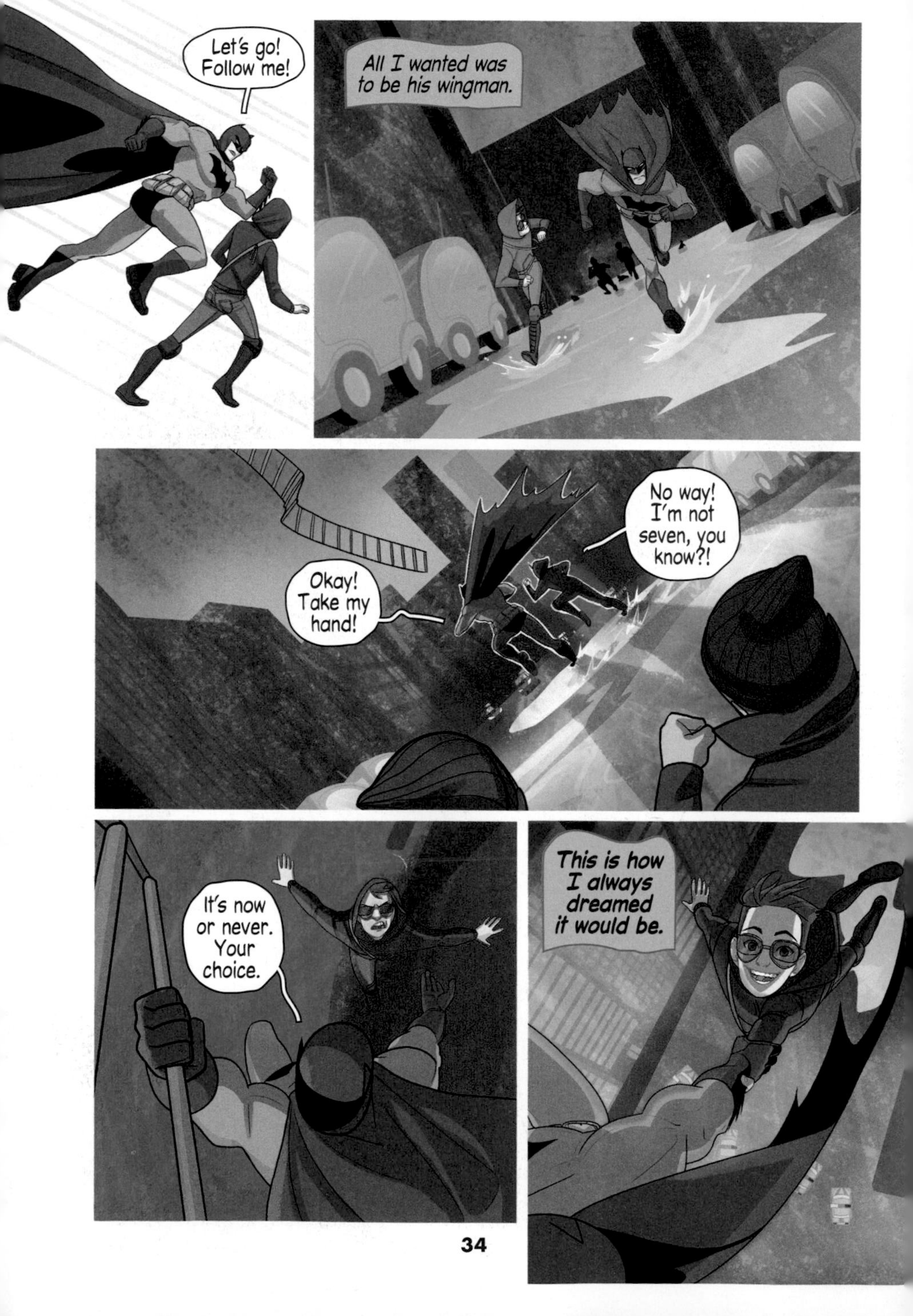
Let's go! Follow me!
All I wanted was to be his wingman.
Okay! Take my hand!
No way! I'm not seven, you know?!
It's now or never. Your choice.
This is how I always dreamed it would be.

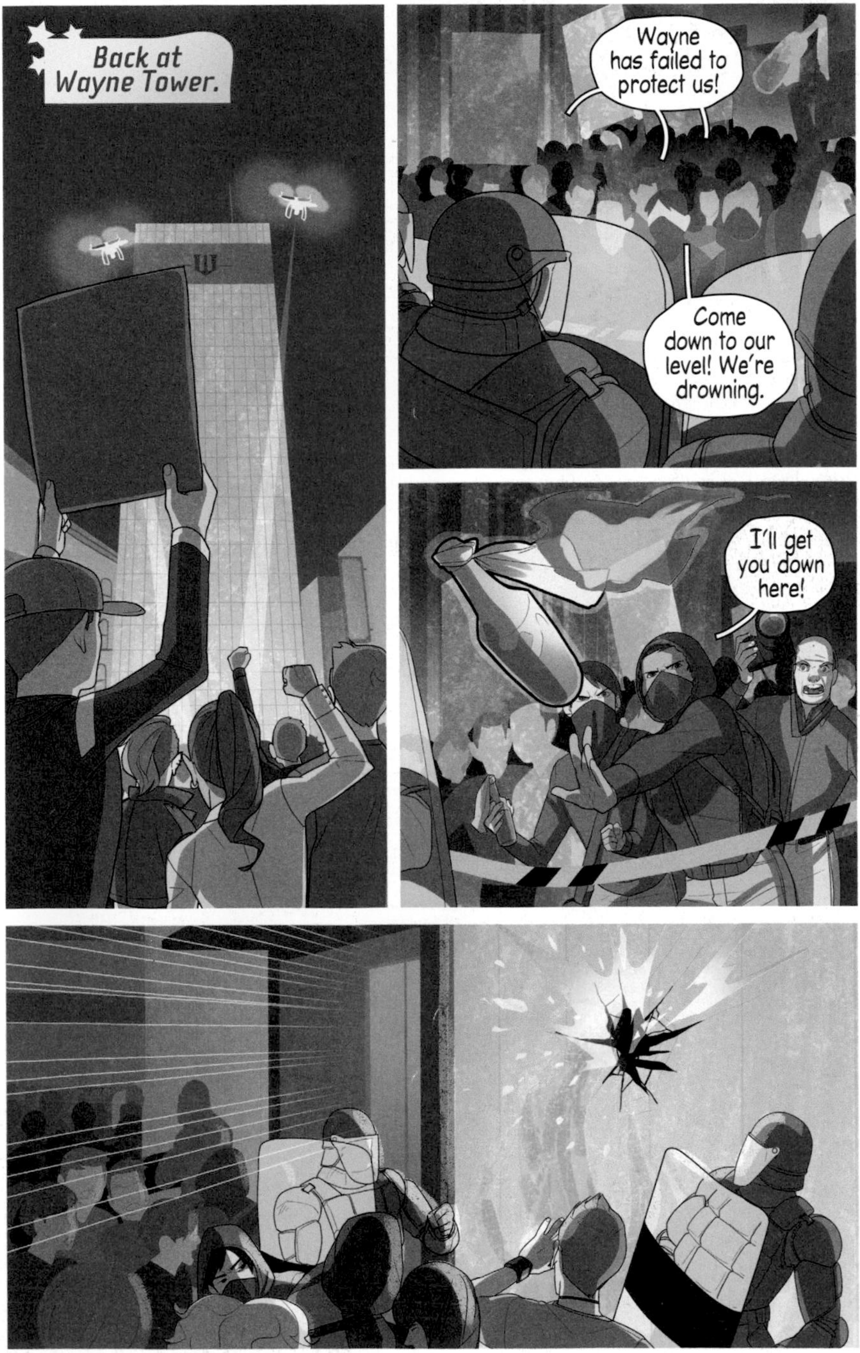

Back at Wayne Tower.
Wayne has failed to protect us!
Come down to our level! We're drowning.
I'll get you down here!

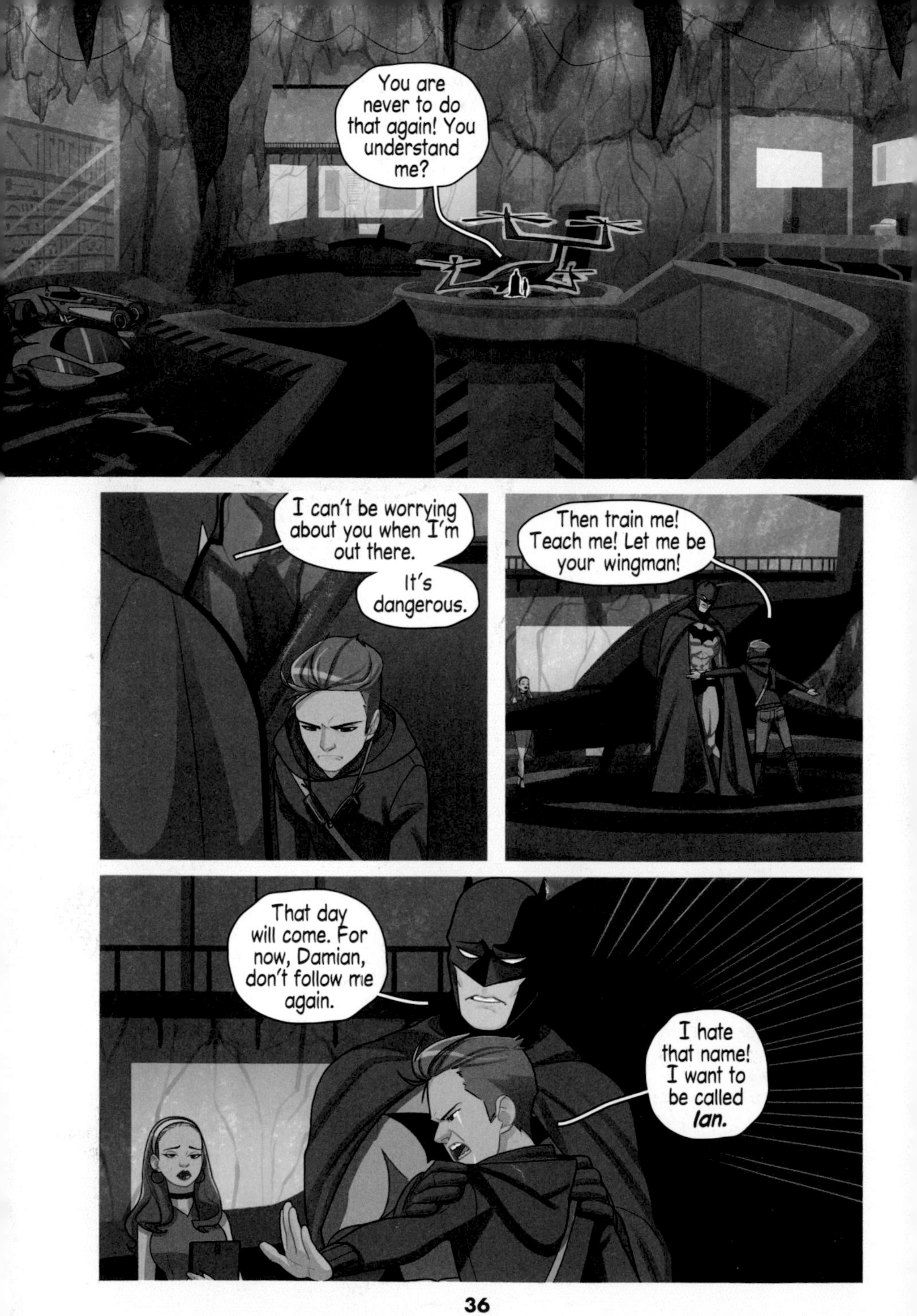
You are never to do that again! You understand me?
I can't be worrying about you when I'm out there.
It's dangerous.
Then train me! Teach me! Let me be your wingman!
That day will come. For now, Damian, don't follow me again.
I hate that name! I want to be called *Ian.*

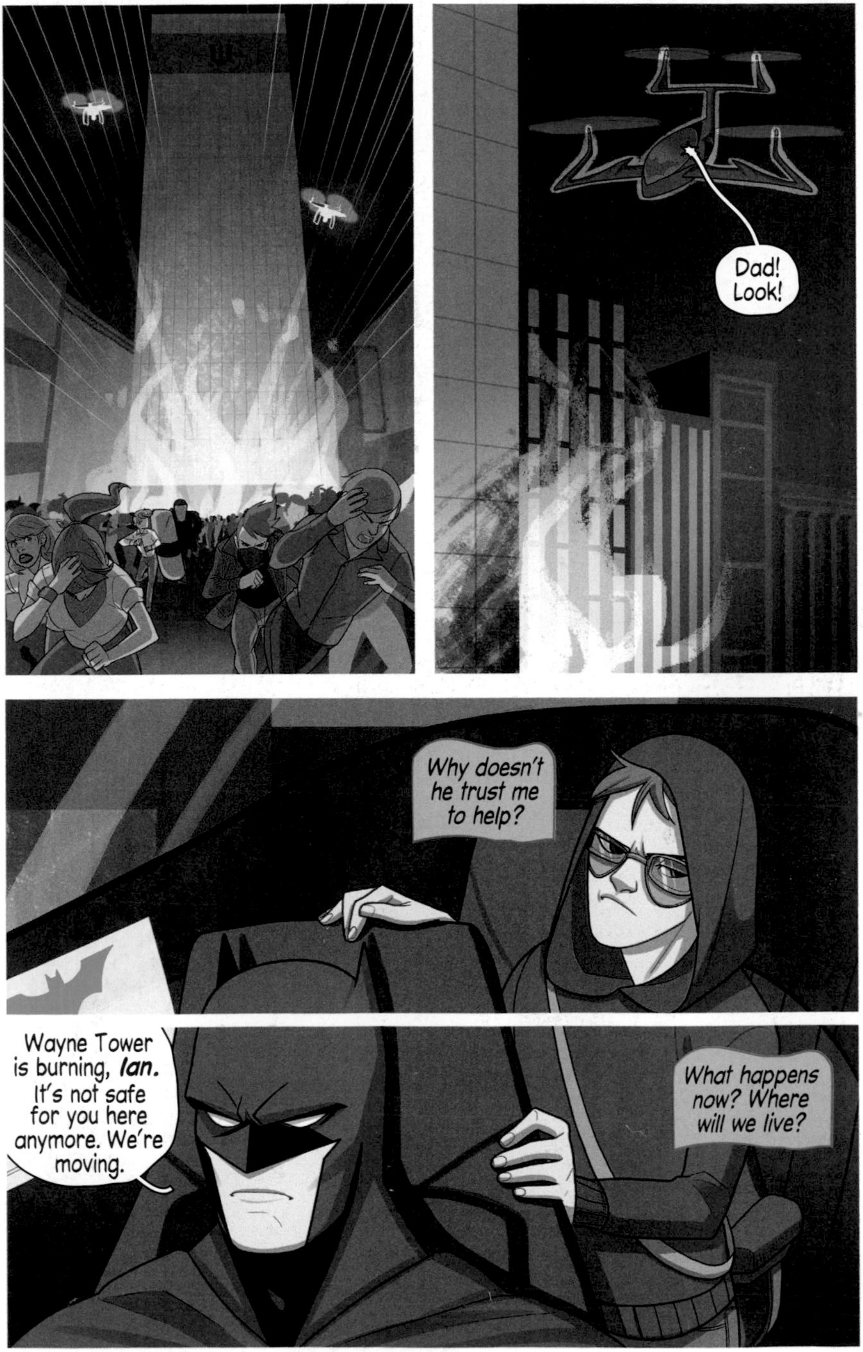
Dad! Look!
Why doesn't he trust me to help?
Wayne Tower is burning, **Ian.** It's not safe for you here anymore. We're moving.
What happens now? Where will we live?

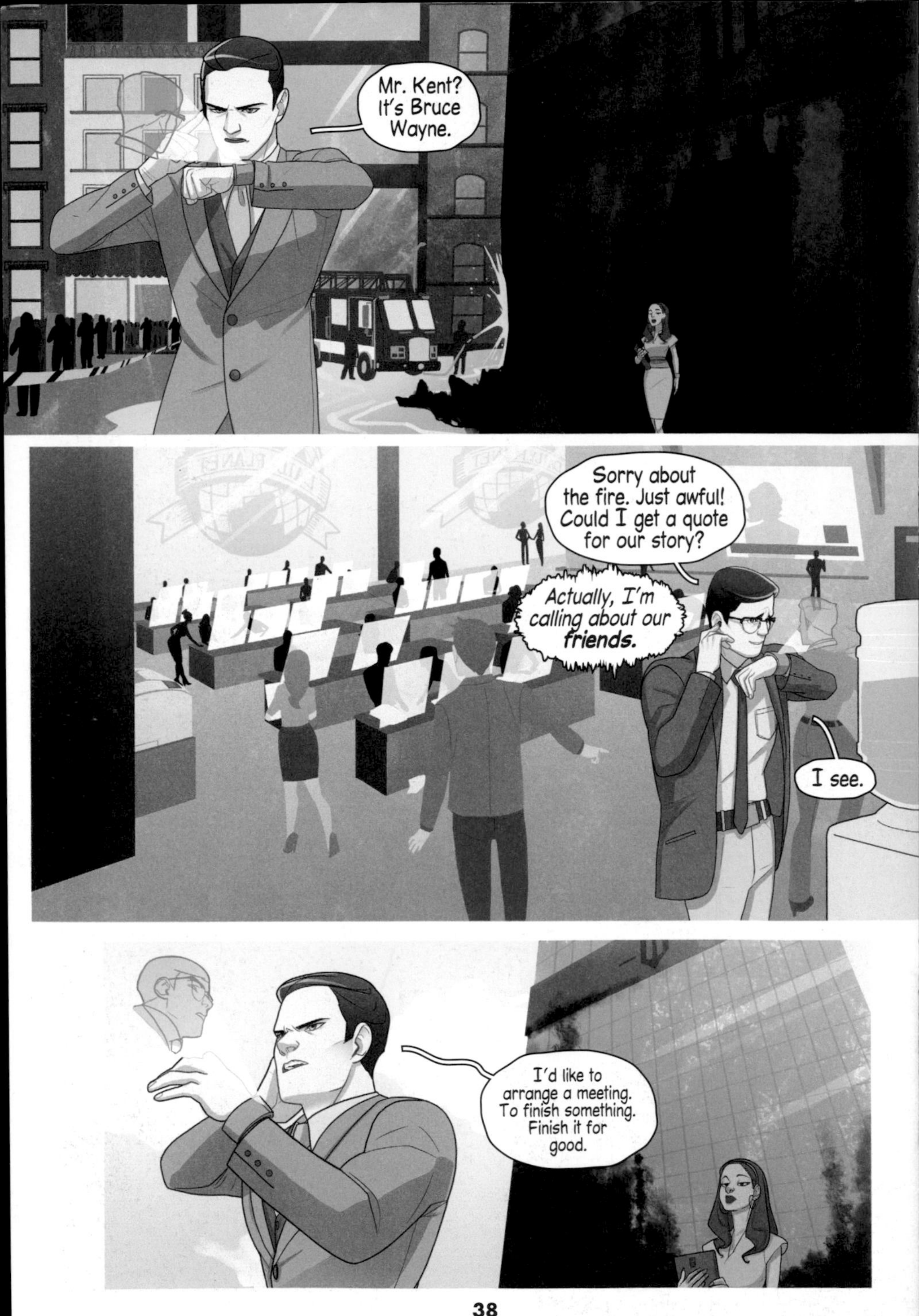
Mr. Kent? It's Bruce Wayne.
Sorry about the fire. Just awful! Could I get a quote for our story?
Actually, I'm calling about our **friends.**
I see.
I'd like to arrange a meeting. To finish something. Finish it for good.

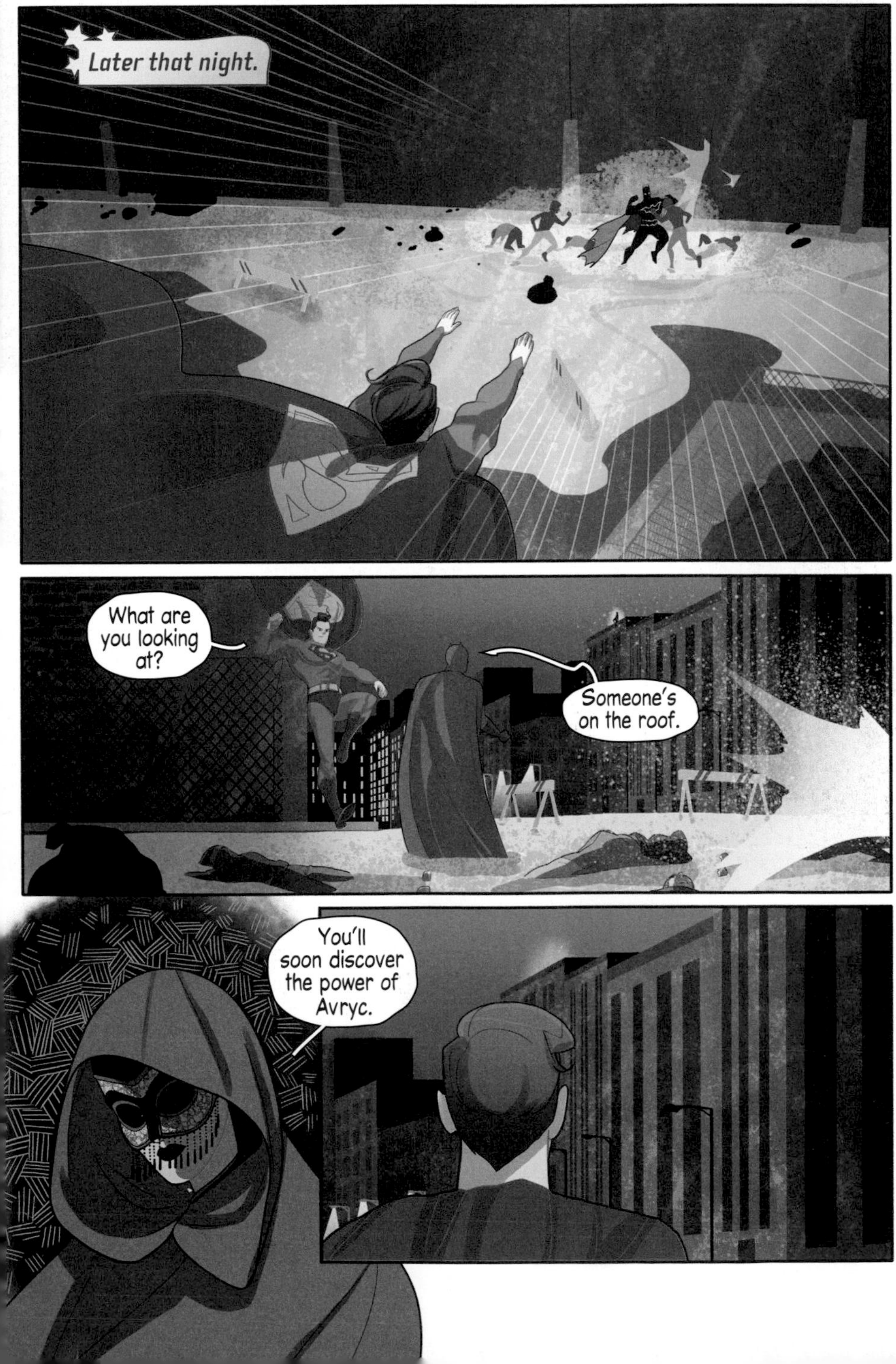
Later that night.
What are you looking at?
Someone's on the roof.
You'll soon discover the power of Avryc.

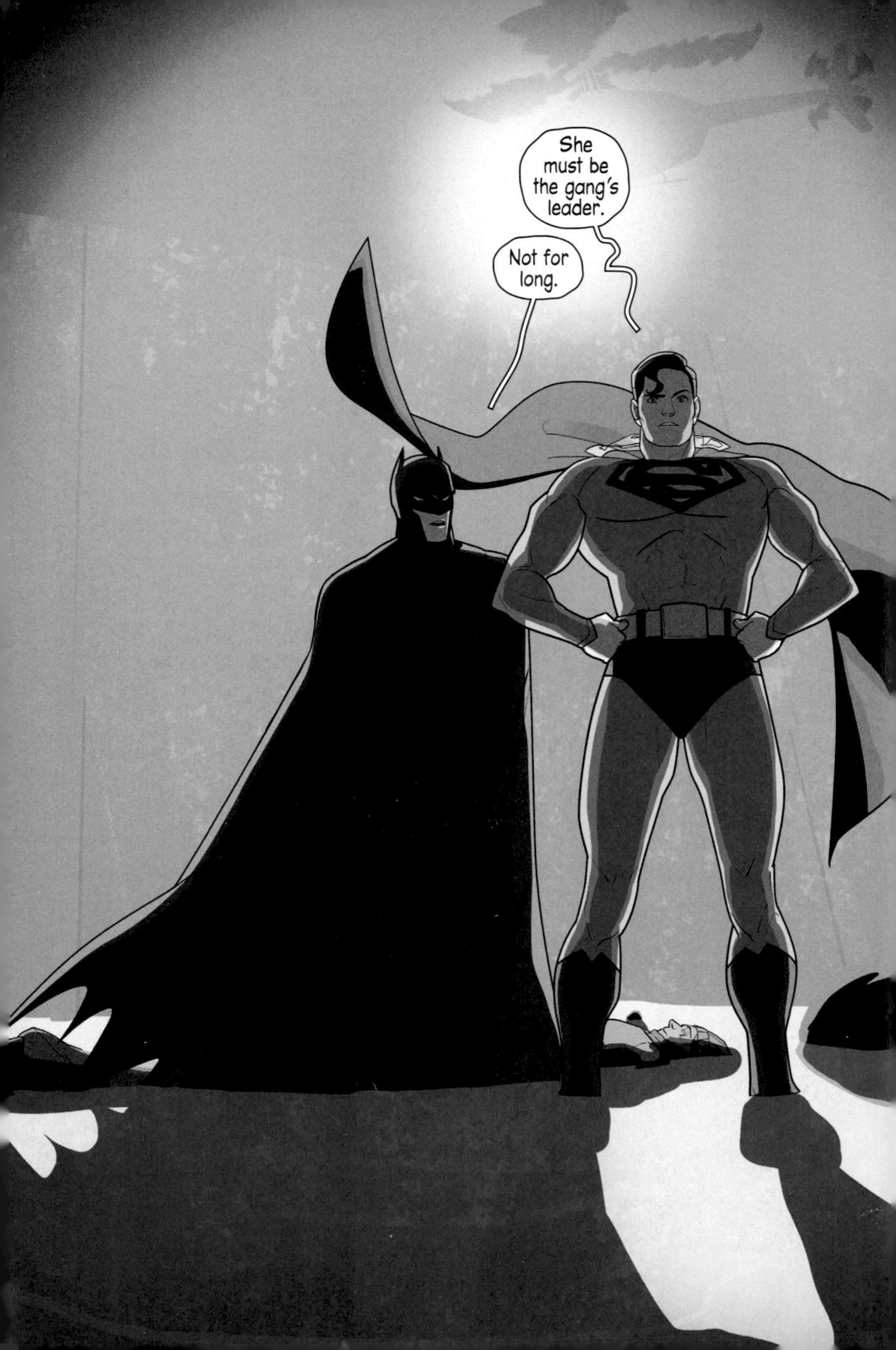
She must be the gang's leader.
Not for long.

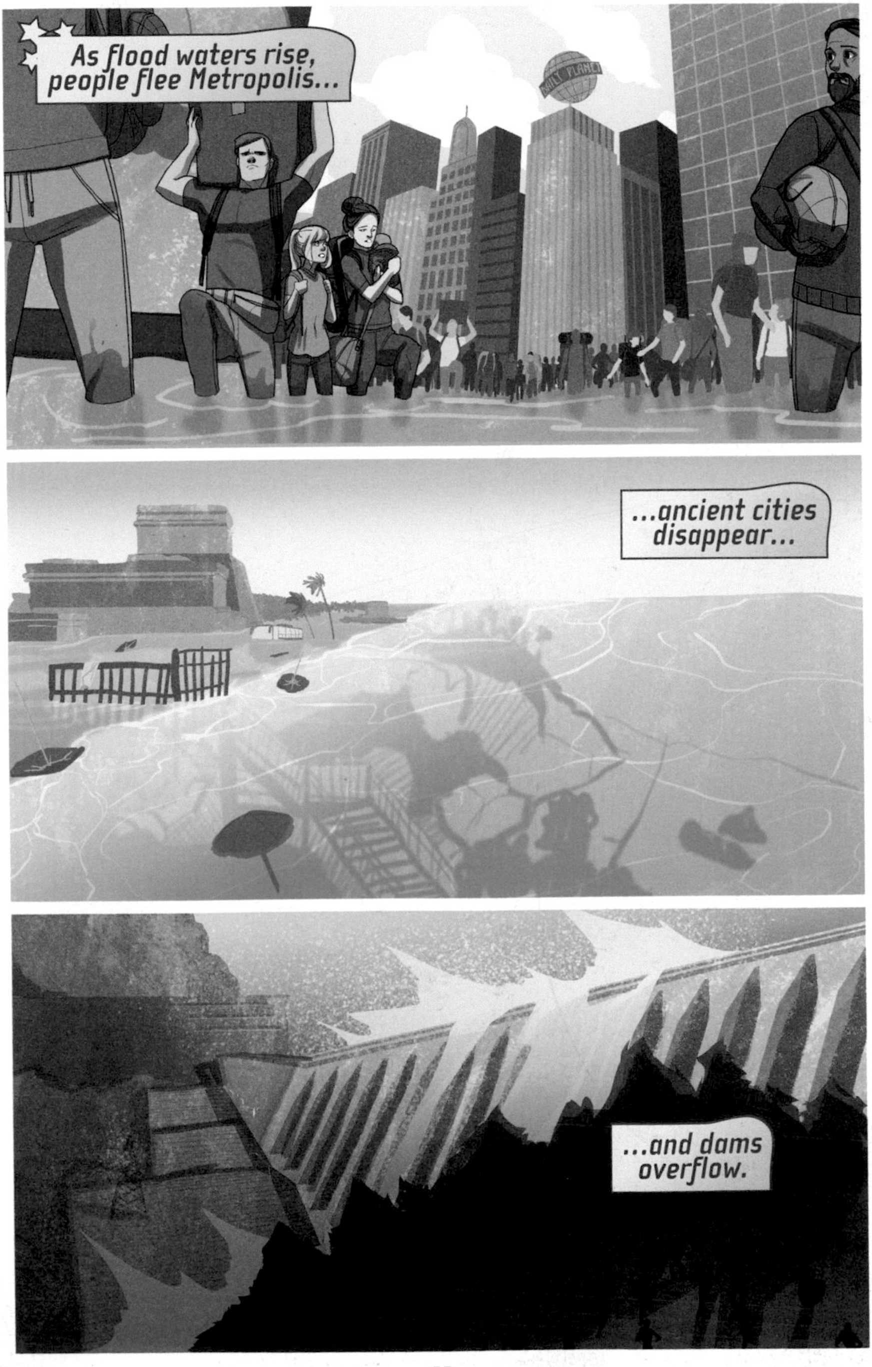
As flood waters rise, people flee Metropolis...
...ancient cities disappear...
...and dams overflow.

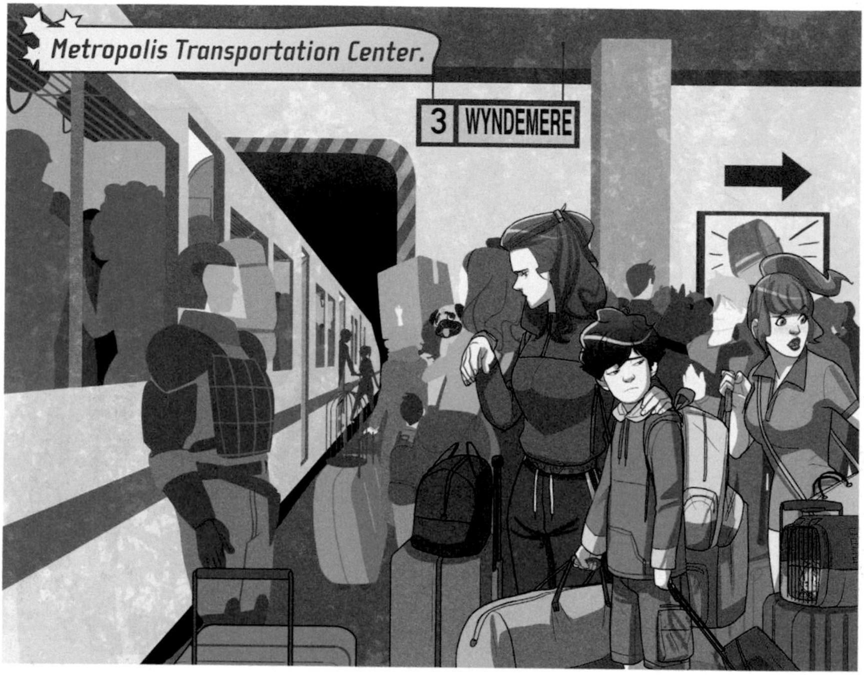
Metropolis Transportation Center.
3 WYNDEMERE

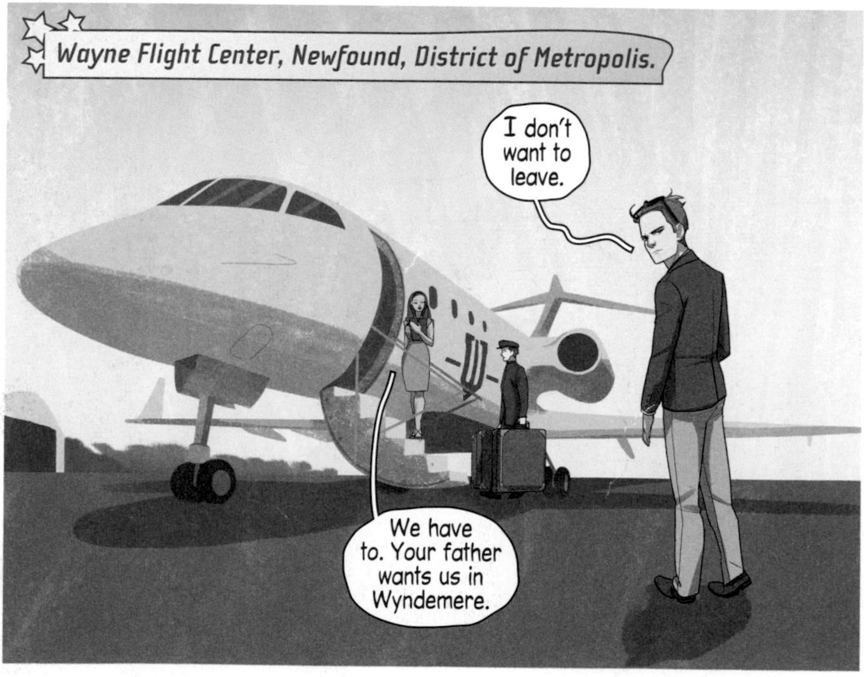
Wayne Flight Center, Newfound, District of Metropolis.
I don't want to leave.
We have to. Your father wants us in Wyndemere.

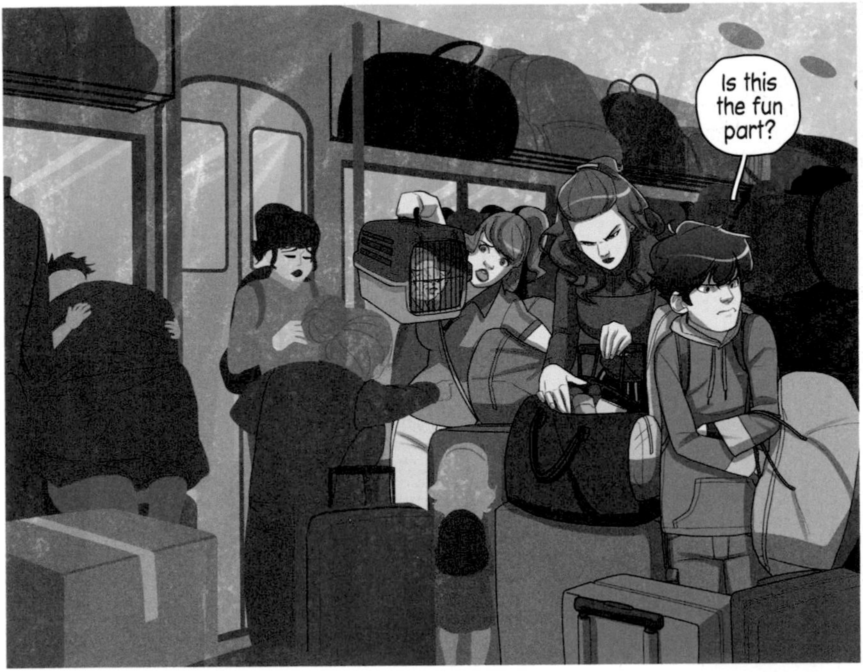
Is this the fun part?

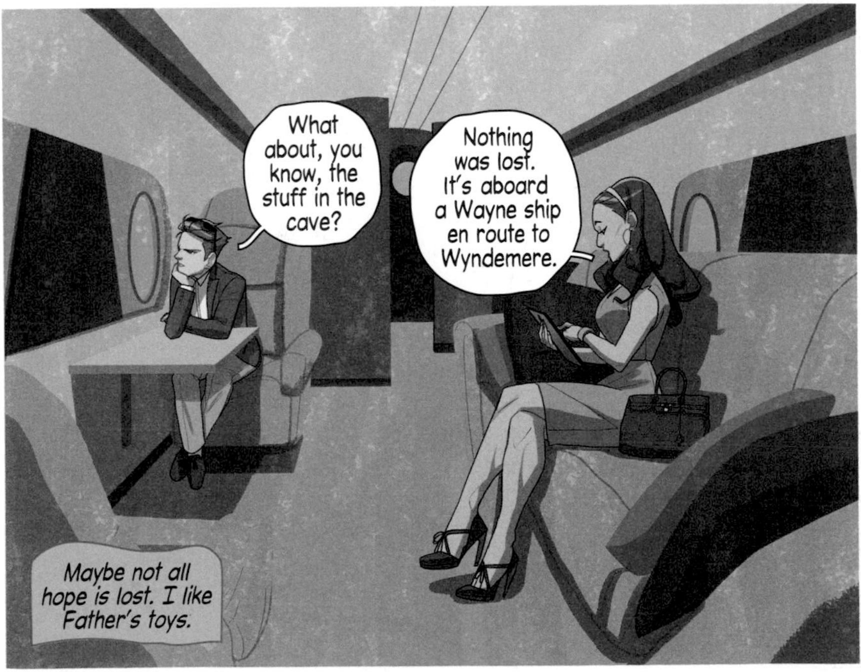
What about, you know, the stuff in the cave?
Nothing was lost. It's aboard a Wayne ship en route to Wyndemere.
Maybe not all hope is lost. I like Father's toys.

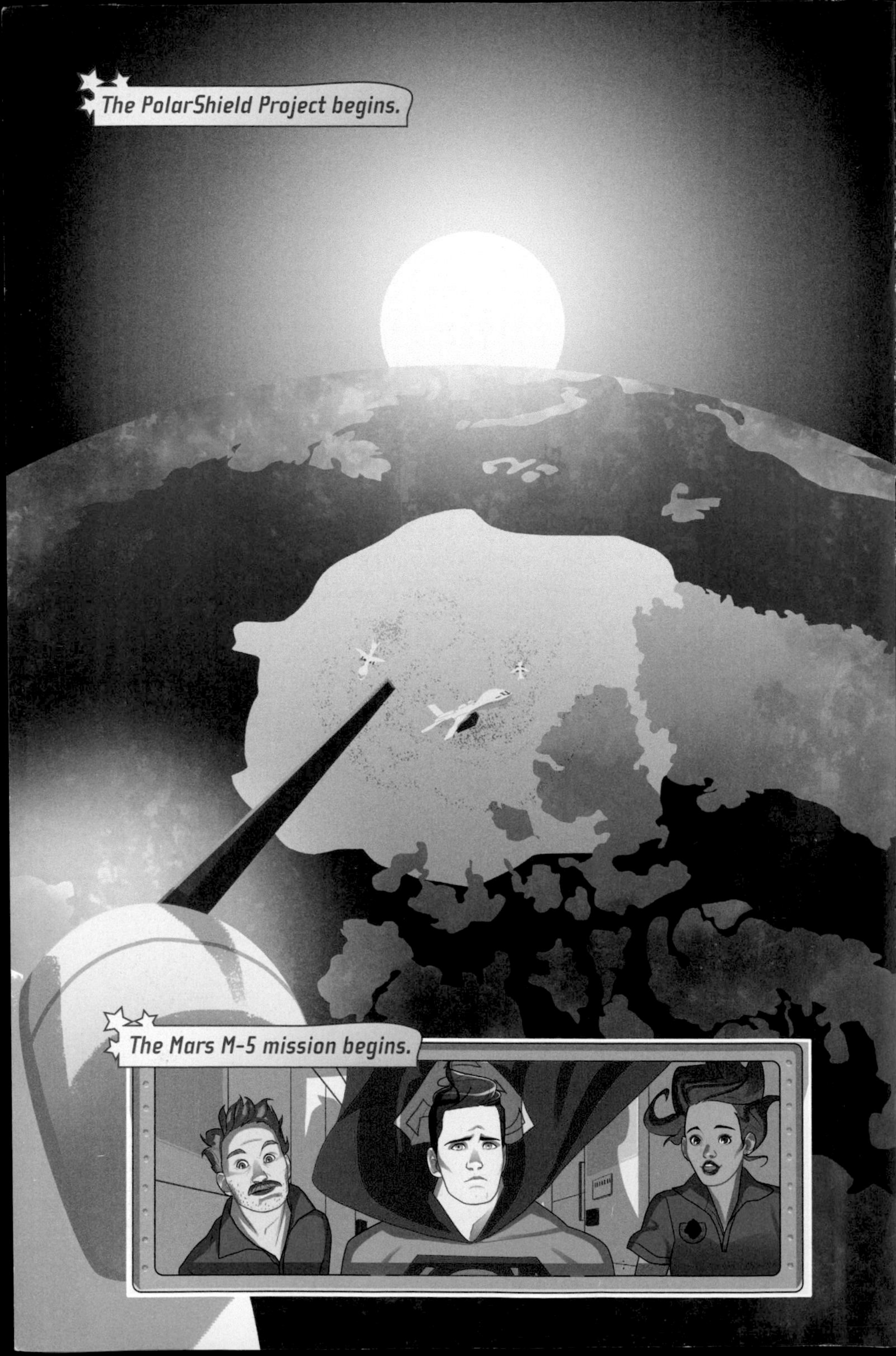
The PolarShield Project begins.
The Mars M-5 mission begins.

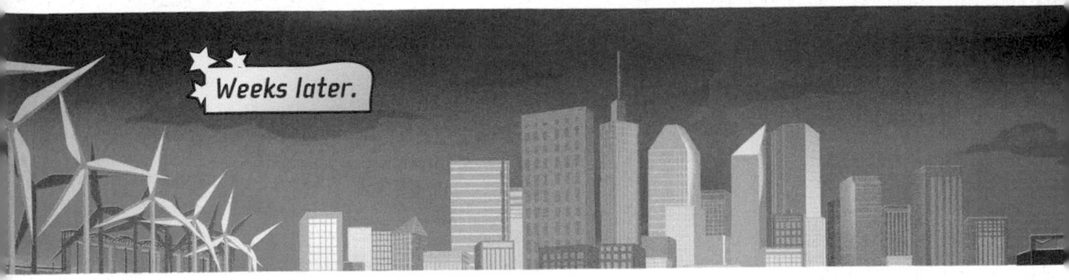
Weeks later.

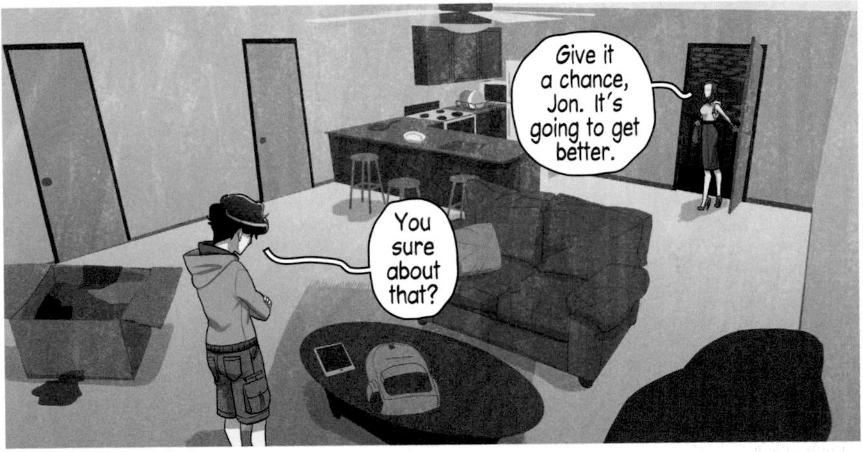
Give it a chance, Jon. It's going to get better.
You sure about that?

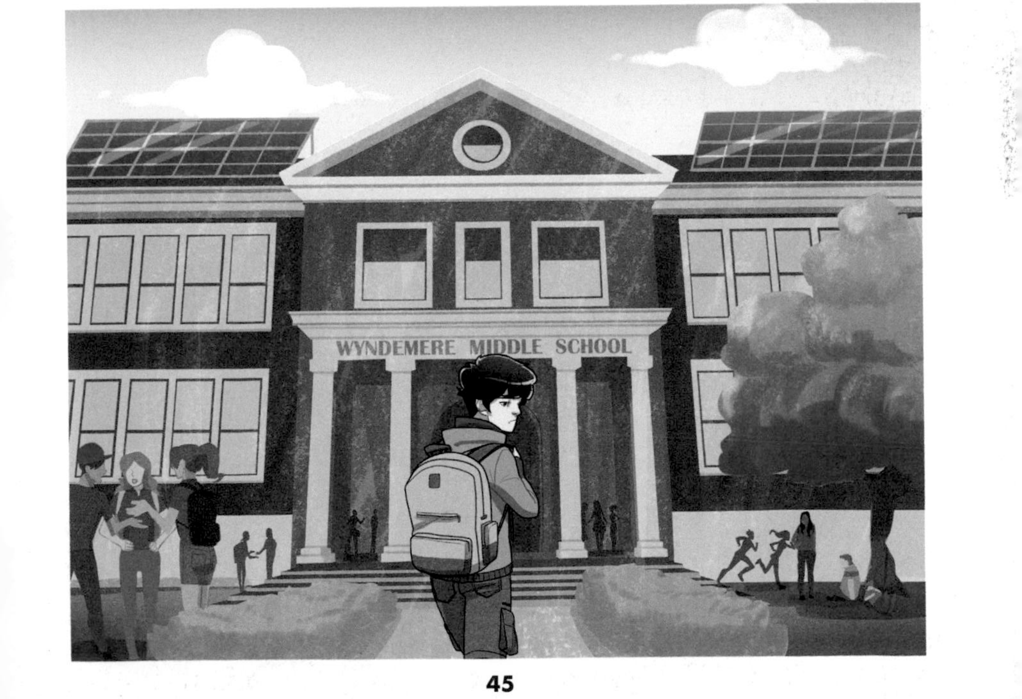
WYNDEMERE MIDDLE SCHOOL

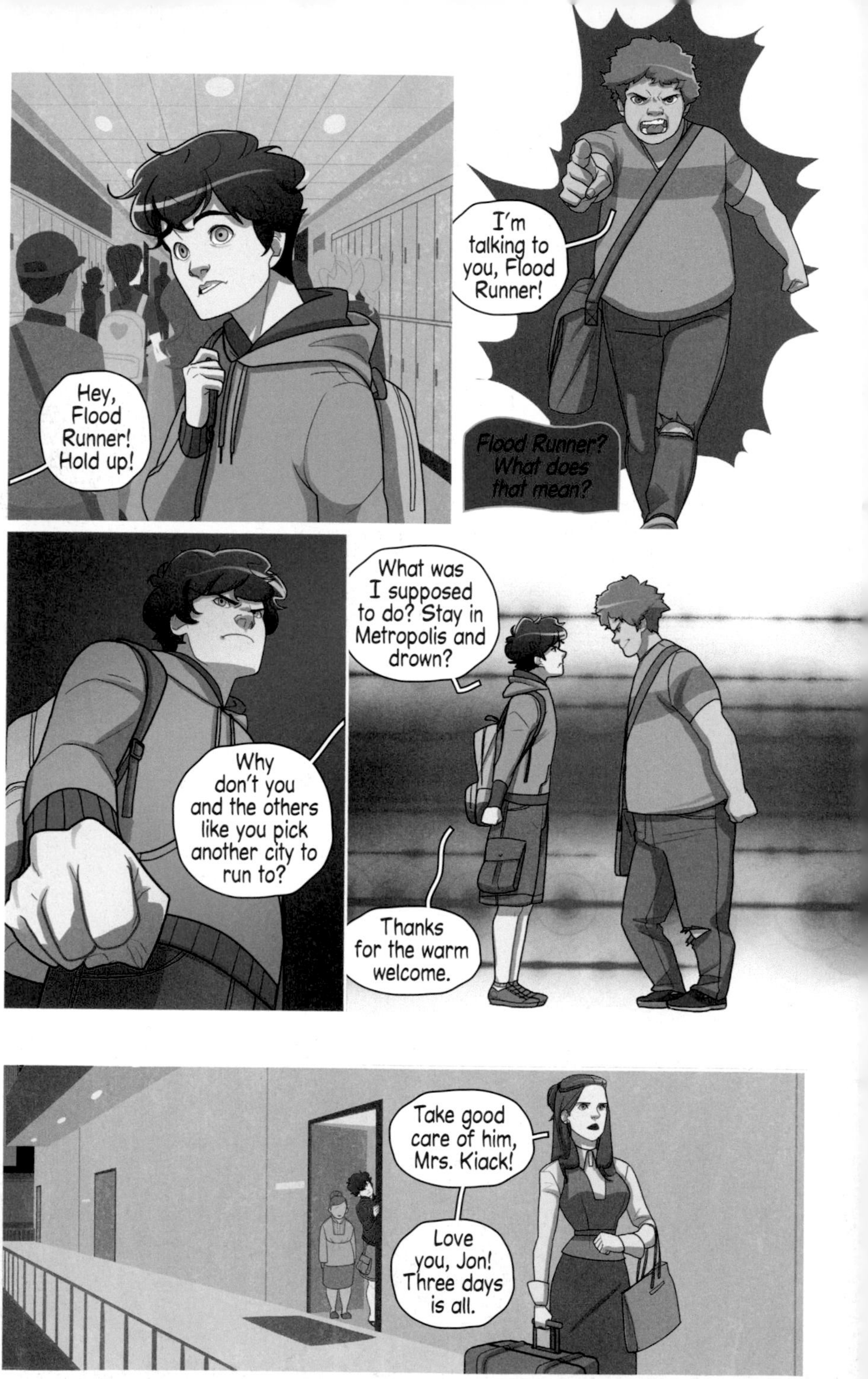

Hey, Flood Runner! Hold up!
I'm talking to you, Flood Runner!
Flood Runner? What does that mean?
Why don't you and the others like you pick another city to run to?
What was I supposed to do? Stay in Metropolis and drown?
Thanks for the warm welcome.
Take good care of him, Mrs. Kiack!
Love you, Jon! Three days is all.

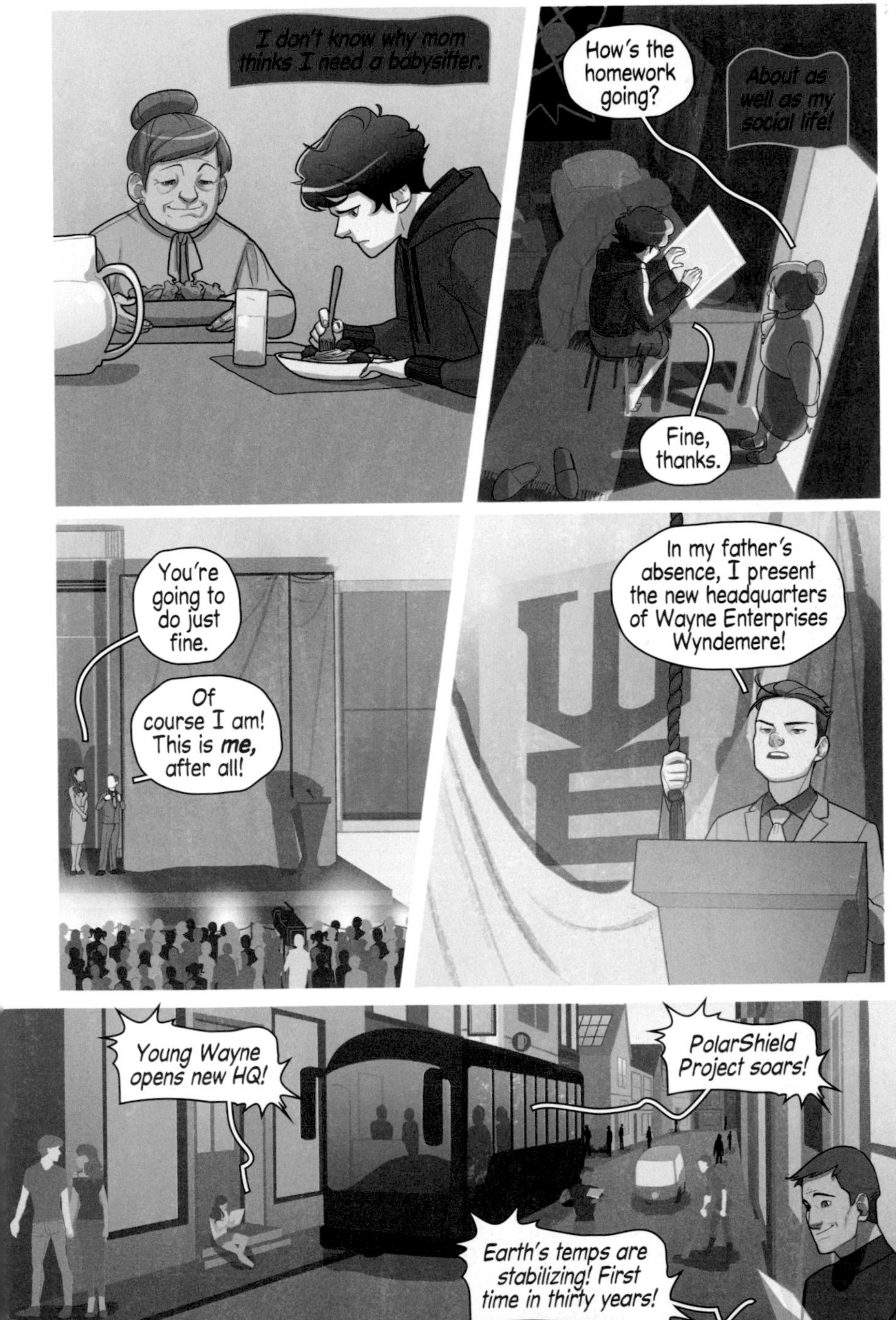
I don't know why mom thinks I need a babysitter.
How's the homework going?
About as well as my social life!
Fine, thanks.
You're going to do just fine.
Of course I am! This is *me,* after all!
In my father's absence, I present the new headquarters of Wayne Enterprises Wyndemere!
Young Wayne opens new HQ!
PolarShield Project soars!
Earth's temps are stabilizing! First time in thirty years!

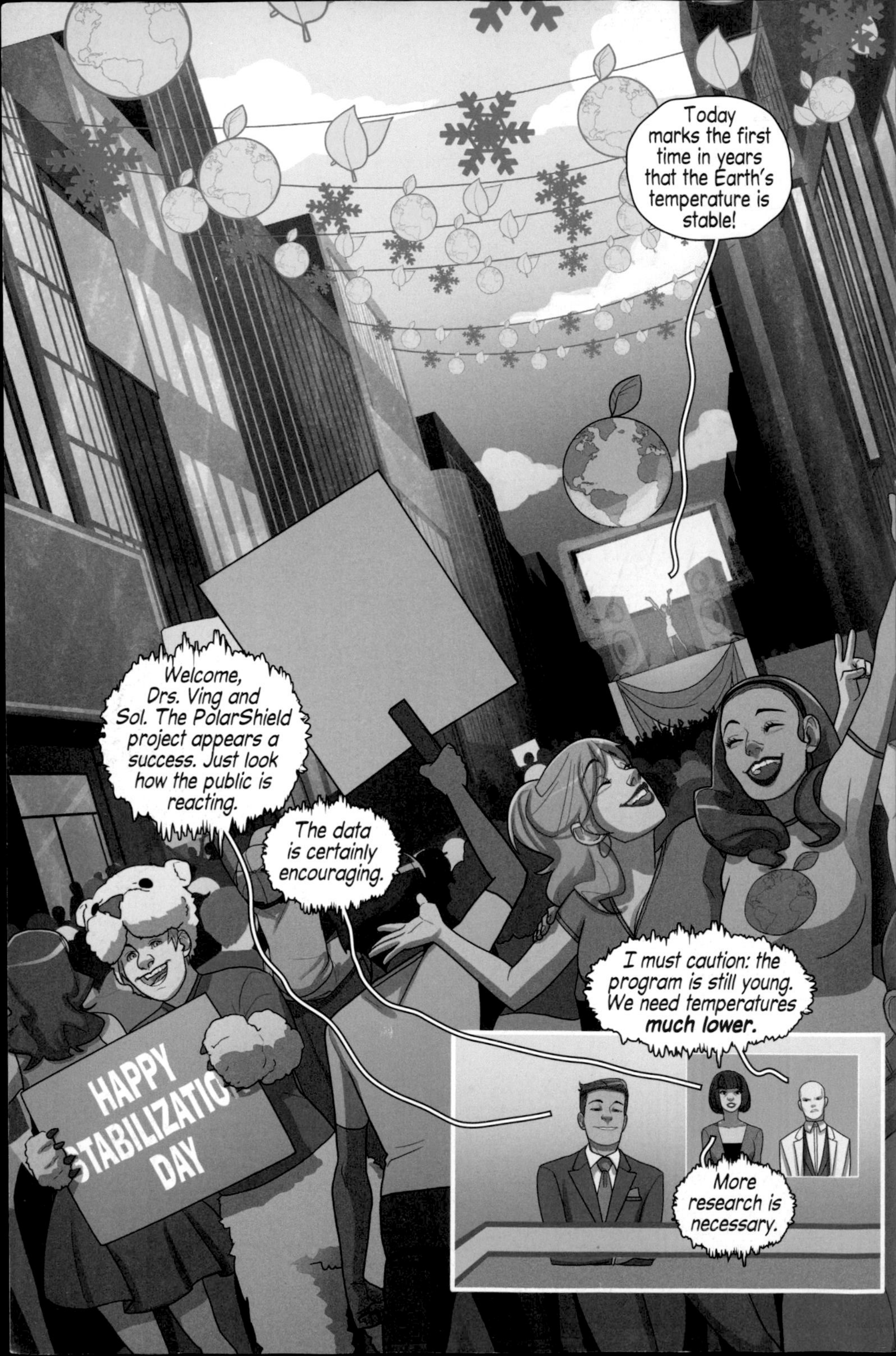
Today marks the first time in years that the Earth's temperature is stable!
Welcome, Drs. Ving and Sol. The PolarShield project appears a success. Just look how the public is reacting.
The data is certainly encouraging.
I must caution: the program is still young. We need temperatures **much lower.**
More research is necessary.
HAPPY STABILIZATIO DAY

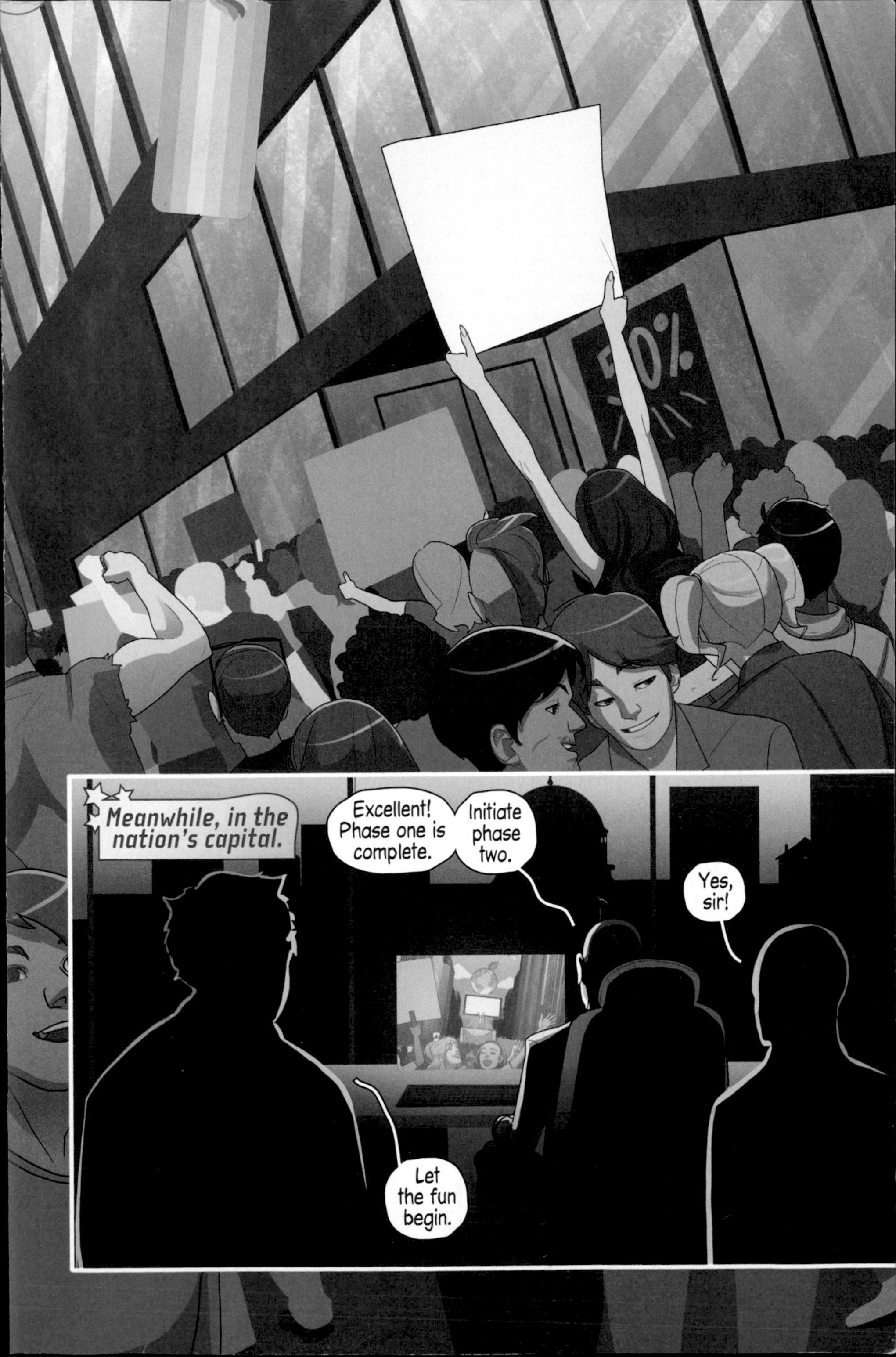
50%
Meanwhile, in the nation's capital.
Excellent! Phase one is complete.
Initiate phase two.
Yes, sir!
Let the fun begin.

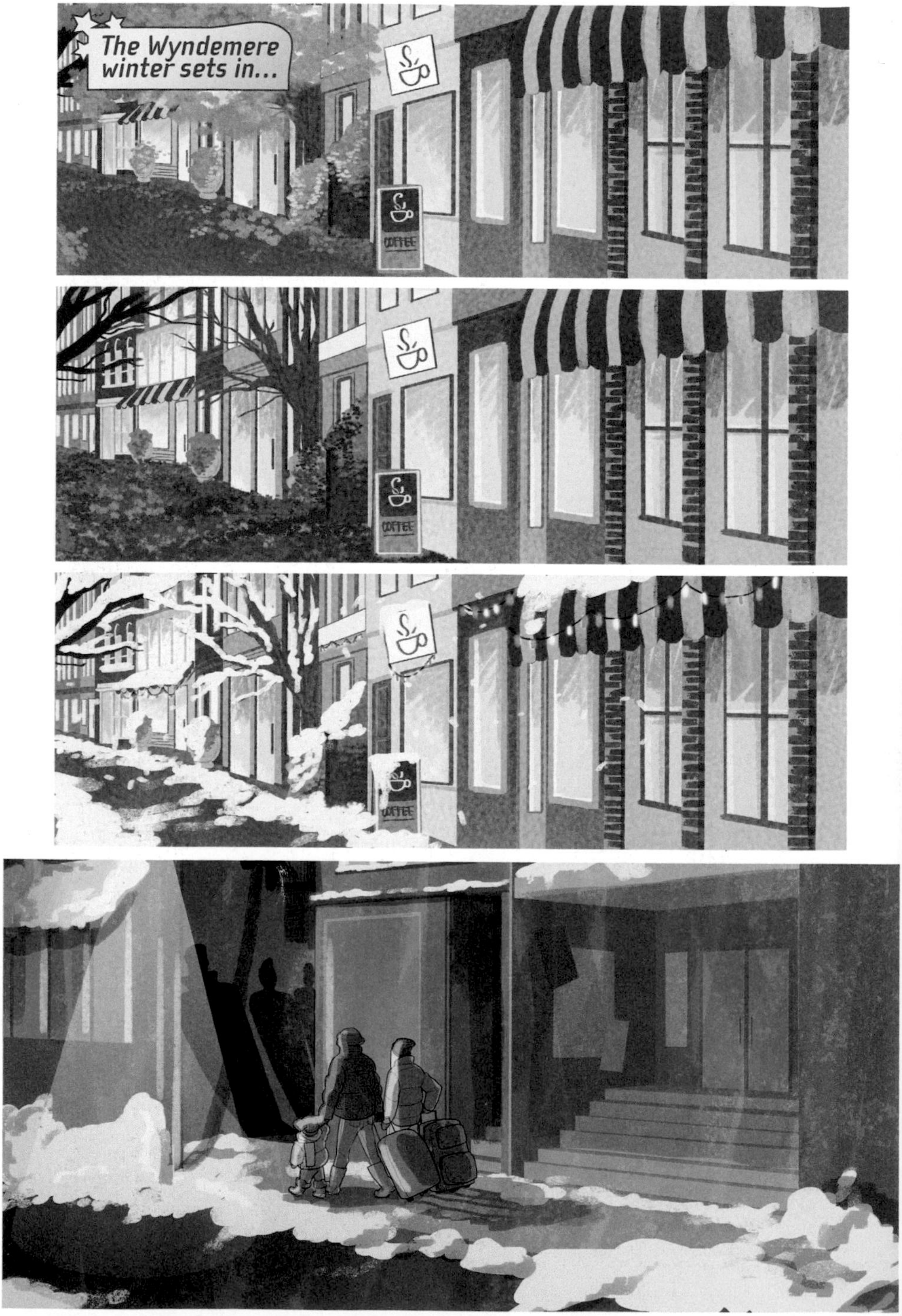
The Wyndemere winter sets in...
COFFEE
COFFEE
COFFEE

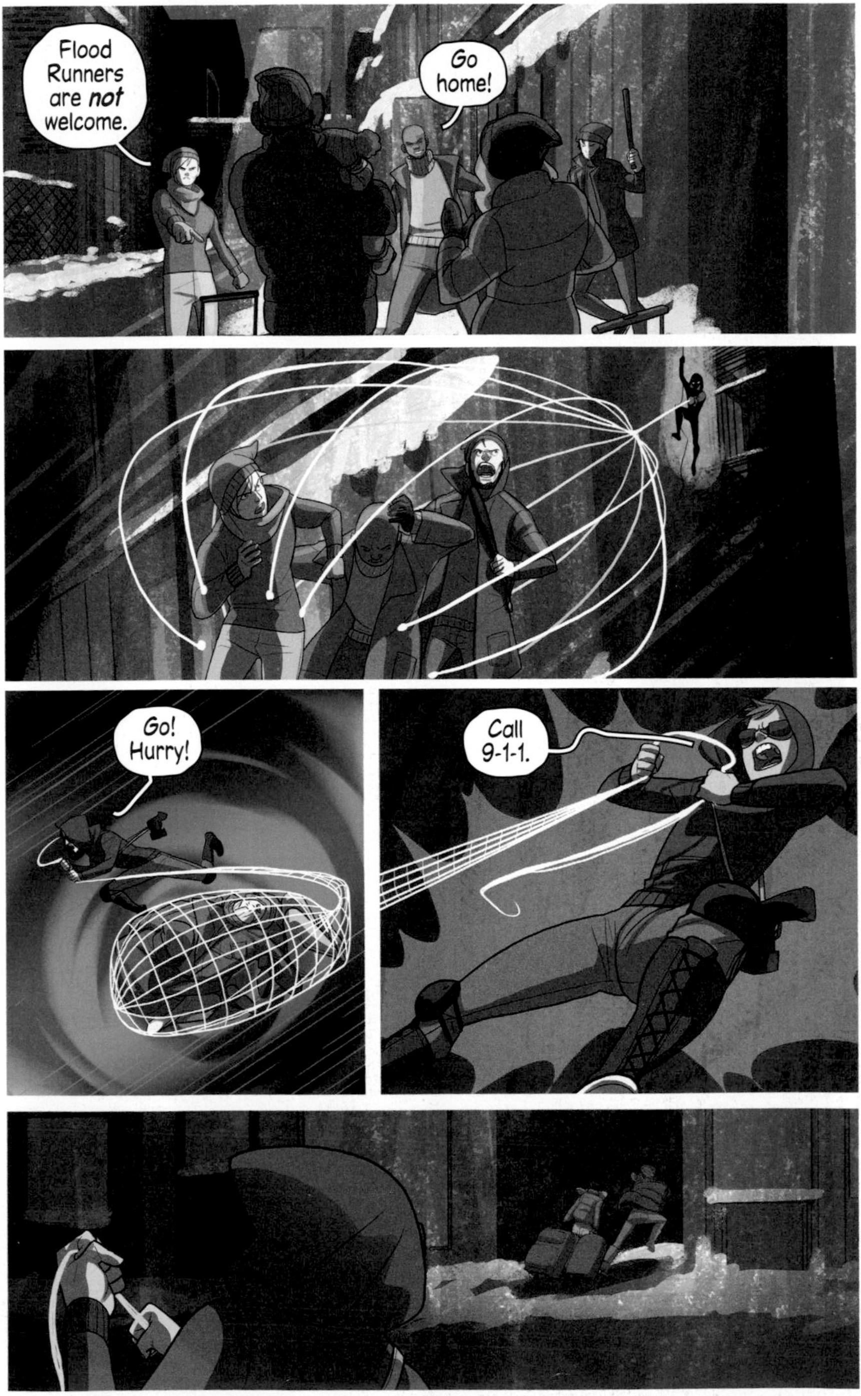
Flood Runners are *not* welcome.
Go home!
Go! Hurry!
Call 9-1-1.

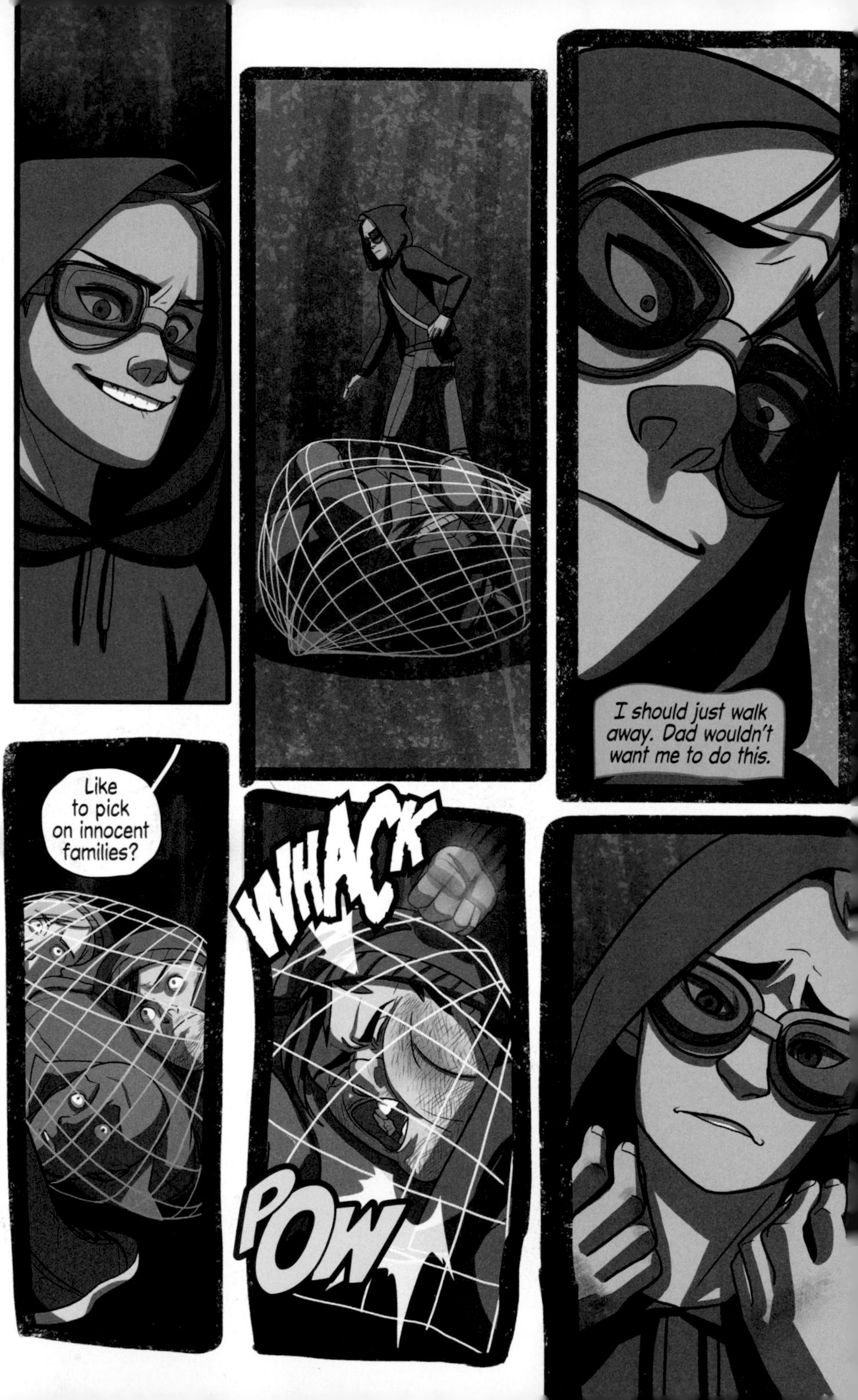
I should just walk away. Dad wouldn't want me to do this.
Like to pick on innocent families?
WHACK
POW

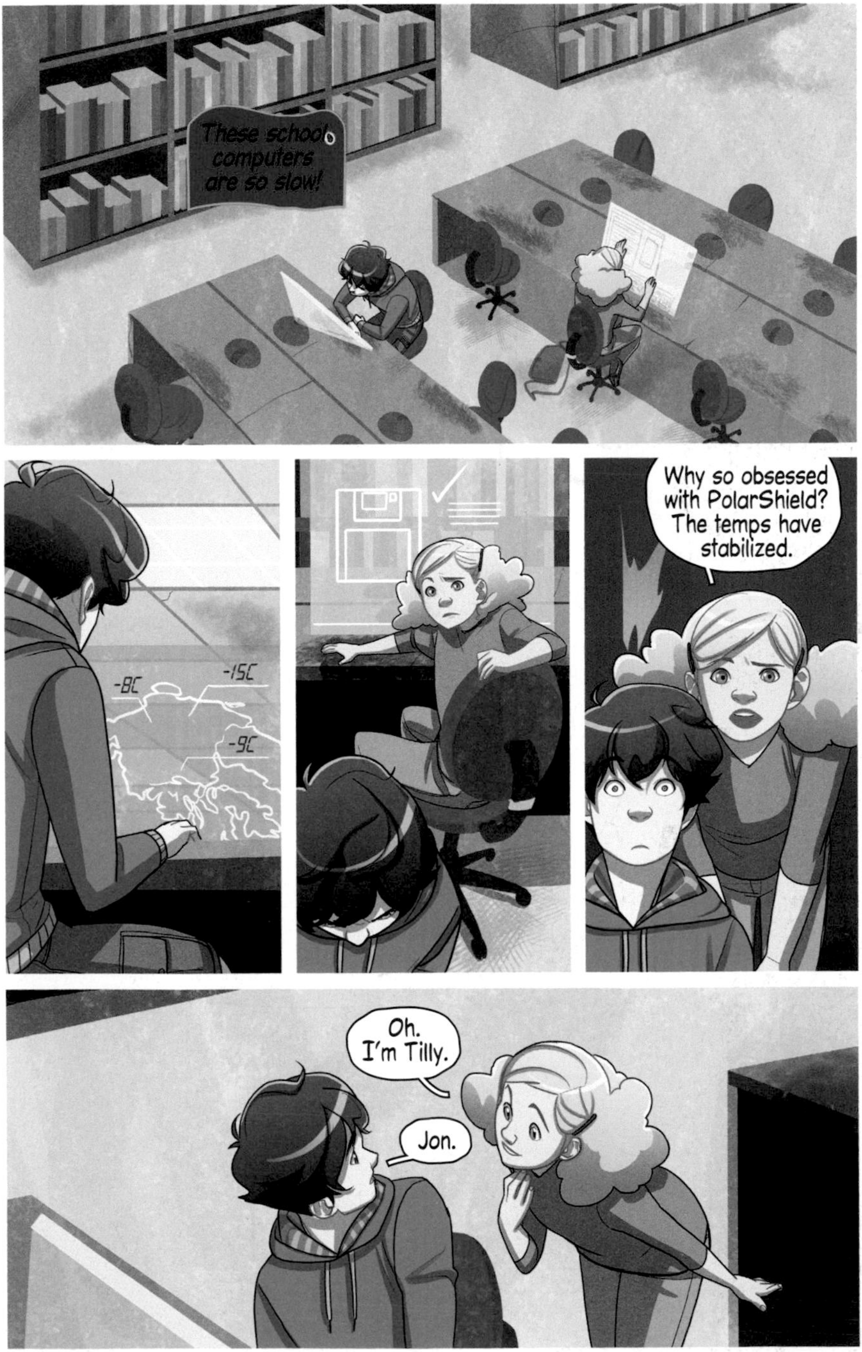
These school computers are so slow!
-8C
-15C
-9C
Why so obsessed with PolarShield? The temps have stabilized.
Oh. I'm Tilly.
Jon.

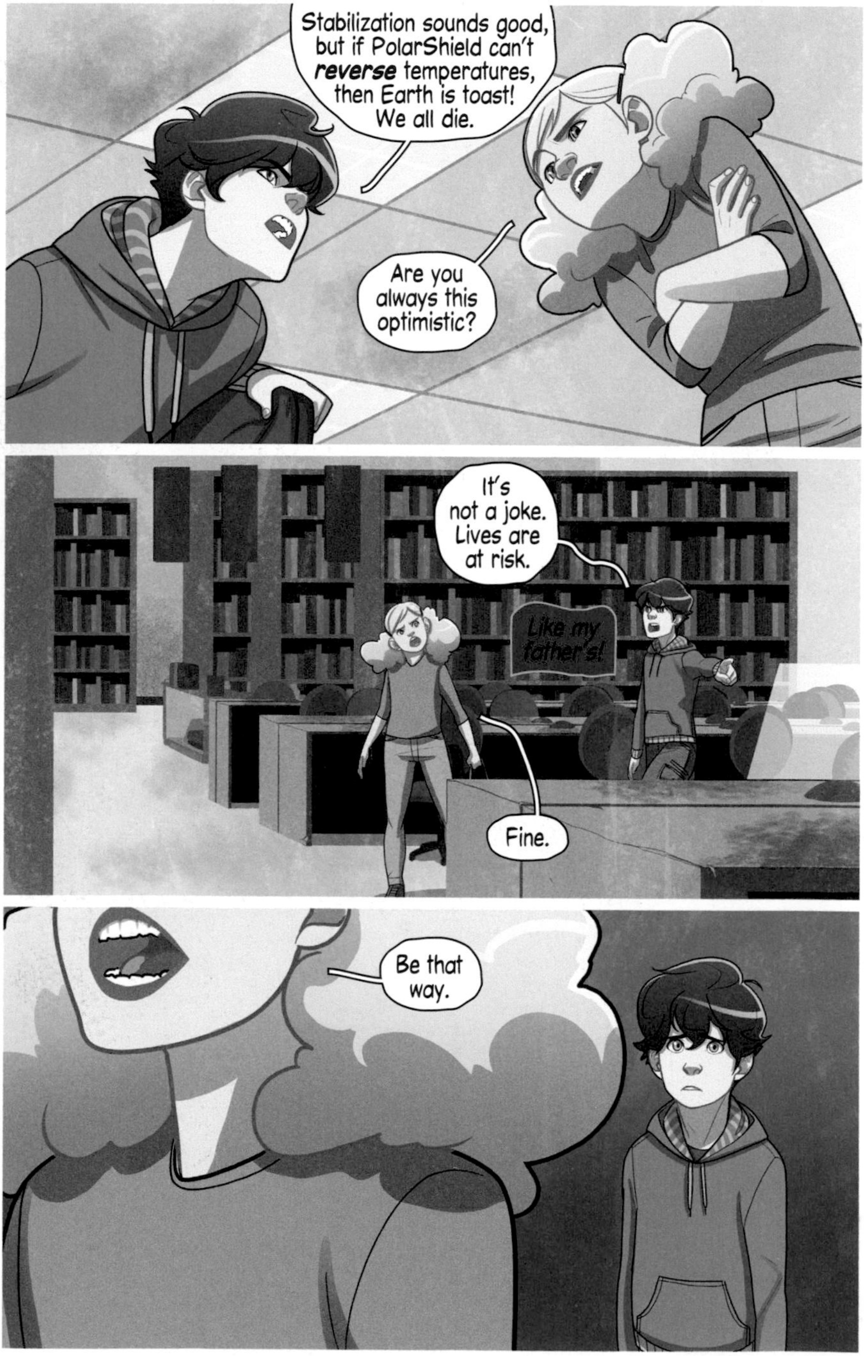
Stabilization sounds good, but if PolarShield can't *reverse* temperatures, then Earth is toast! We all die.
Are you always this optimistic?
It's not a joke. Lives are at risk.
Like my father's!
Fine.
Be that way.

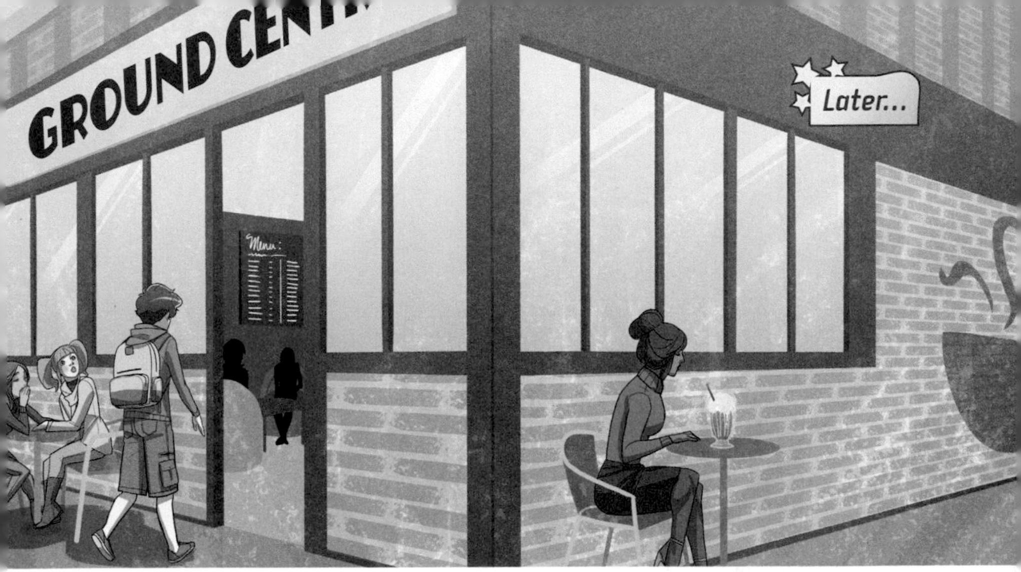
Later...

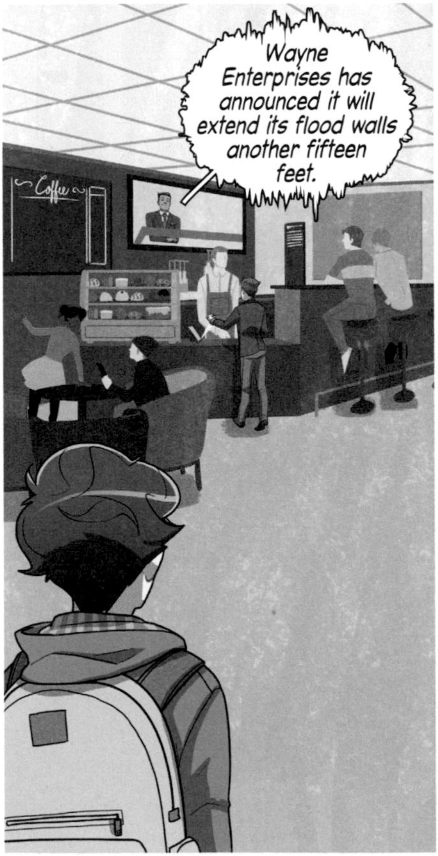
Wayne Enterprises has announced it will extend its flood walls another fifteen feet.
Coffee

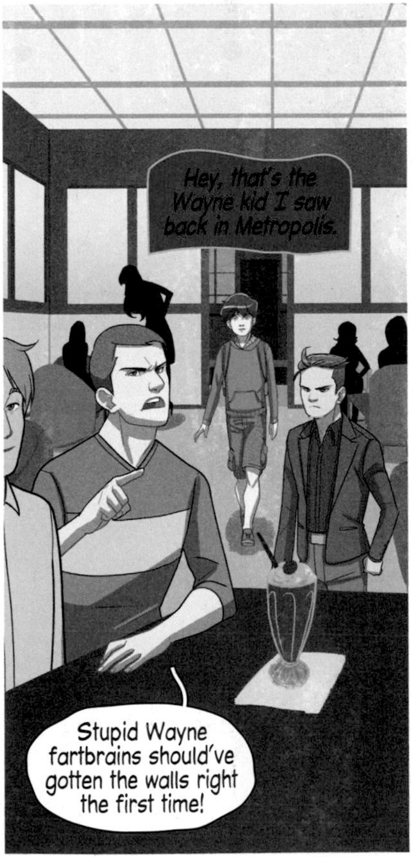
Hey, that's the Wayne kid I saw back in Metropolis.
Stupid Wayne fartbrains should've gotten the walls right the first time!

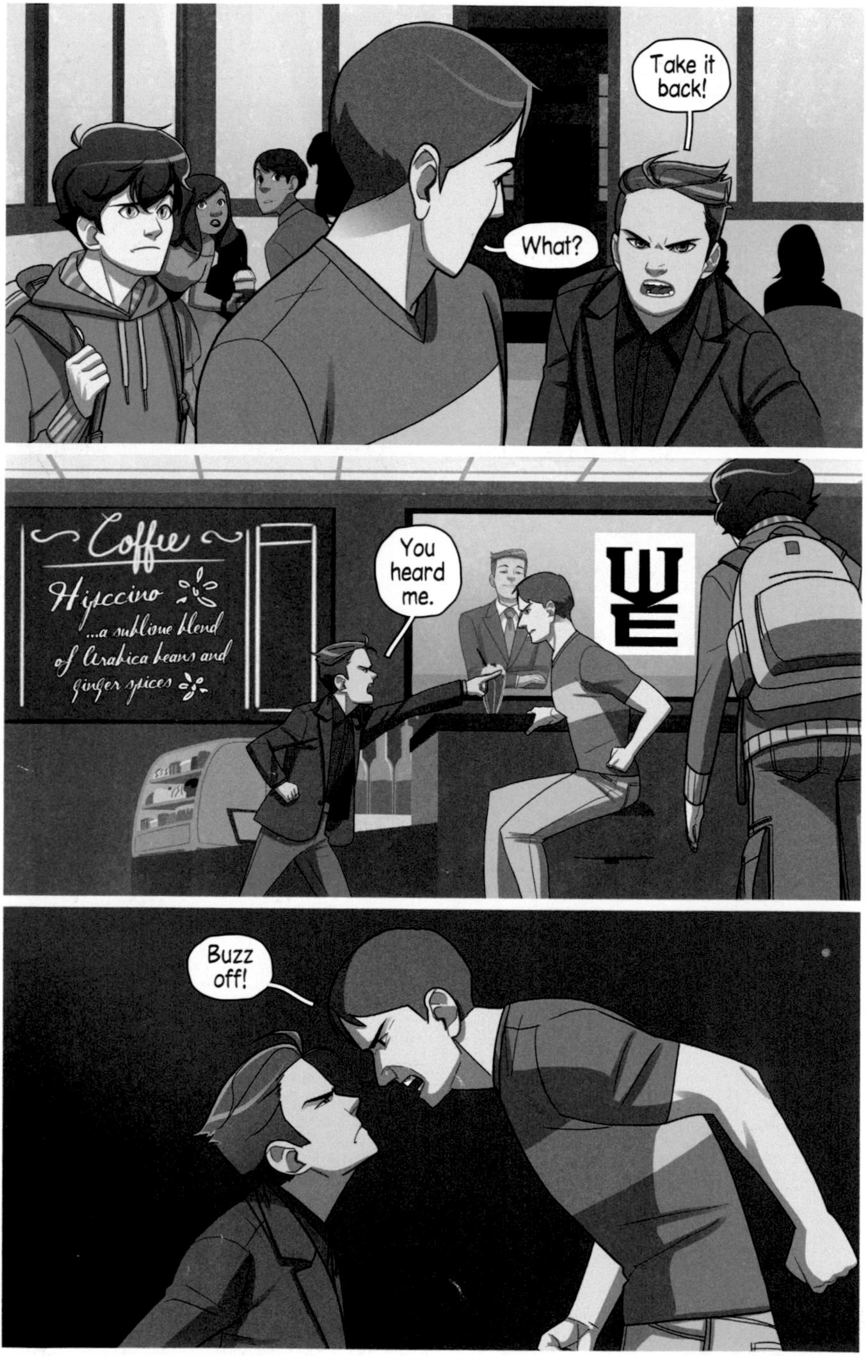
Take it back!
What?
Coffee
Hipccino
...a sublime blend of Arabica beans and ginger spices
You heard me.
Buzz off!

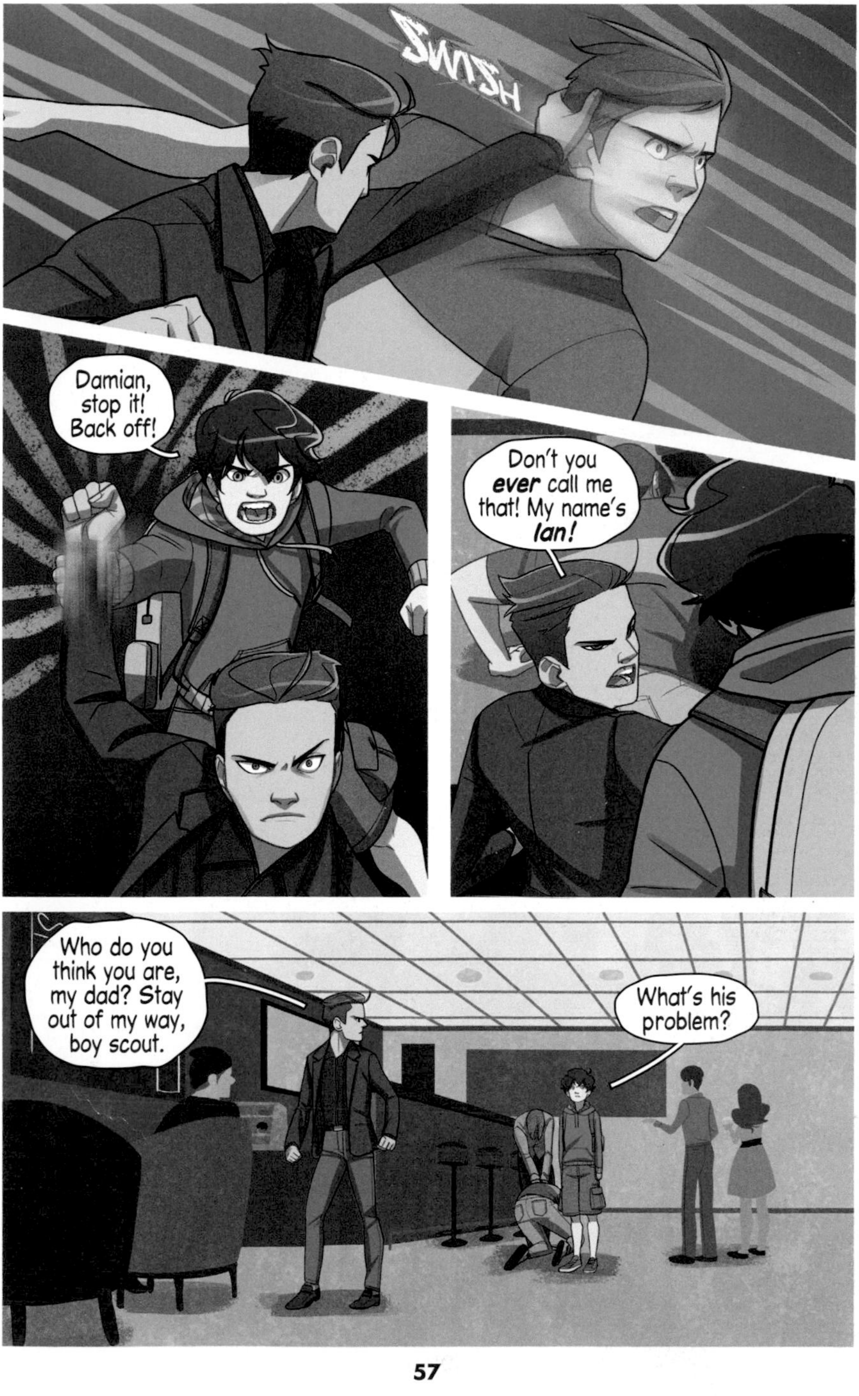
SWISH
Damian, stop it! Back off!
Don't you **ever** call me that! My name's ***Ian!***
Who do you think you are, my dad? Stay out of my way, boy scout.
What's his problem?

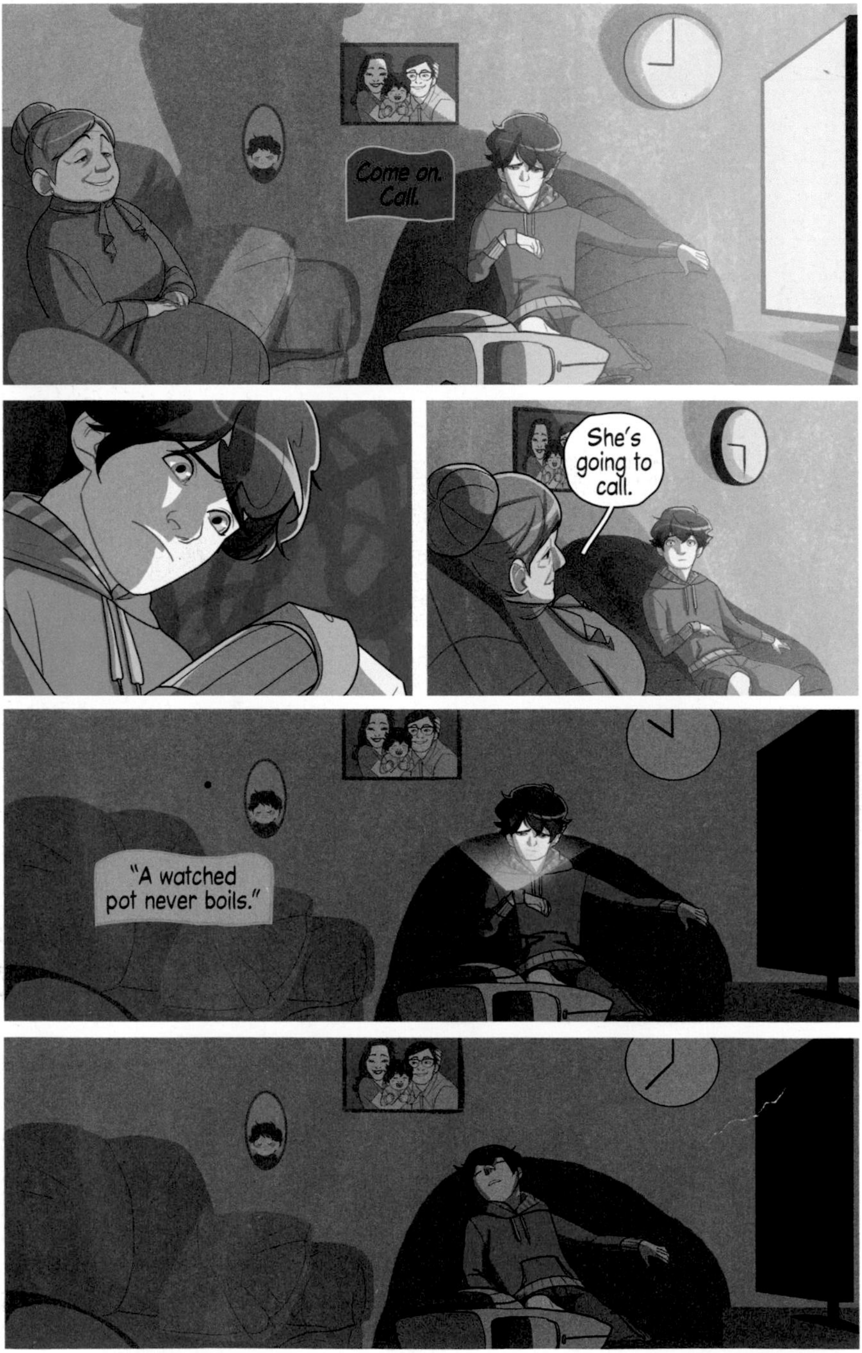
Come on. Call.
She's going to call.
"A watched pot never boils."

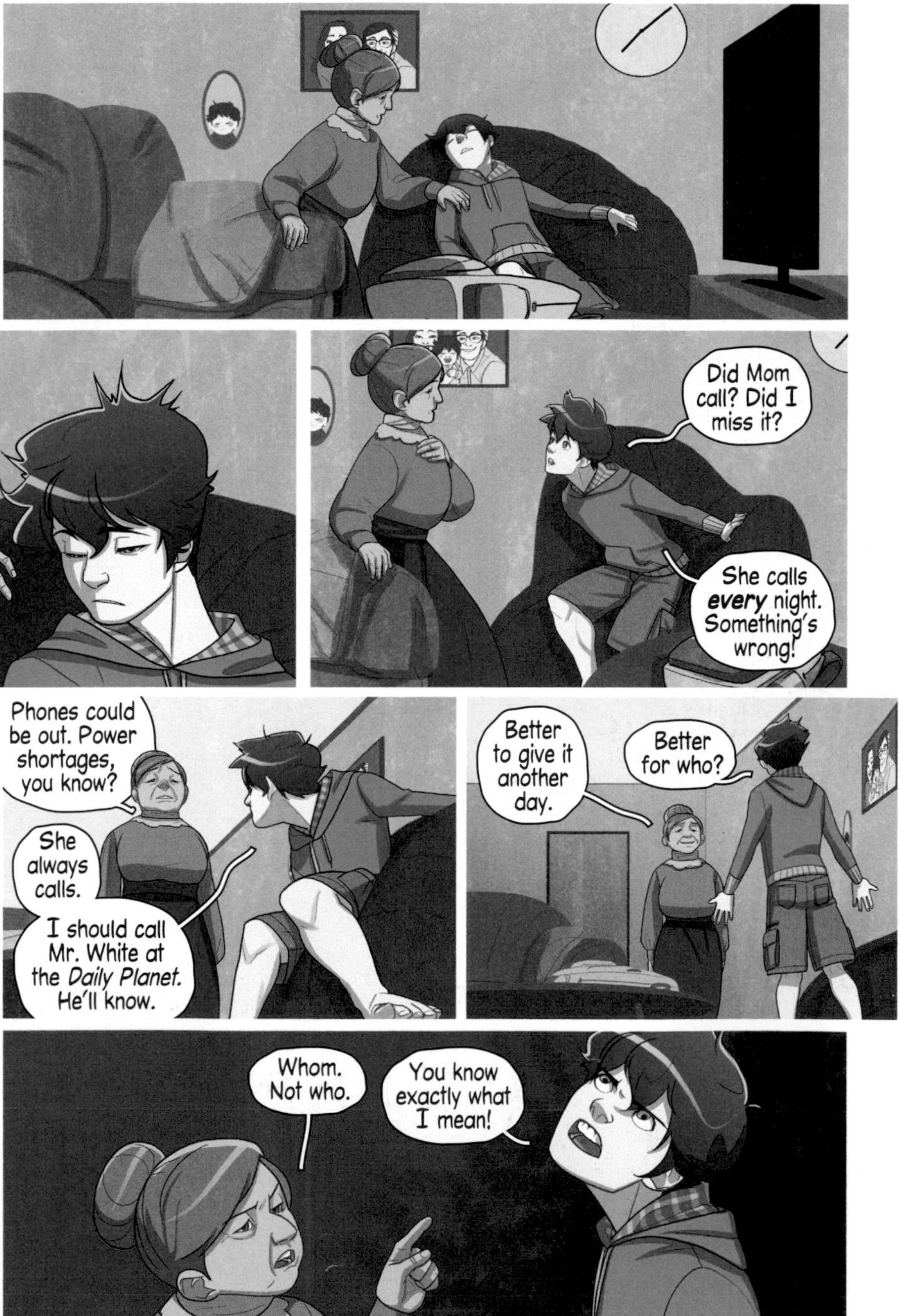

Did Mom call? Did I miss it?
She calls **every** night. Something's wrong!
Phones could be out. Power shortages, you know?
She always calls.
I should call Mr. White at the *Daily Planet*. He'll know.
Better to give it another day.
Better for who?
Whom. Not who.
You know exactly what I mean!

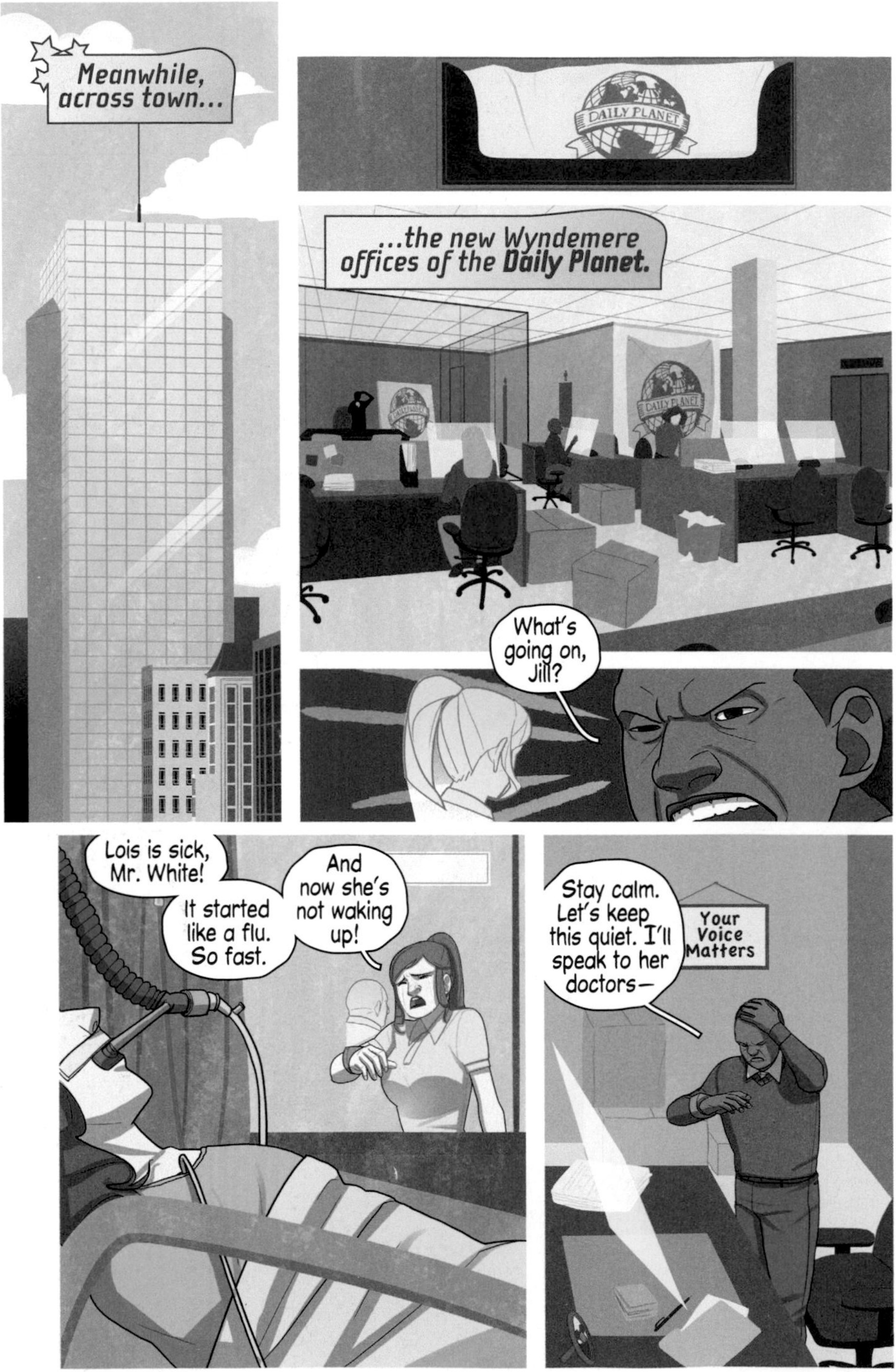
Meanwhile, across town...
DAILY PLANET
...the new Wyndemere offices of the Daily Planet.
DAILY PLANET
What's going on, Jill?
Lois is sick, Mr. White!
It started like a flu. So fast.
And now she's not waking up!
Stay calm. Let's keep this quiet. I'll speak to her doctors—
Your Voice Matters

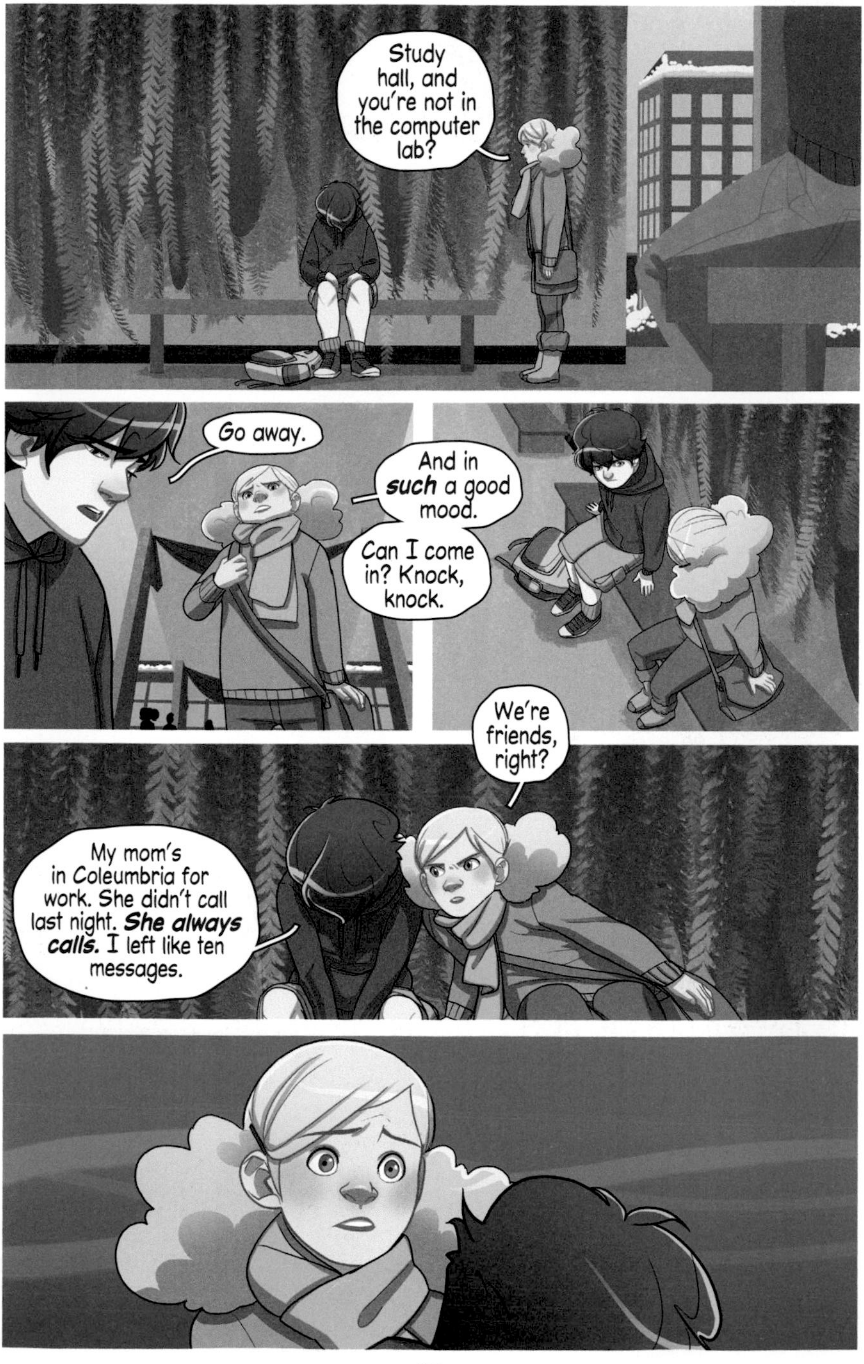
Study hall, and you're not in the computer lab?
Go away.
And in **such** a good mood.
Can I come in? Knock, knock.
We're friends, right?
My mom's in Coleumbria for work. She didn't call last night. ***She always calls.*** I left like ten messages.

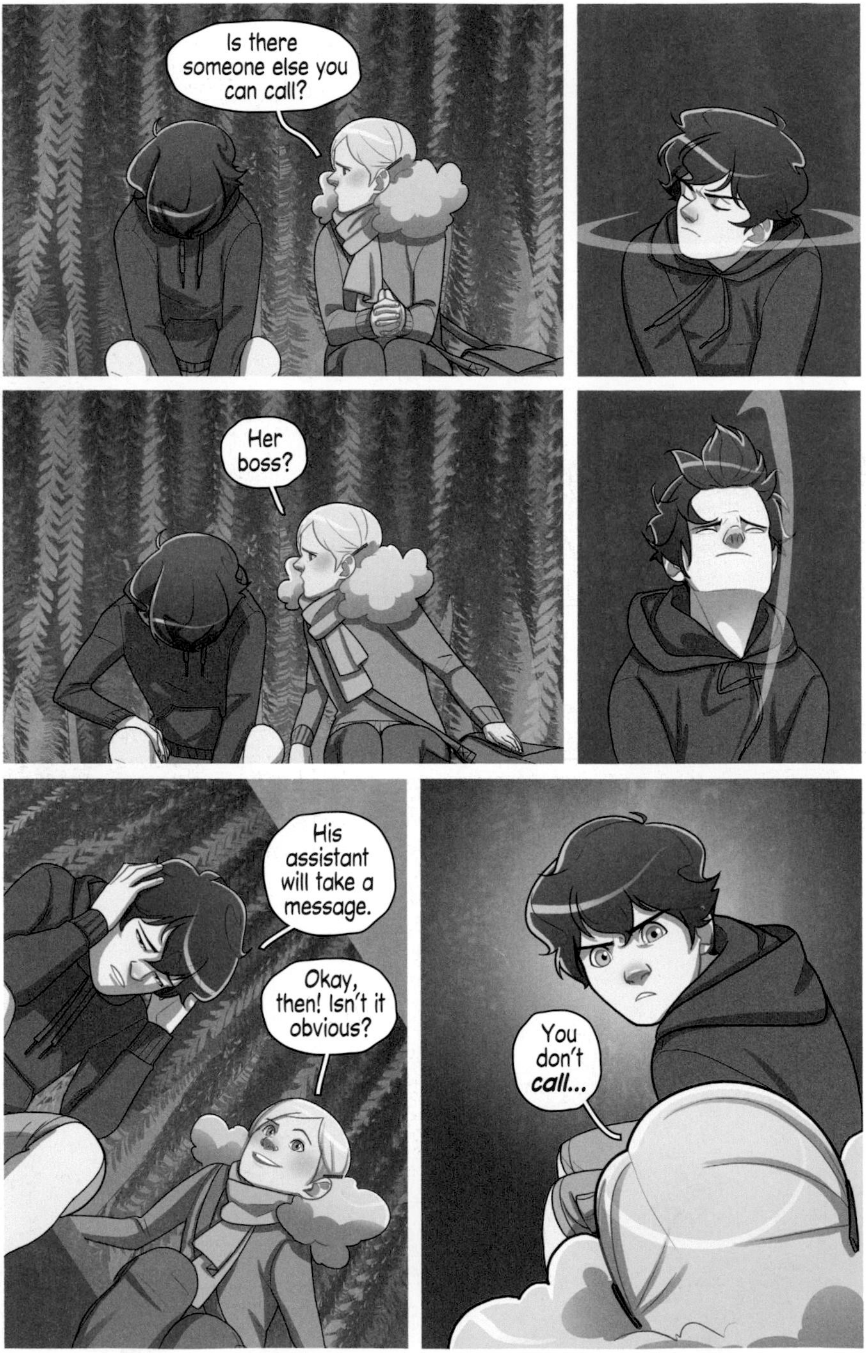

Is there someone else you can call?
Her boss?
His assistant will take a message.
Okay, then! Isn't it obvious?
You don't call...

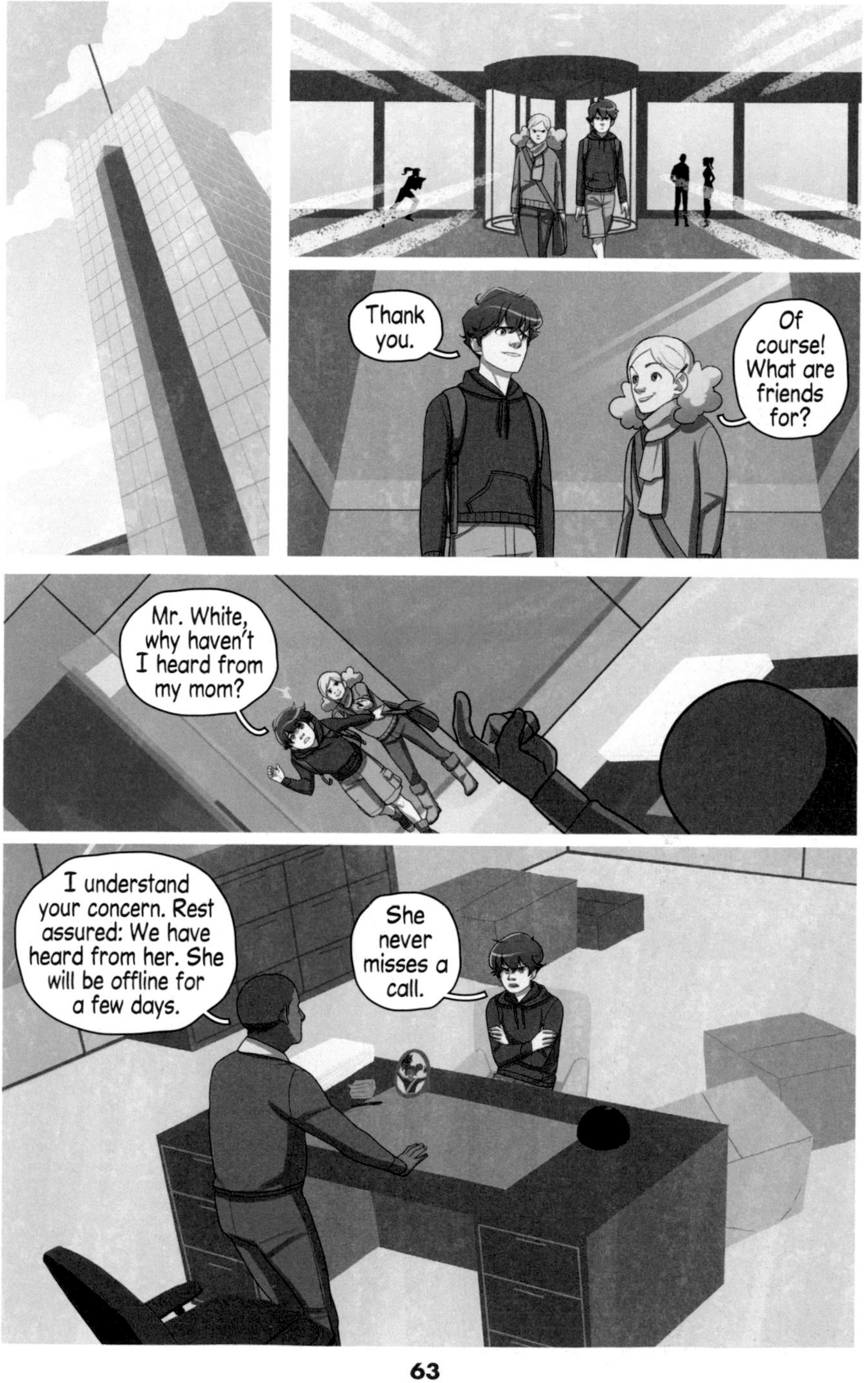
Thank you.
Of course! What are friends for?
Mr. White, why haven't I heard from my mom?
I understand your concern. Rest assured: We have heard from her. She will be offline for a few days.
She never misses a call.

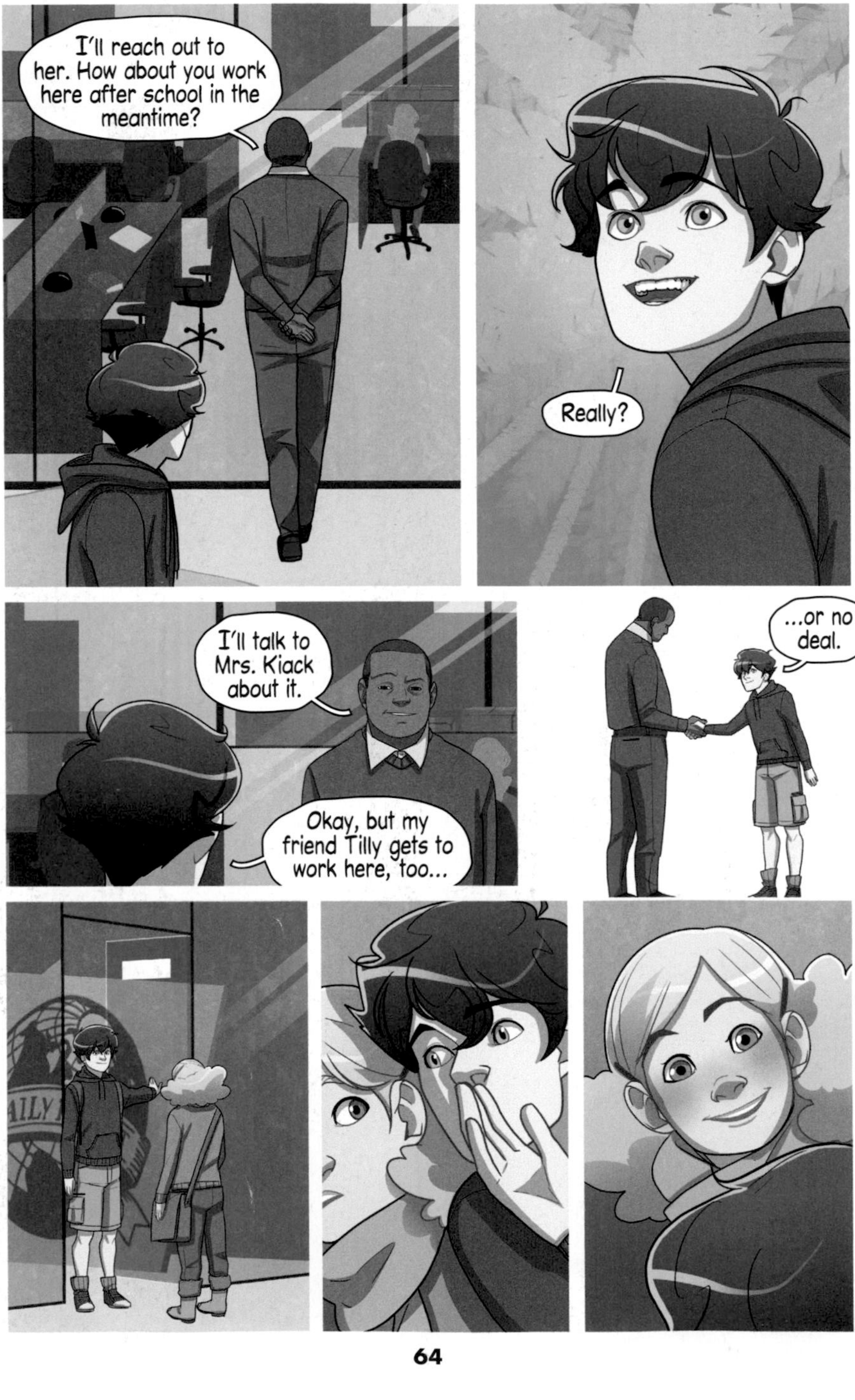
I'll reach out to her. How about you work here after school in the meantime?
Really?
I'll talk to Mrs. Kiack about it.
Okay, but my friend Tilly gets to work here, too...
...or no deal.

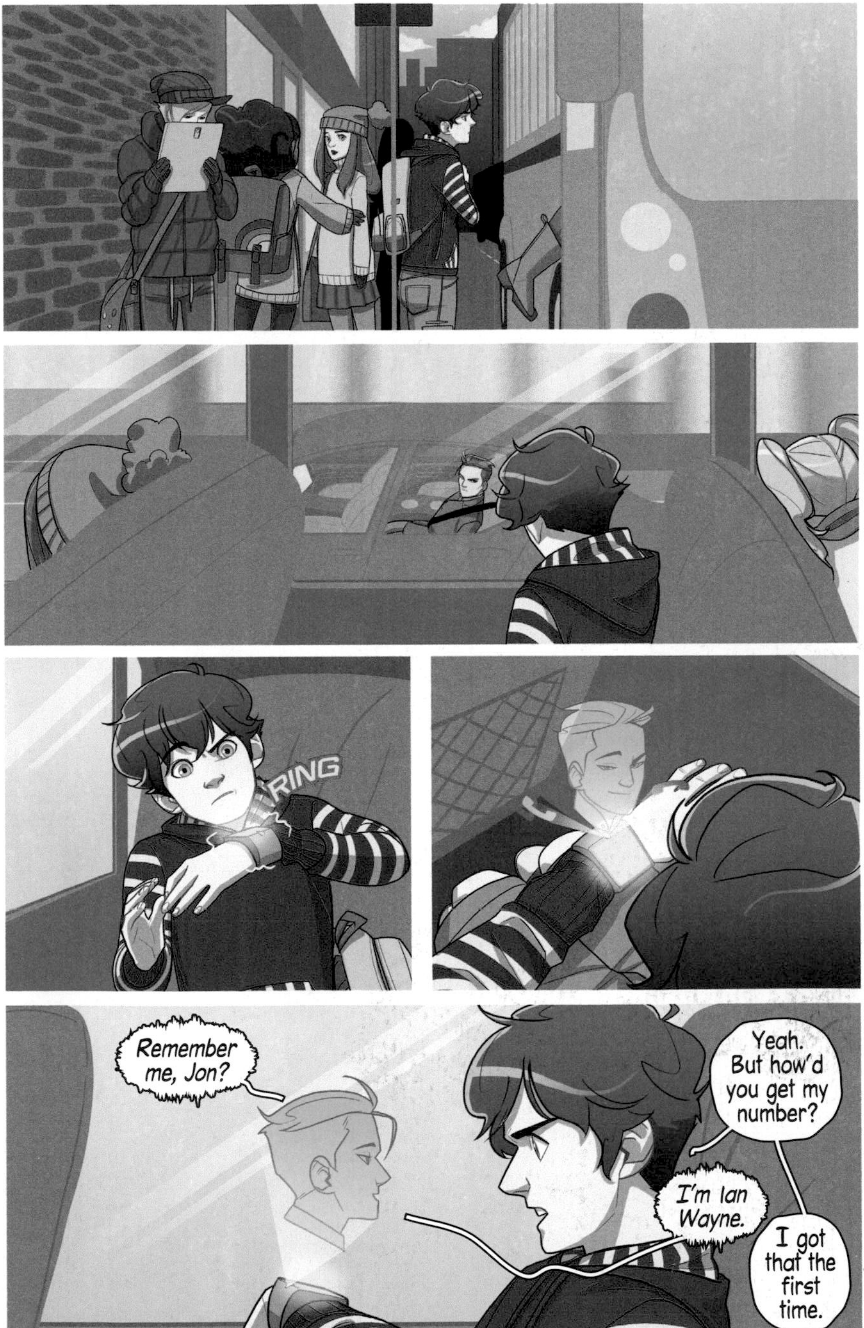
RING
Remember me, Jon?
Yeah. But how'd you get my number?
I'm Ian Wayne.
I got that the first time.

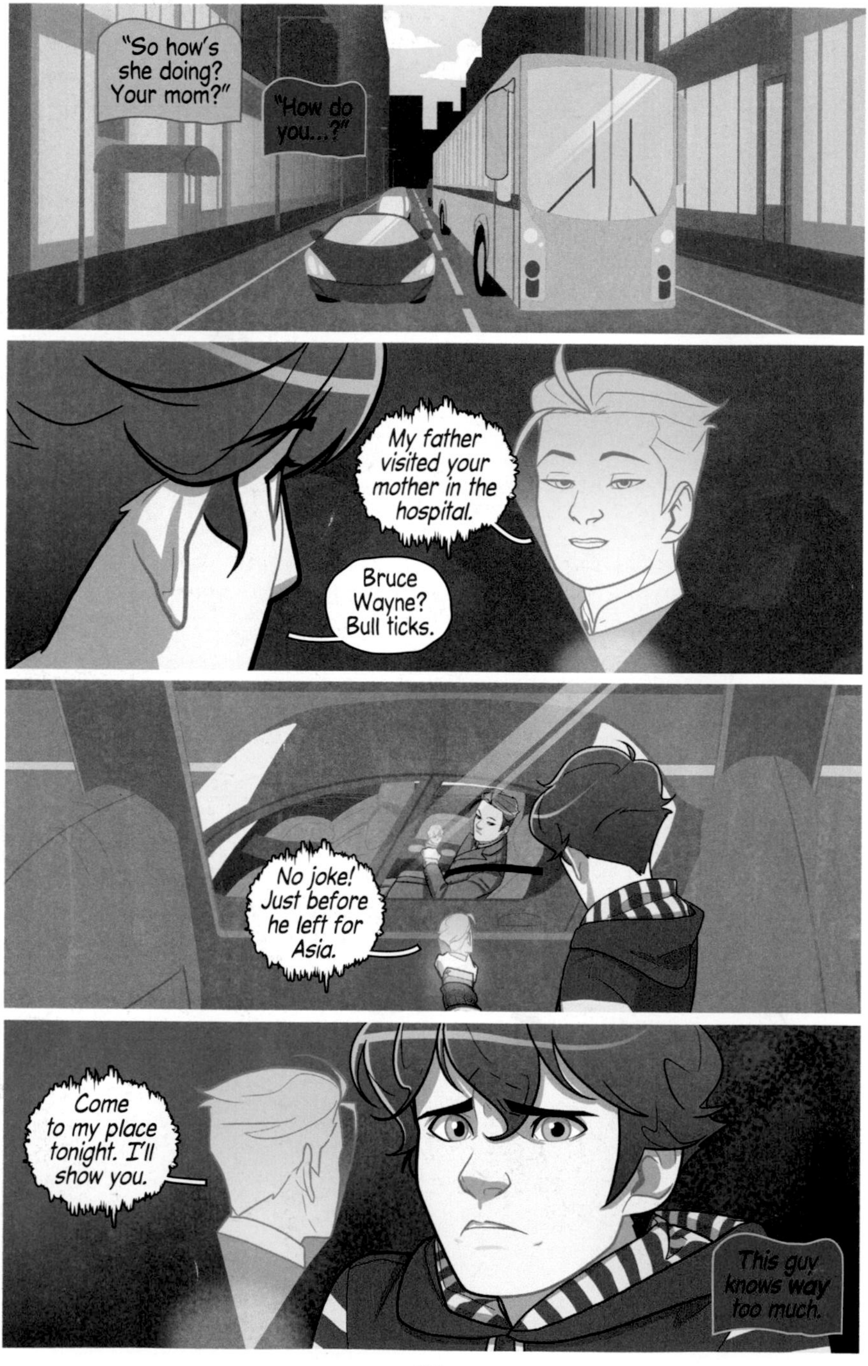
"So how's she doing? Your mom?"
"How do you...?"
My father visited your mother in the hospital.
Bruce Wayne? Bull ticks.
No joke! Just before he left for Asia.
Come to my place tonight. I'll show you.
This guy knows way too much.

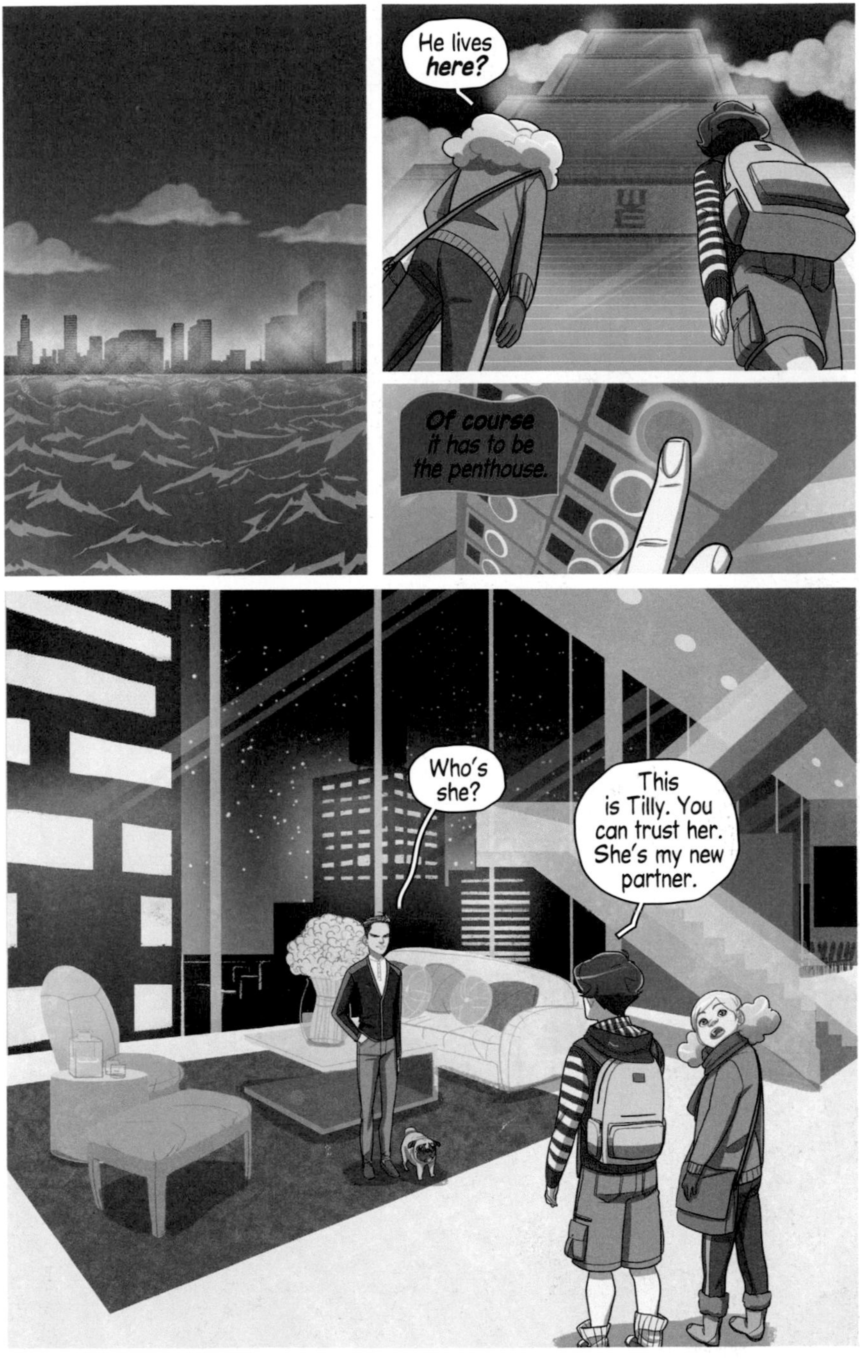
He lives here?
Of course it has to be the penthouse.
Who's she?
This is Tilly. You can trust her. She's my new partner.

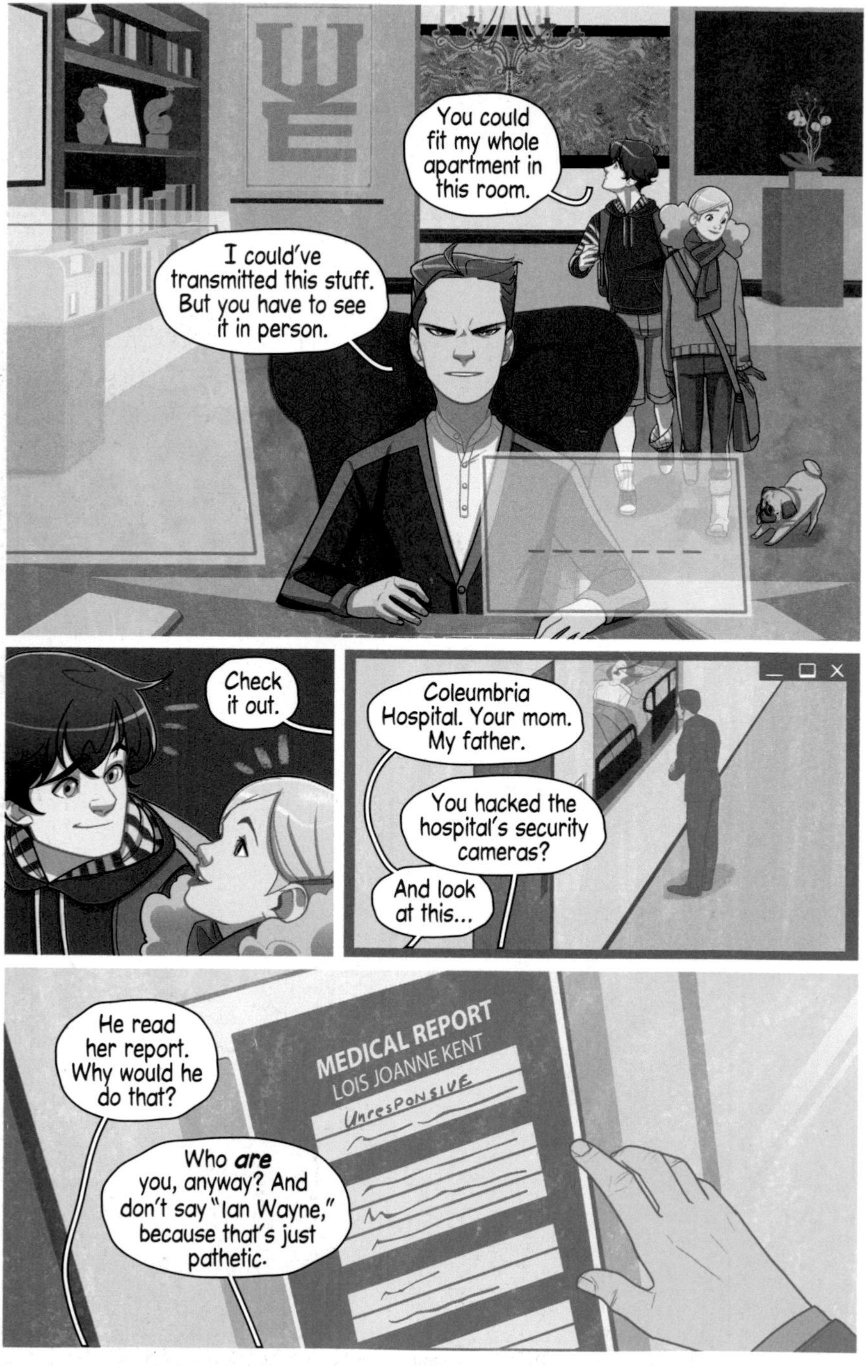
You could fit my whole apartment in this room.
I could've transmitted this stuff. But you have to see it in person.
Check it out.
Coleumbria Hospital. Your mom. My father.
You hacked the hospital's security cameras?
And look at this...
MEDICAL REPORT
LOIS JOANNE KENT
UnresPONSIVE
He read her report. Why would he do that?
Who *are* you, anyway? And don't say "Ian Wayne," because that's just pathetic.

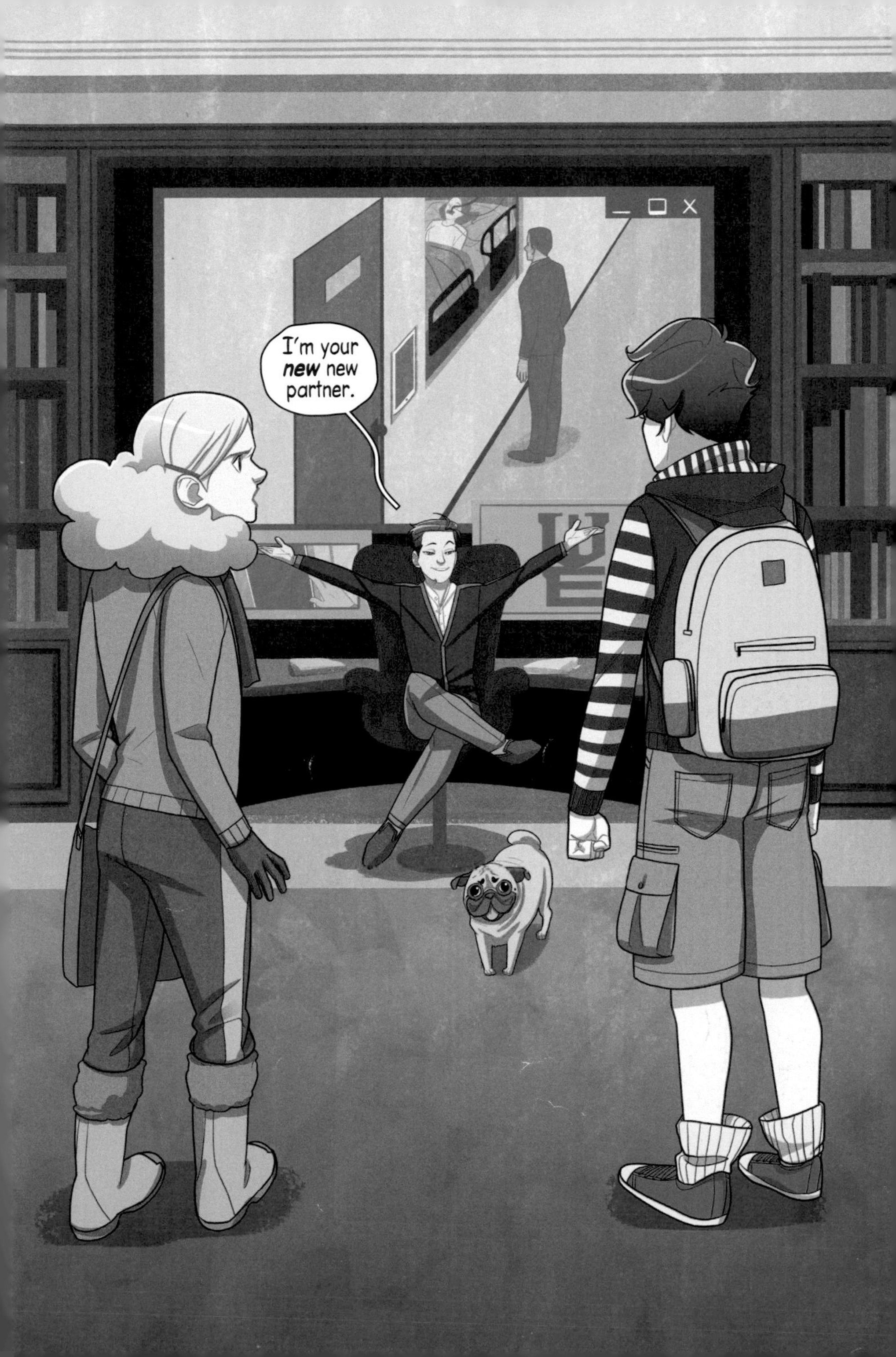
I'm your *new* new partner.

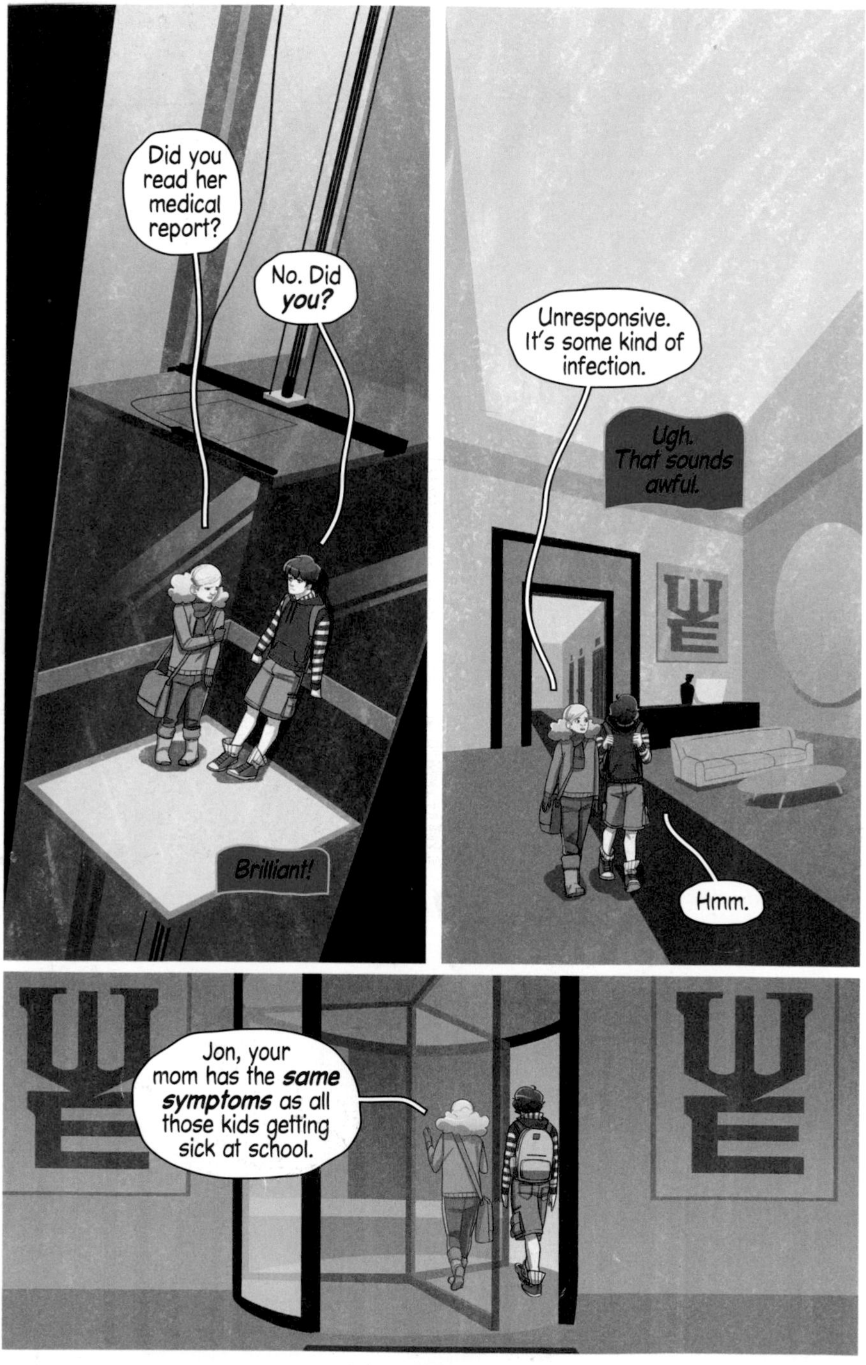
Did you read her medical report?
No. Did *you?*
Brilliant!
Unresponsive. It's some kind of infection.
Ugh. That sounds awful.
Hmm.
Jon, your mom has the ***same symptoms*** as all those kids getting sick at school.

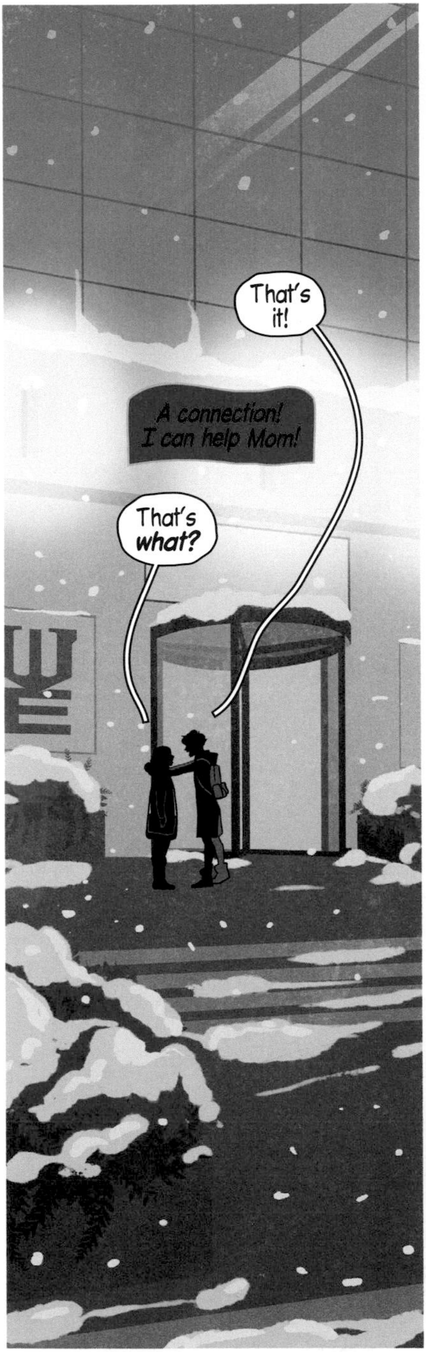
A connection!
I can help Mom!
That's it!
That's what?

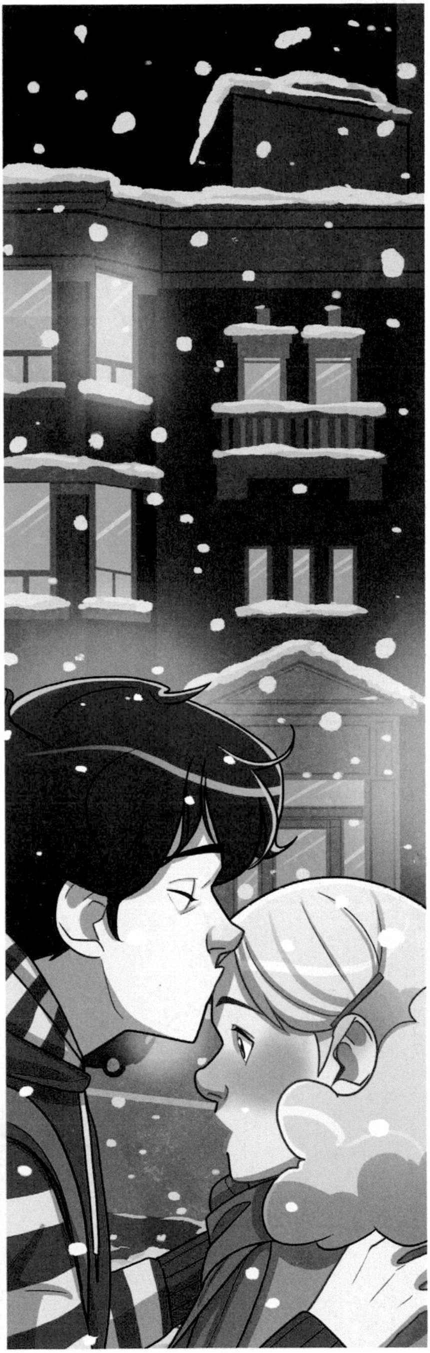

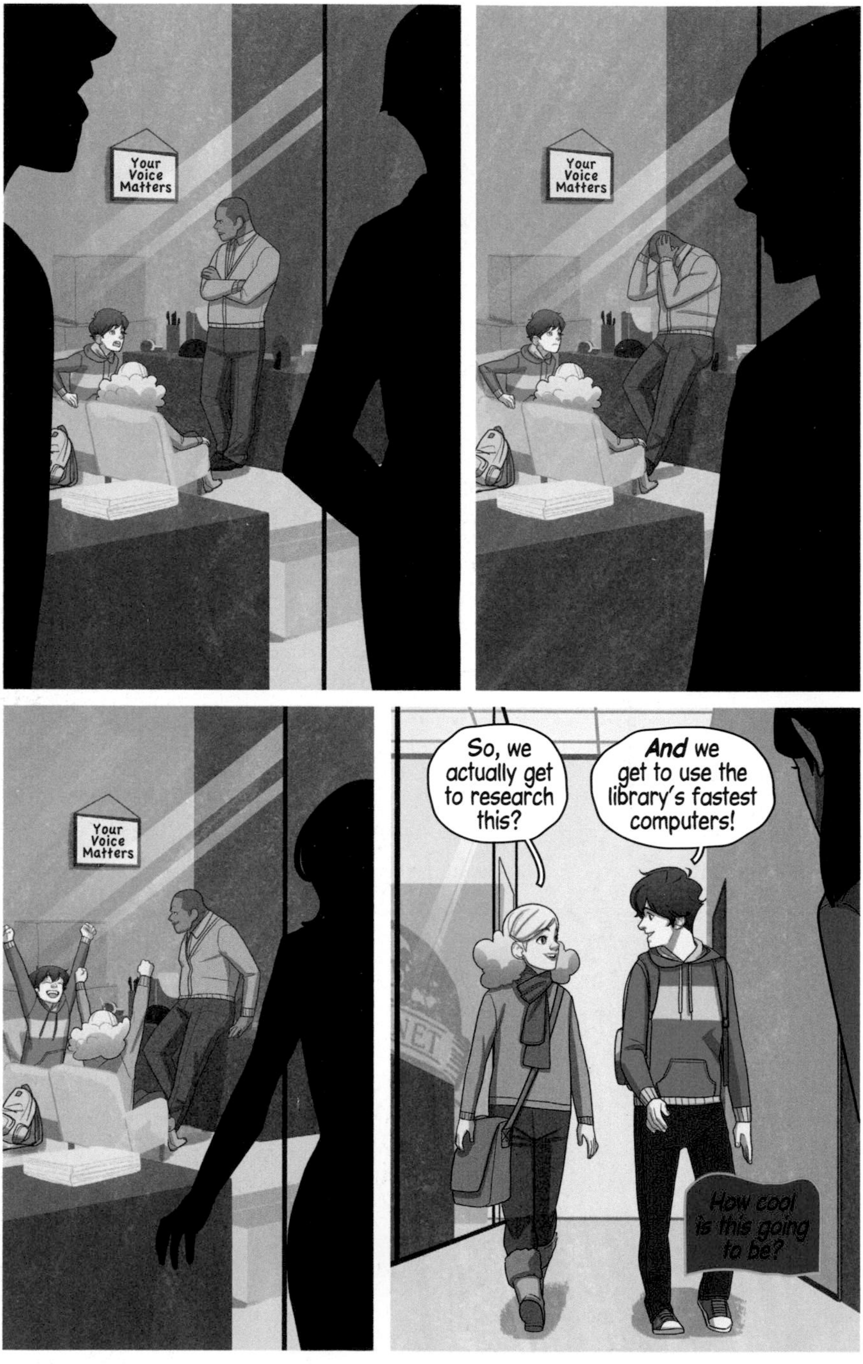
Your Voice Matters
Your Voice Matters
Your Voice Matters
So, we actually get to research this?
And we get to use the library's fastest computers!
How cool is this going to be?

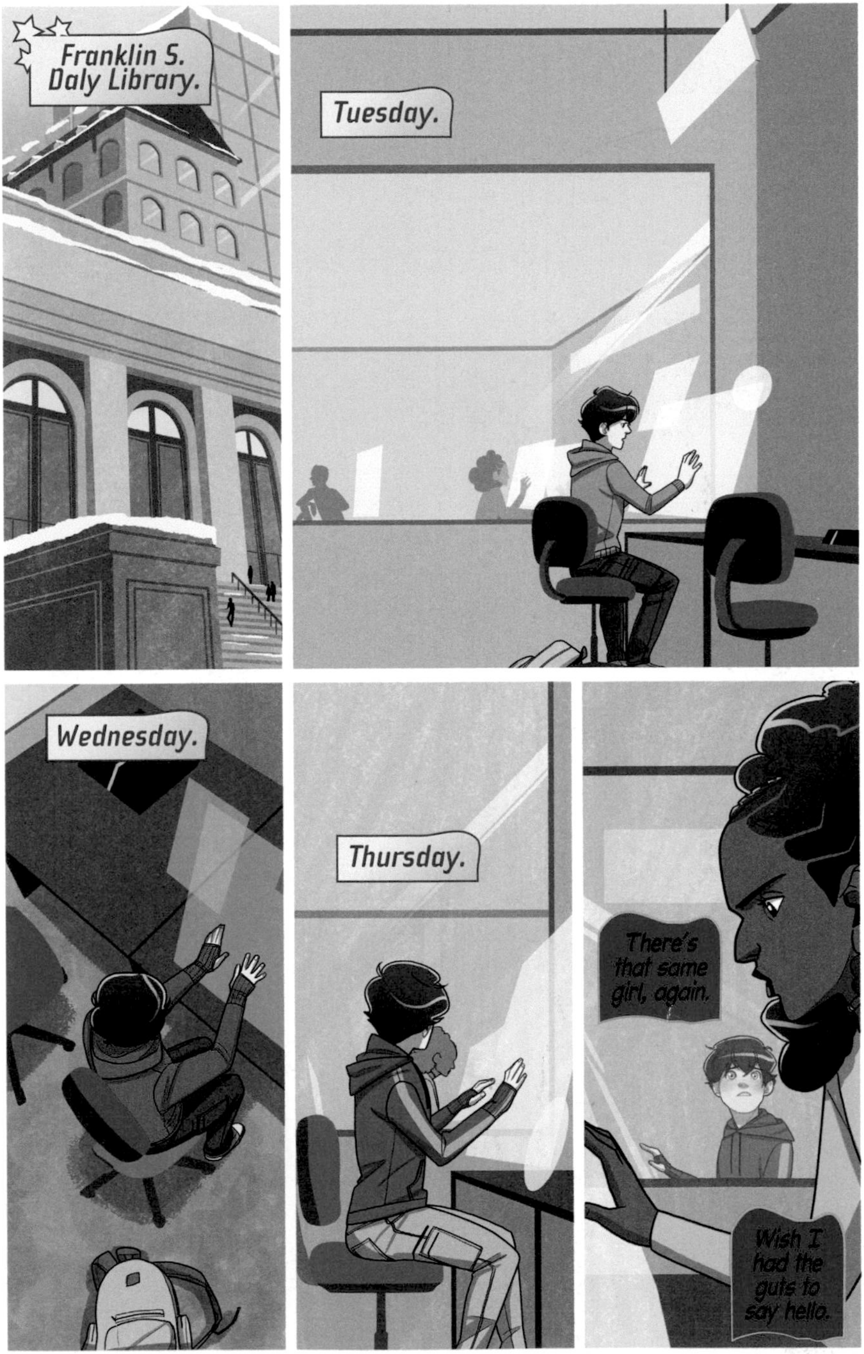
Franklin S. Daly Library.
Tuesday.
Wednesday.
Thursday.
There's that same girl, again.
Wish I had the guts to say hello.

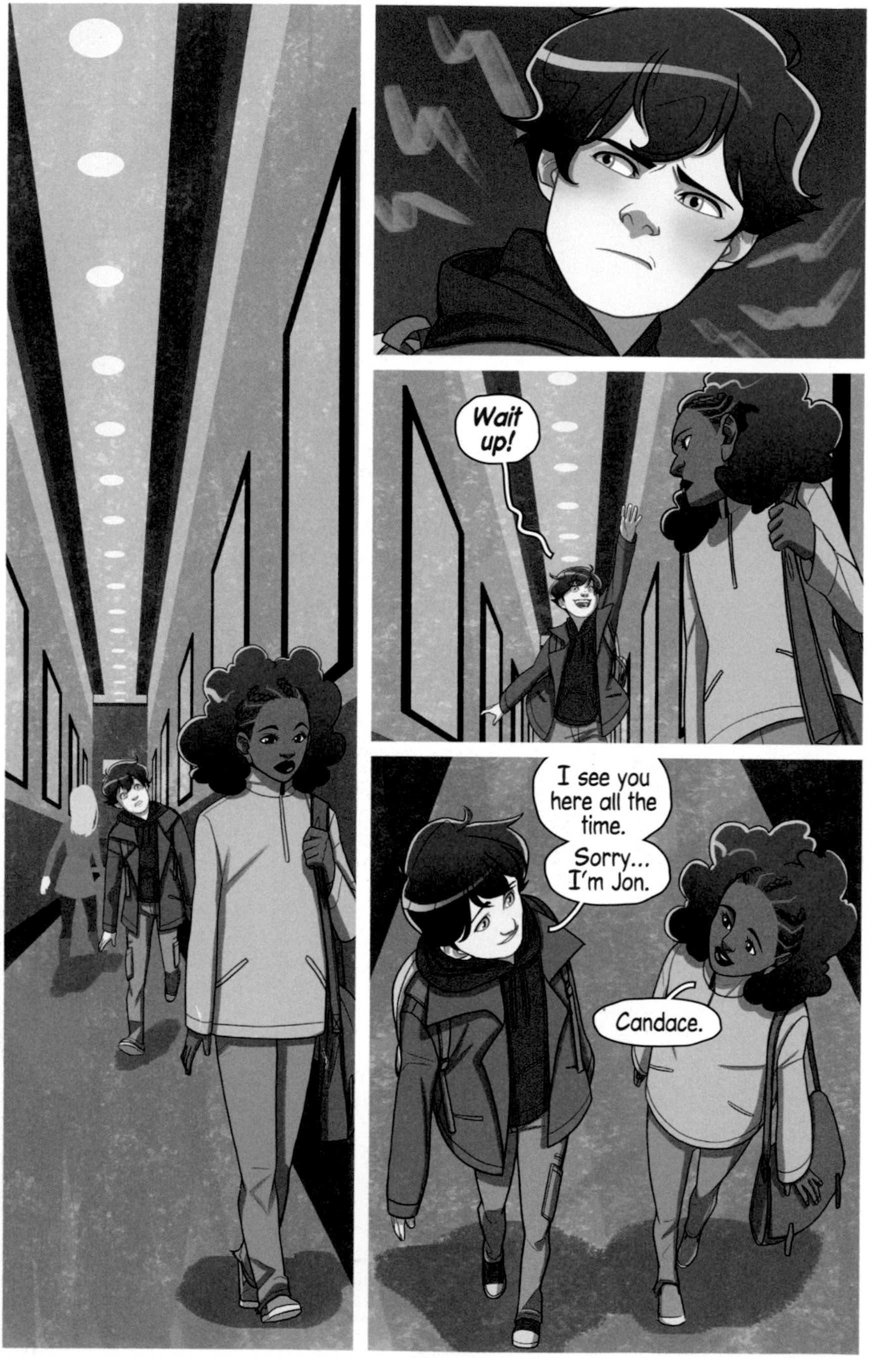
Wait up!
I see you here all the time.
Sorry... I'm Jon.
Candace.

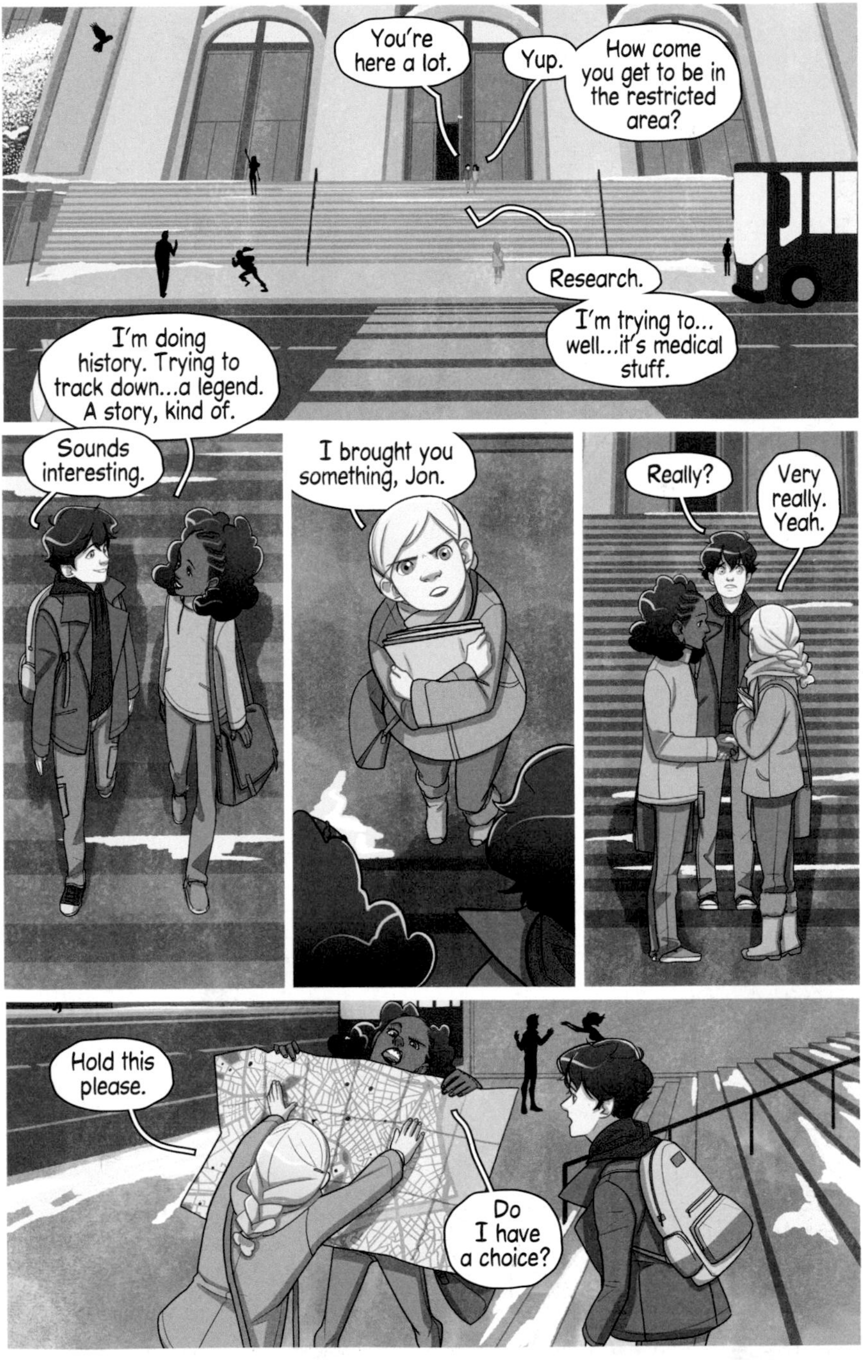
You're here a lot.
Yup.
How come you get to be in the restricted area?
Research.
I'm trying to... well...it's medical stuff.
I'm doing history. Trying to track down...a legend. A story, kind of.
Sounds interesting.
I brought you something, Jon.
Really?
Very really. Yeah.
Hold this please.
Do I have a choice?

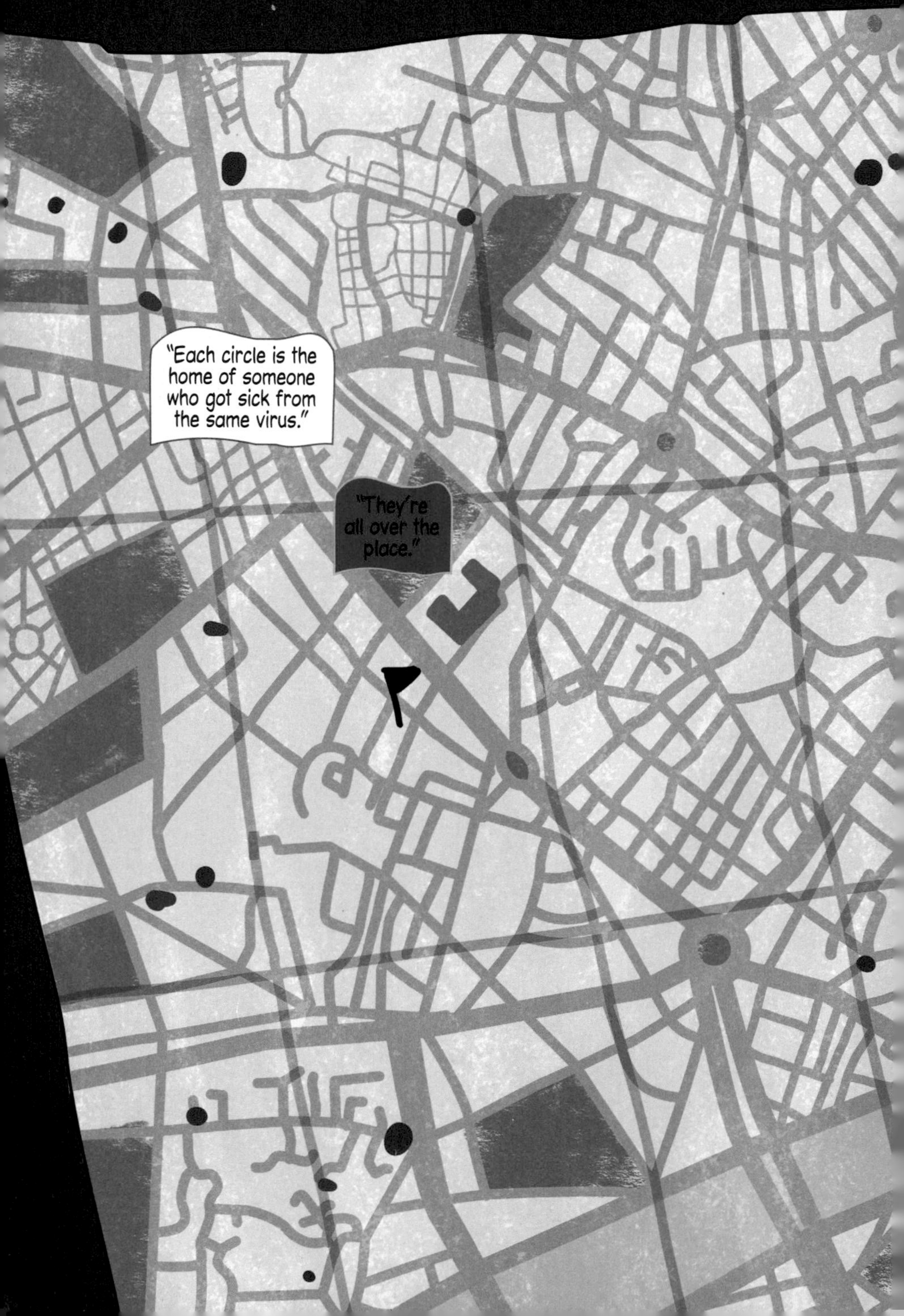
"Each circle is the home of someone who got sick from the same virus."
"They're all over the place."

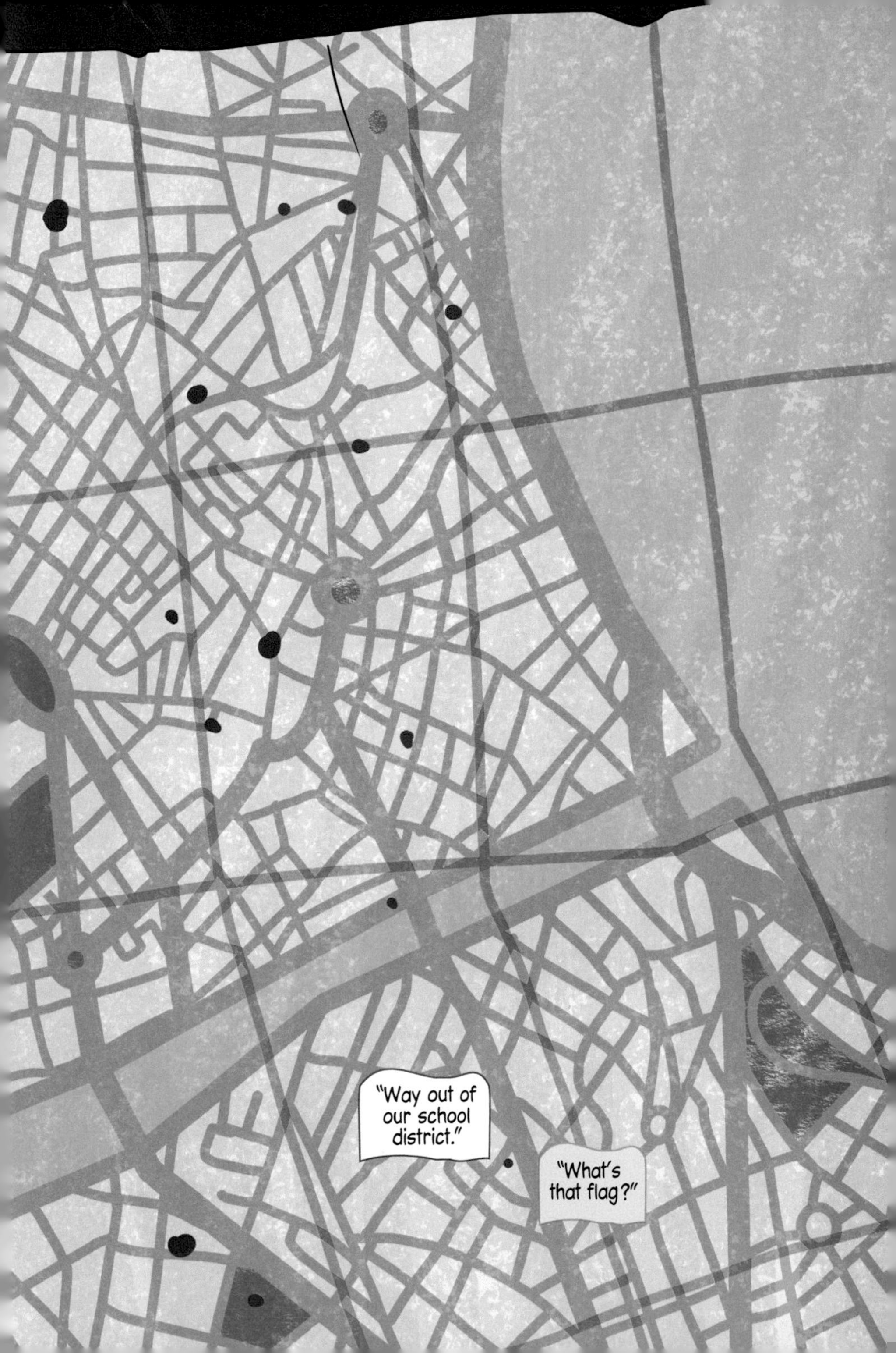
"Way out of our school district."
"What's that flag?"

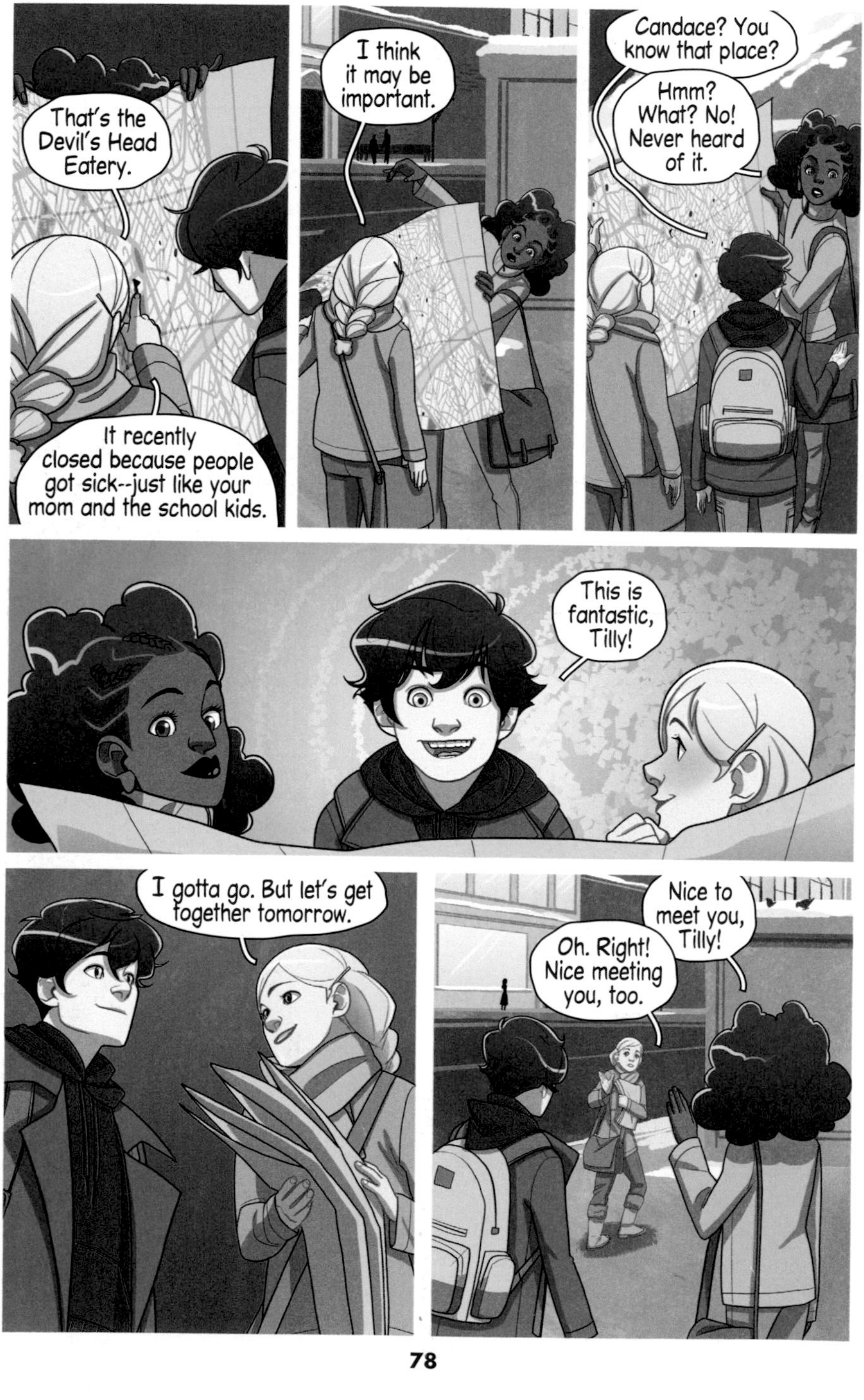
That's the Devil's Head Eatery.
It recently closed because people got sick--just like your mom and the school kids.
I think it may be important.
Candace? You know that place?
Hmm? What? No! Never heard of it.
This is fantastic, Tilly!
I gotta go. But let's get together tomorrow.
Nice to meet you, Tilly!
Oh. Right! Nice meeting you, too.

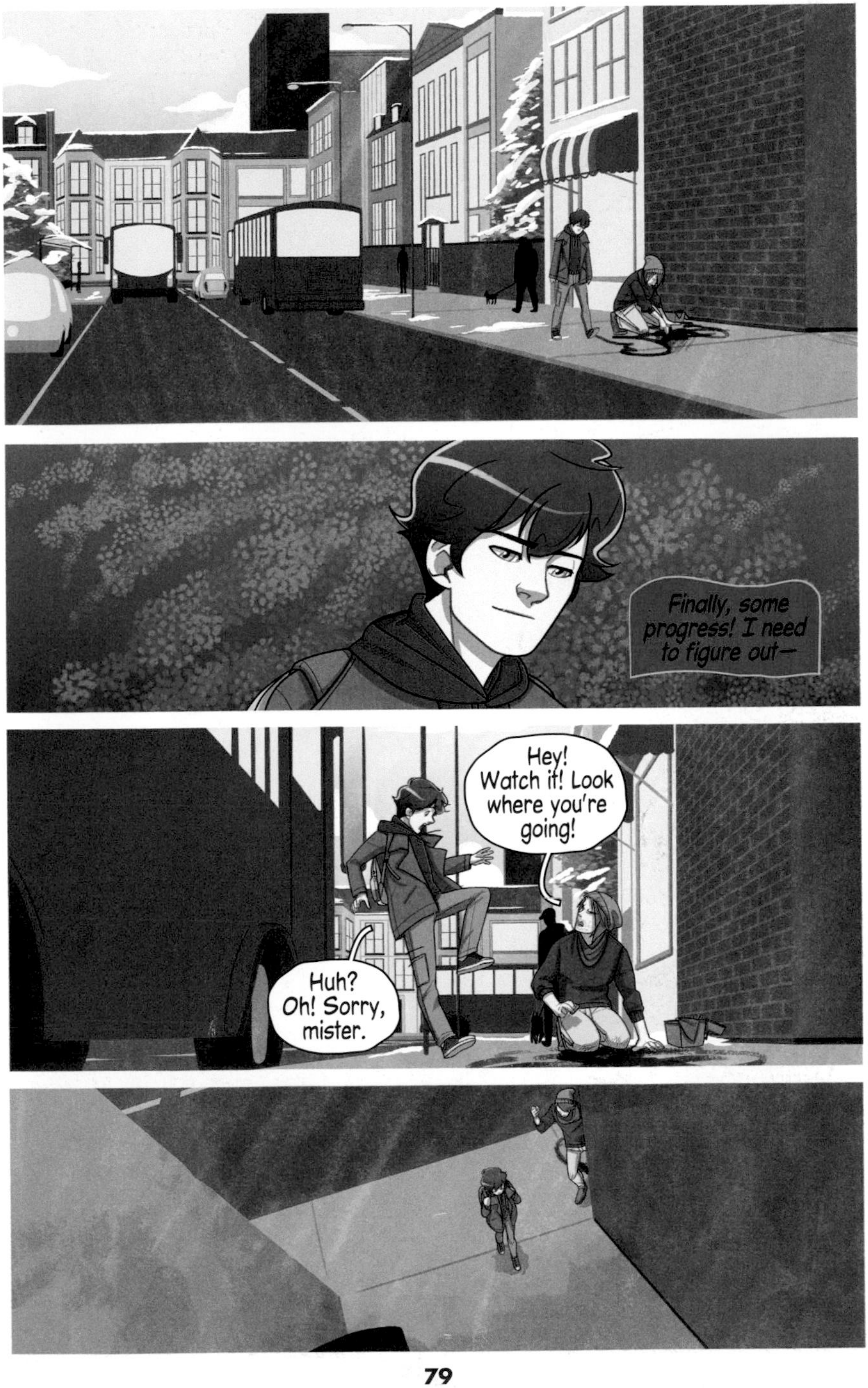
Finally, some progress! I need to figure out—
Hey! Watch it! Look where you're going!
Huh? Oh! Sorry, mister.

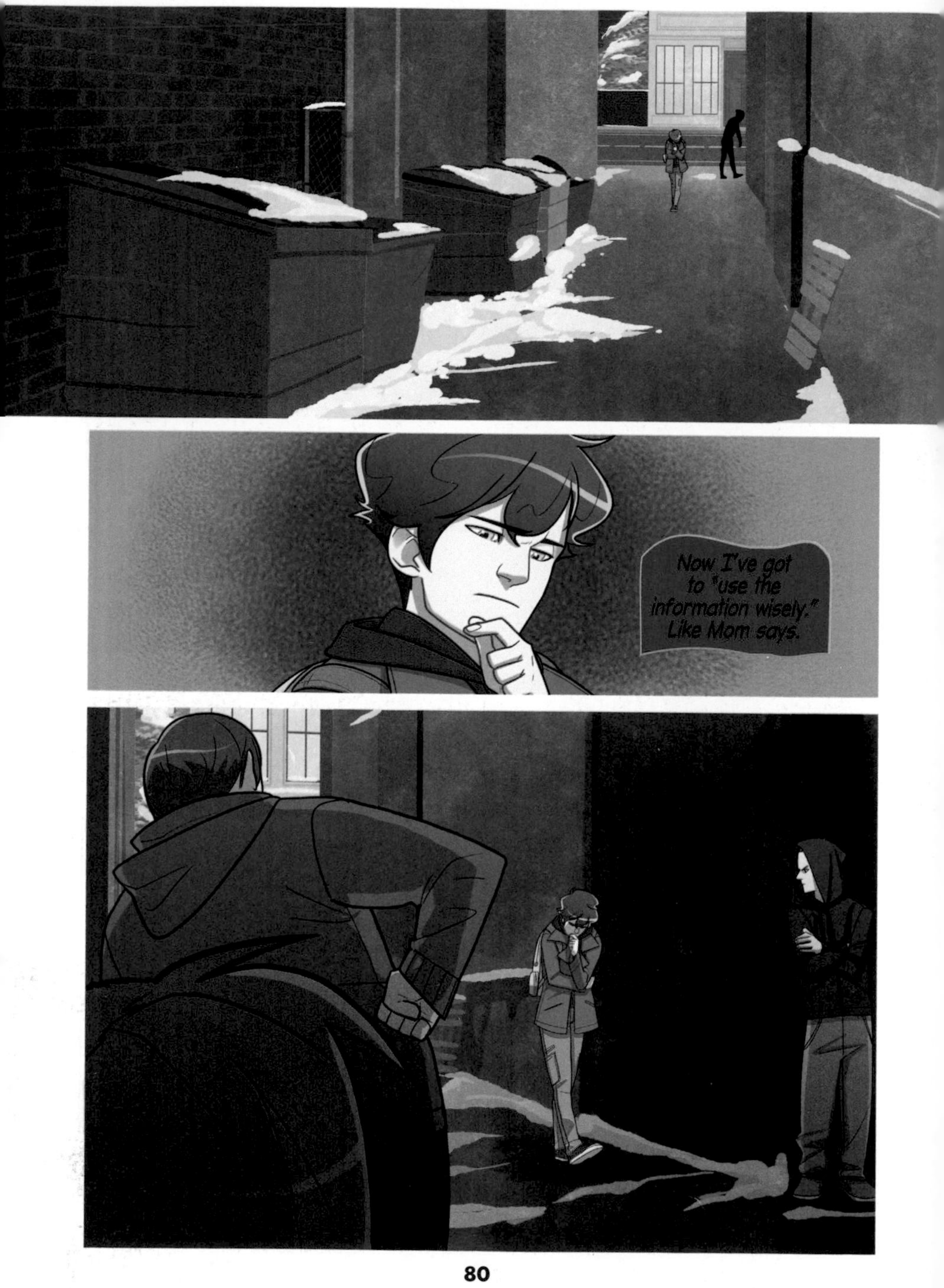
Now I've got to "use the information wisely." Like Mom says.

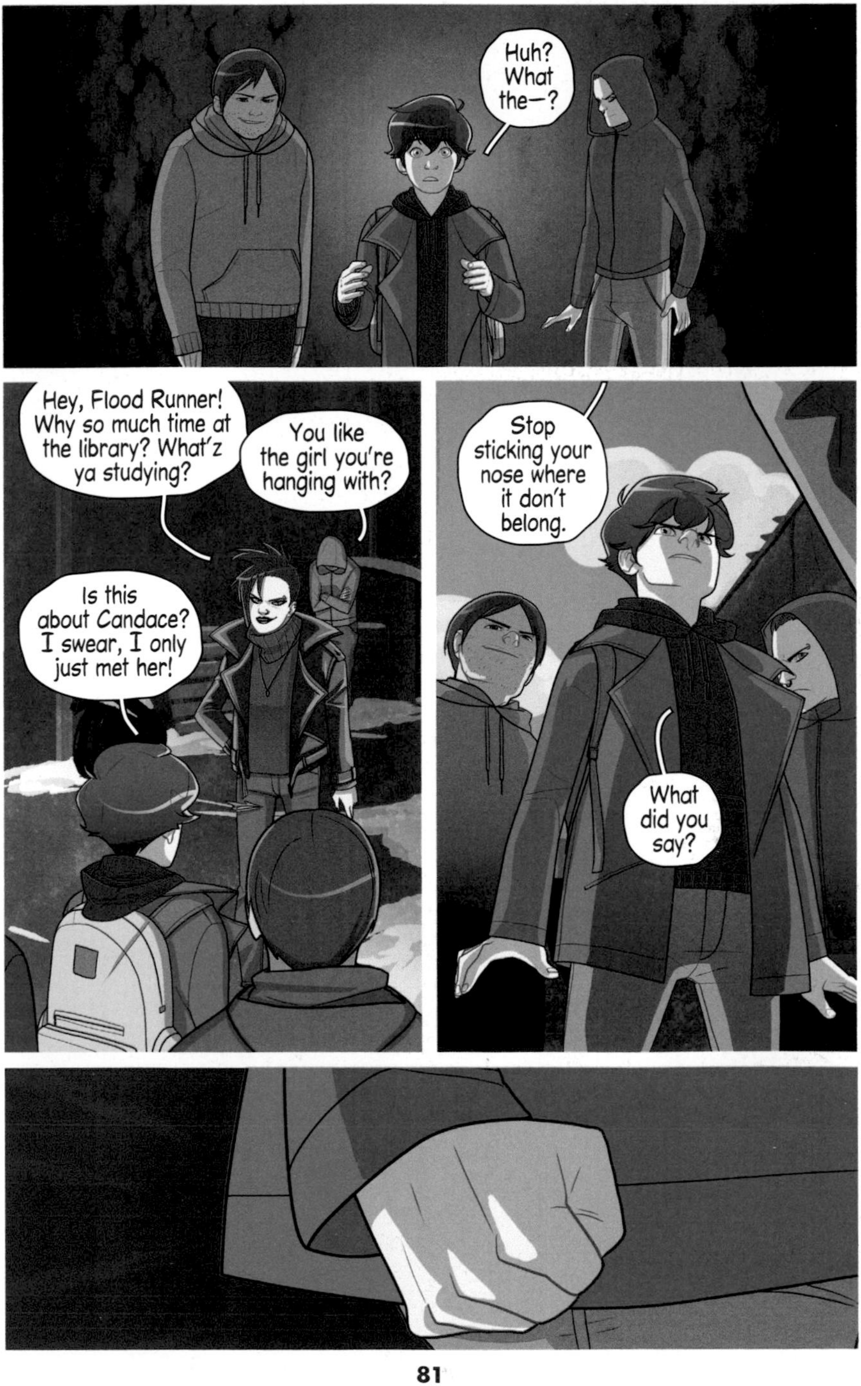
Huh? What the—?
Hey, Flood Runner! Why so much time at the library? What'z ya studying?
You like the girl you're hanging with?
Is this about Candace? I swear, I only just met her!
Stop sticking your nose where it don't belong.
What did you say?

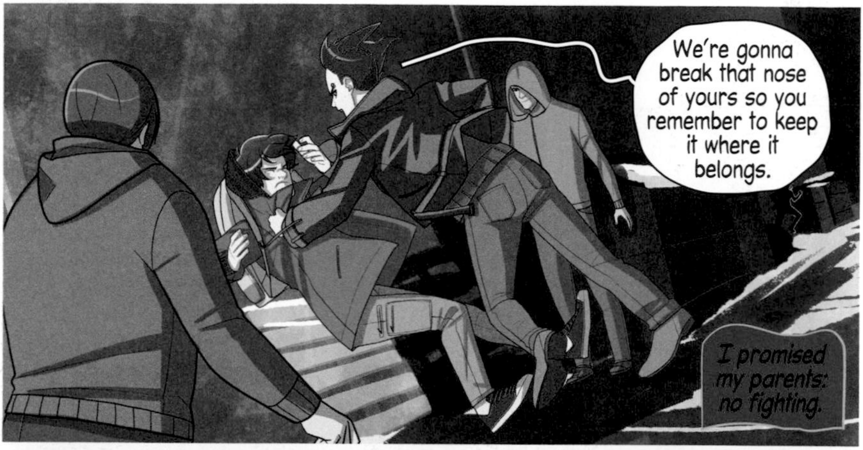
We're gonna break that nose of yours so you remember to keep it where it belongs.
I promised my parents: no fighting.

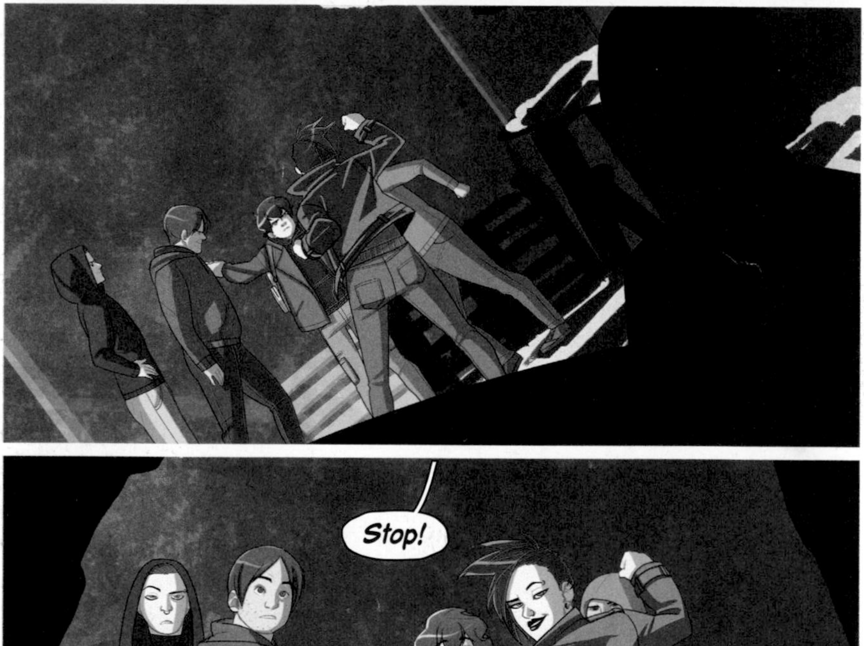

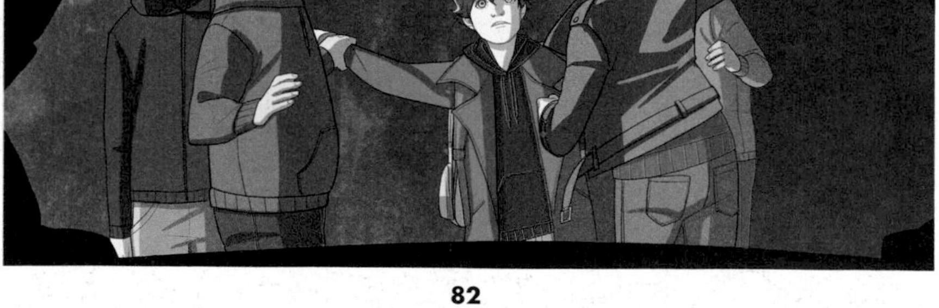
Stop!

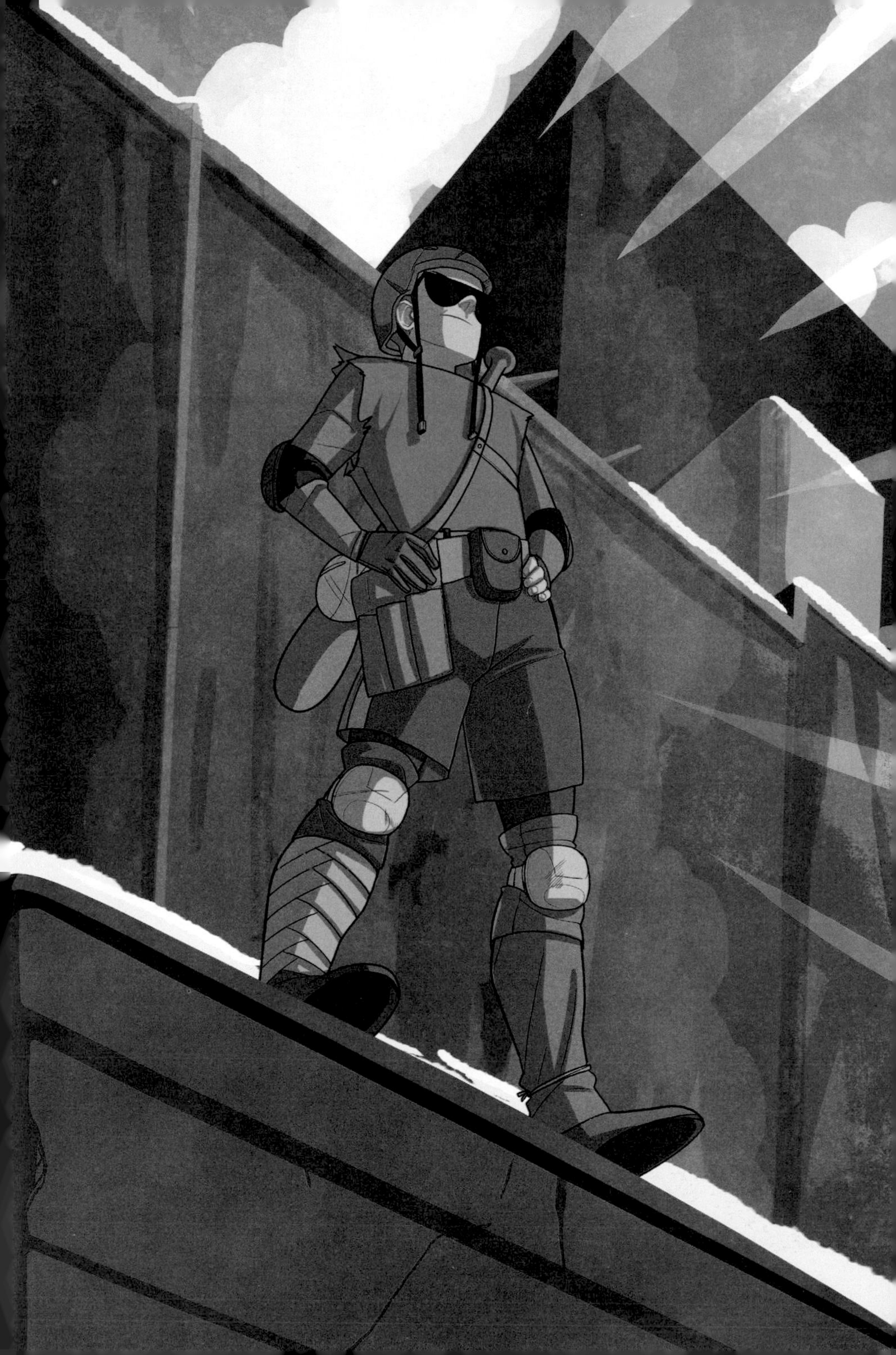

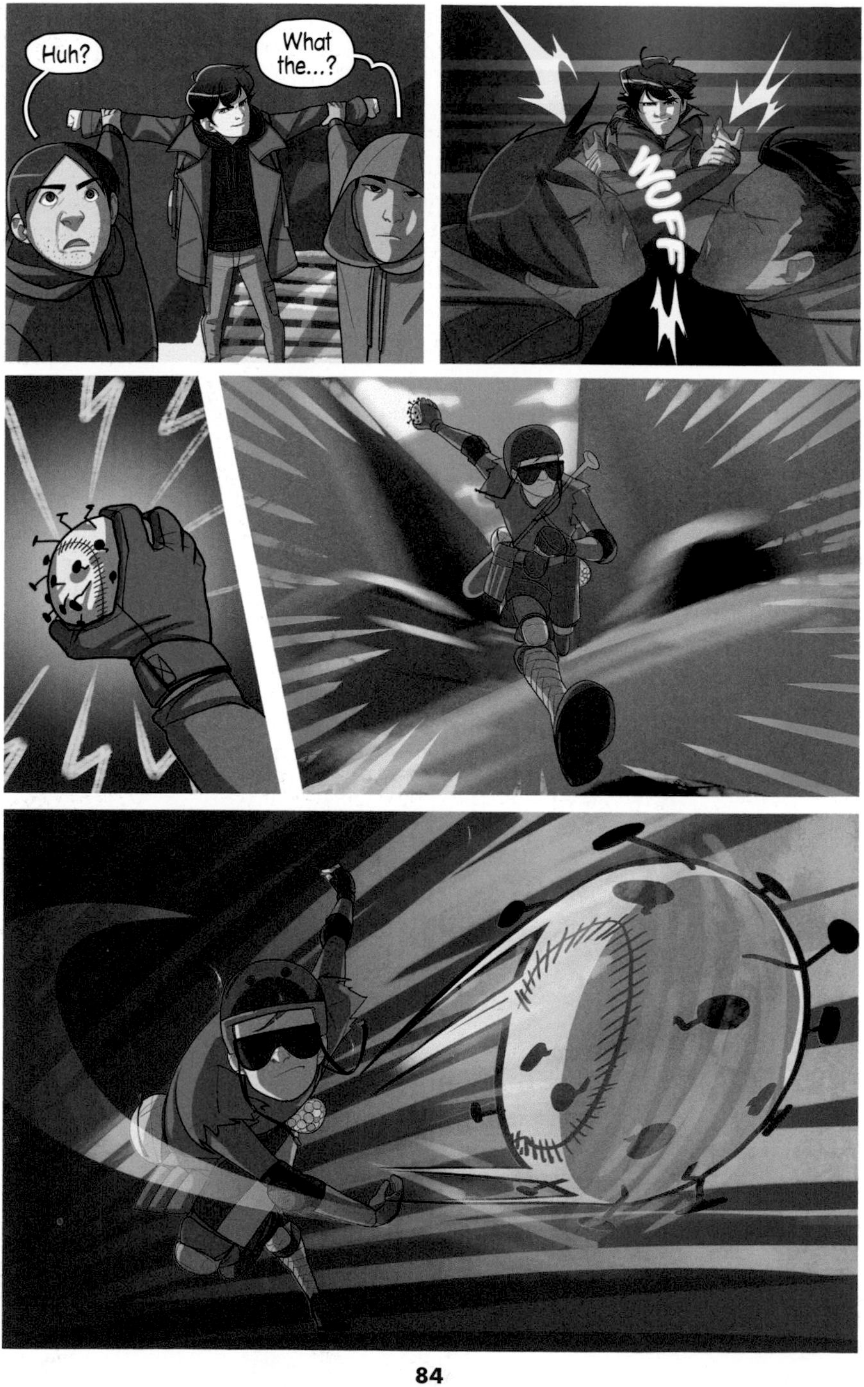
Huh?
What the...?
WUFF

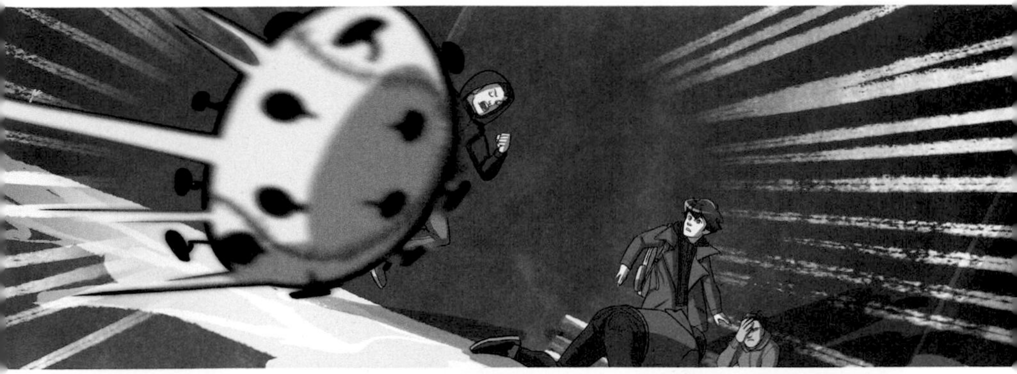

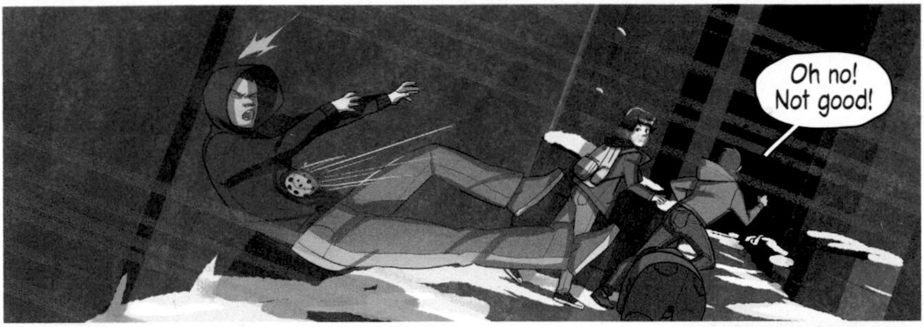
Oh no!
Not good!

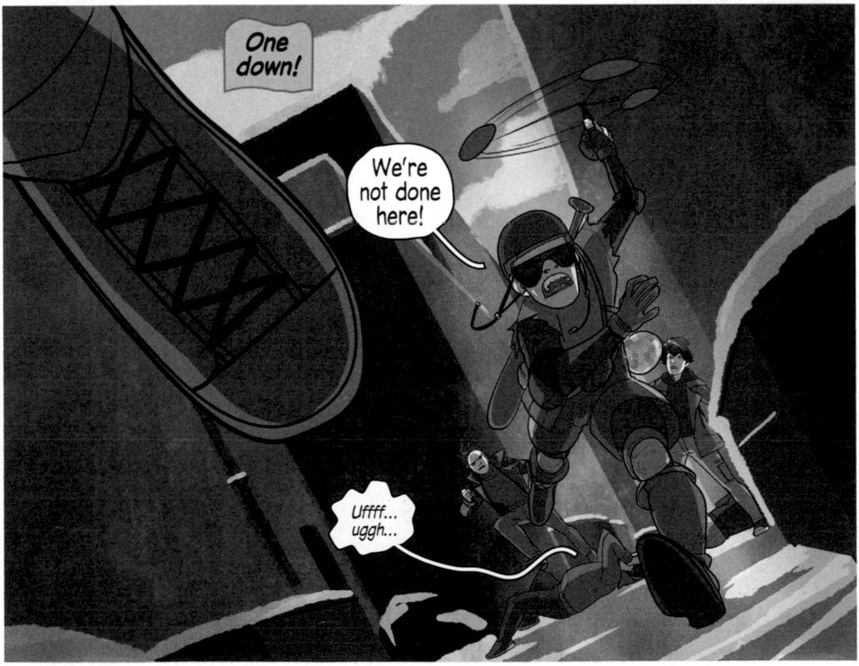
One down!
We're not done here!
Uffff... uggh...

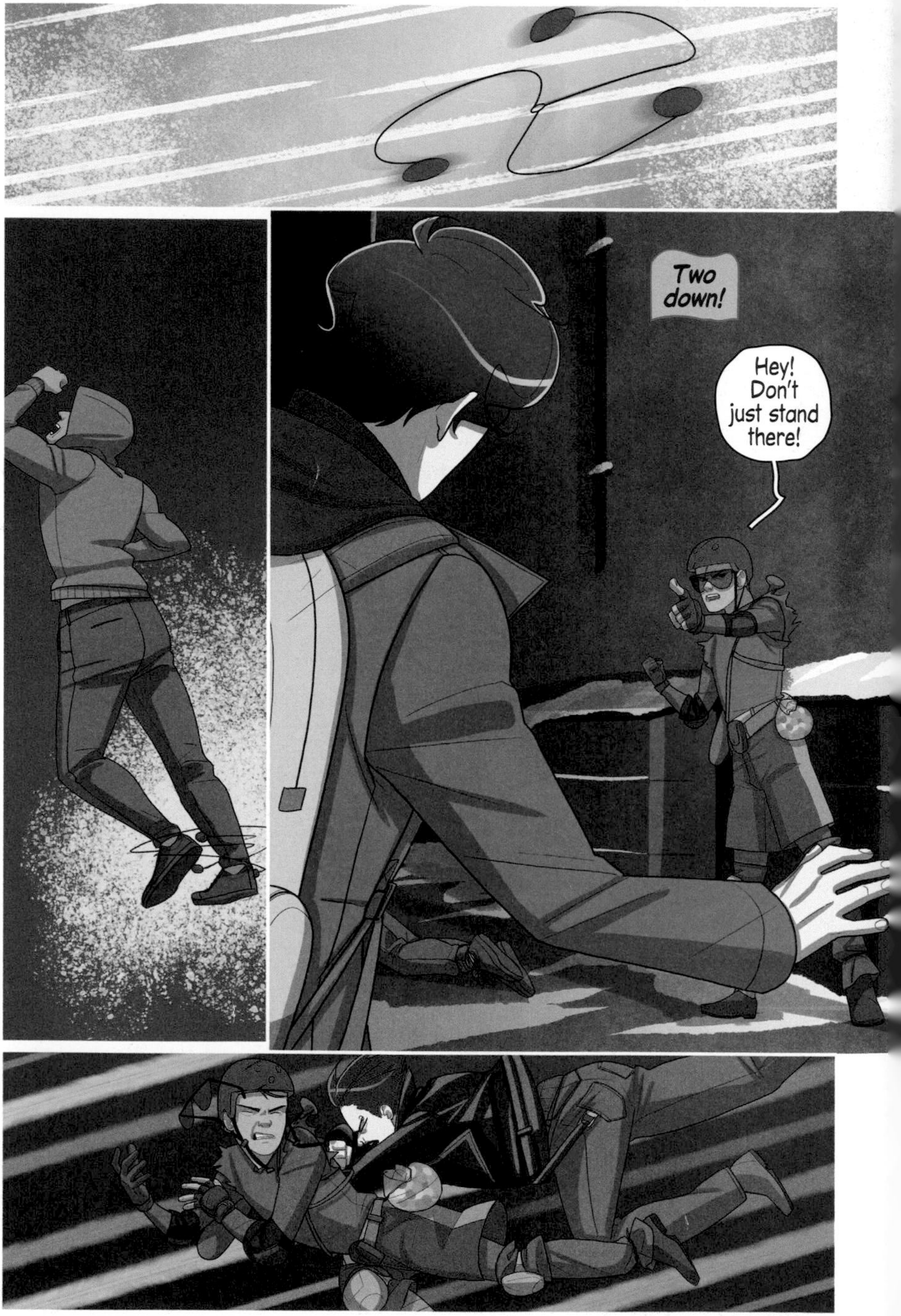
Two down!
Hey! Don't just stand there!

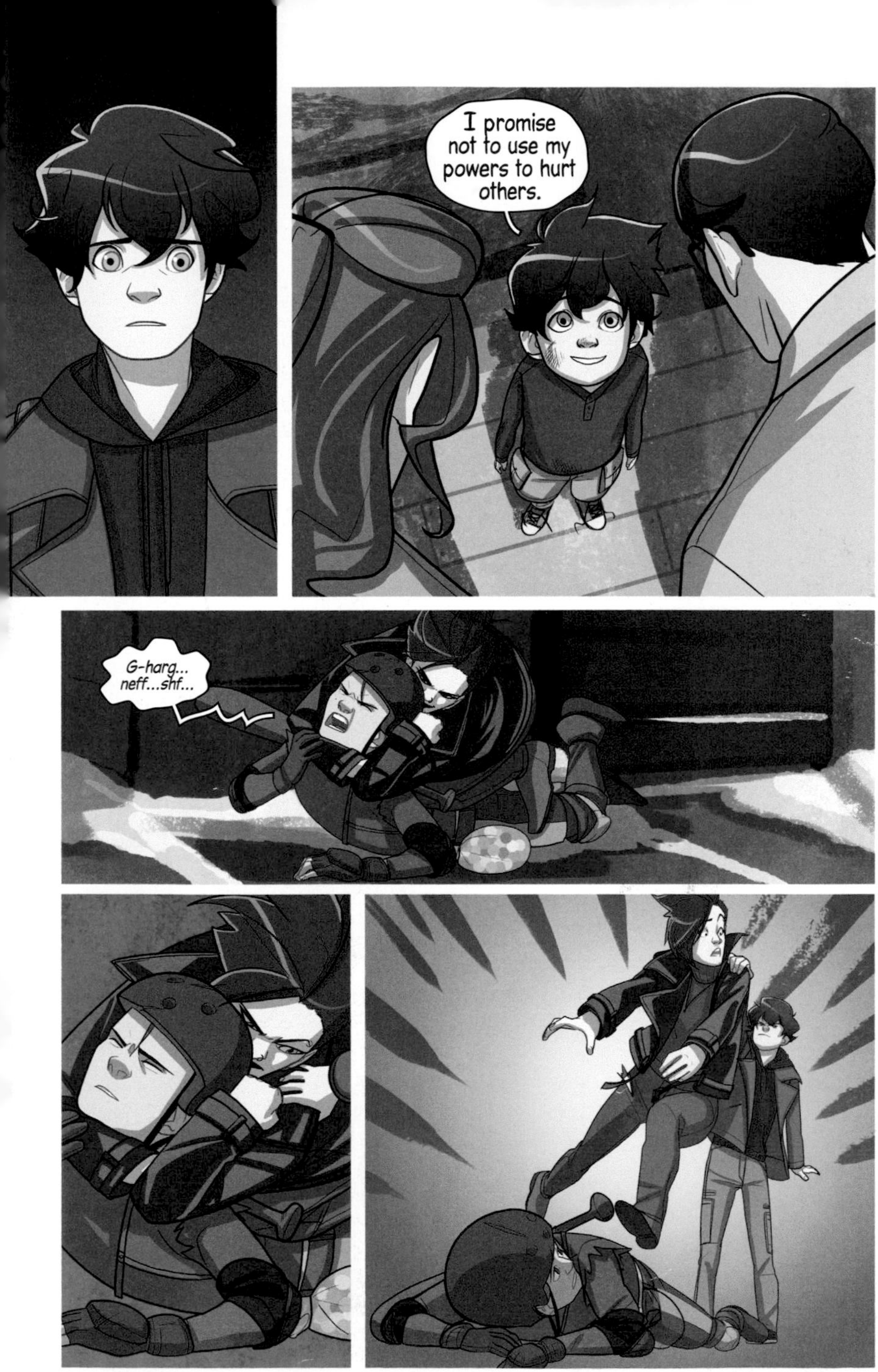
I promise not to use my powers to hurt others.
G-harg... neff...shf...

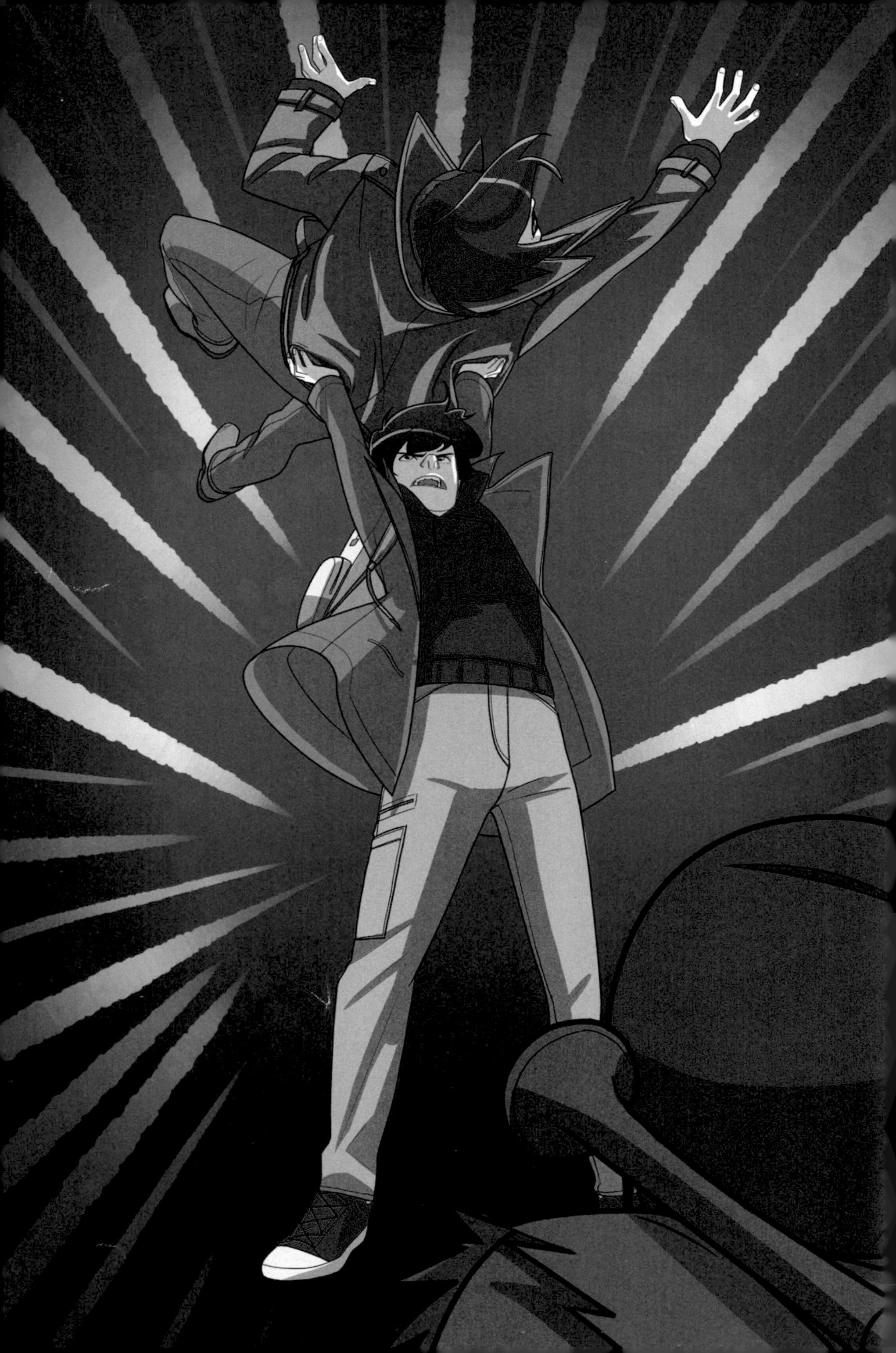

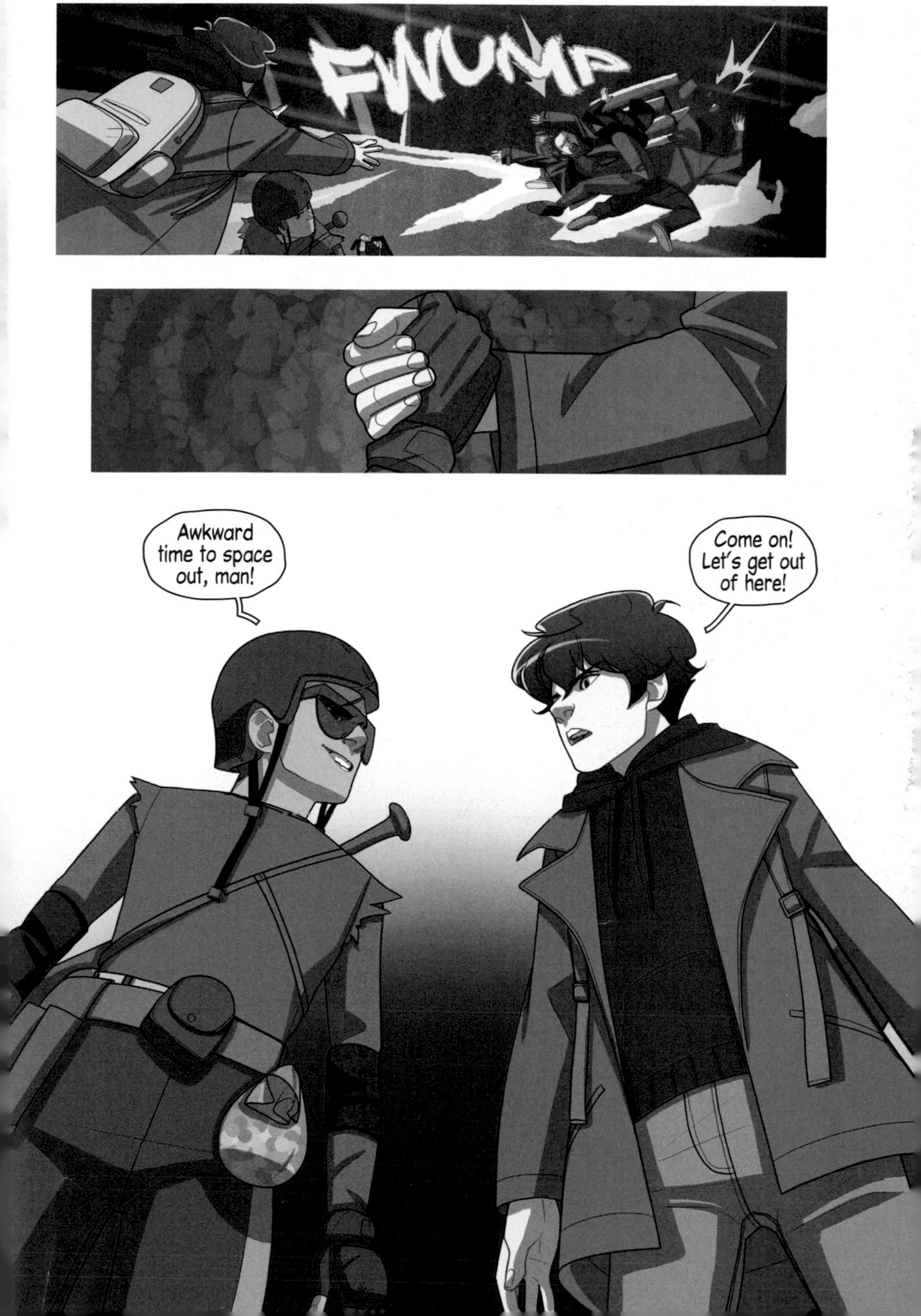
FWUMP
Awkward time to space out, man!
Come on! Let's get out of here!

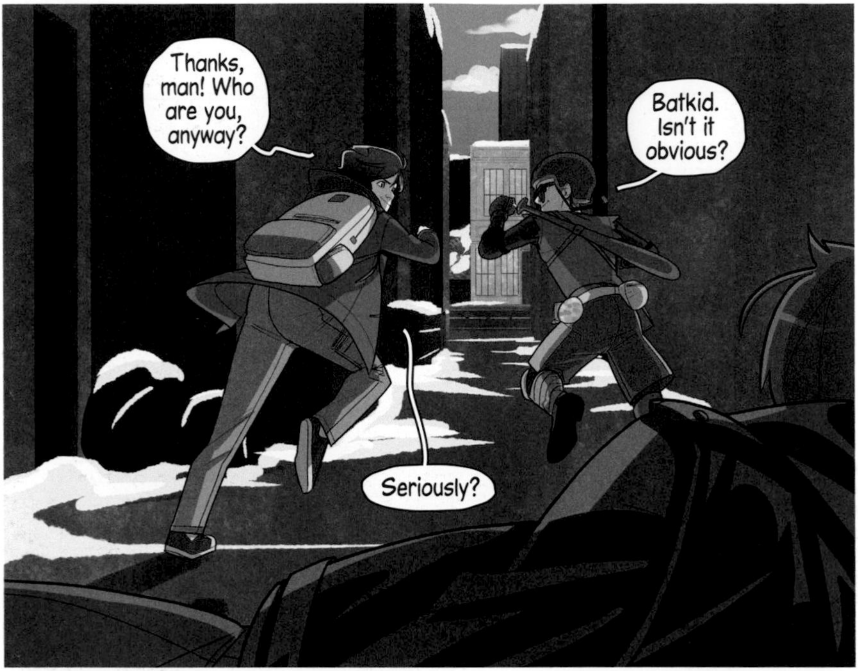
Thanks, man! Who are you, anyway?
Batkid. Isn't it obvious?
Seriously?

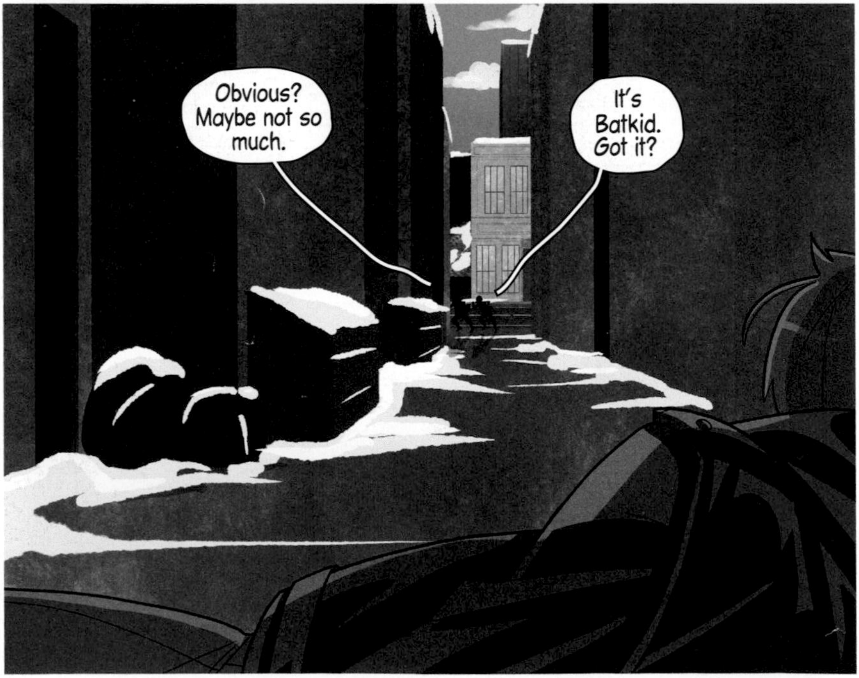
Obvious? Maybe not so much.
It's Batkid. Got it?

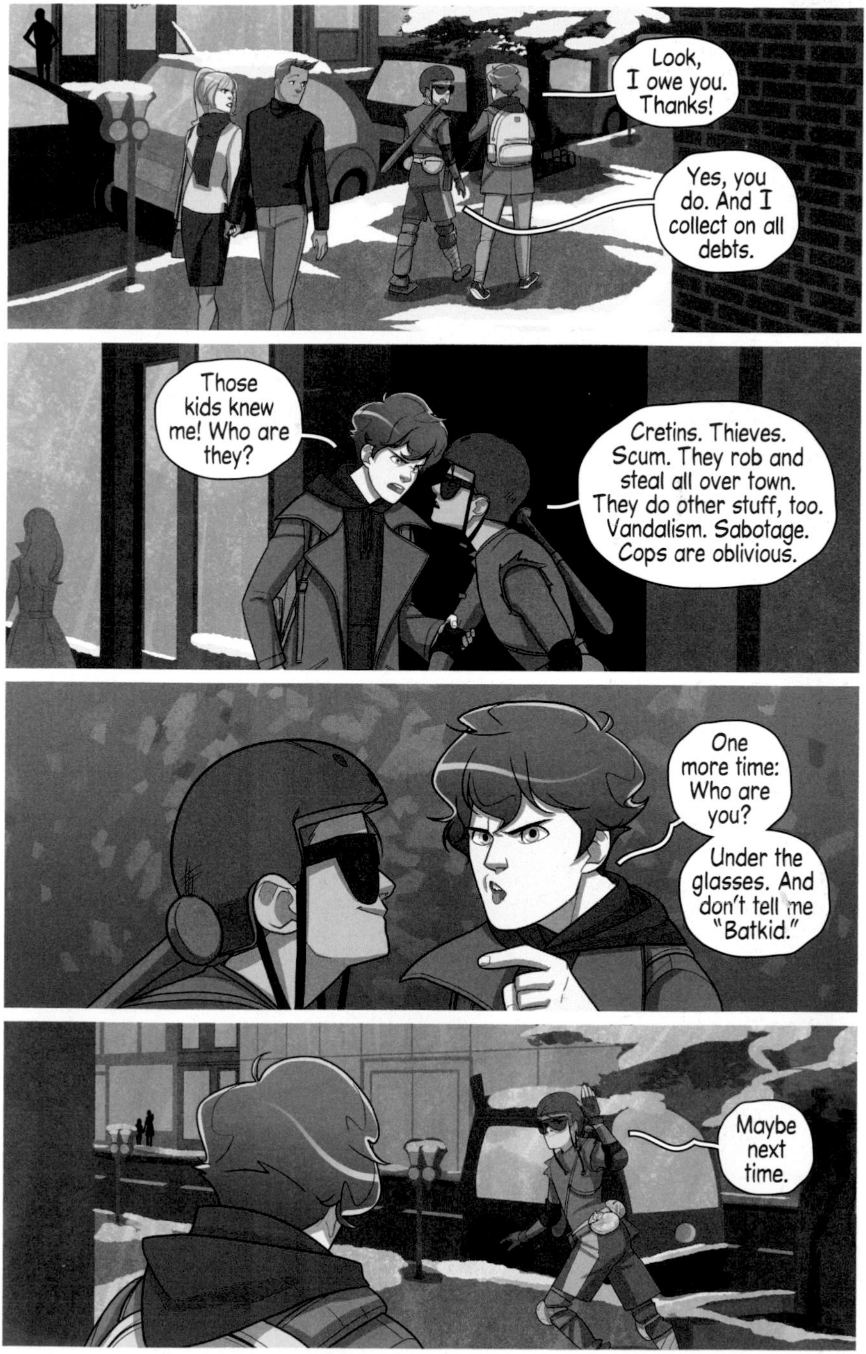
Look, I owe you. Thanks!
Yes, you do. And I collect on all debts.
Those kids knew me! Who are they?
Cretins. Thieves. Scum. They rob and steal all over town. They do other stuff, too. Vandalism. Sabotage. Cops are oblivious.
One more time: Who are you?
Under the glasses. And don't tell me "Batkid."
Maybe next time.

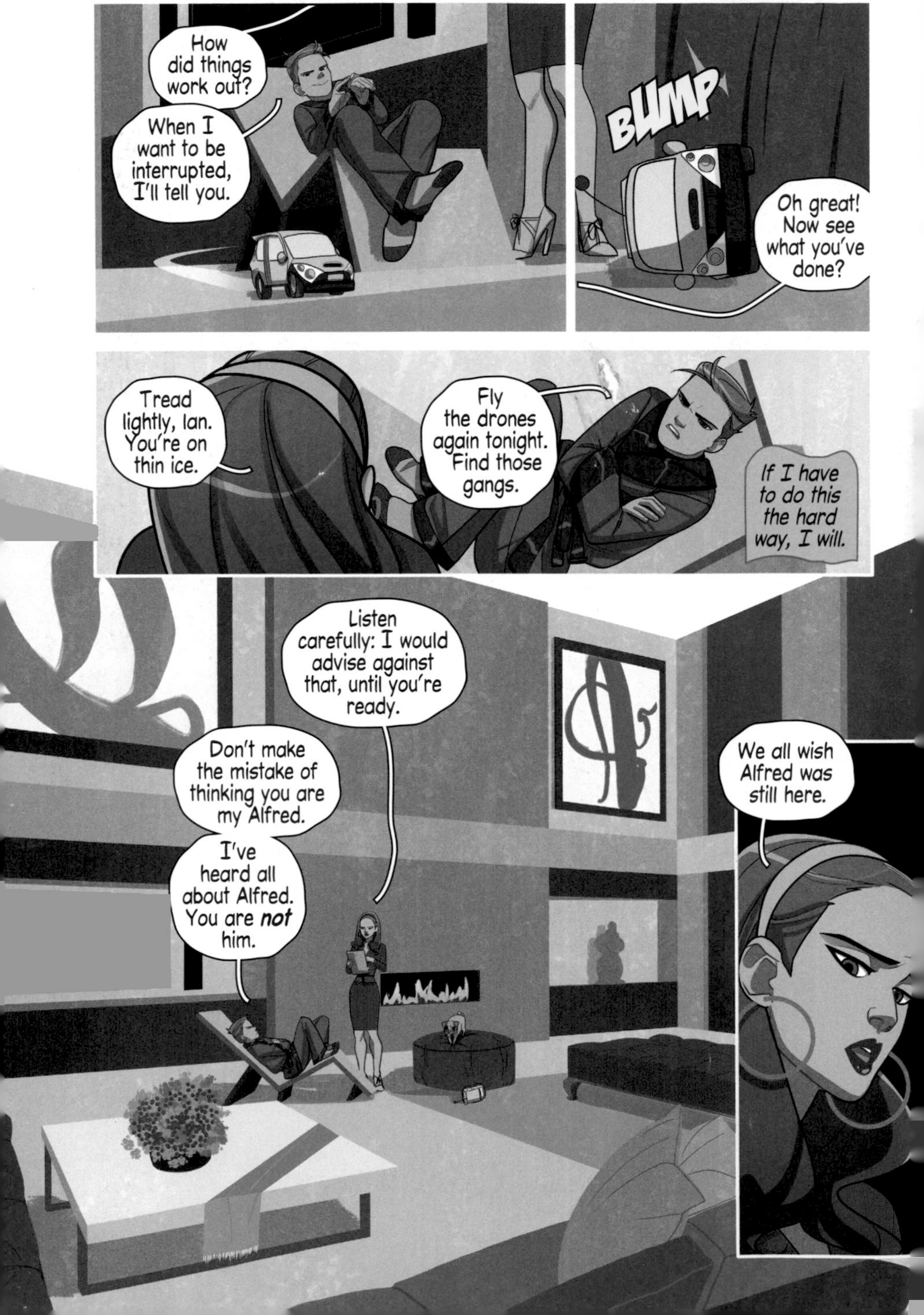
How did things work out?
When I want to be interrupted, I'll tell you.
BUMP
Oh great! Now see what you've done?
Tread lightly, Ian. You're on thin ice.
Fly the drones again tonight. Find those gangs.
If I have to do this the hard way, I will.
Listen carefully: I would advise against that, until you're ready.
Don't make the mistake of thinking you are my Alfred.
I've heard all about Alfred. You are *not* him.
We all wish Alfred was still here.

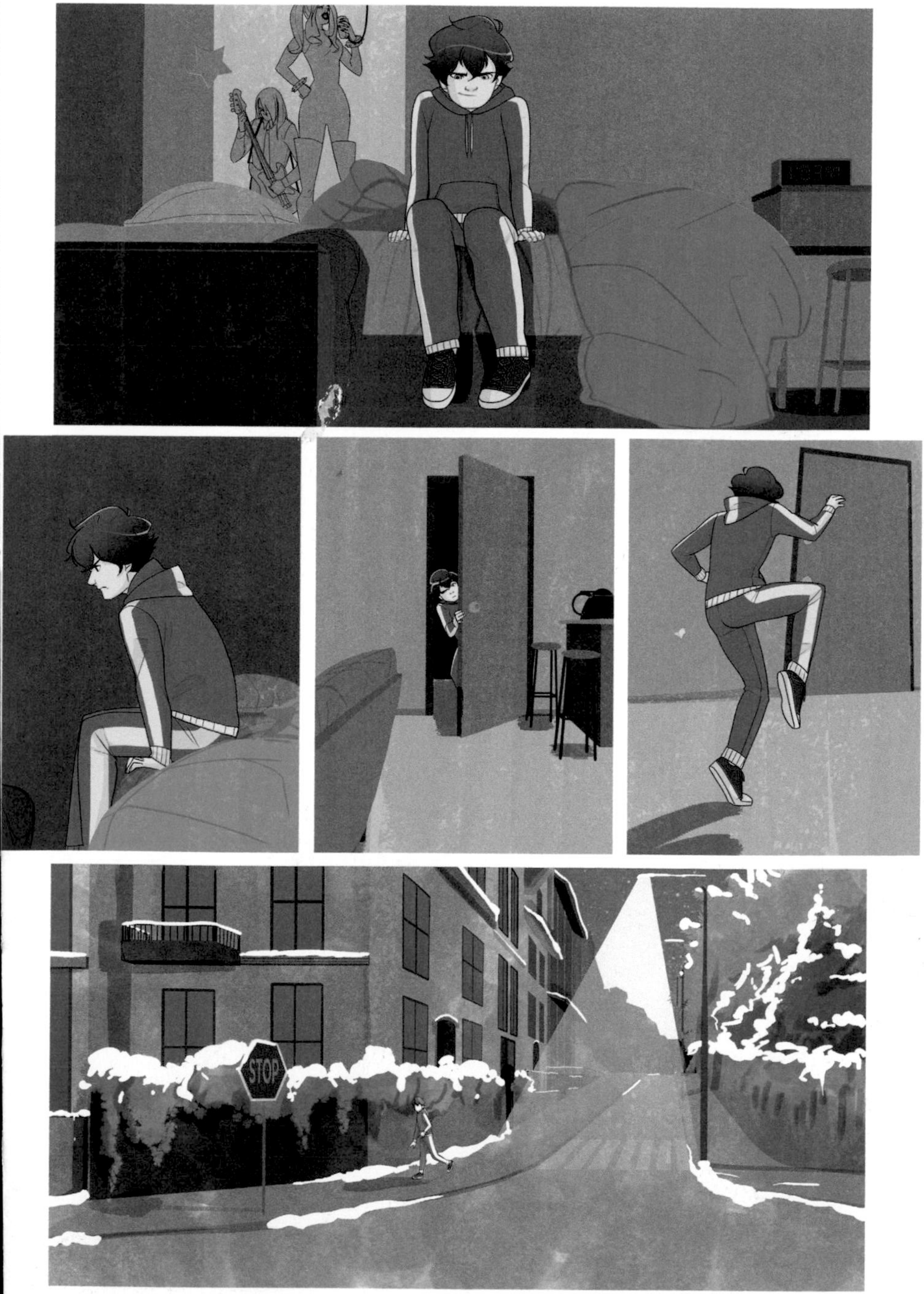
STOP

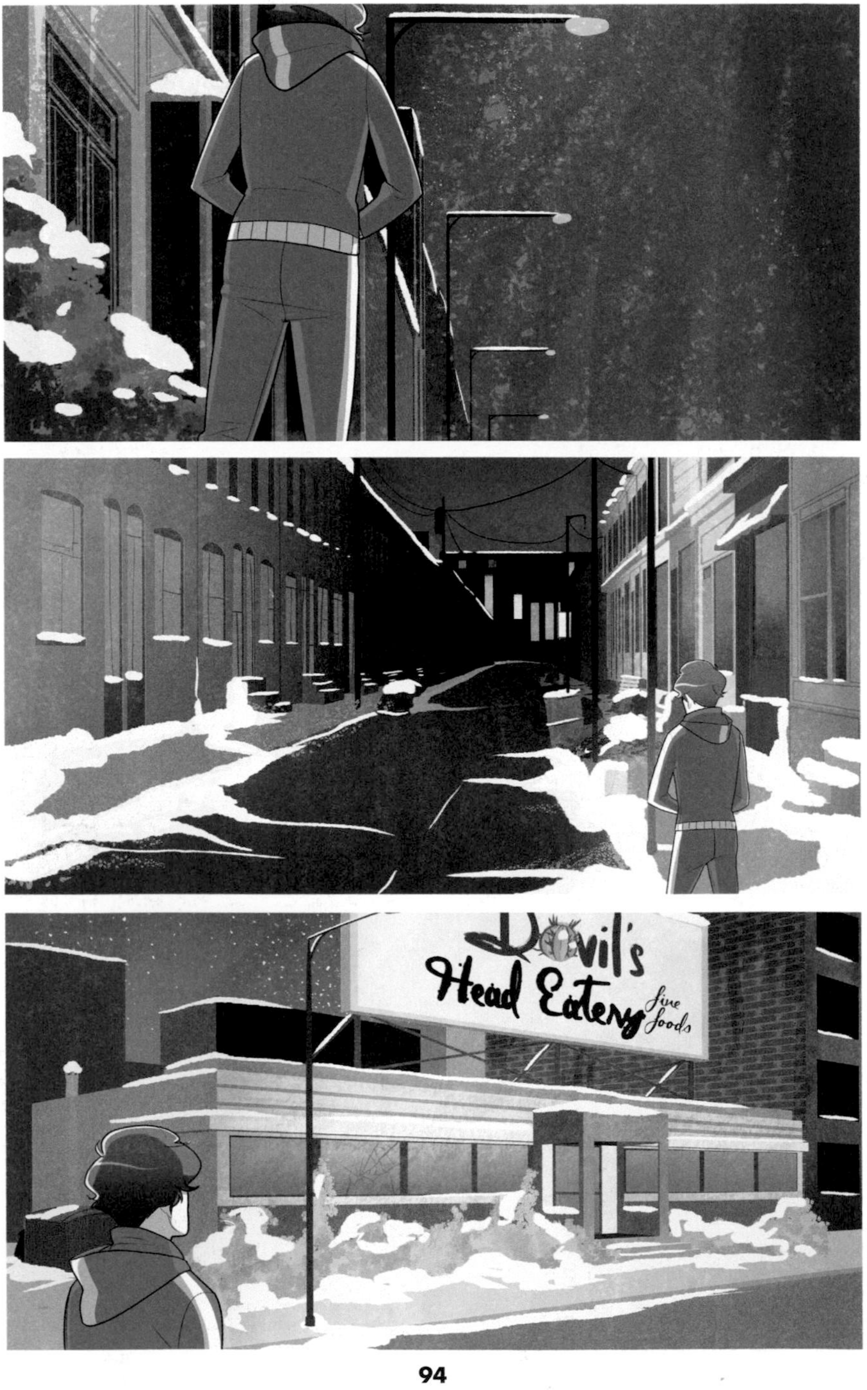
Devil's
Head Eatery
fine foods

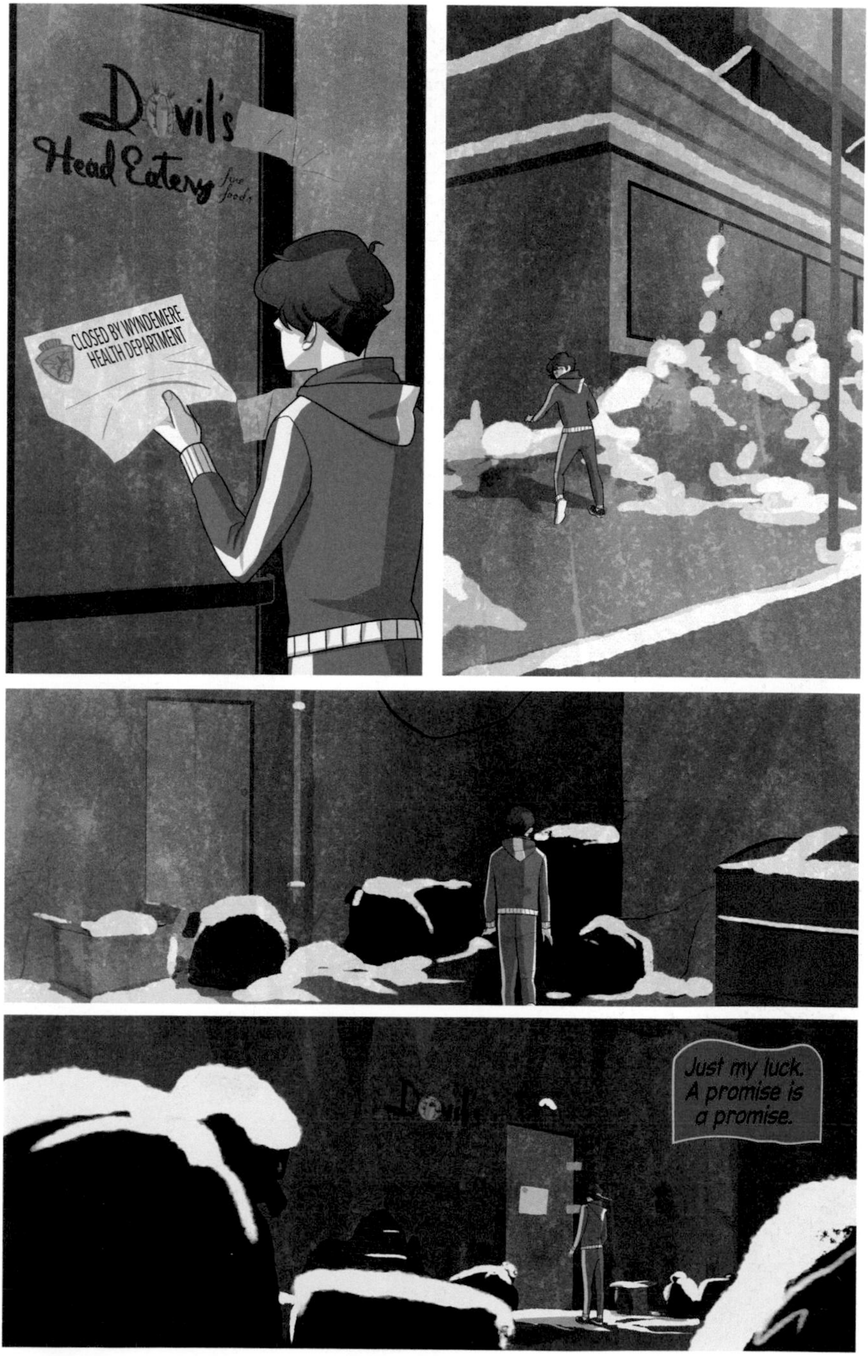
Devil's
Head Eatery
fine foods
CLOSED BY WYNDEMERE HEALTH DEPARTMENT
Just my luck. A promise is a promise.

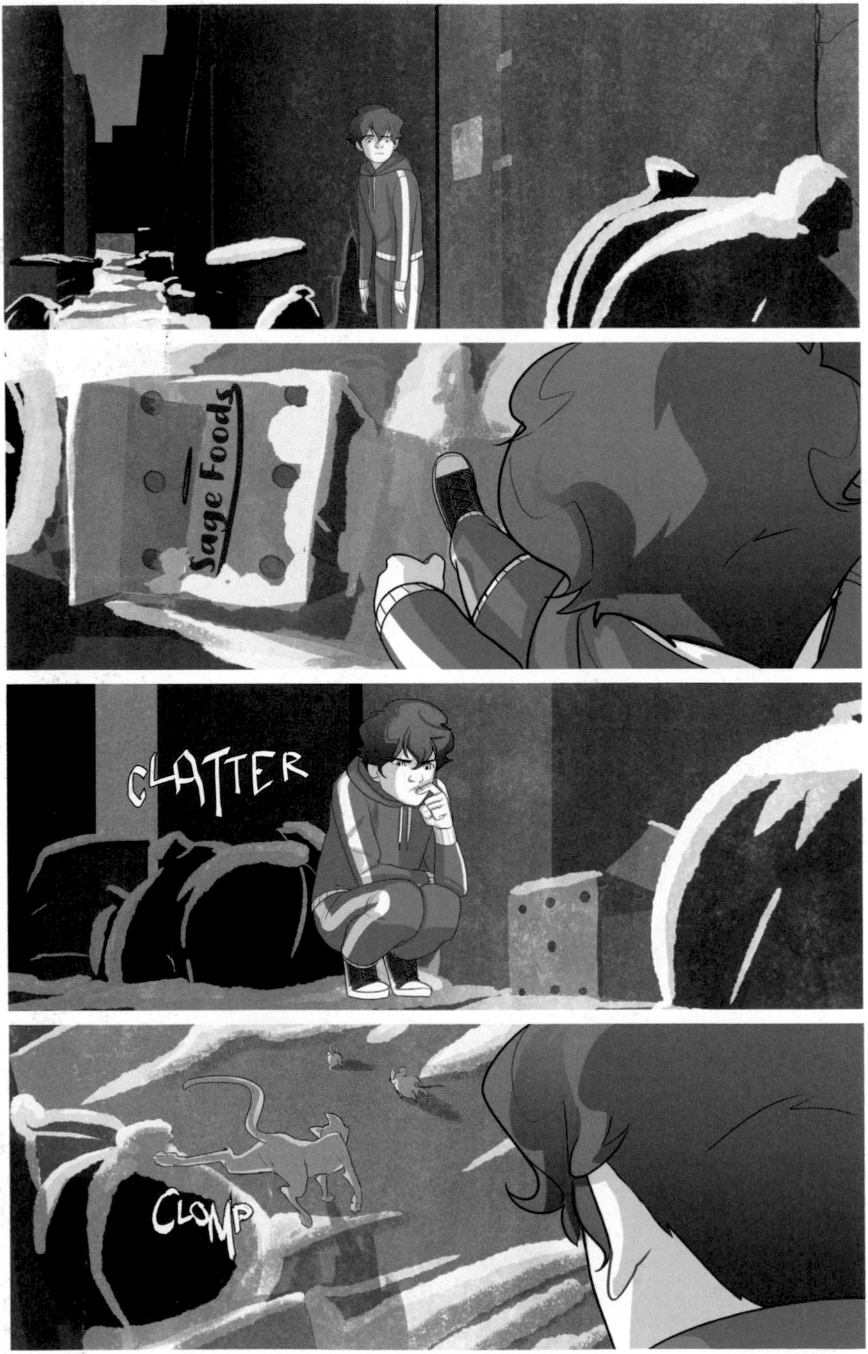
Sage Foods
CLATTER
CLOMP

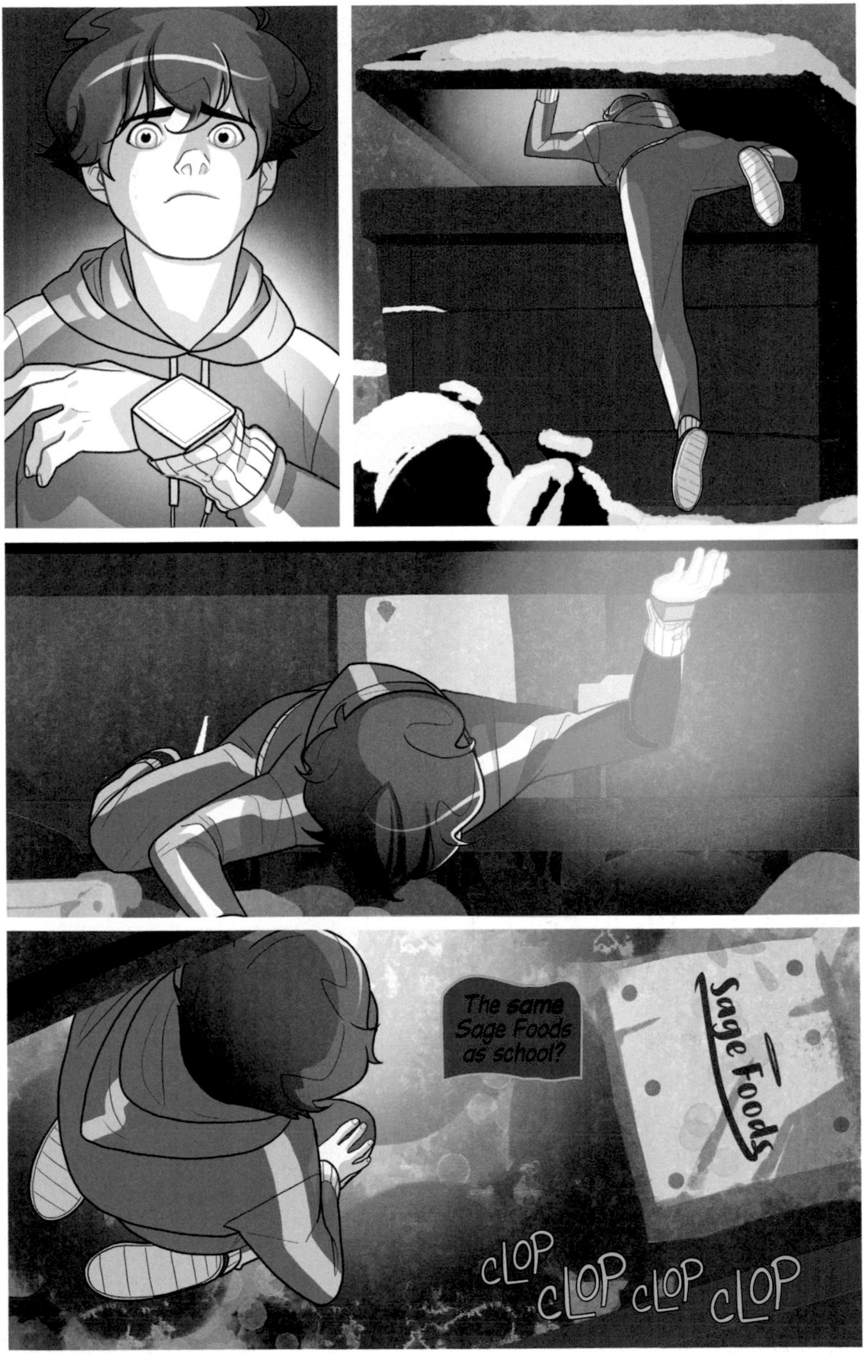
The same Sage Foods as school?
Sage Foods
CLOP CLOP CLOP CLOP

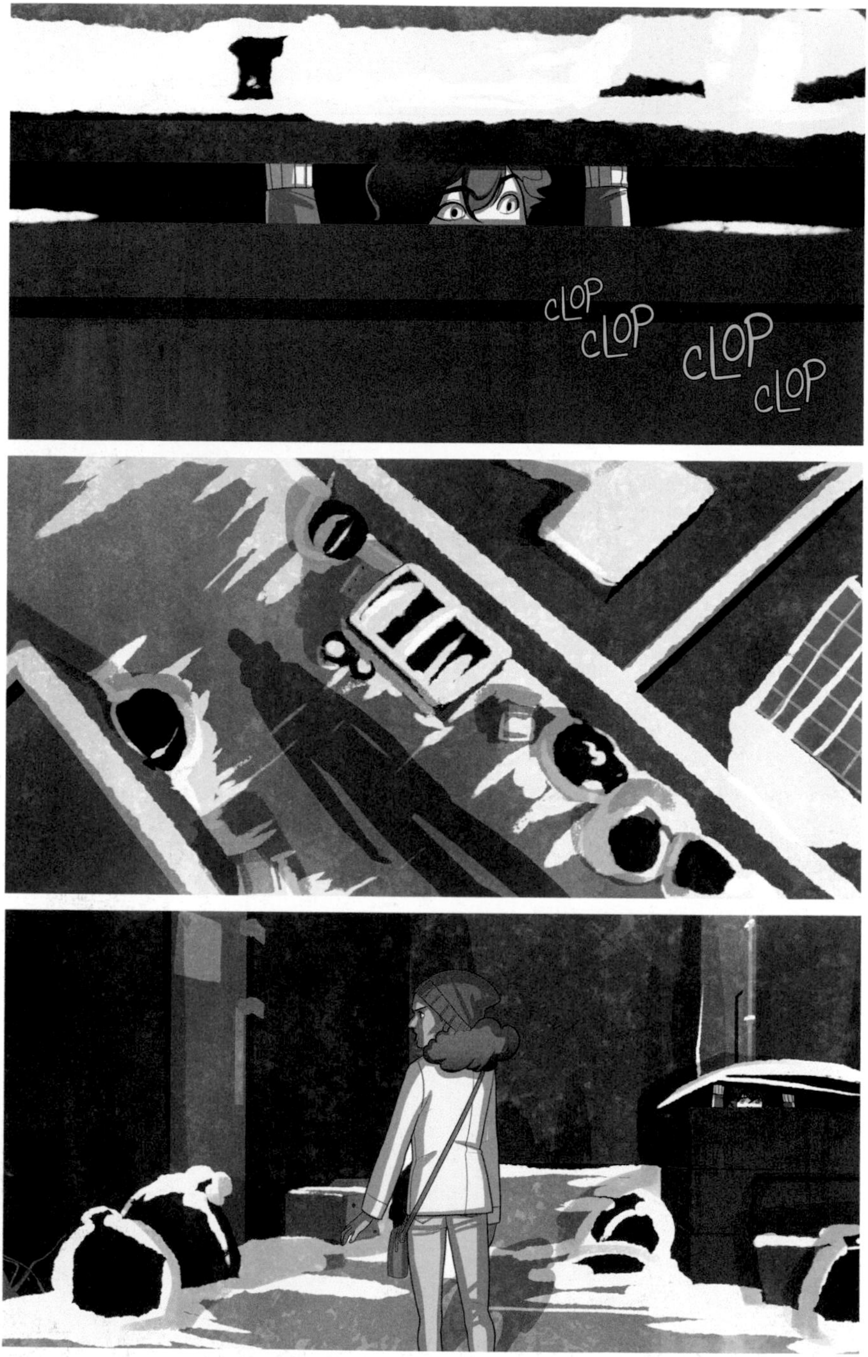
CLOP
CLOP
CLOP
CLOP

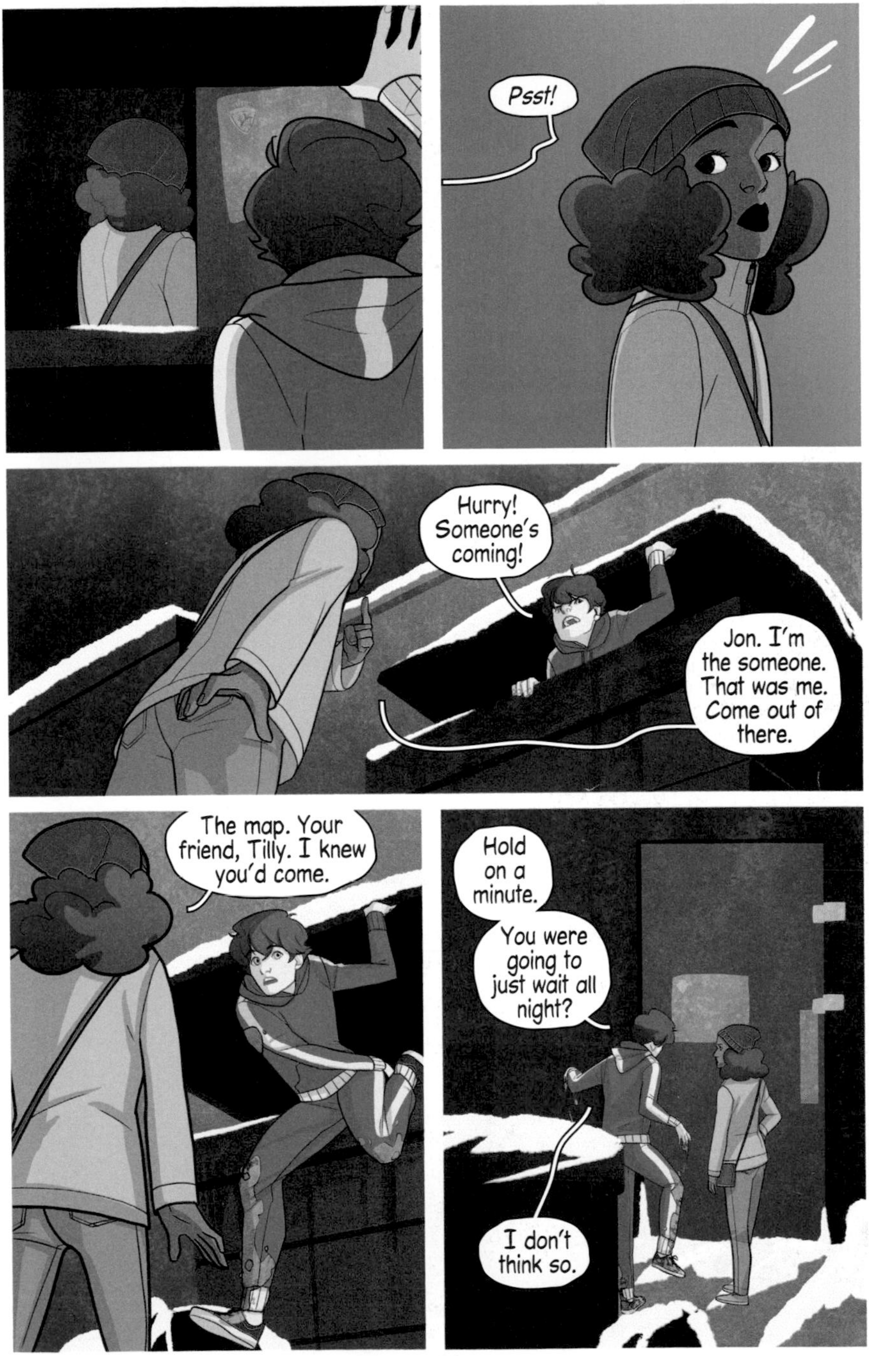

Psst!
Hurry! Someone's coming!
Jon. I'm the someone. That was me. Come out of there.
The map. Your friend, Tilly. I knew you'd come.
Hold on a minute.
You were going to just wait all night?
I don't think so.

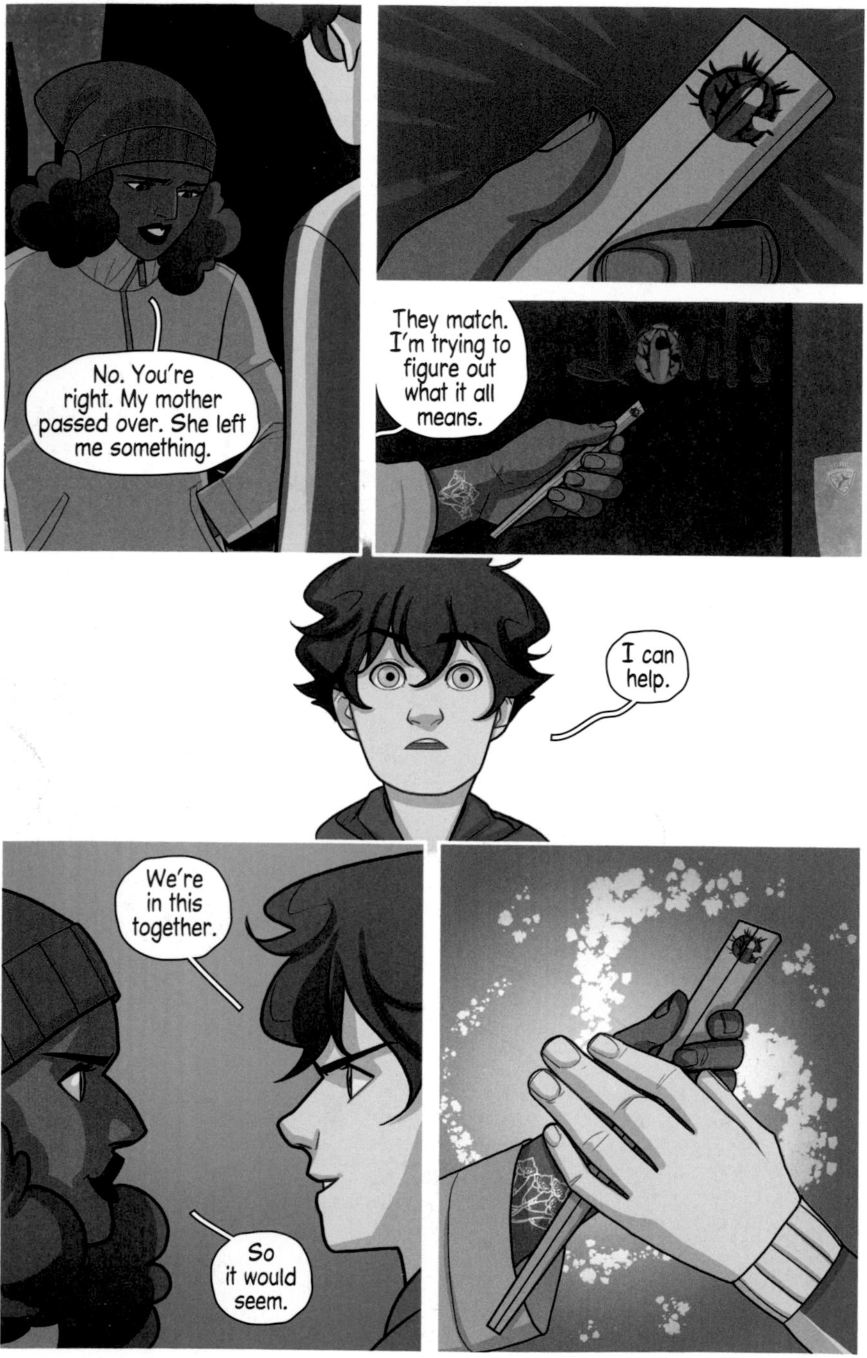
No. You're right. My mother passed over. She left me something.
They match. I'm trying to figure out what it all means.
I can help.
We're in this together.
So it would seem.

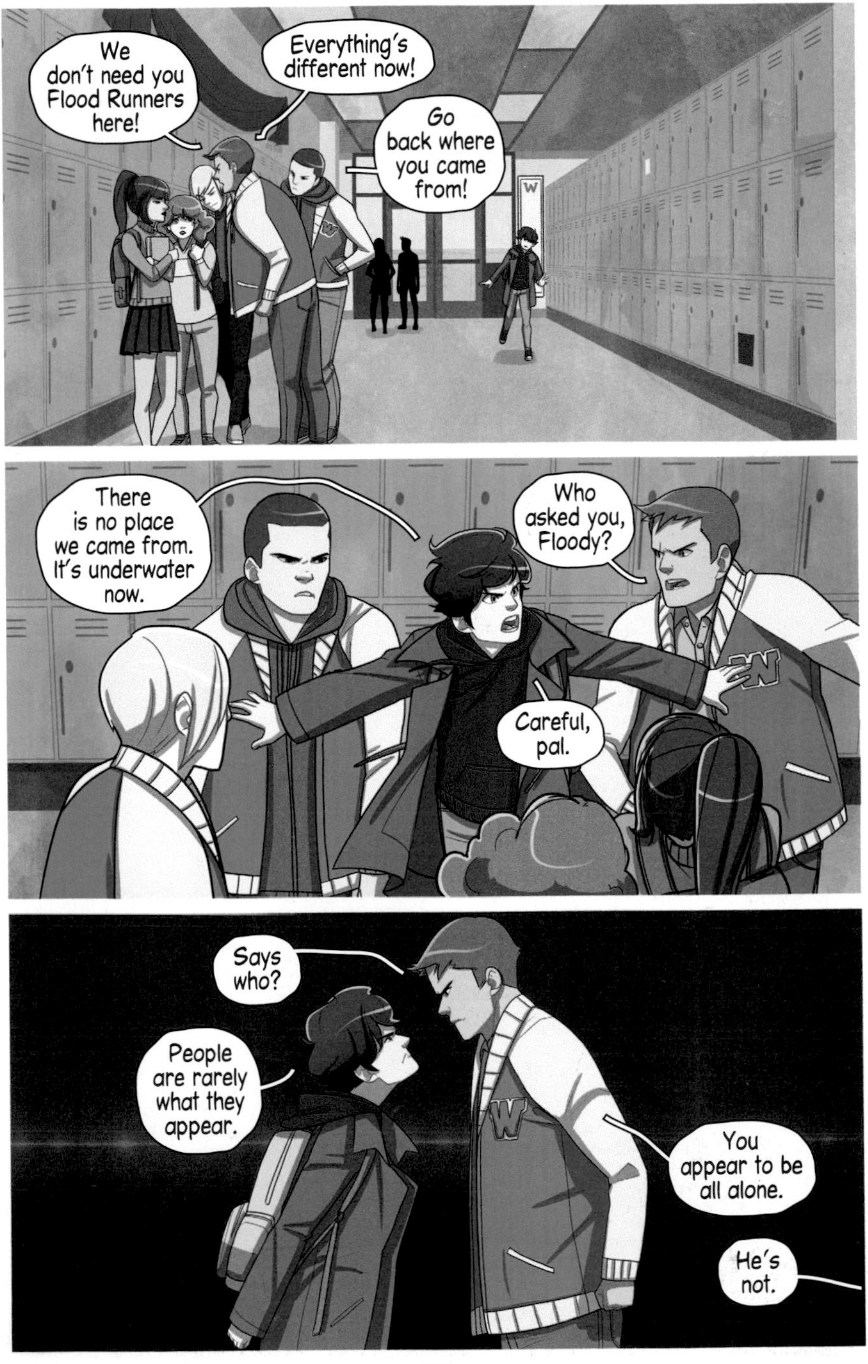
We don't need you Flood Runners here!
Everything's different now!
Go back where you came from!
W
There is no place we came from. It's underwater now.
Who asked you, Floody?
Careful, pal.
Says who?
People are rarely what they appear.
You appear to be all alone.
He's not.

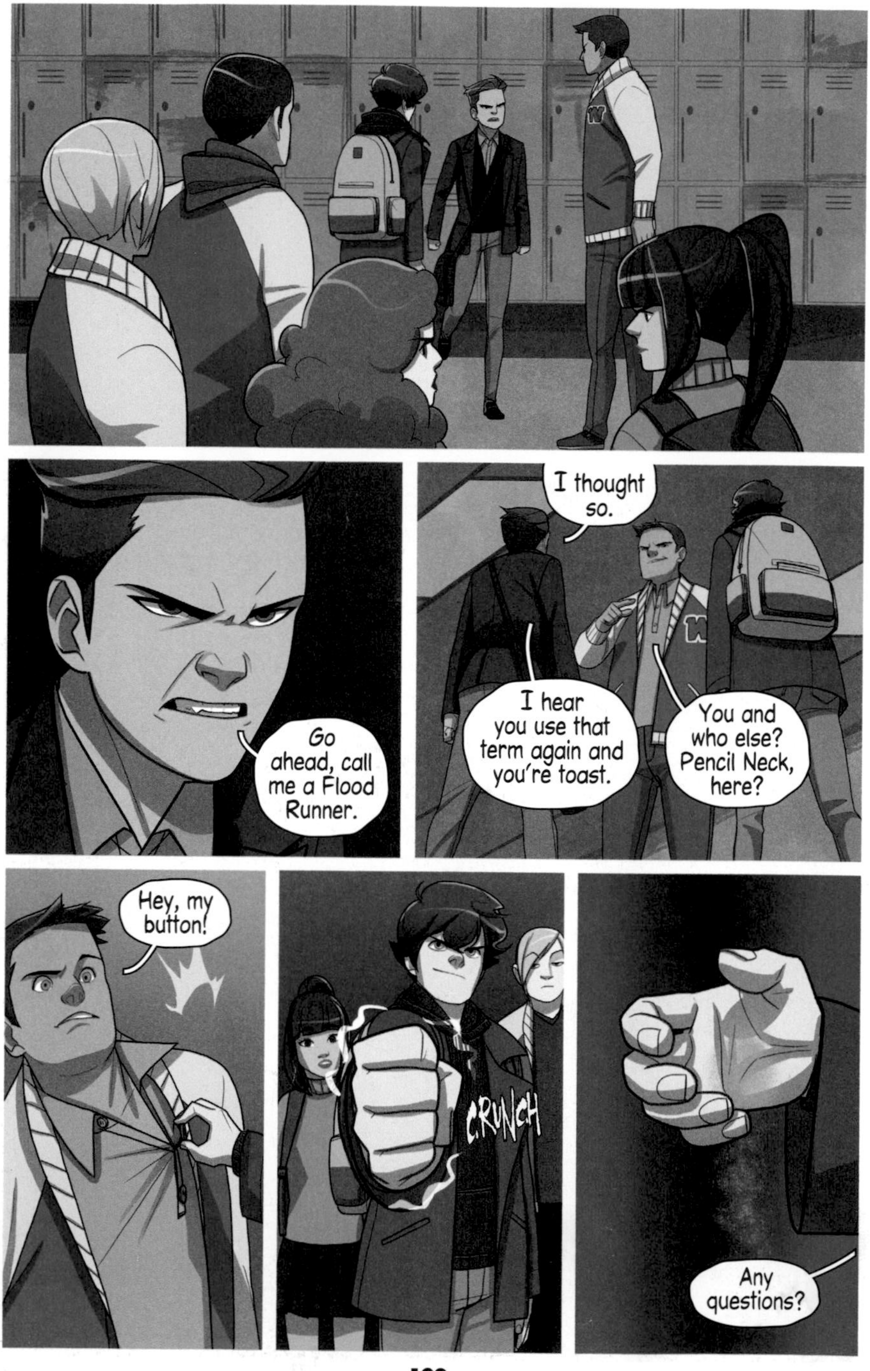
Go ahead, call me a Flood Runner.
I thought so.
I hear you use that term again and you're toast.
You and who else? Pencil Neck, here?
Hey, my button!
CRUNCH
Any questions?

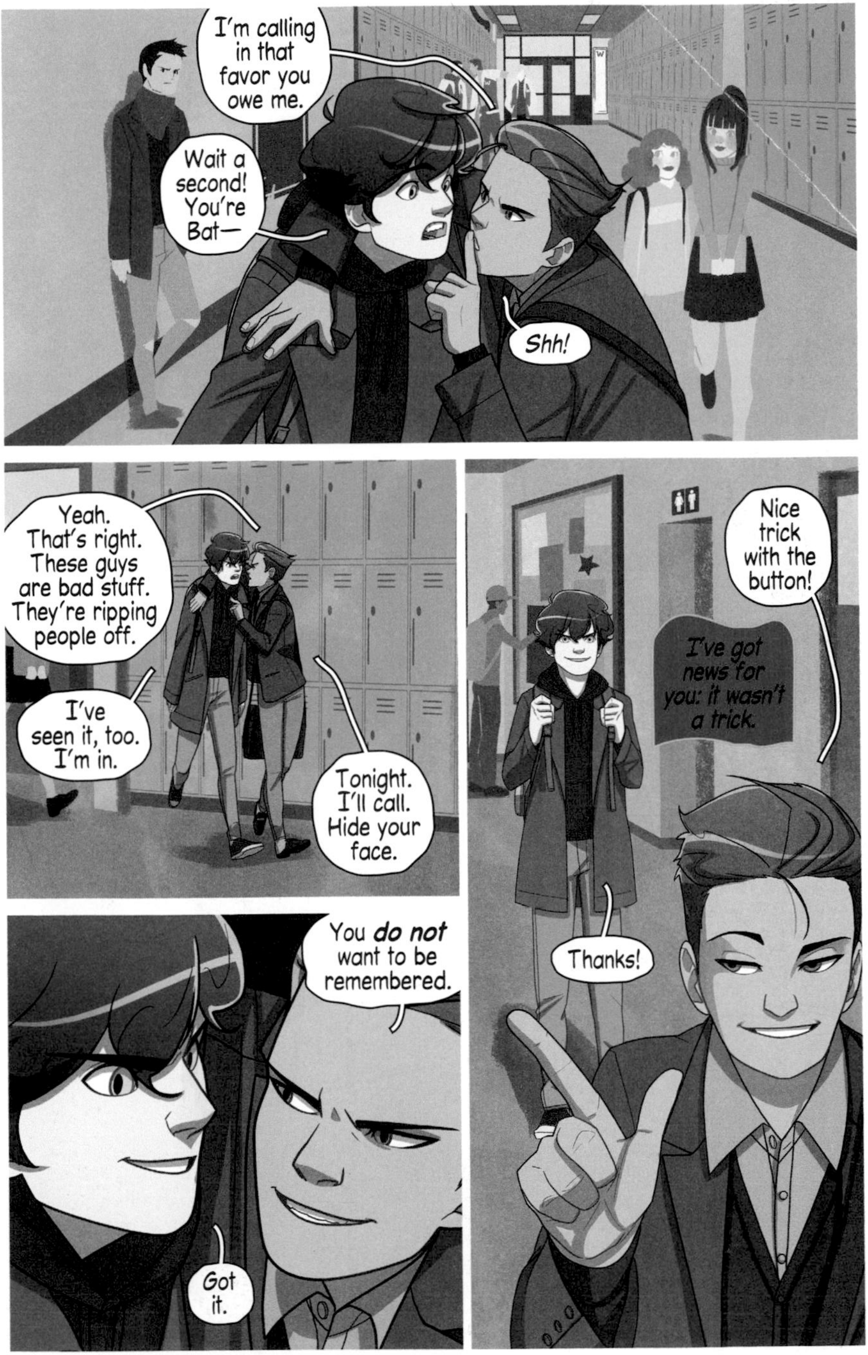
I'm calling in that favor you owe me.
Wait a second! You're Bat—
Shh!
Yeah. That's right. These guys are bad stuff. They're ripping people off.
I've seen it, too. I'm in.
Tonight. I'll call. Hide your face.
You **do not** want to be remembered.
Got it.
Nice trick with the button!
I've got news for you: it wasn't a trick.
Thanks!

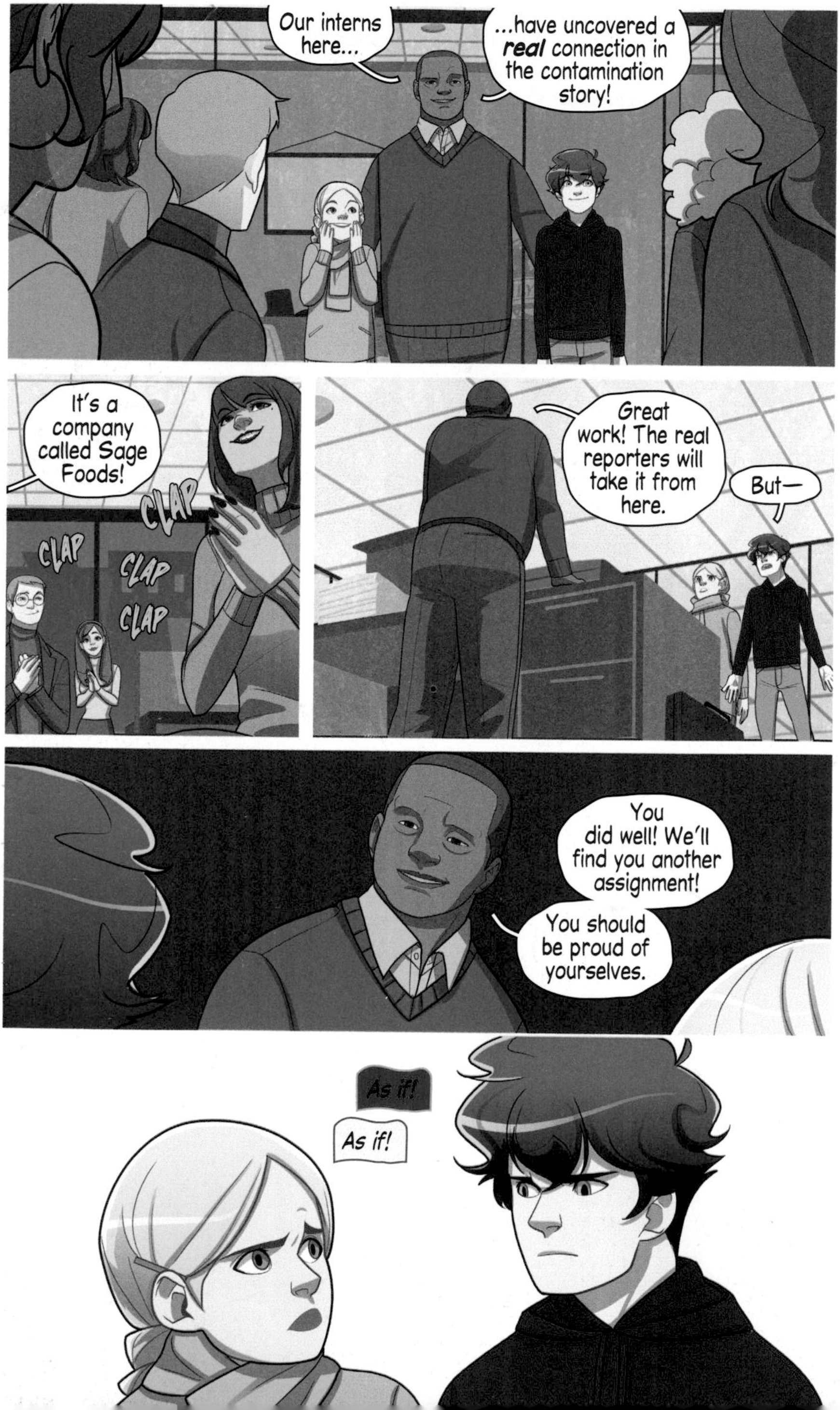
Our interns here...
...have uncovered a **real** connection in the contamination story!
It's a company called Sage Foods!
CLAP
CLAP
CLAP
CLAP
Great work! The real reporters will take it from here.
But—
You did well! We'll find you another assignment!
You should be proud of yourselves.
As if!
As if!

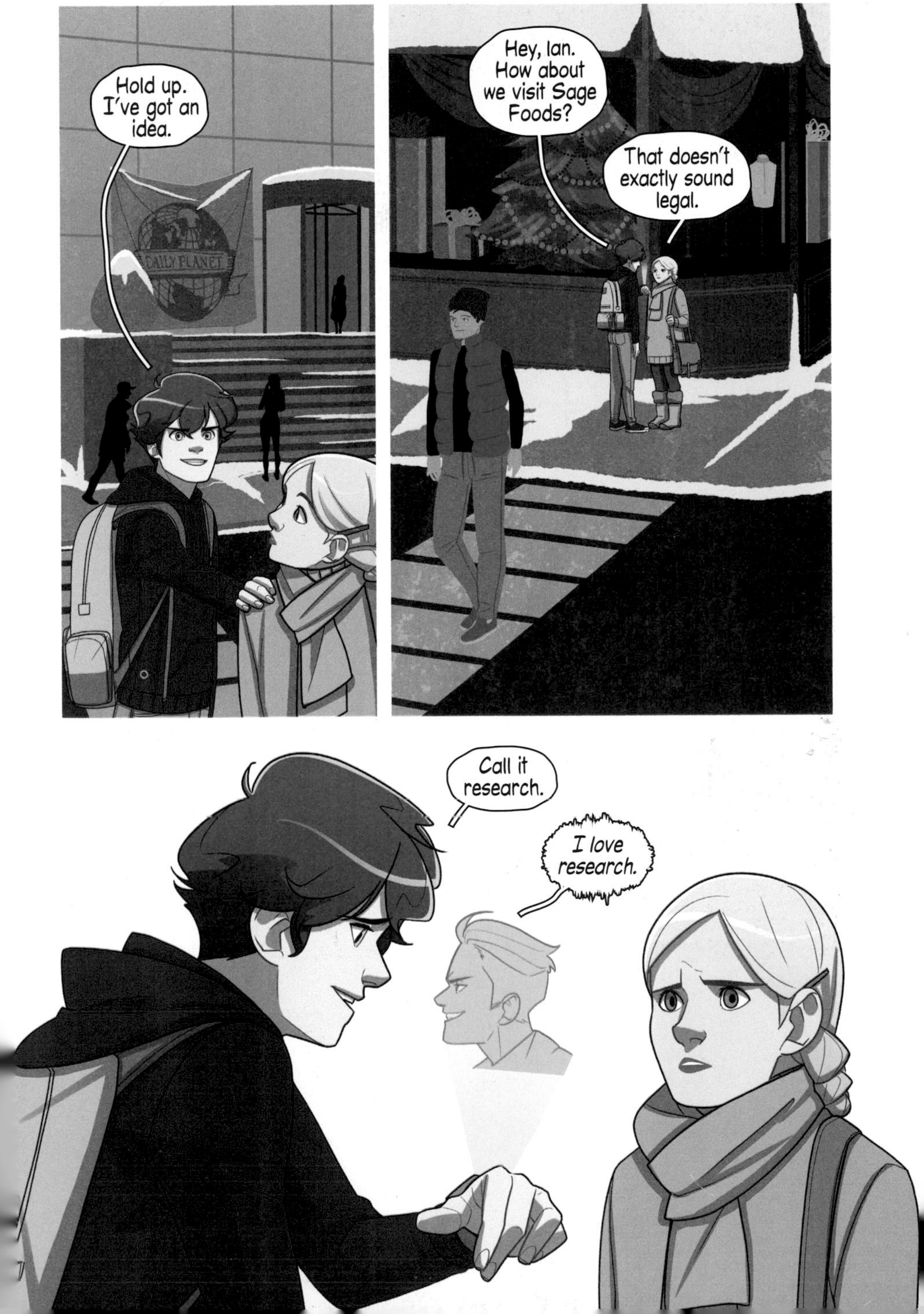
Hold up. I've got an idea.
DAILY PLANET
Hey, Ian. How about we visit Sage Foods?
That doesn't exactly sound legal.
Call it research.
I love research.

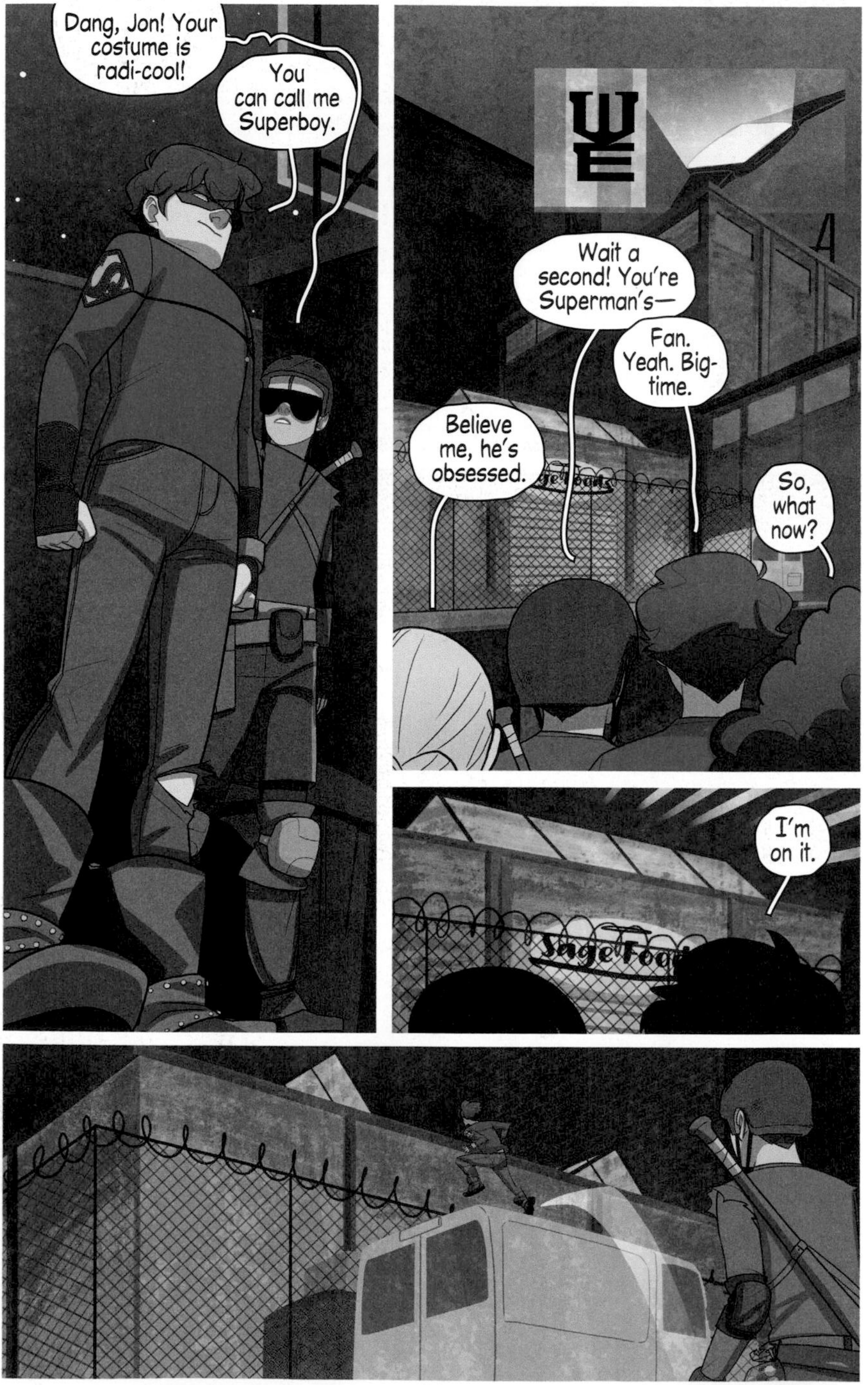
Dang, Jon! Your costume is radi-cool!
You can call me Superboy.
WE
Wait a second! You're Superman's—
Fan. Yeah. Big-time.
Believe me, he's obsessed.
So, what now?
I'm on it.

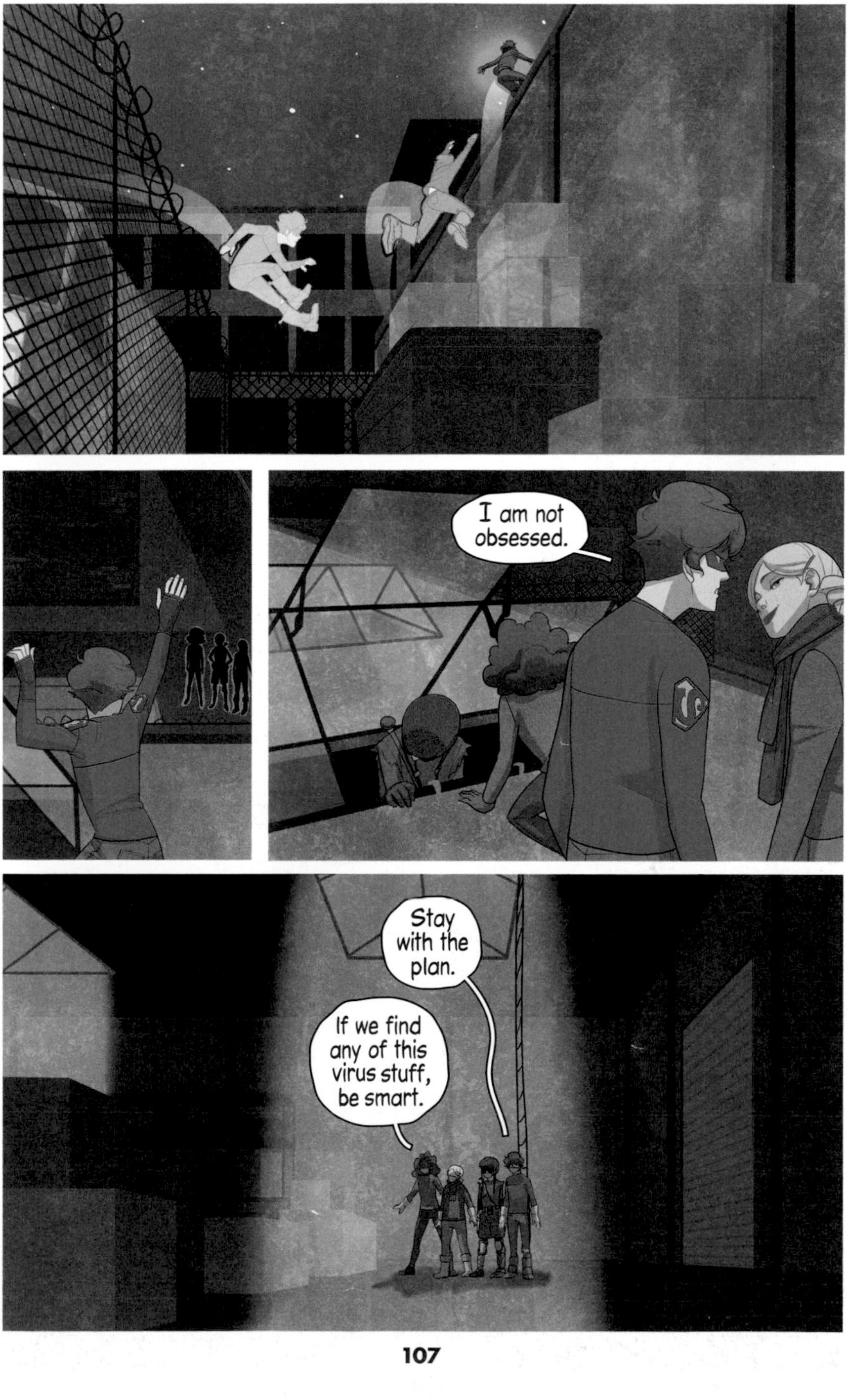
I am not obsessed.
Stay with the plan.
If we find any of this virus stuff, be smart.

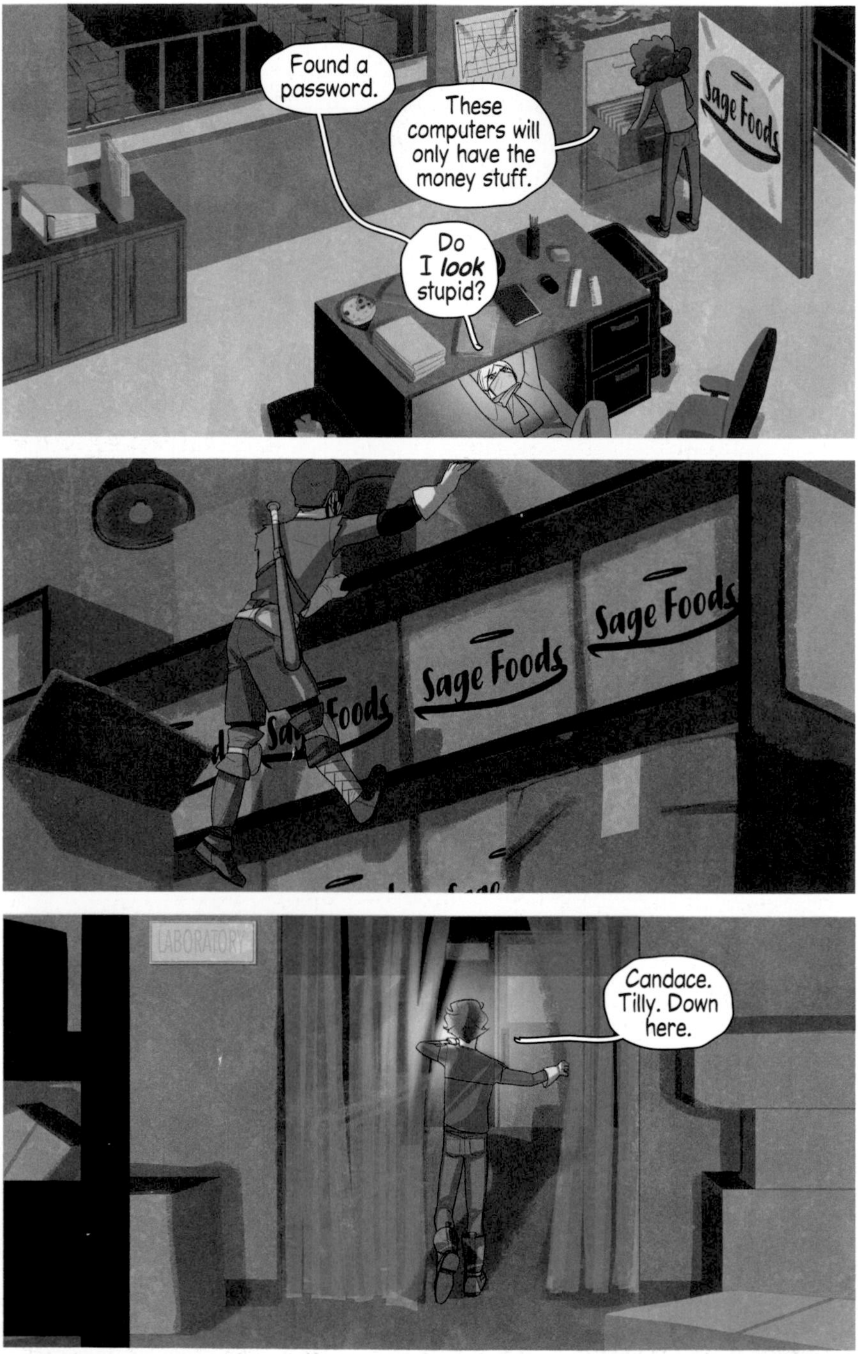
Found a password.
These computers will only have the money stuff.
Do I *look* stupid?
Sage Foods
Sage Foods
Sage Foods
LABORATORY
Candace. Tilly. Down here.

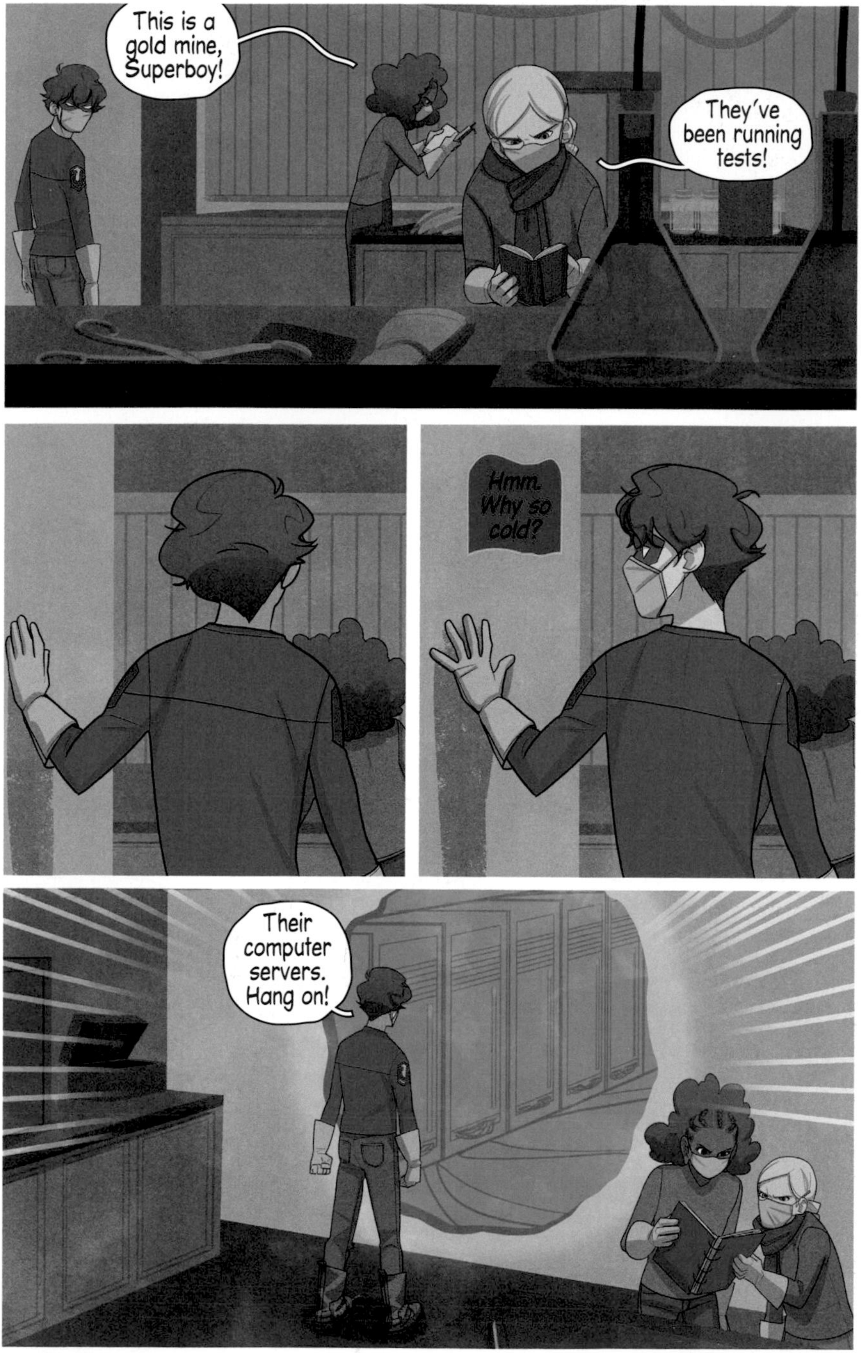
This is a gold mine, Superboy!
They've been running tests!
Hmm. Why so cold?
Their computer servers. Hang on!

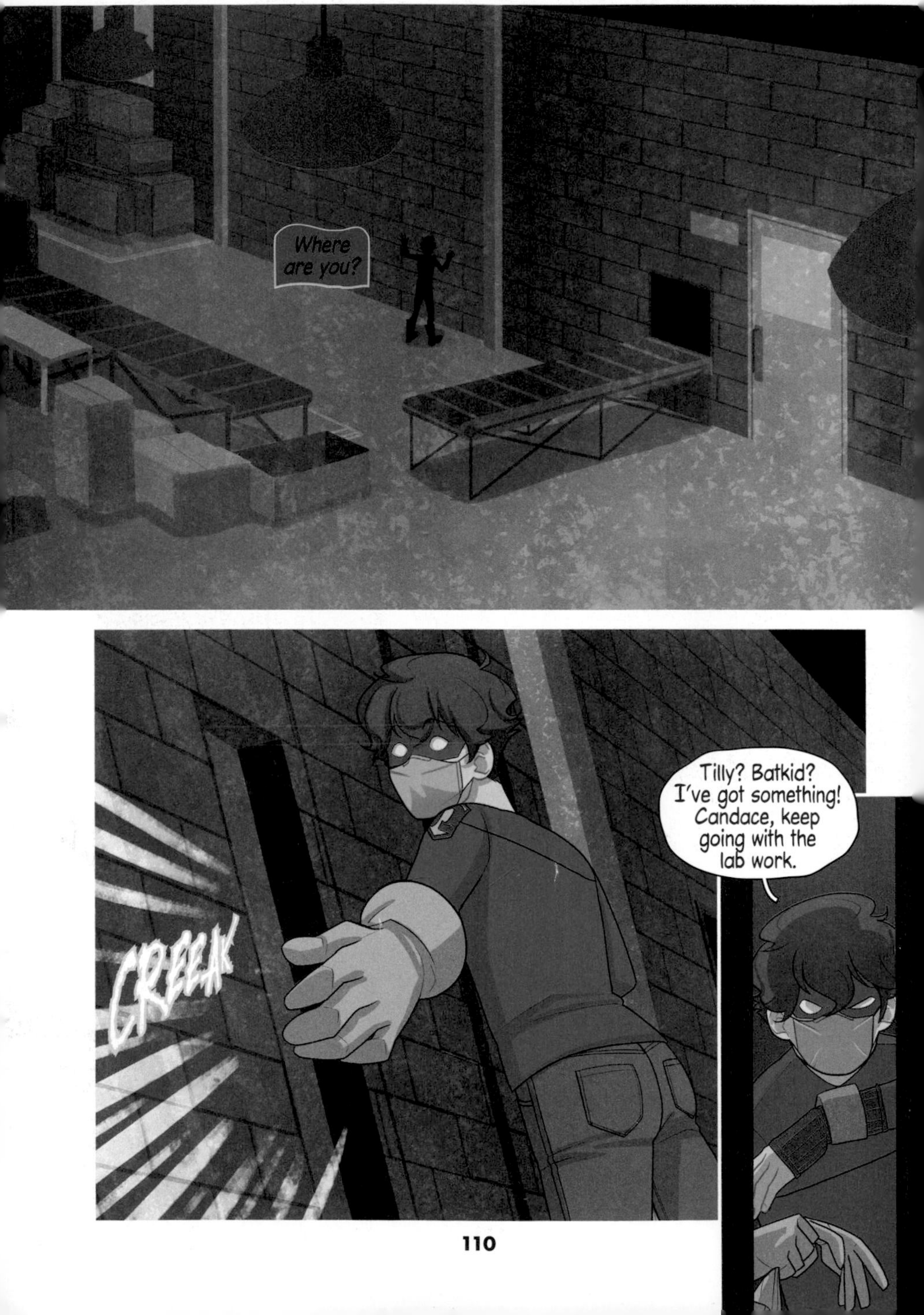
Where are you?
CREEAK
Tilly? Batkid? I've got something! Candace, keep going with the lab work.

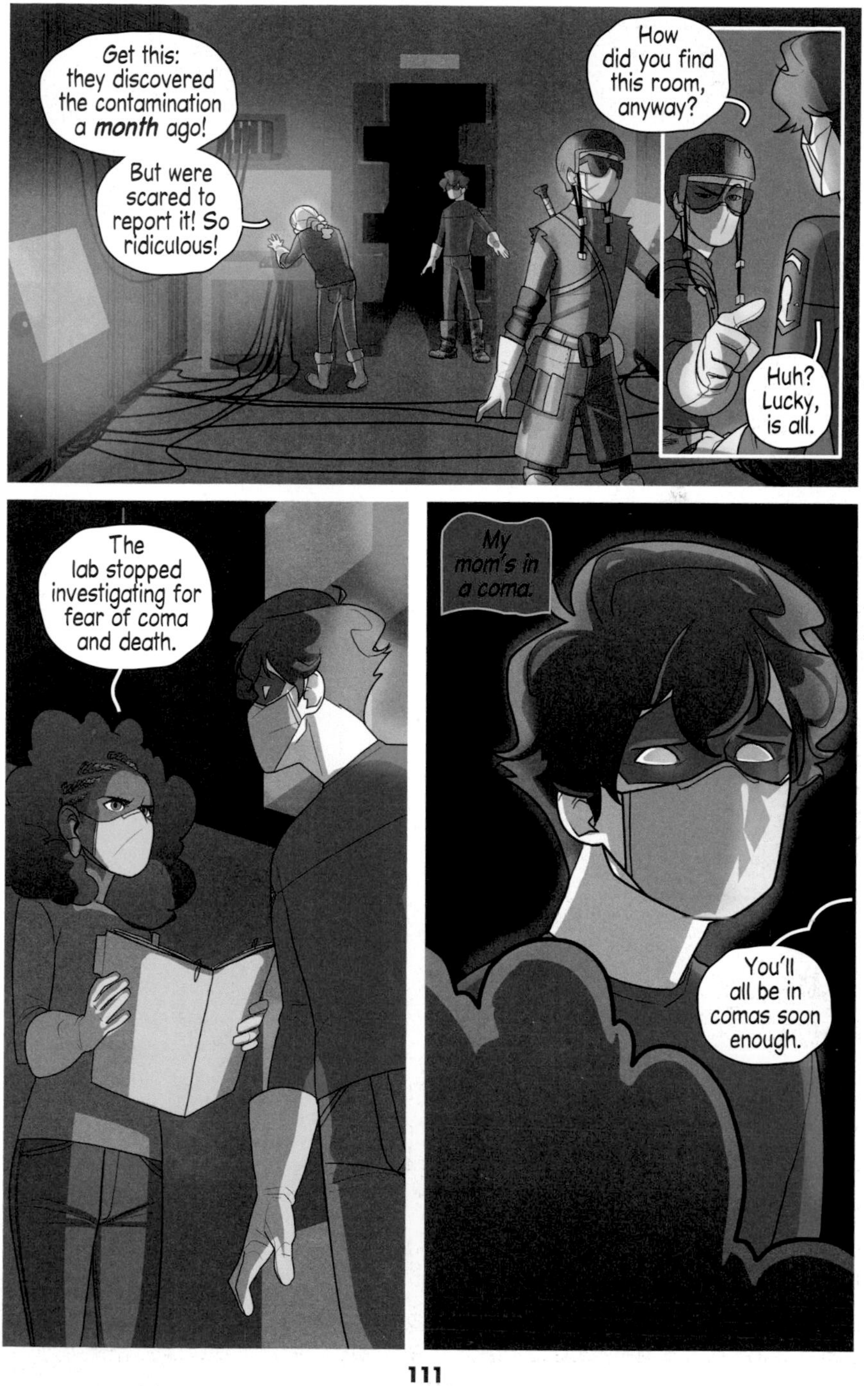
Get this: they discovered the contamination a *month* ago!
But were scared to report it! So ridiculous!
How did you find this room, anyway?
Huh? Lucky, is all.
The lab stopped investigating for fear of coma and death.
My mom's in a coma.
You'll all be in comas soon enough.

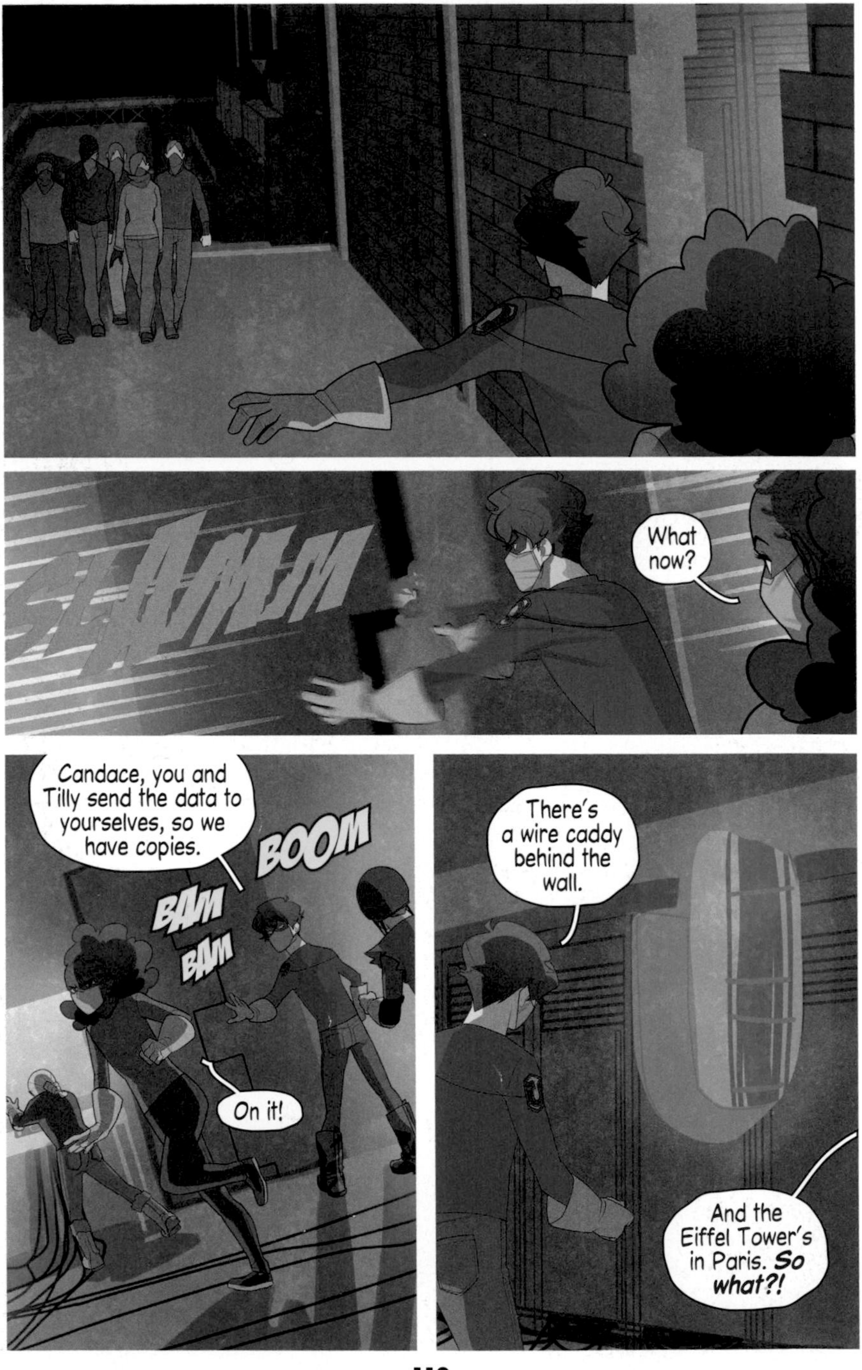
SLAMM
What now?
Candace, you and Tilly send the data to yourselves, so we have copies.
BOOM
BAM
BAM
On it!
There's a wire caddy behind the wall.
And the Eiffel Tower's in Paris. *So what?!*

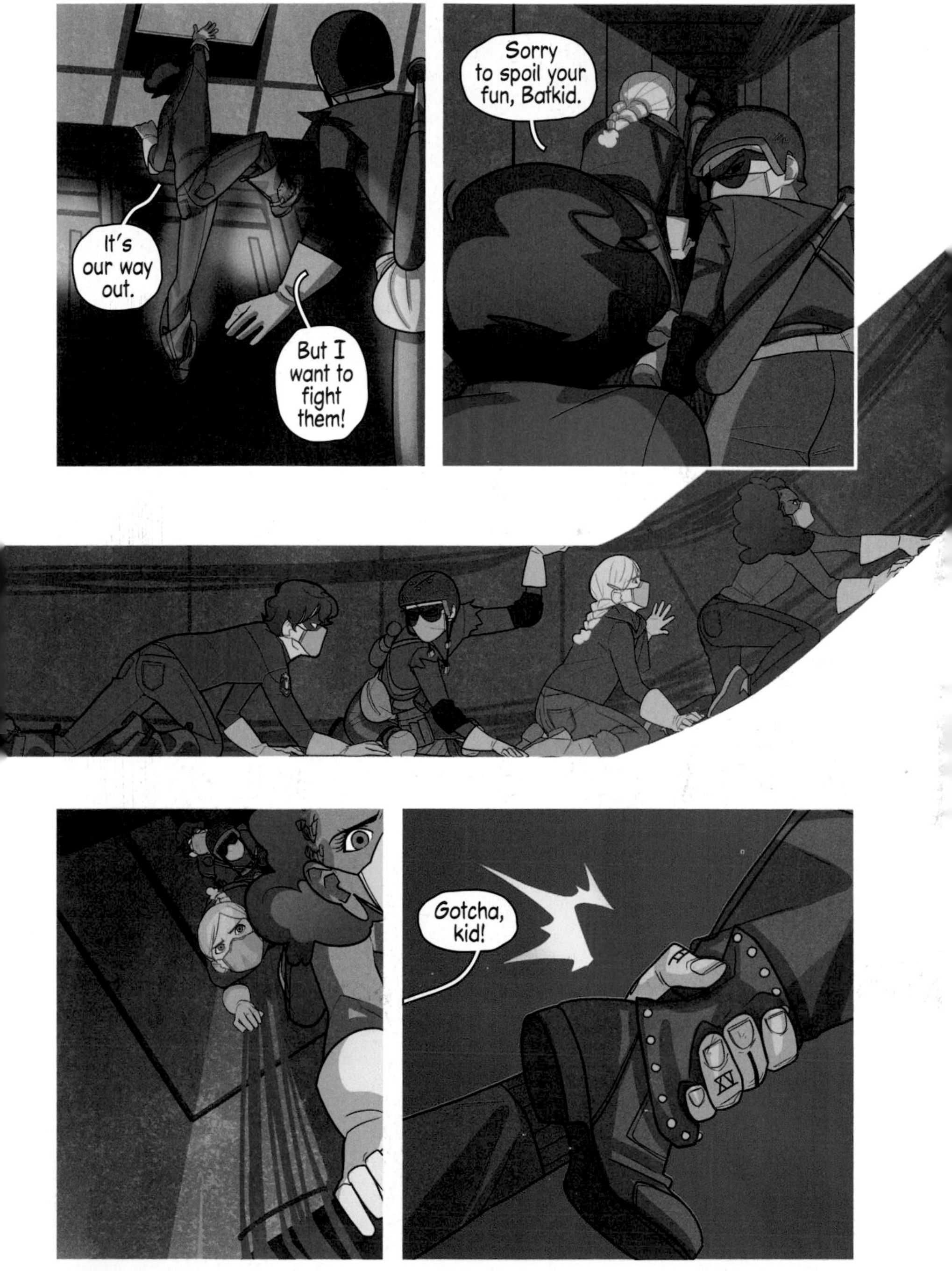
It's our way out.
But I want to fight them!
Sorry to spoil your fun, Batkid.
Gotcha, kid!

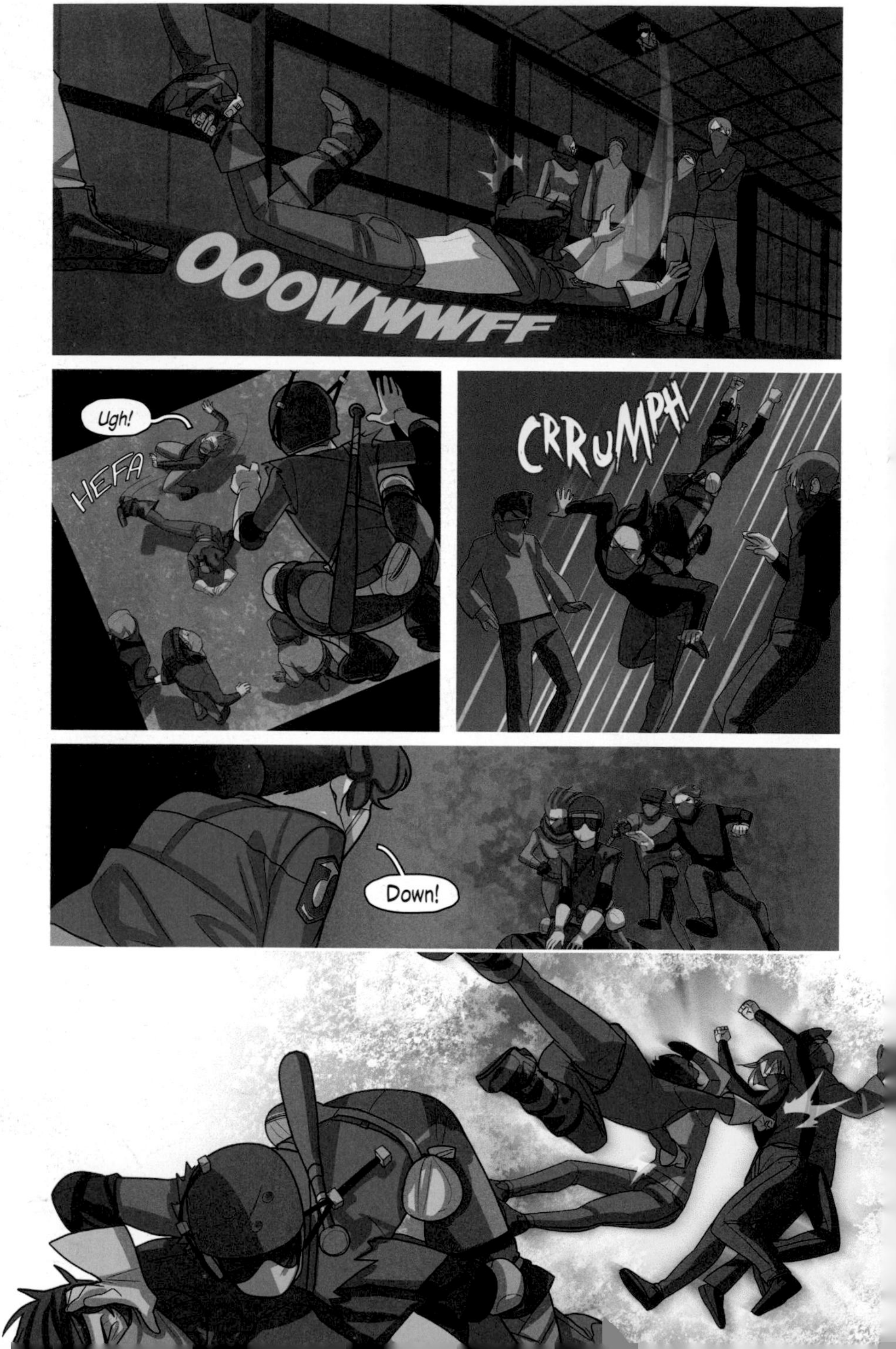
OOOWWWWFF
Ugh!
HEFA
CRRUMPH
Down!

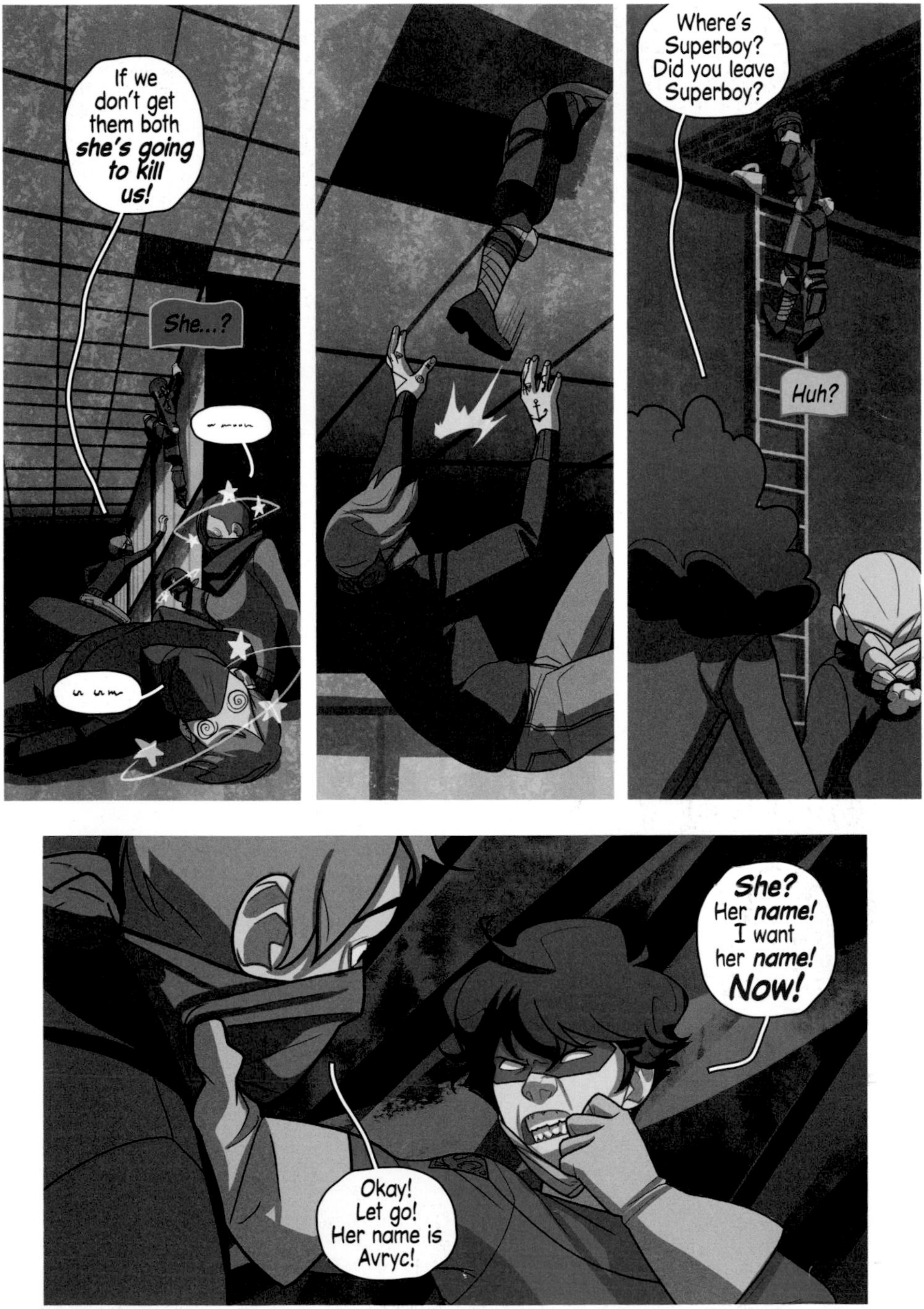
If we don't get them both *she's going to kill us!*
She...?
Where's Superboy? Did you leave Superboy?
Huh?
She? Her *name!* I want her *name!* *Now!*
Okay! Let go! Her name is Avryc!

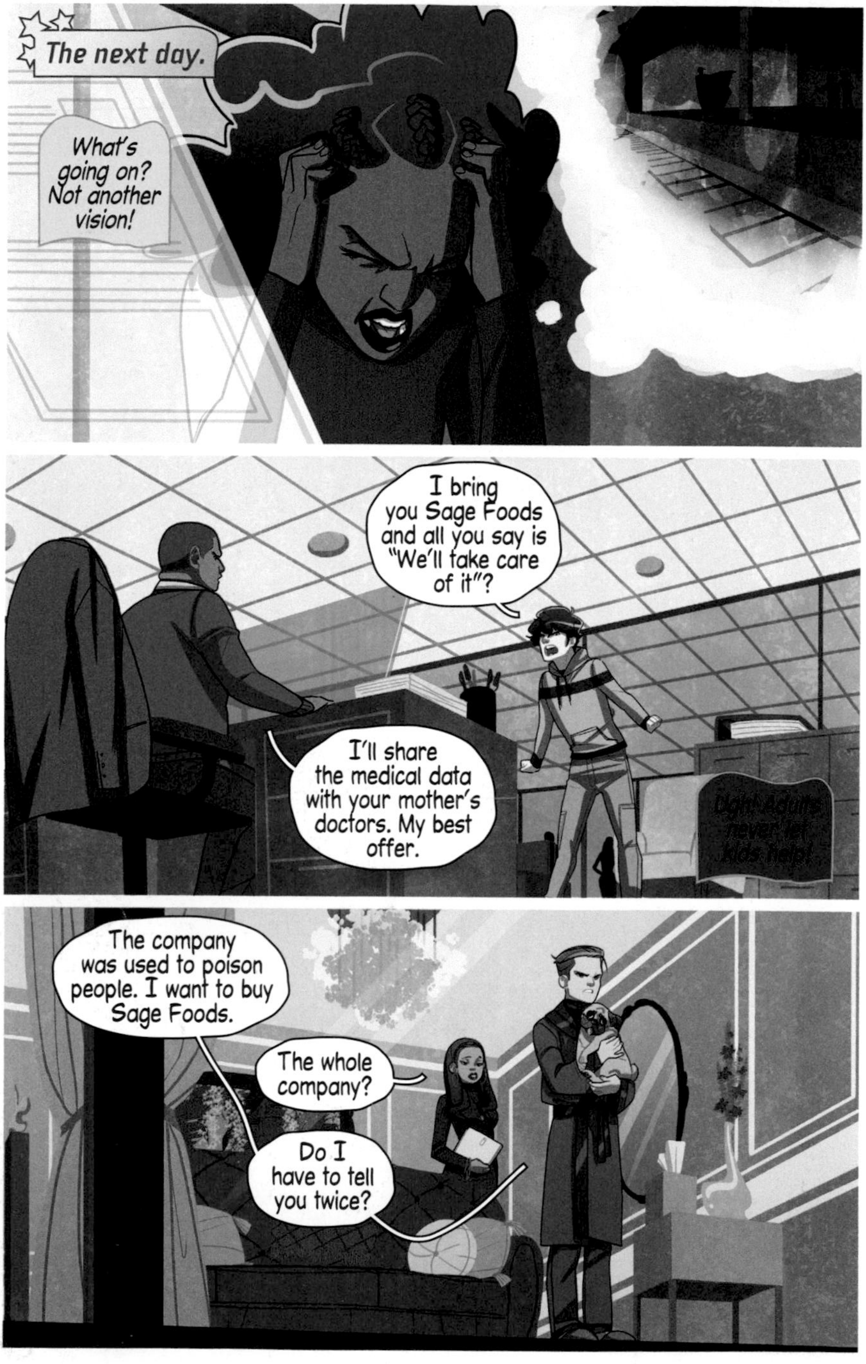

The next day.
What's going on? Not another vision!
I bring you Sage Foods and all you say is "We'll take care of it"?
I'll share the medical data with your mother's doctors. My best offer.
The company was used to poison people. I want to buy Sage Foods.
The whole company?
Do I have to tell you twice?

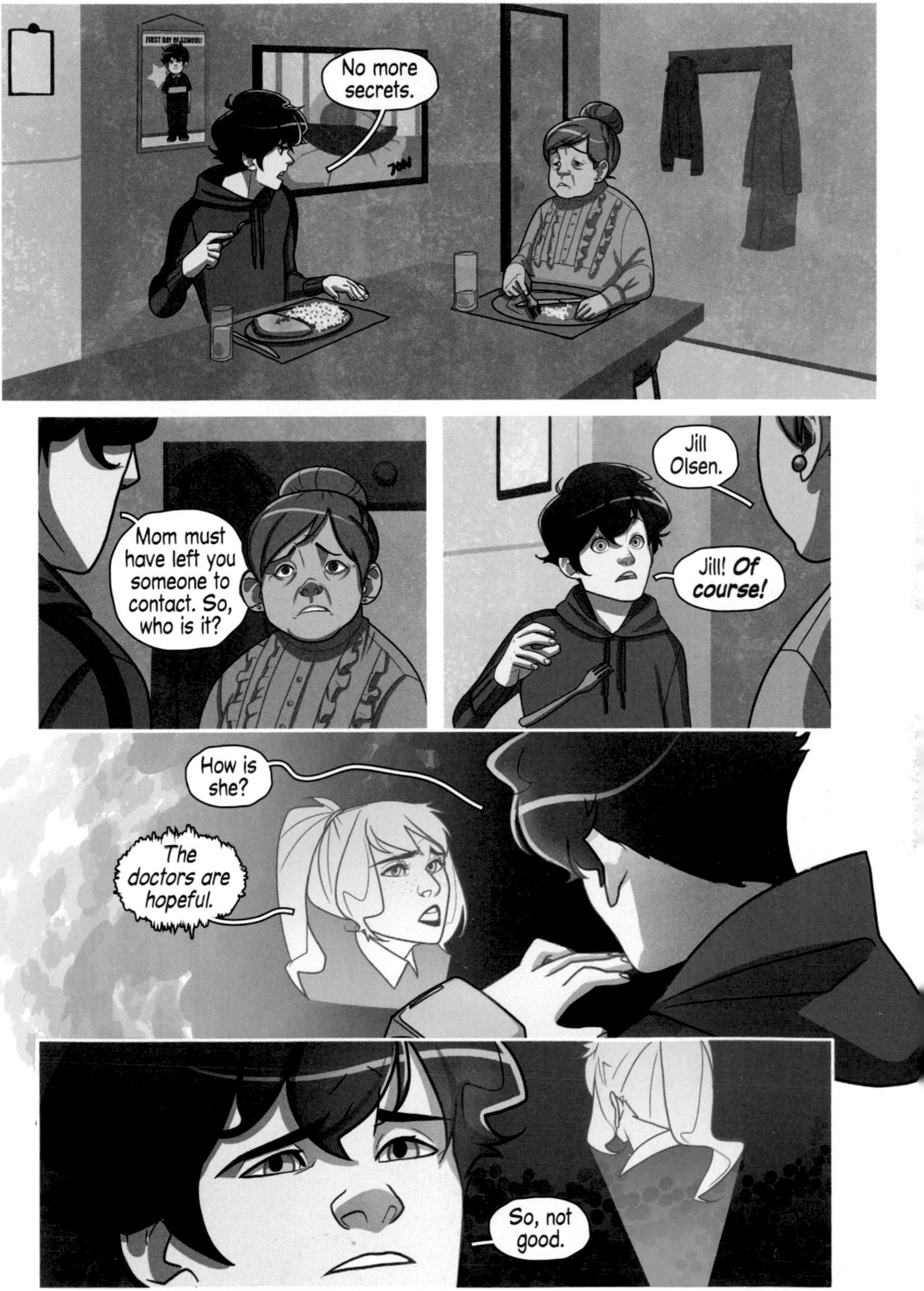
FIRST DAY OF SCHOOL!
No more secrets.
Mom must have left you someone to contact. So, who is it?
Jill Olsen.
Jill! Of course!
How is she?
The doctors are hopeful.
So, not good.

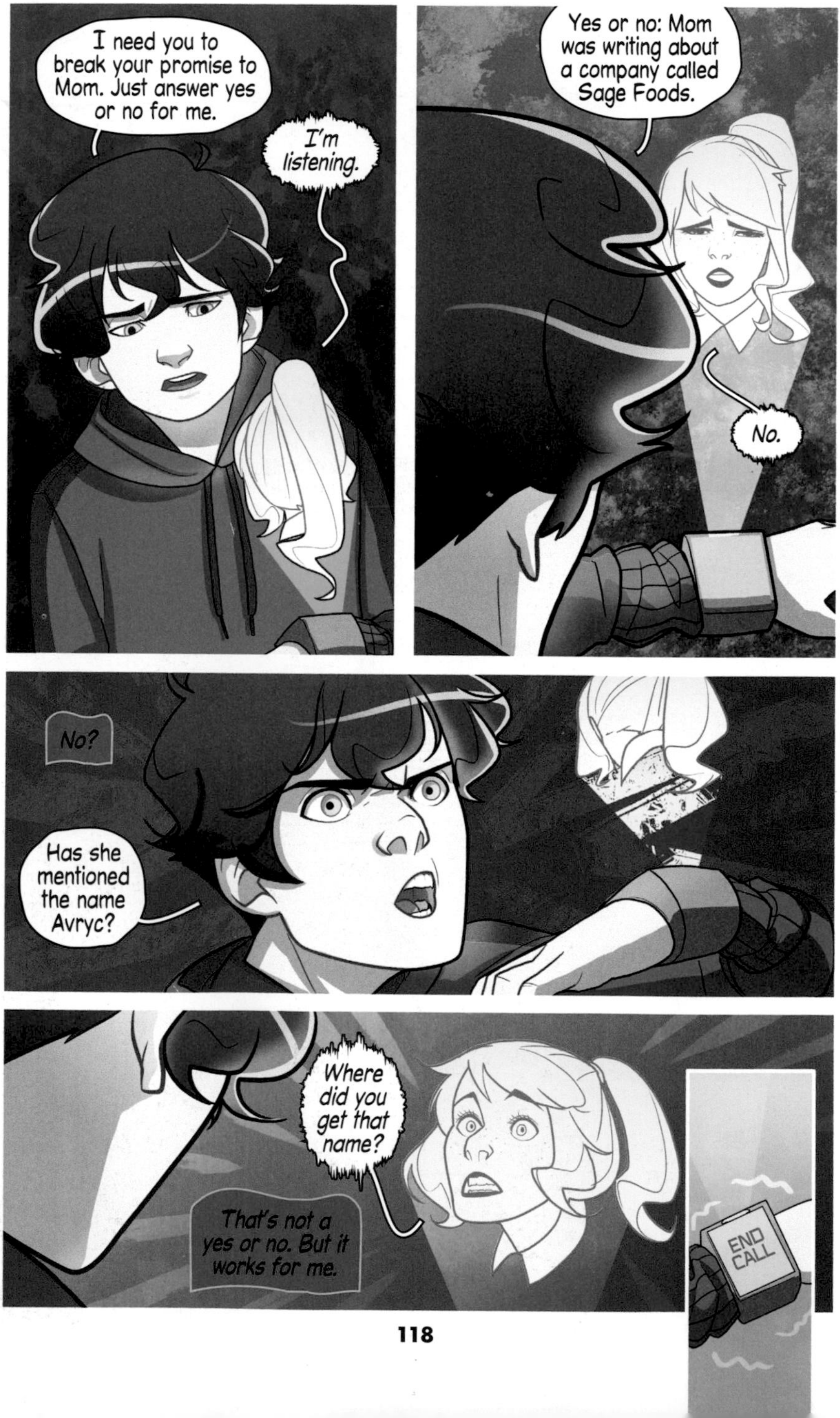
I need you to break your promise to Mom. Just answer yes or no for me.
I'm listening.
Yes or no: Mom was writing about a company called Sage Foods.
No.
No?
Has she mentioned the name Avryc?
Where did you get that name?
That's not a yes or no. But it works for me.
END CALL

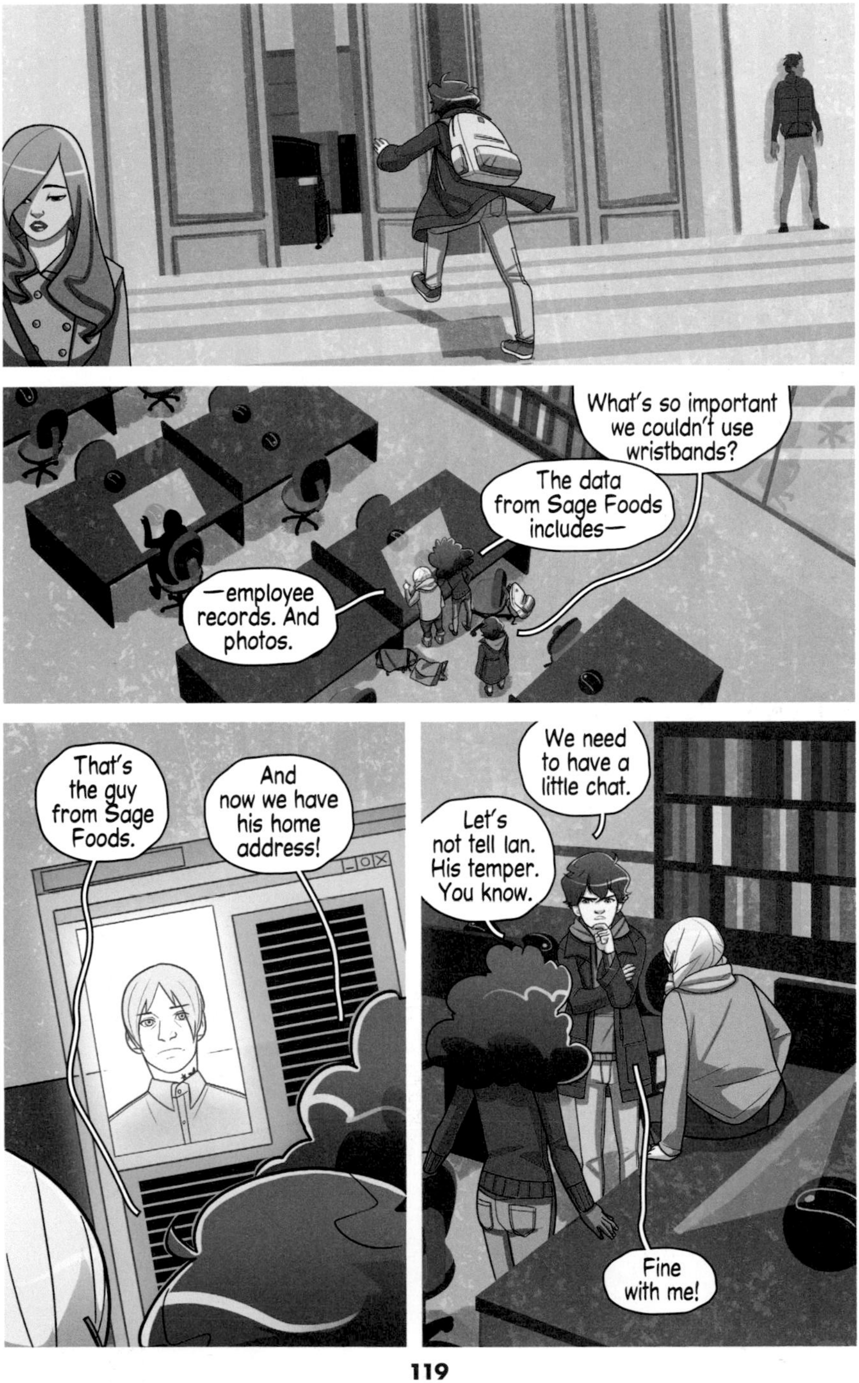

What's so important we couldn't use wristbands?
The data from Sage Foods includes—
—employee records. And photos.
That's the guy from Sage Foods.
And now we have his home address!
We need to have a little chat.
Let's not tell Ian. His temper. You know.
Fine with me!

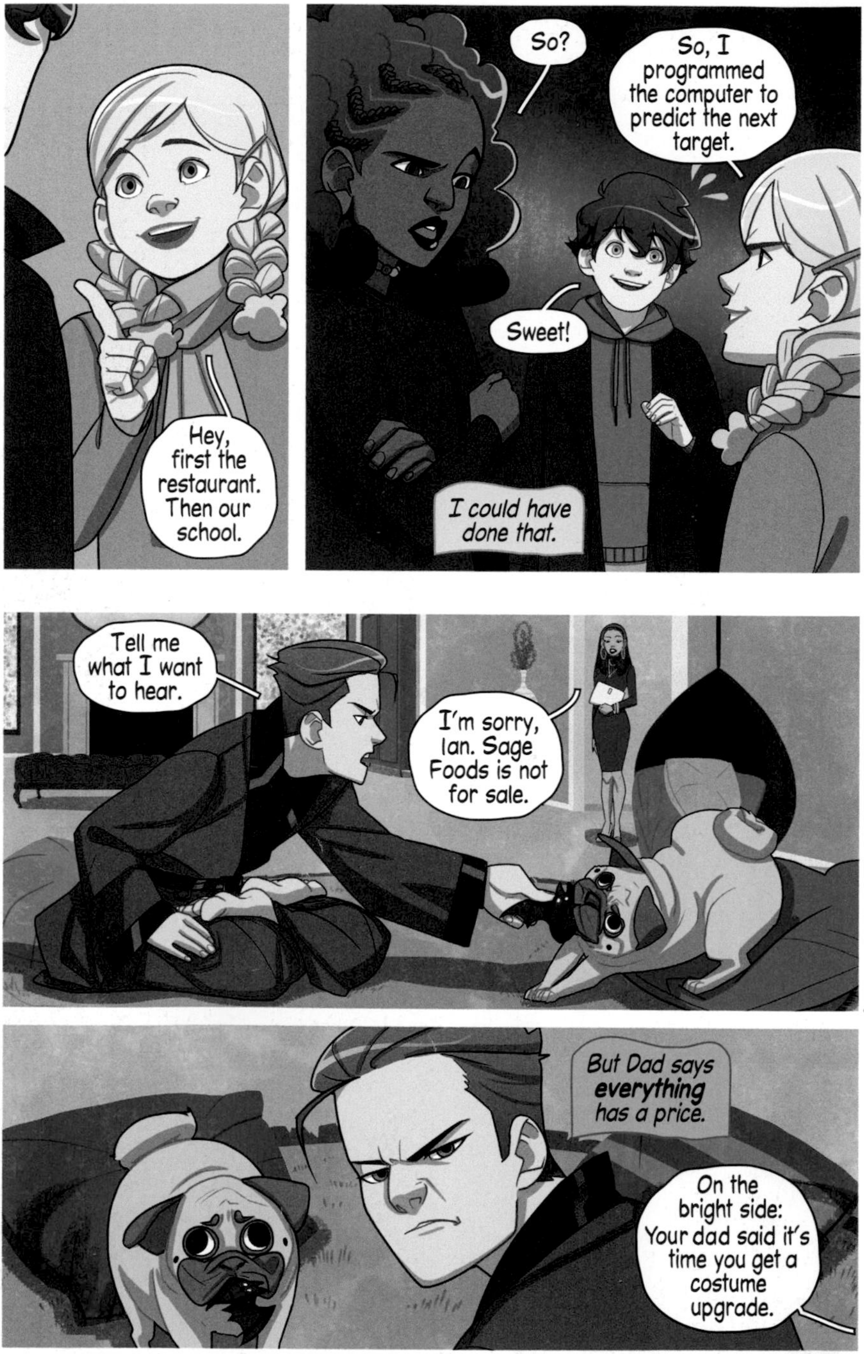

Hey, first the restaurant. Then our school.
So?
So, I programmed the computer to predict the next target.
Sweet!
I could have done that.
Tell me what I want to hear.
I'm sorry, Ian. Sage Foods is not for sale.
But Dad says **everything** has a price.
On the bright side: Your dad said it's time you get a costume upgrade.

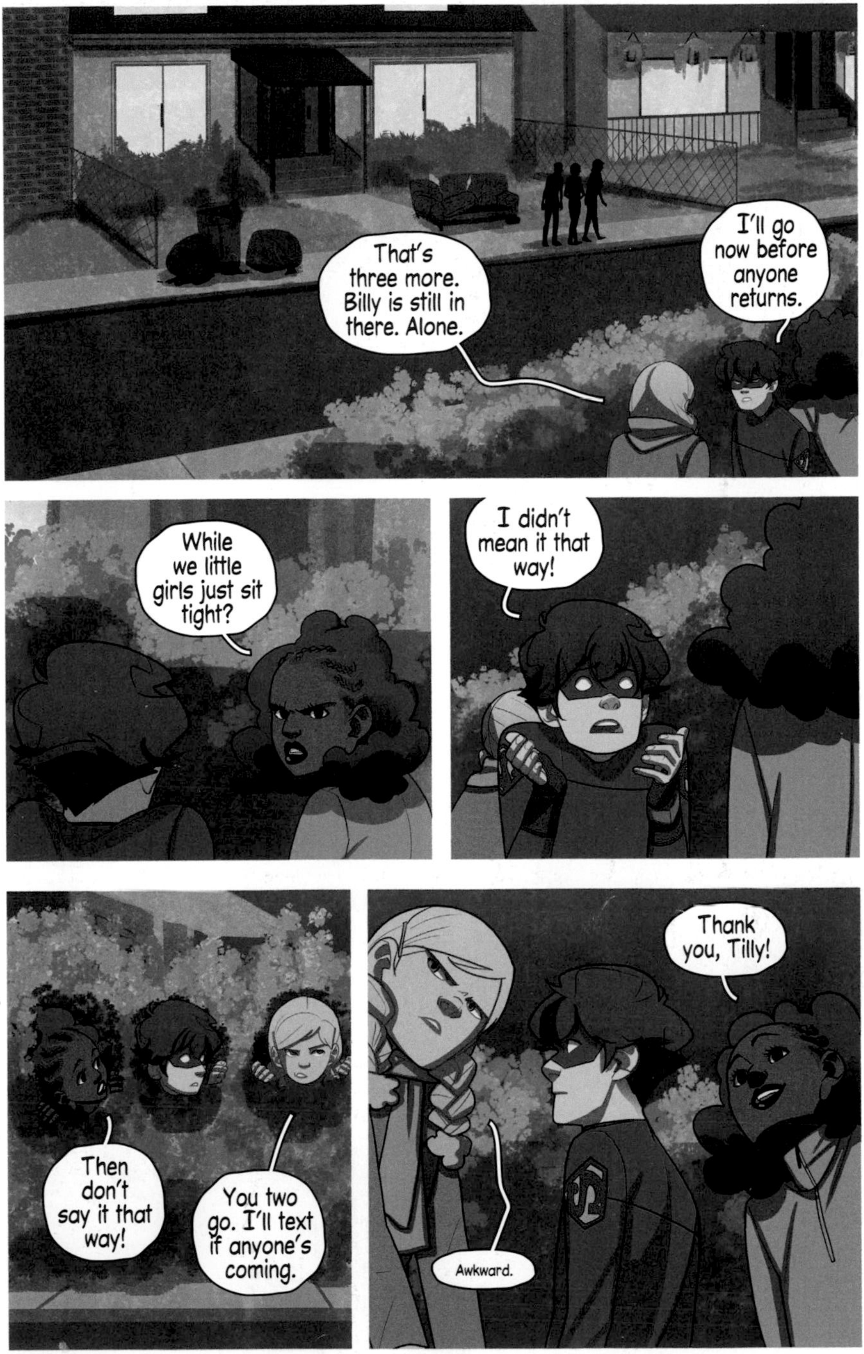
That's three more. Billy is still in there. Alone.
I'll go now before anyone returns.
While we little girls just sit tight?
I didn't mean it that way!
Then don't say it that way!
You two go. I'll text if anyone's coming.
Awkward.
Thank you, Tilly!

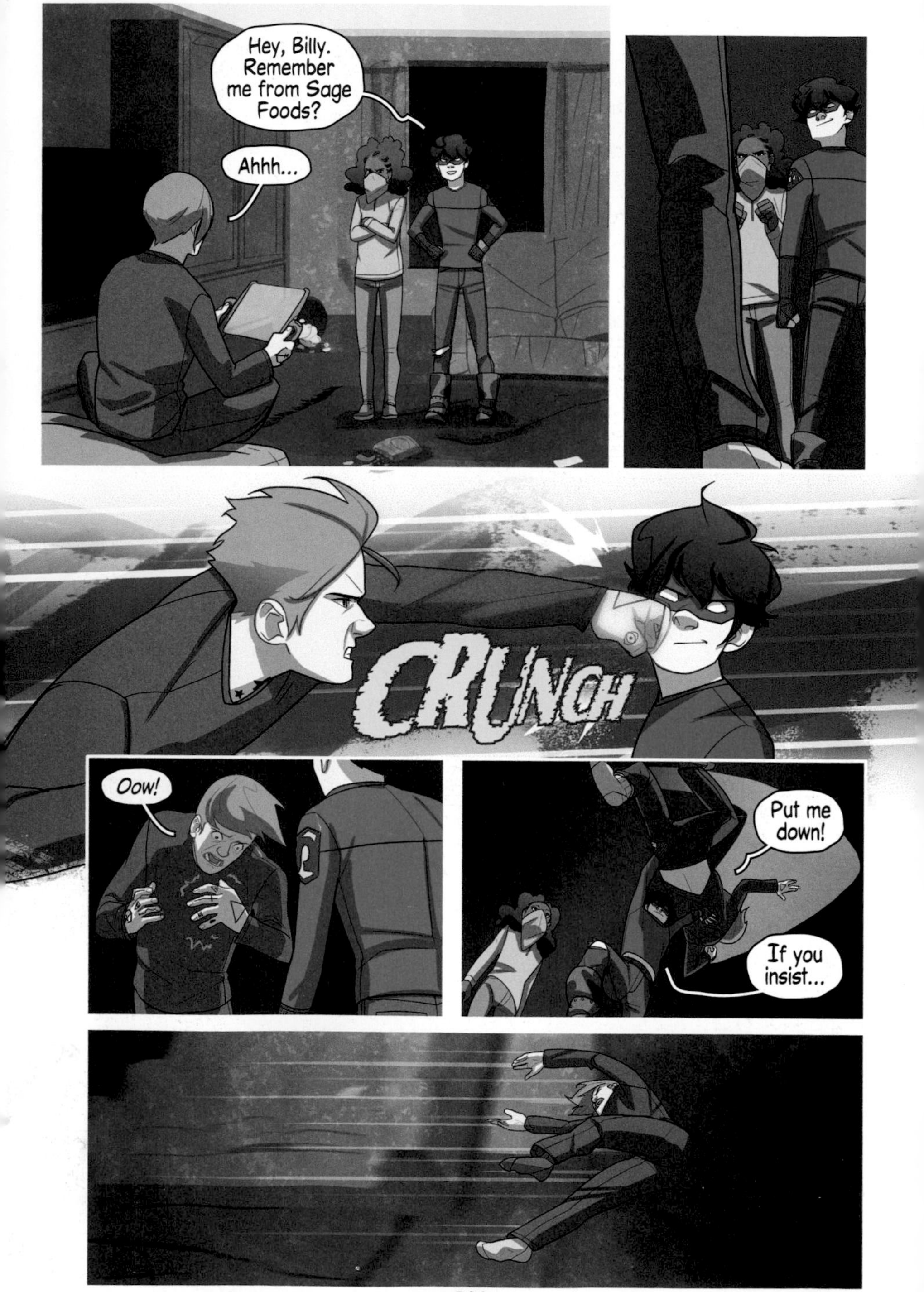
Hey, Billy. Remember me from Sage Foods?
Ahhh...
CRUNCH
Oow!
Put me down!
If you insist...

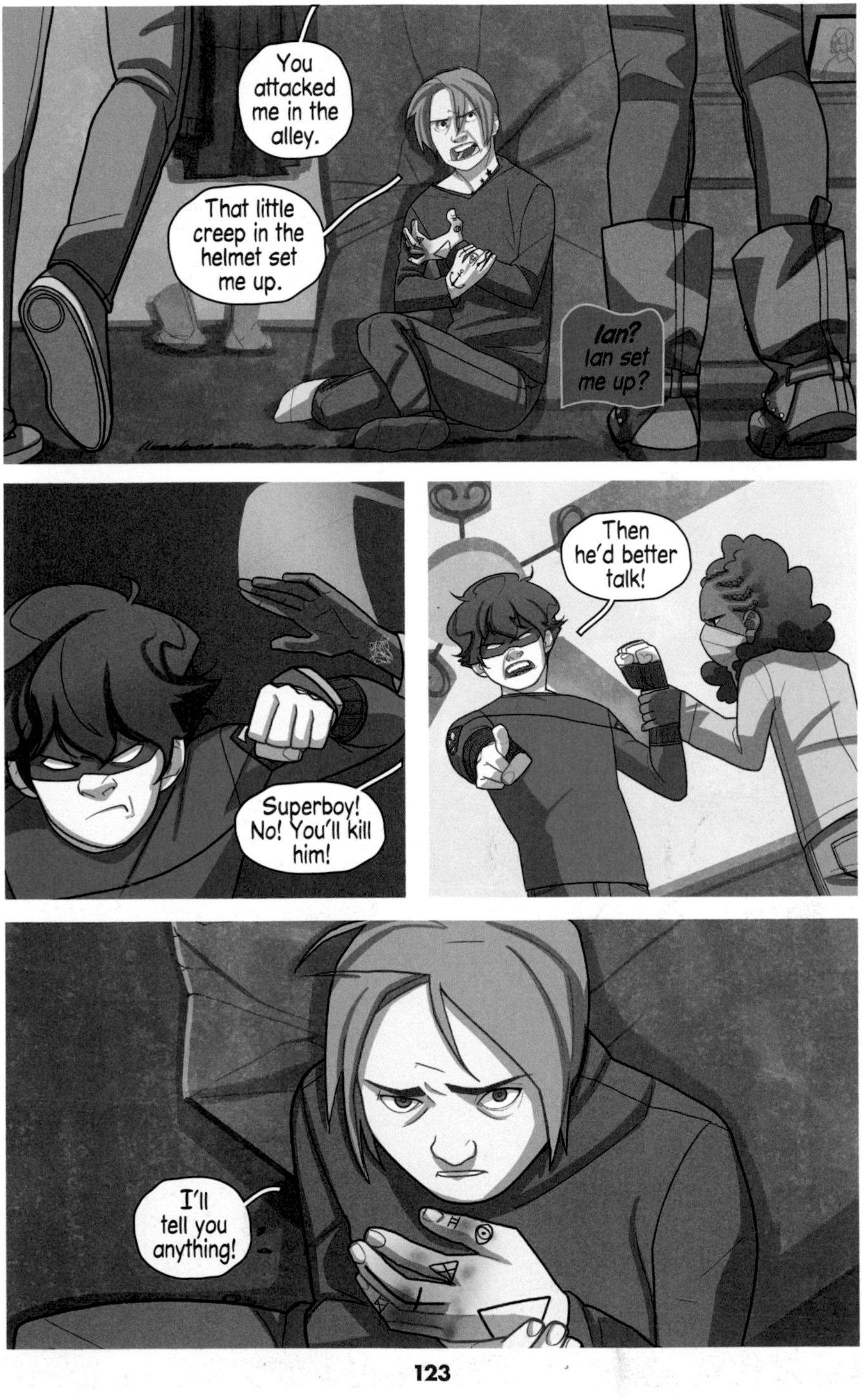

You attacked me in the alley.
That little creep in the helmet set me up.
Ian? Ian set me up?
Superboy! No! You'll kill him!
Then he'd better talk!
I'll tell you anything!

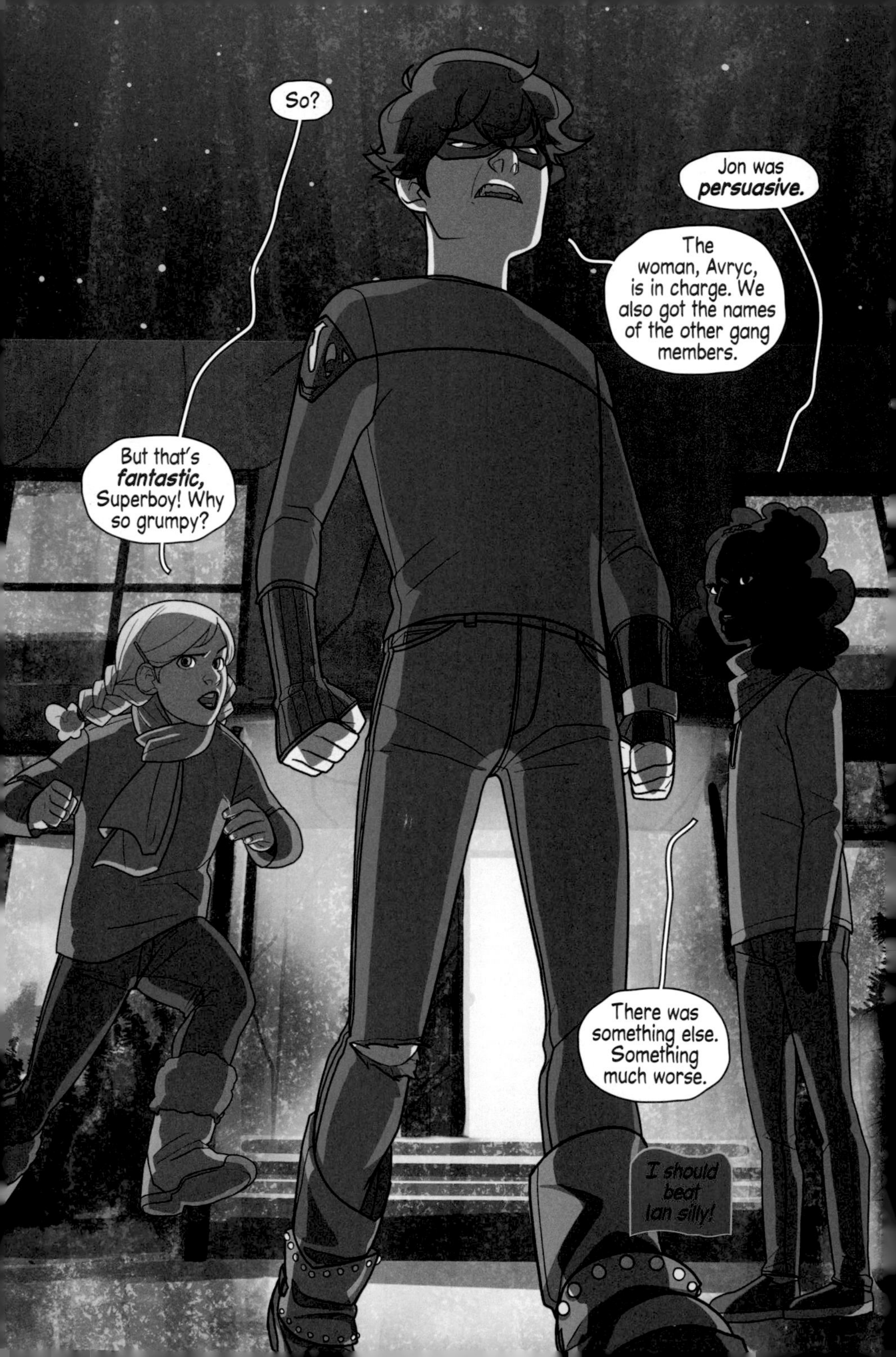
So?
But that's *fantastic,* Superboy! Why so grumpy?
Jon was **persuasive.**
The woman, Avryc, is in charge. We also got the names of the other gang members.
There was something else. Something much worse.
I should beat Ian silly!

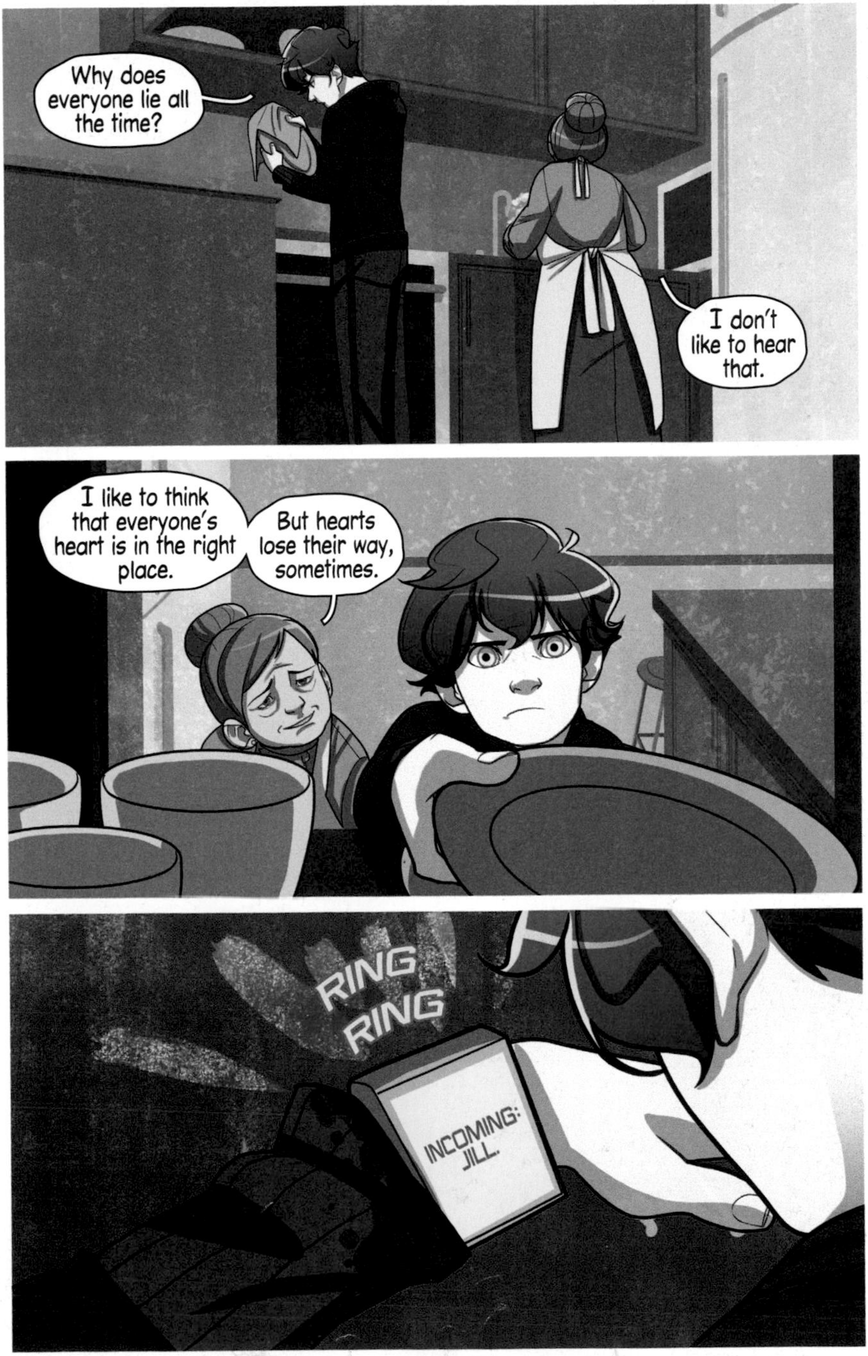
Why does everyone lie all the time?
I don't like to hear that.
I like to think that everyone's heart is in the right place.
But hearts lose their way, sometimes.
RING
RING
INCOMING: JILL.

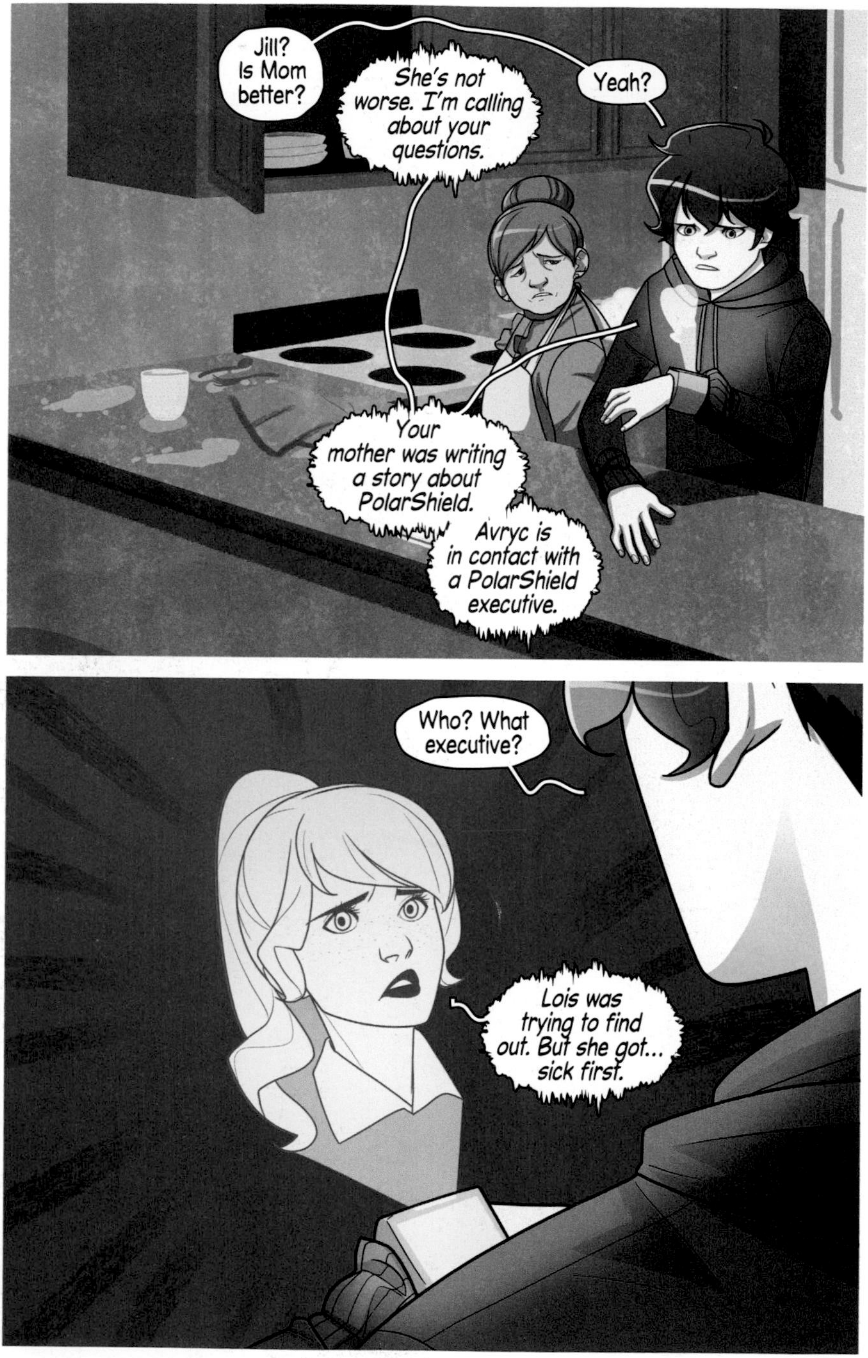
Jill? Is Mom better?
She's not worse. I'm calling about your questions.
Yeah?
Your mother was writing a story about PolarShield.
Avryc is in contact with a PolarShield executive.
Who? What executive?
Lois was trying to find out. But she got... sick first.

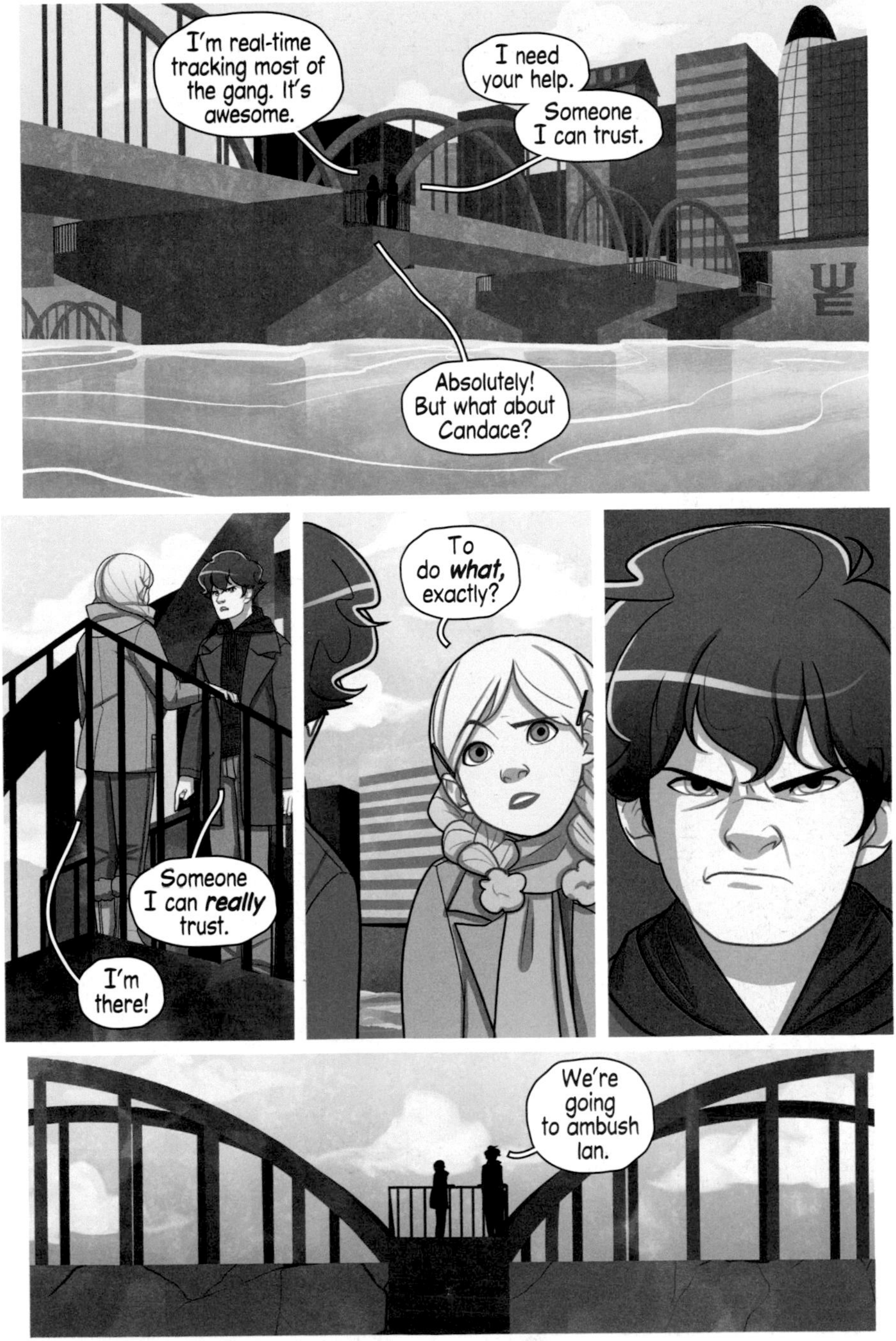
I'm real-time tracking most of the gang. It's awesome.
I need your help.
Someone I can trust.
Absolutely! But what about Candace?
Someone I can *really* trust.
I'm there!
To do ***what,*** exactly?
We're going to ambush Ian.

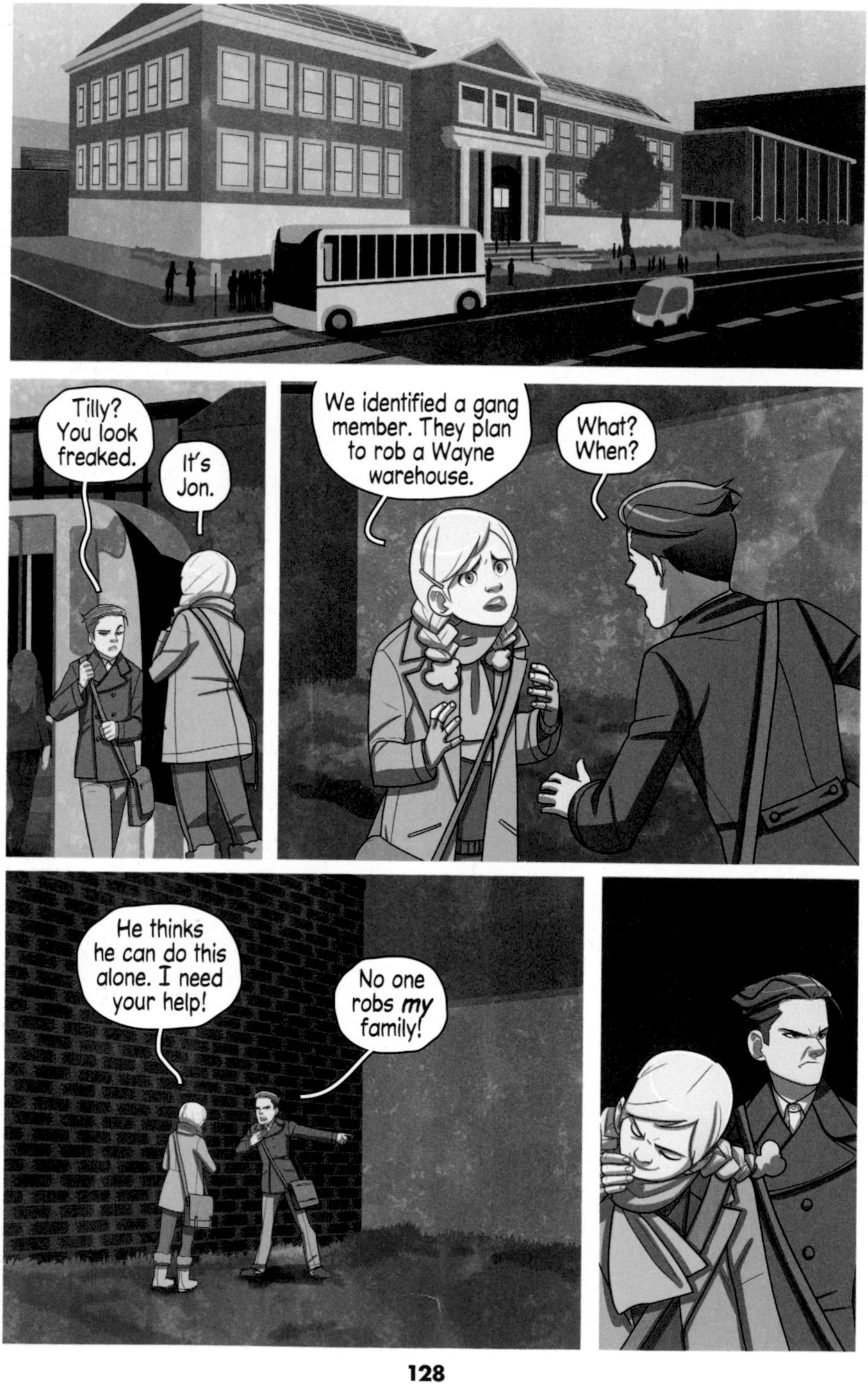
Tilly? You look freaked.
It's Jon.
We identified a gang member. They plan to rob a Wayne warehouse.
What? When?
He thinks he can do this alone. I need your help!
No one robs *my* family!

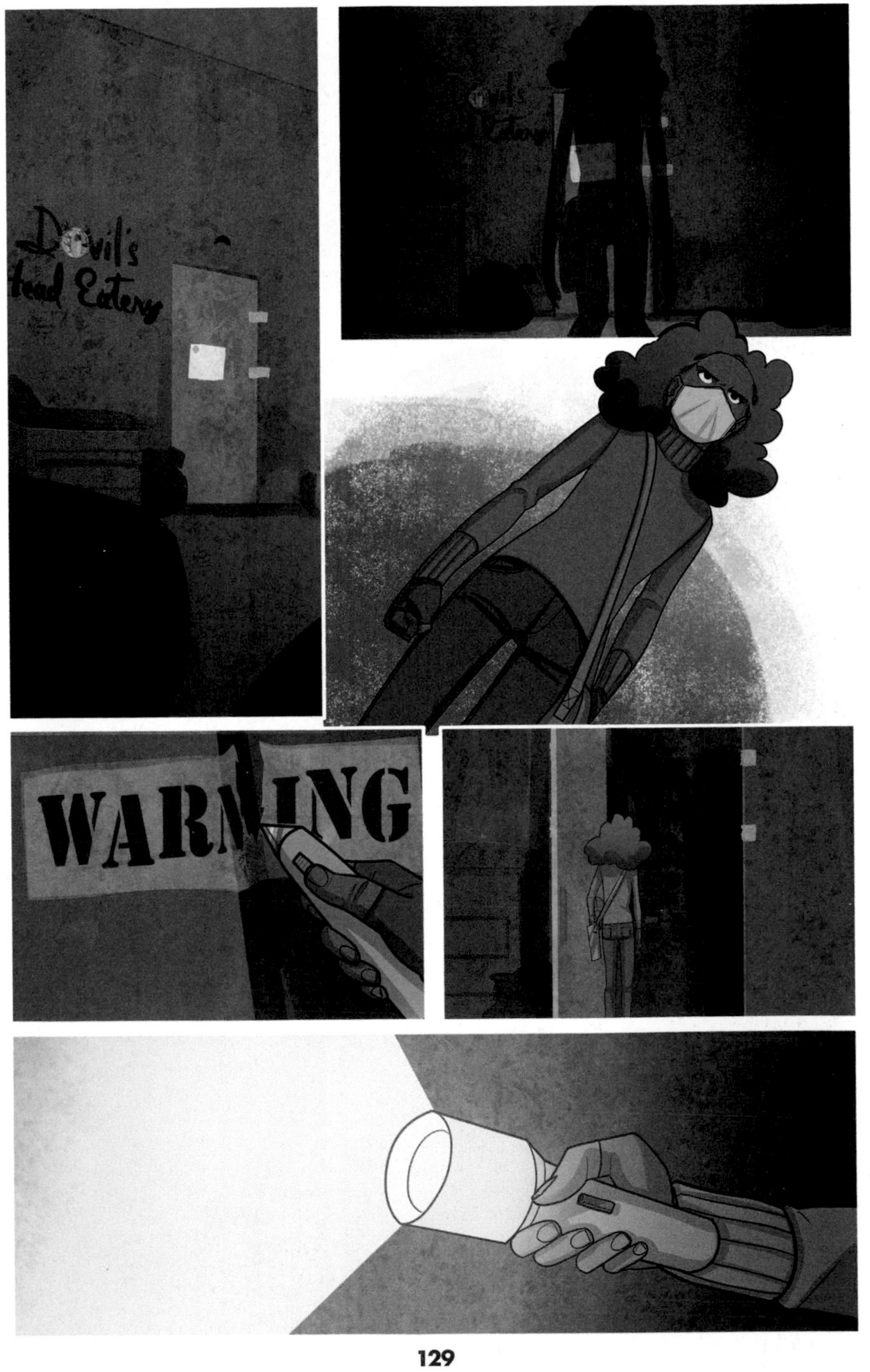
WARNING

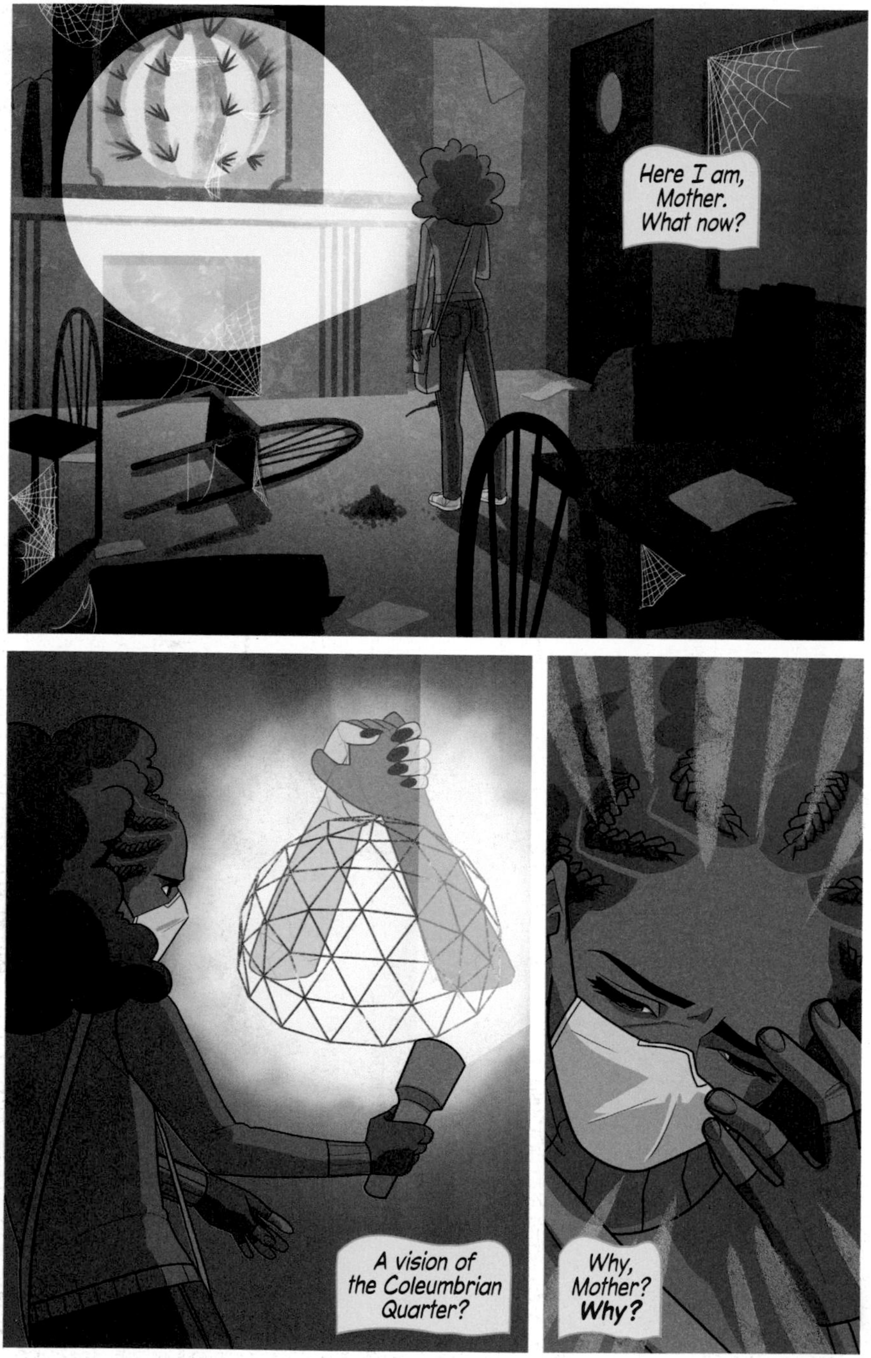
Here I am, Mother. What now?
A vision of the Coleumbrian Quarter?
Why, Mother? **Why?**

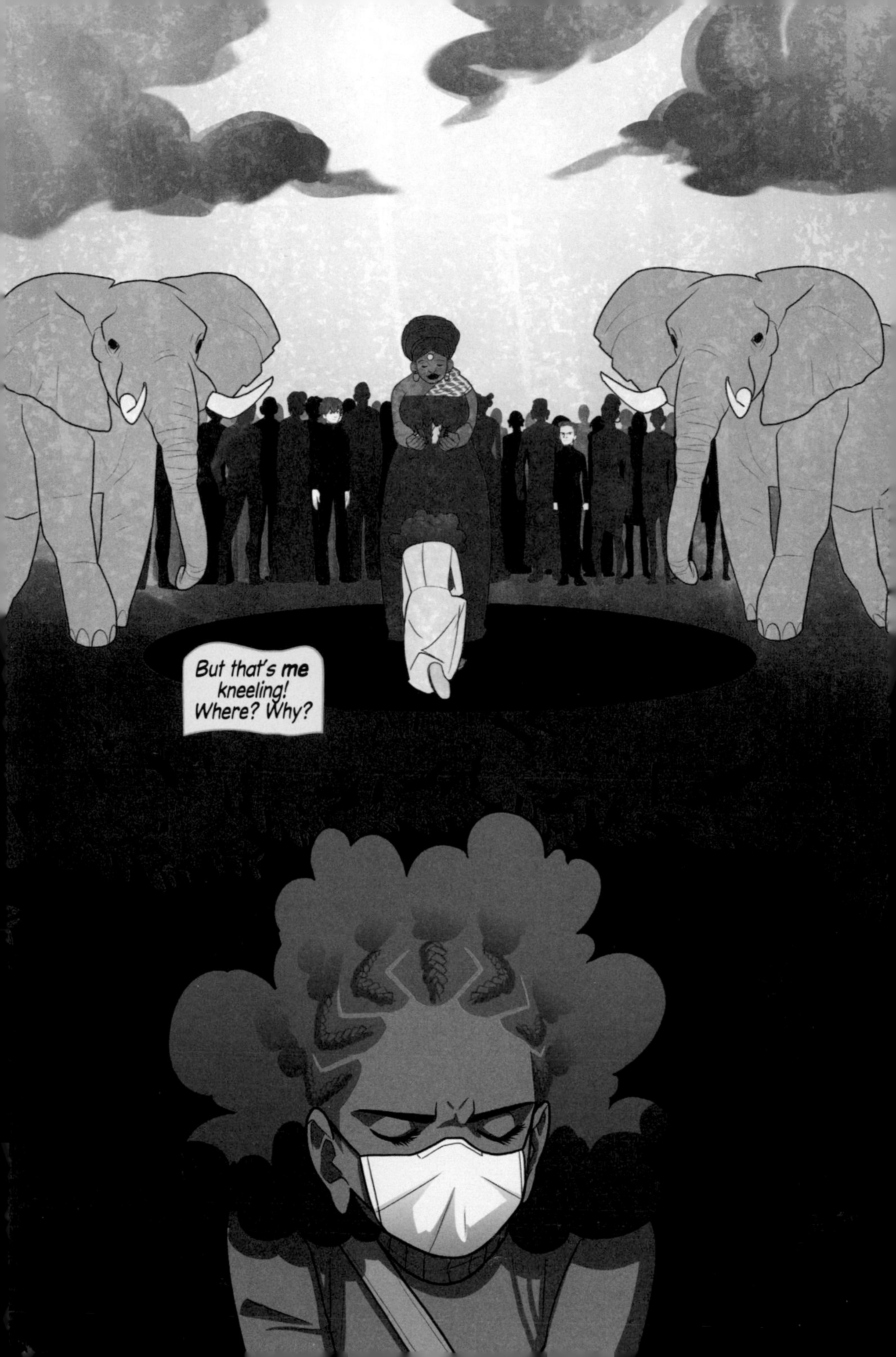
But that's me kneeling! Where? Why?

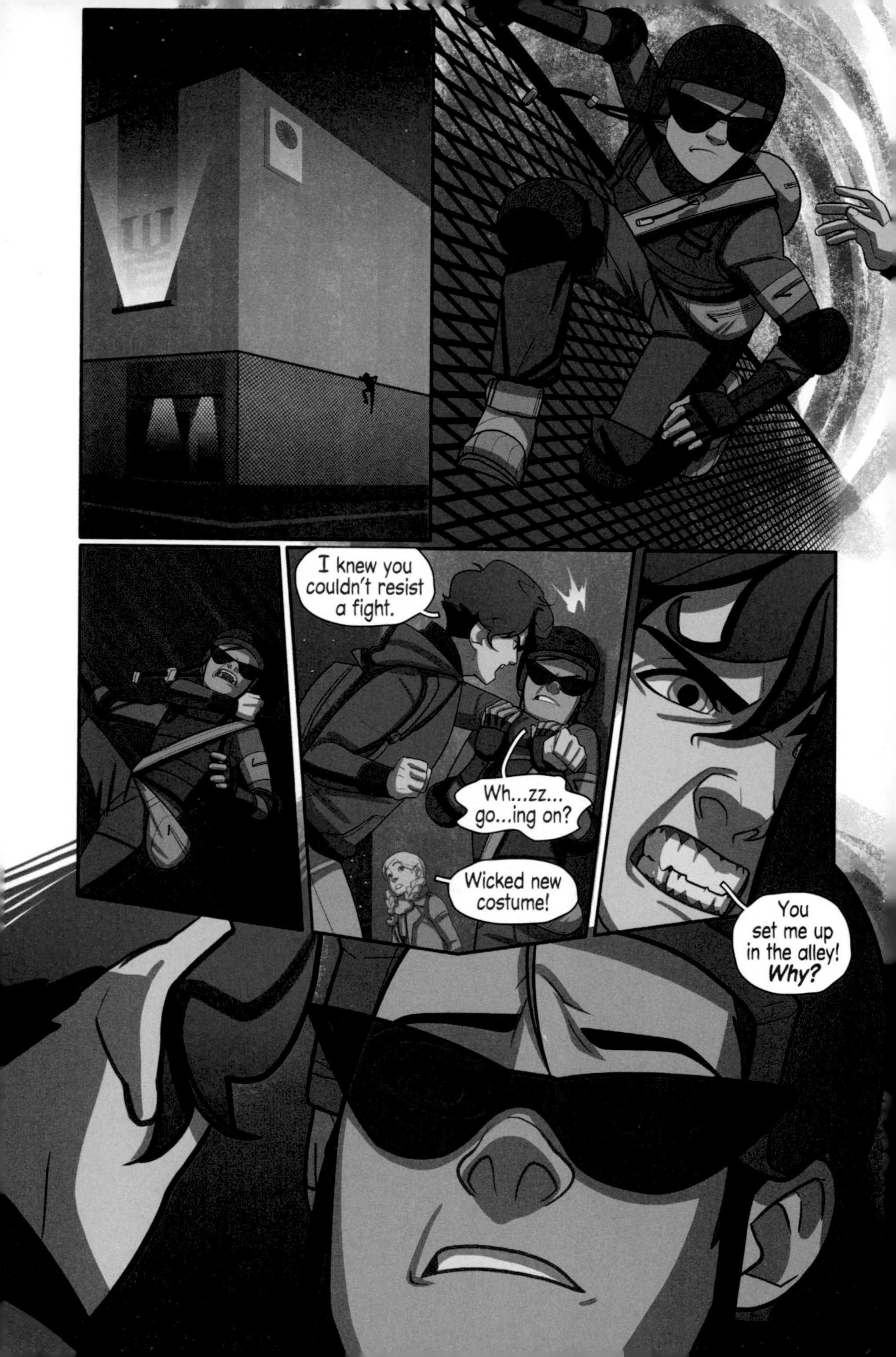
I knew you couldn't resist a fight.
Wh...zz... go...ing on?
Wicked new costume!
You set me up in the alley! *Why?*

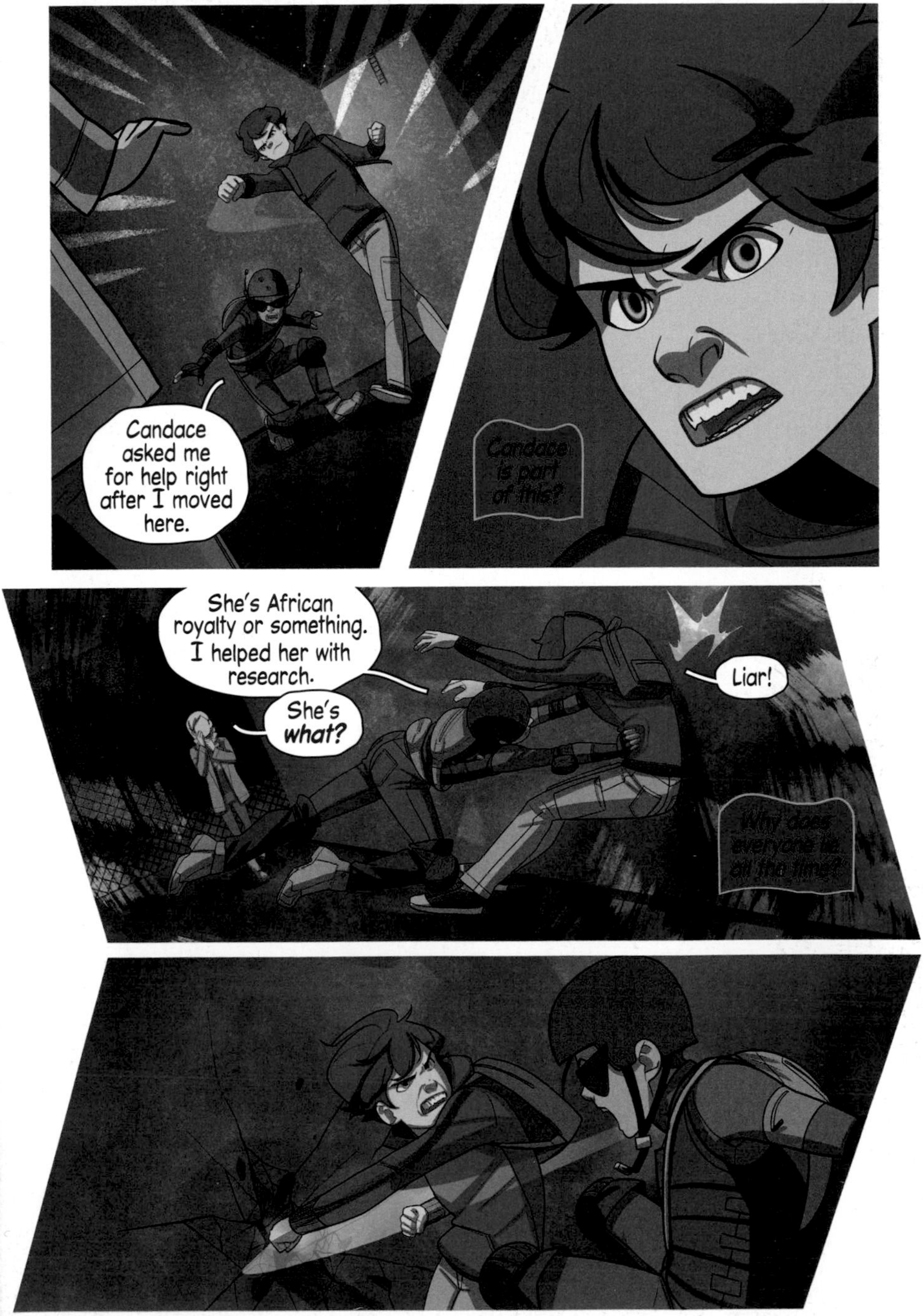
Candace asked me for help right after I moved here.
Candace is part of this?
She's African royalty or something. I helped her with research.
She's *what?*
Liar!
Why does everyone lie all the time?

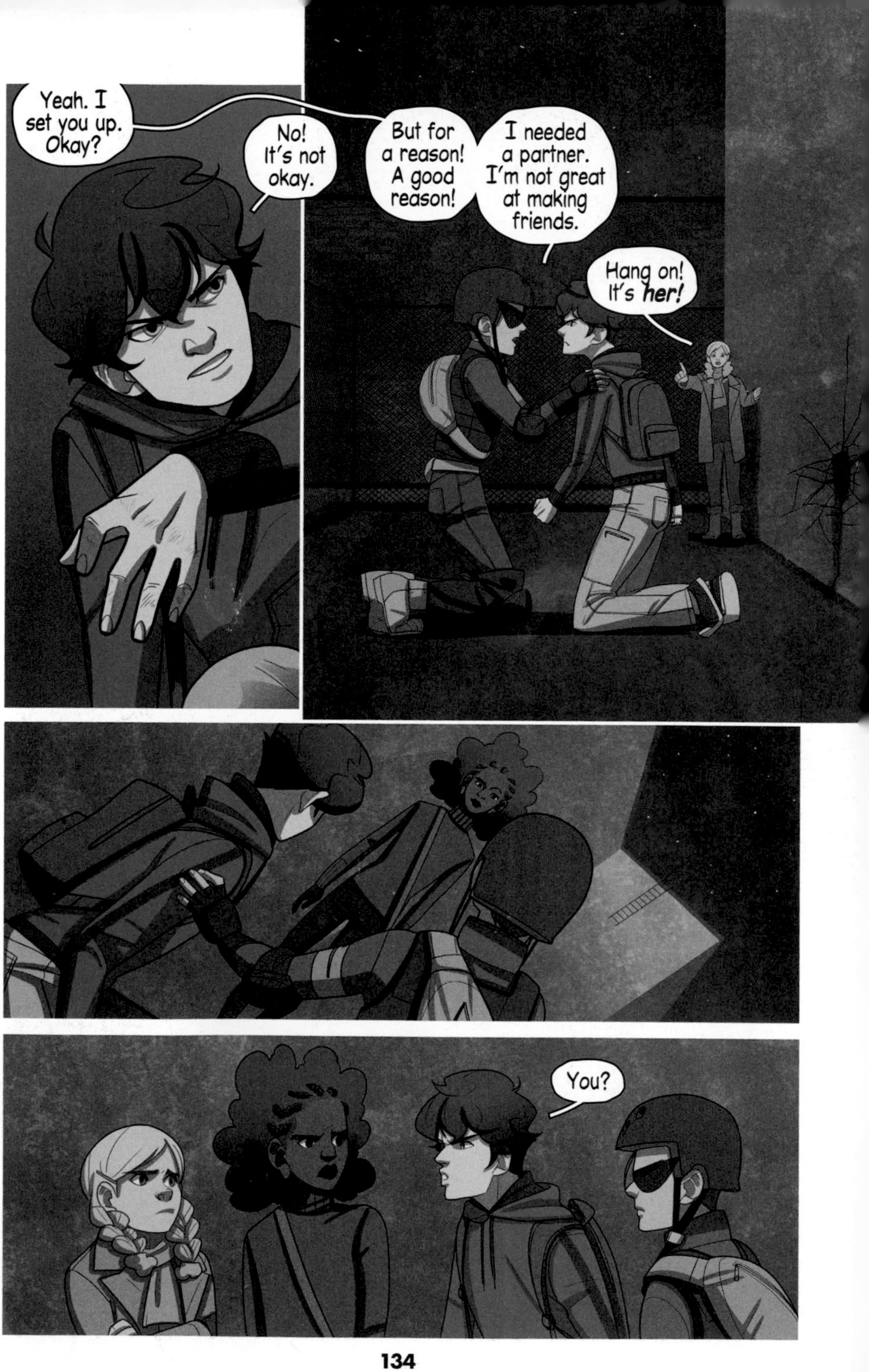
Yeah. I set you up. Okay?
No! It's not okay.
But for a reason! A good reason!
I needed a partner. I'm not great at making friends.
Hang on! It's her!
You?

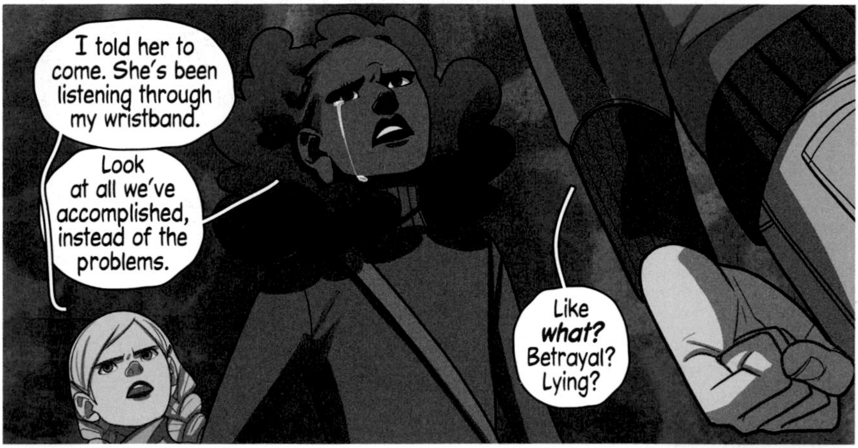

I told her to come. She's been listening through my wristband.
Look at all we've accomplished, instead of the problems.
Like *what?* Betrayal? Lying?

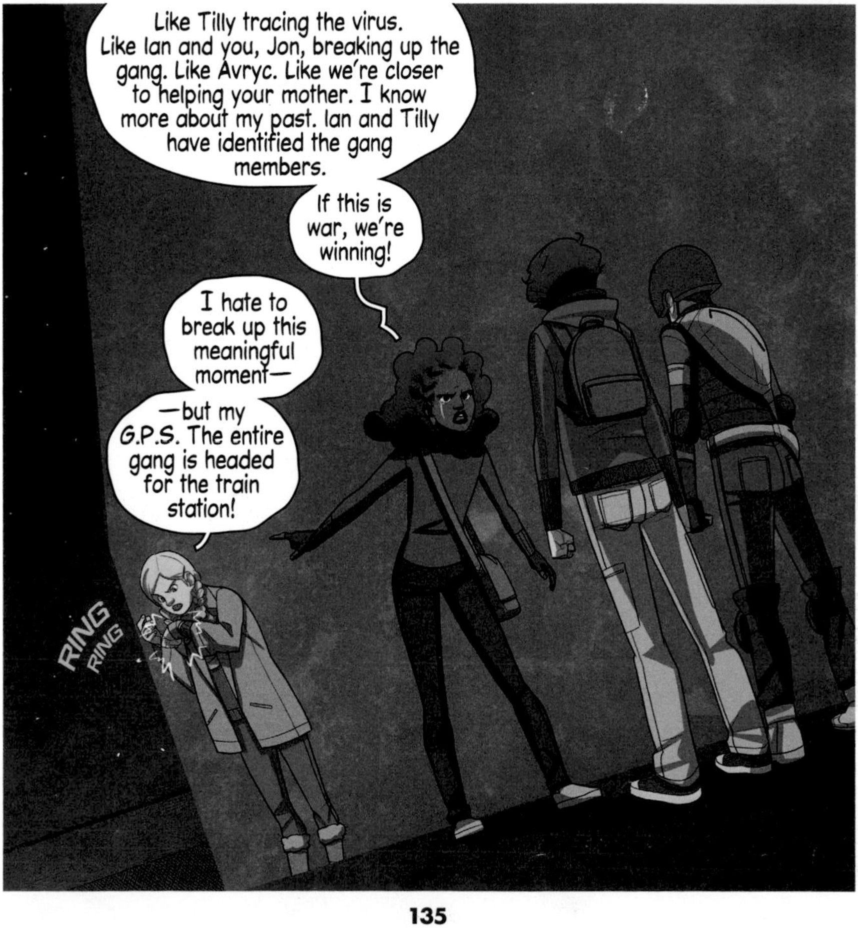

Like Tilly tracing the virus. Like Ian and you, Jon, breaking up the gang. Like Avryc. Like we're closer to helping your mother. I know more about my past. Ian and Tilly have identified the gang members.
If this is war, we're winning!
I hate to break up this meaningful moment—
—but my G.P.S. The entire gang is headed for the train station!
RING
RING

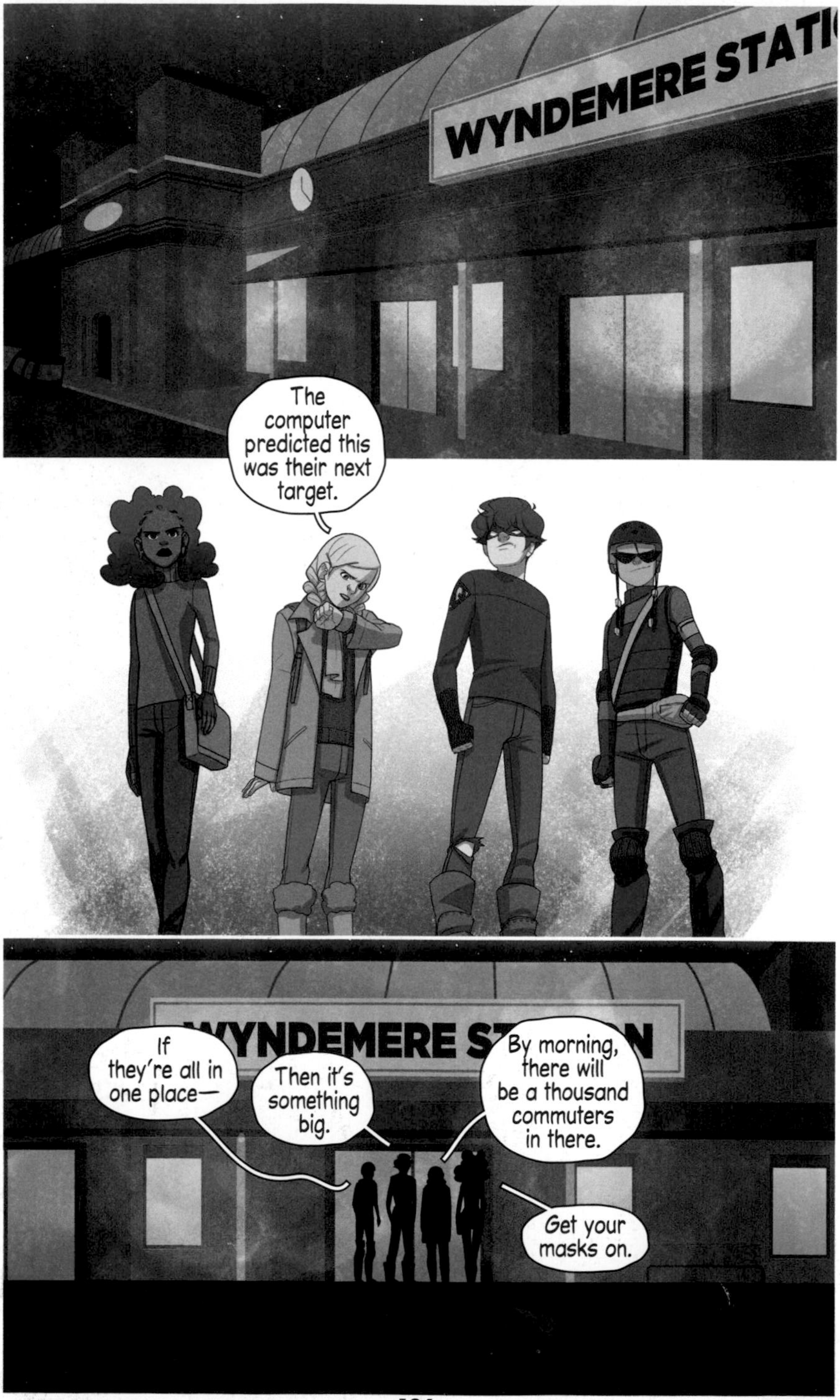
WYNDEMERE STATI
The computer predicted this was their next target.
WYNDEMERE ST N
If they're all in one place—
Then it's something big.
By morning, there will be a thousand commuters in there.
Get your masks on.

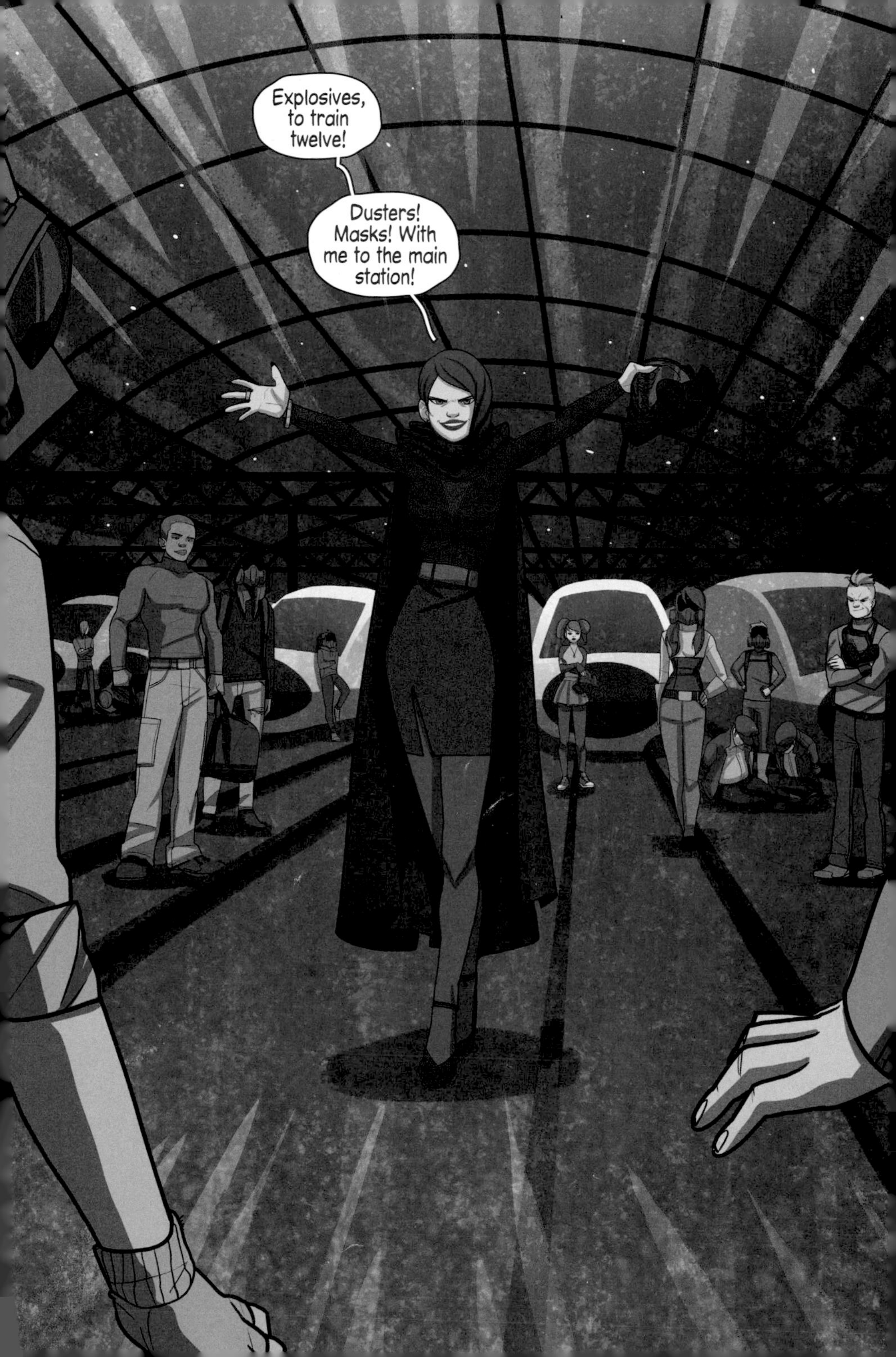
Explosives, to train twelve!
Dusters! Masks! With me to the main station!

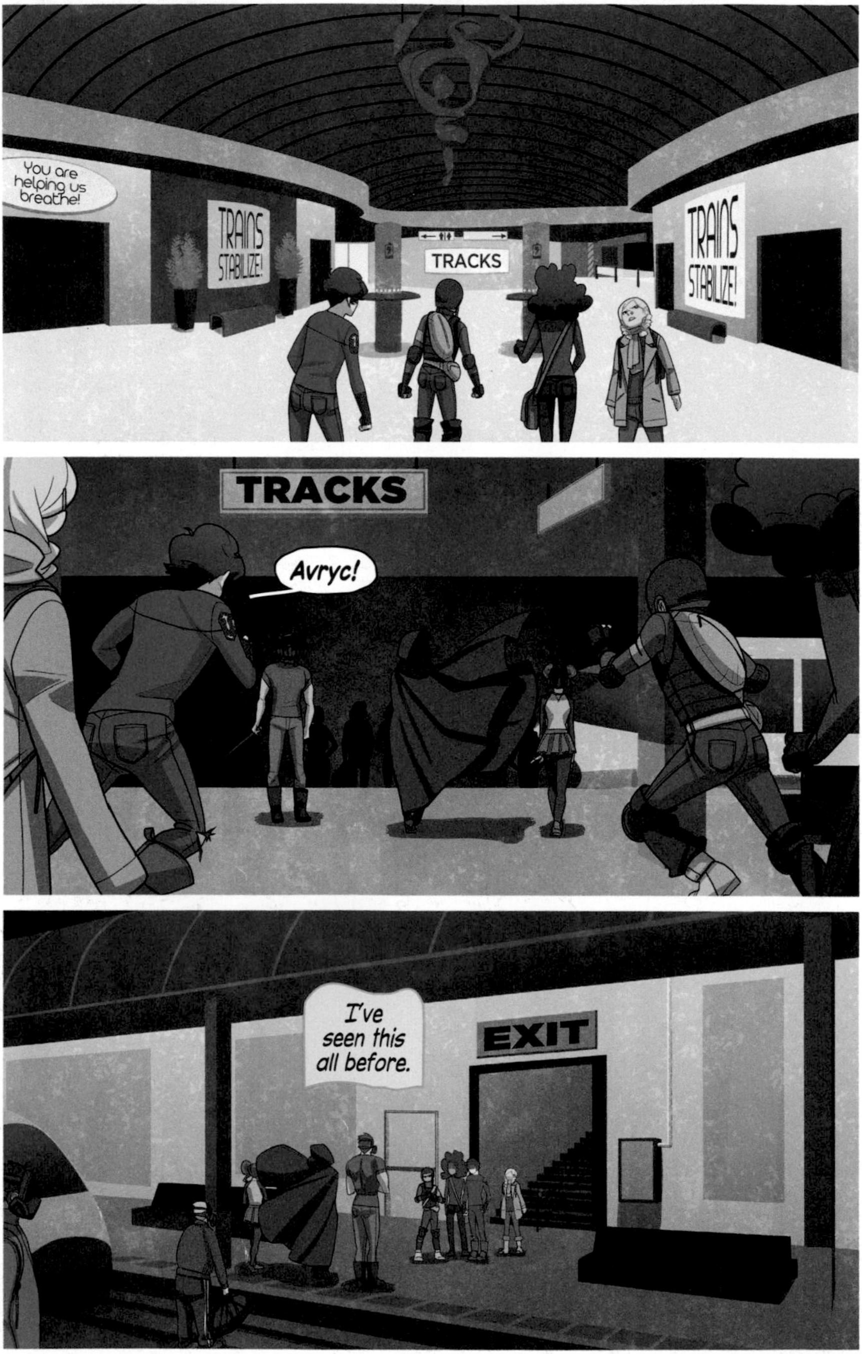
You are helping us breathe!
TRAINS STABILIZE!
TRACKS
TRAINS STABILIZE!
TRACKS
Avryc!
I've seen this all before.
EXIT

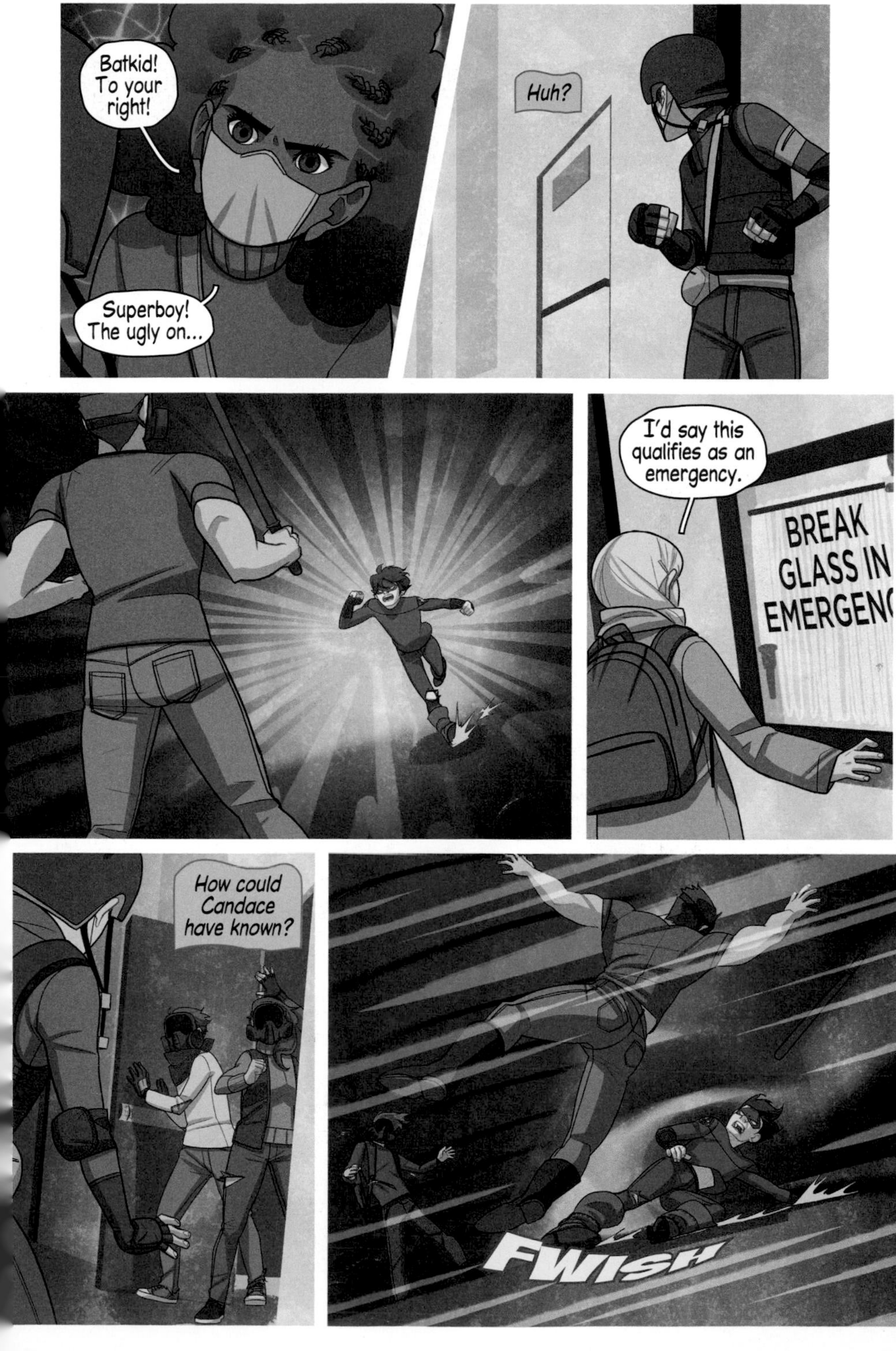
Batkid! To your right!
Superboy! The ugly on...
Huh?
I'd say this qualifies as an emergency.
BREAK GLASS IN EMERGENC
How could Candace have known?
FWISH

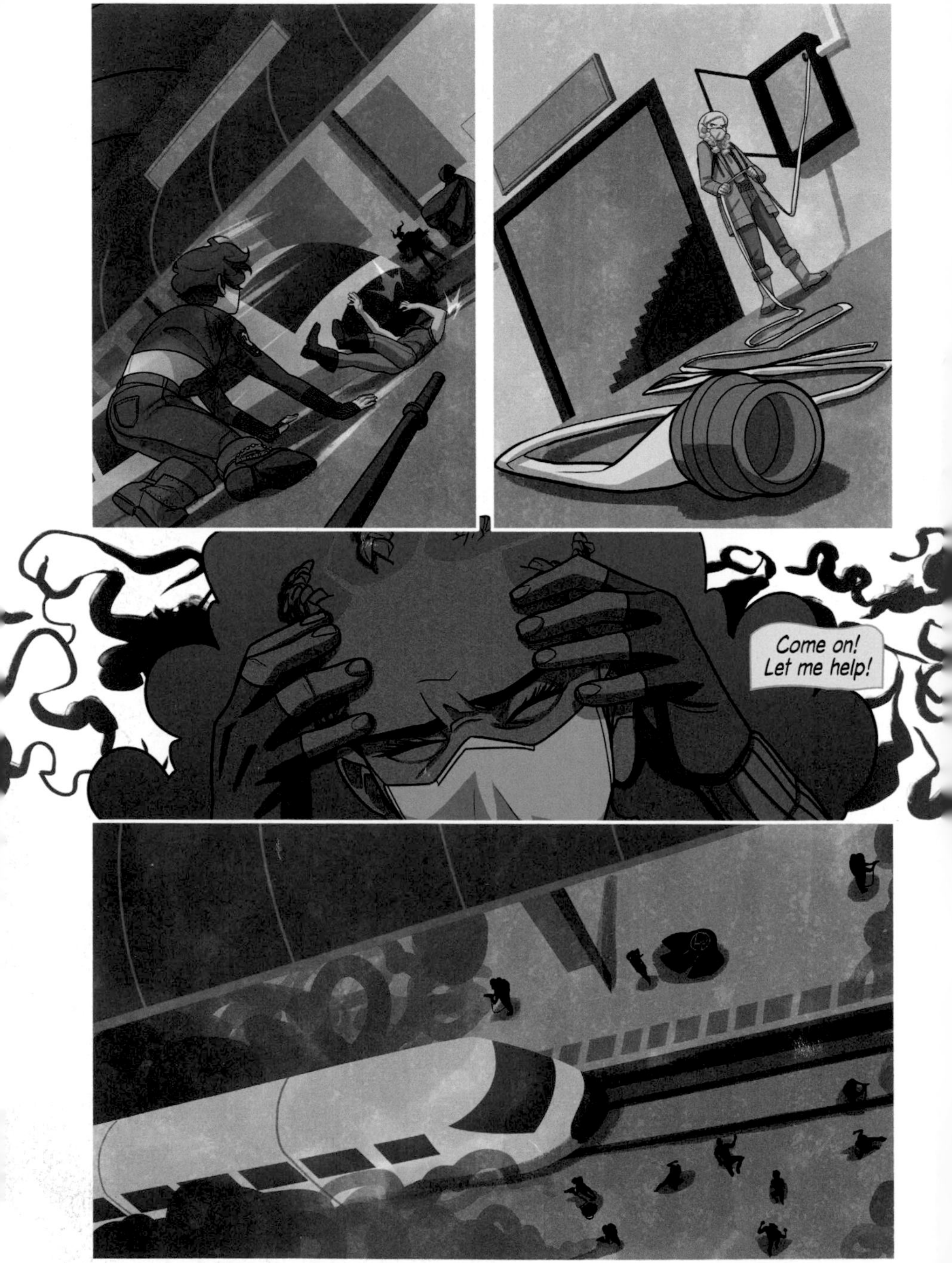
Come on!
Let me help!

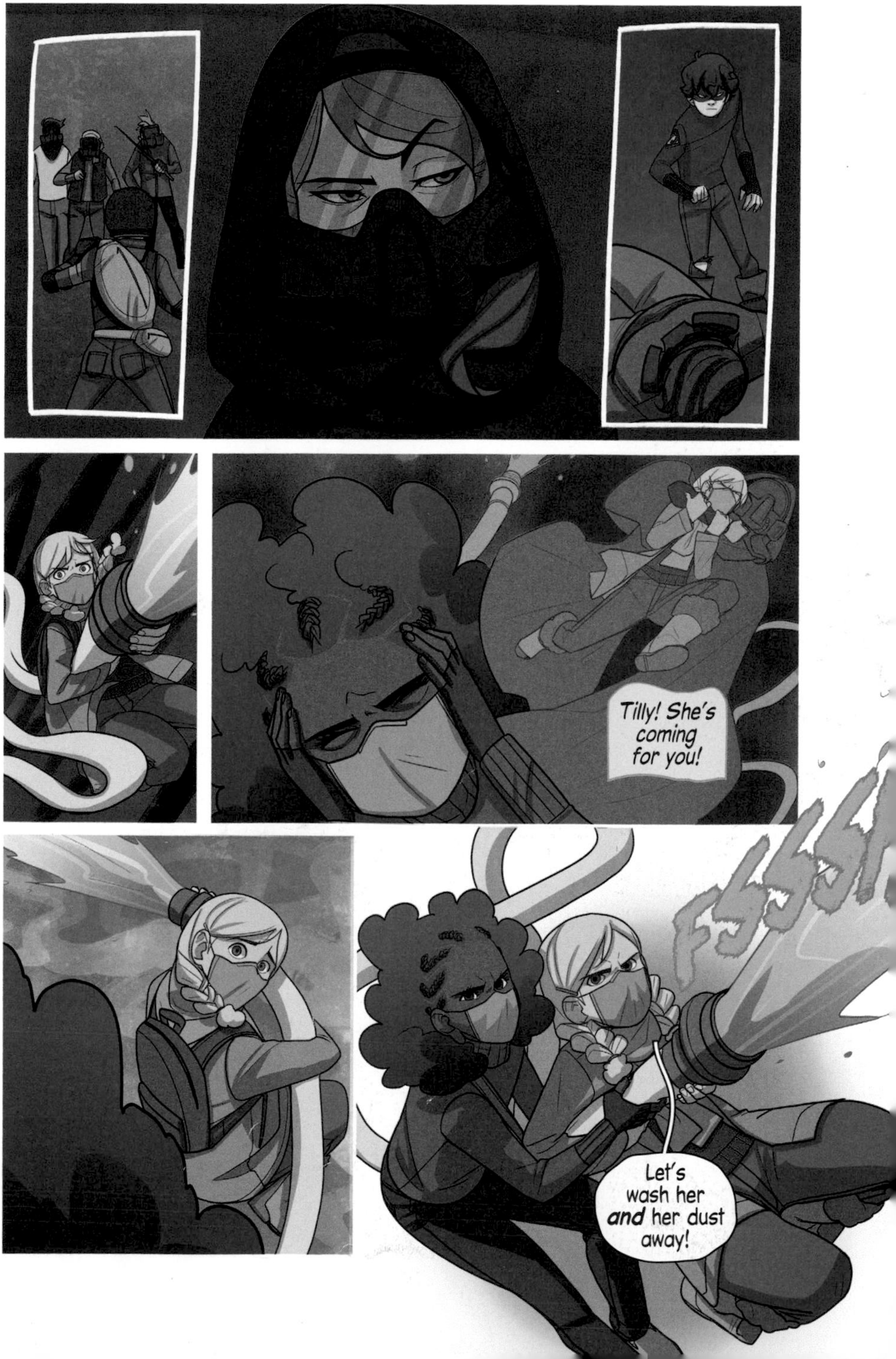
Tilly! She's coming for you!
Let's wash her *and* her dust away!

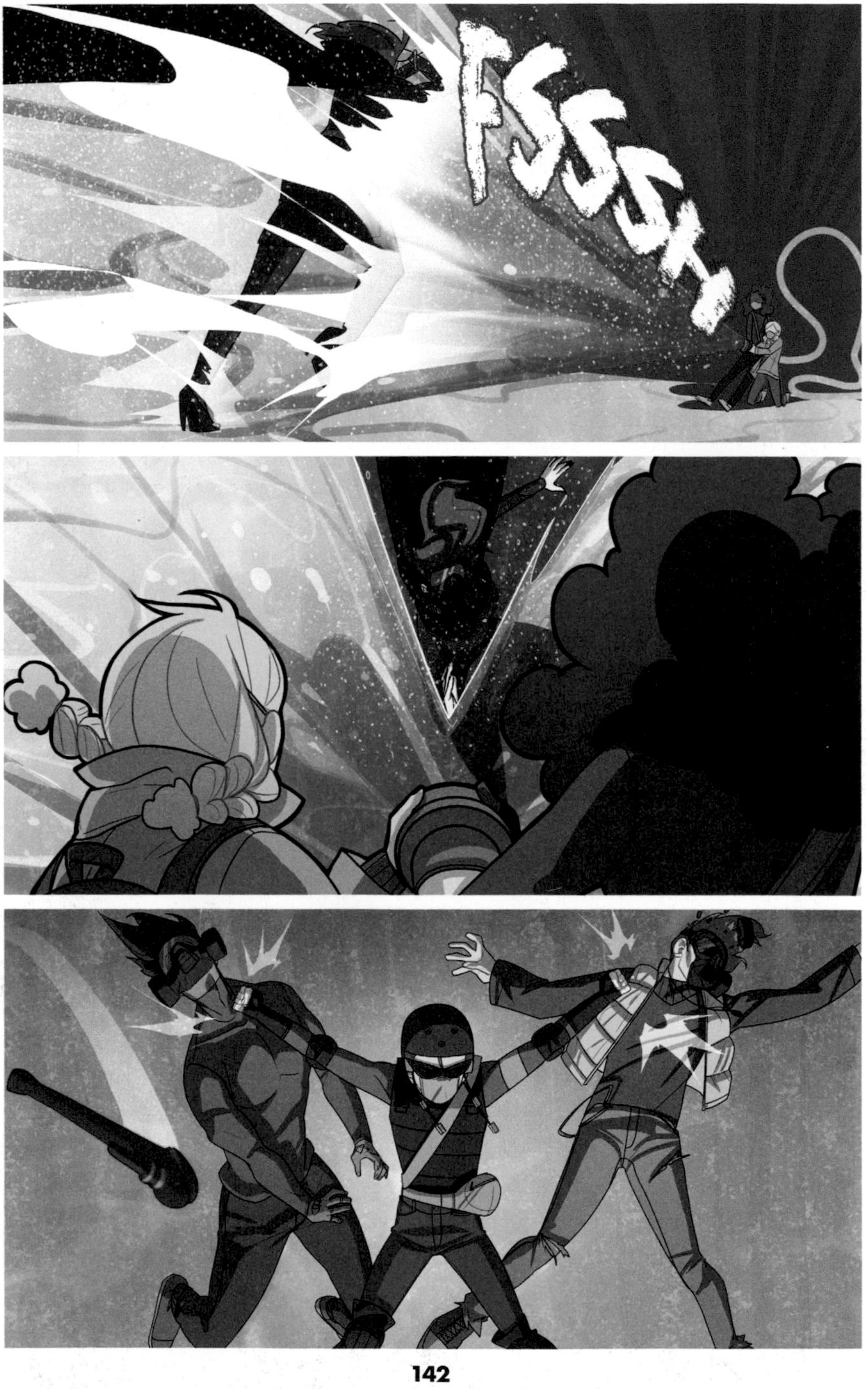
FSSSHT

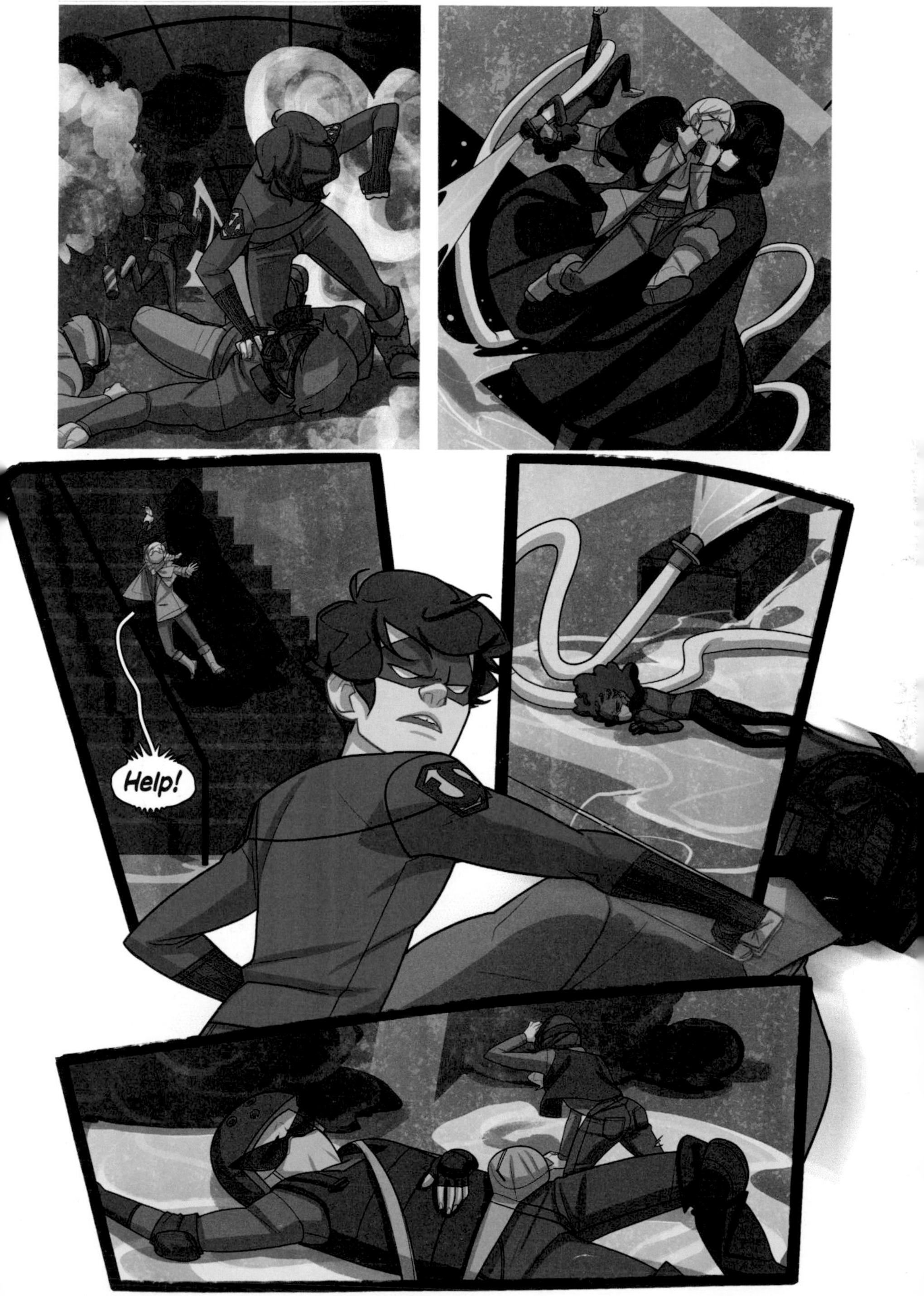
Help!

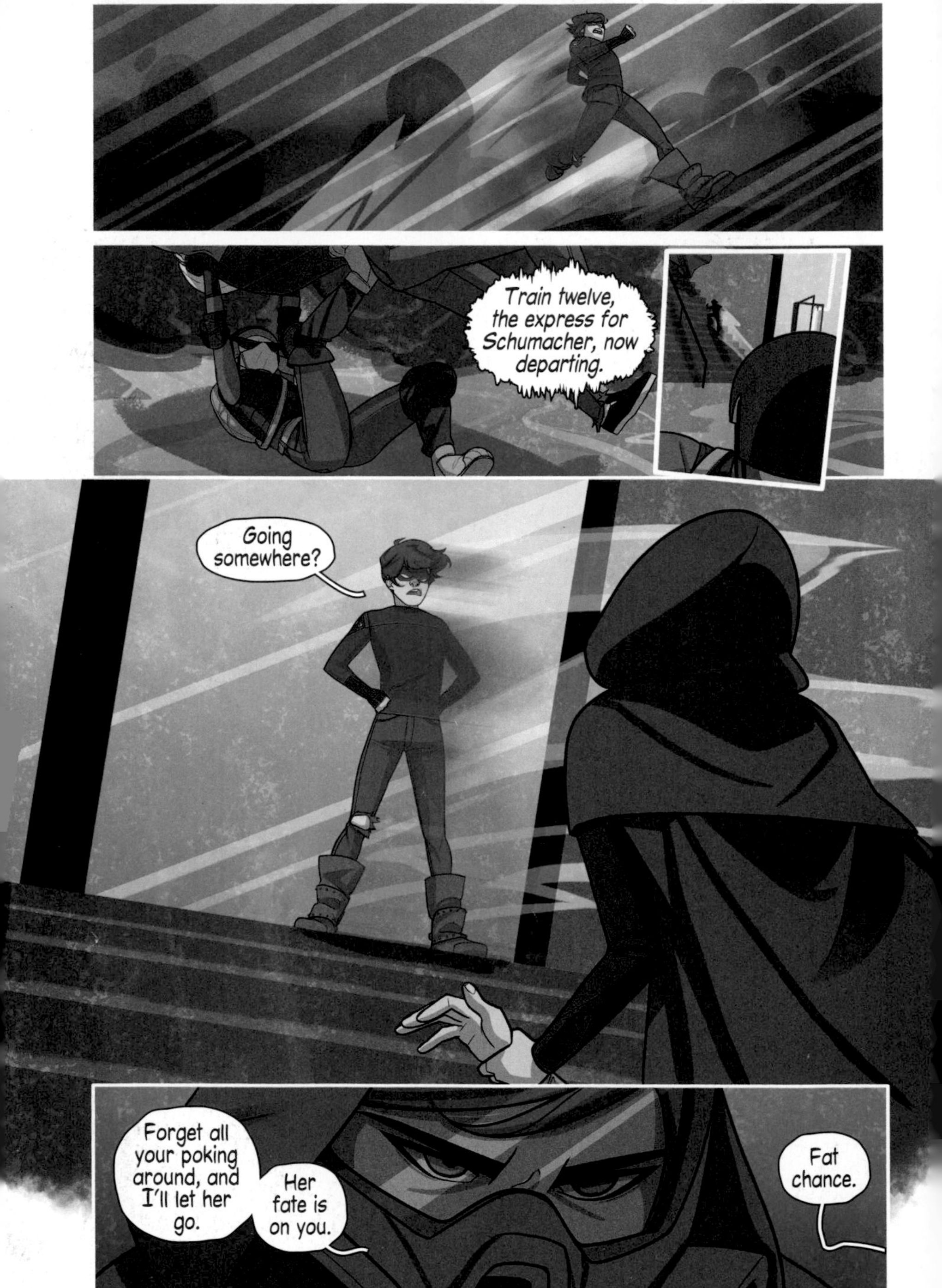
Train twelve, the express for Schumacher, now departing.
Going somewhere?
Forget all your poking around, and I'll let her go.
Her fate is on you.
Fat chance.

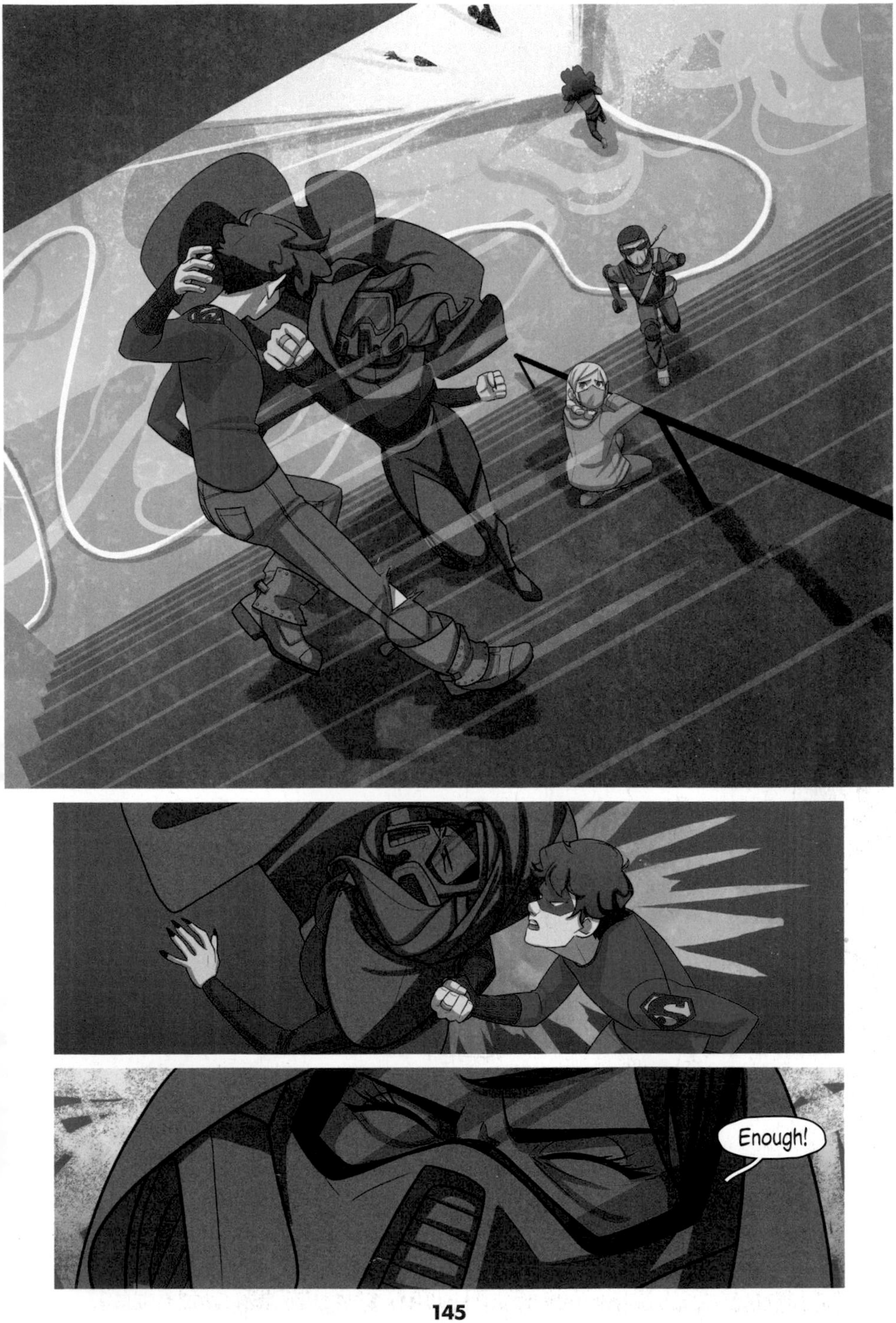
Enough!

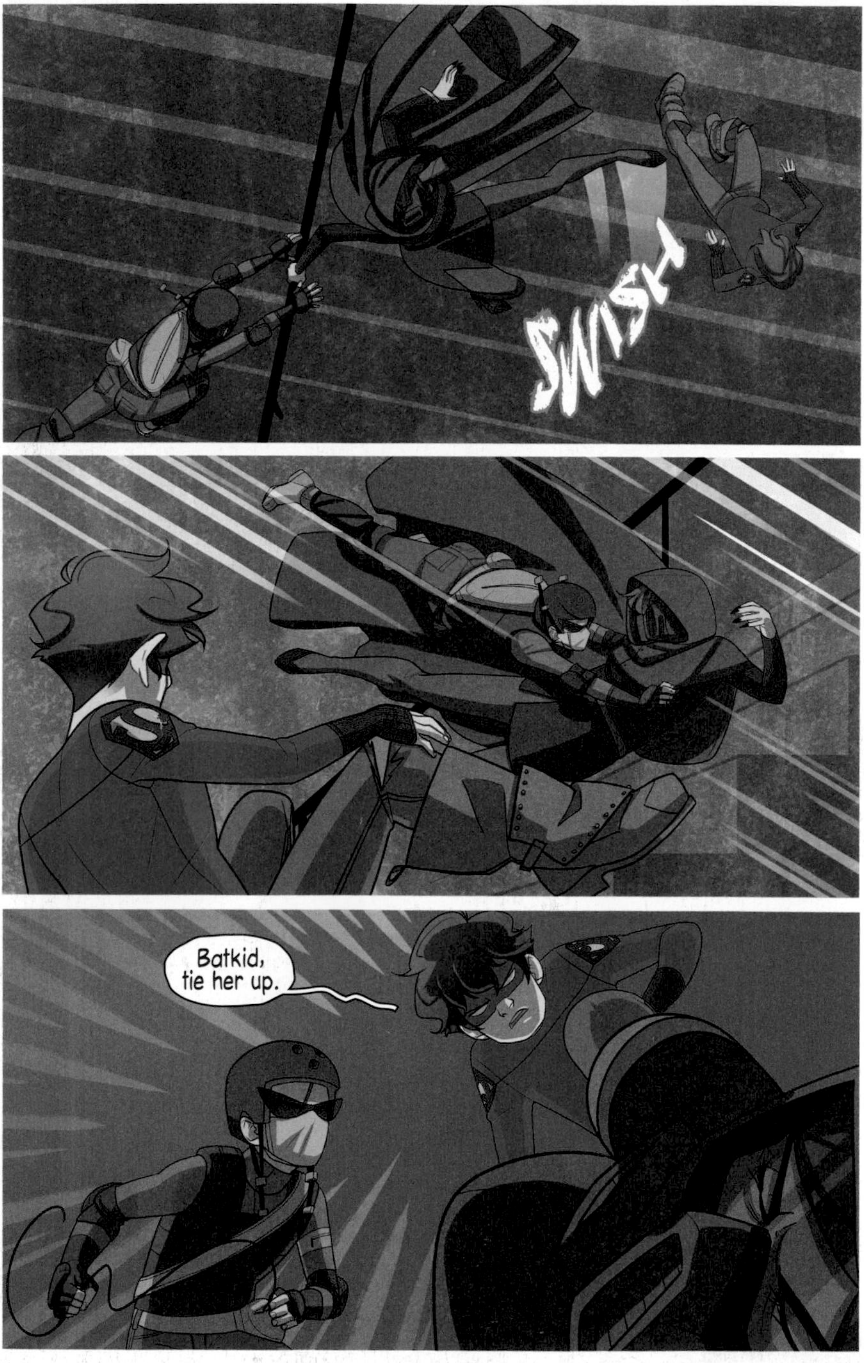
SWISH
Batkid, tie her up.

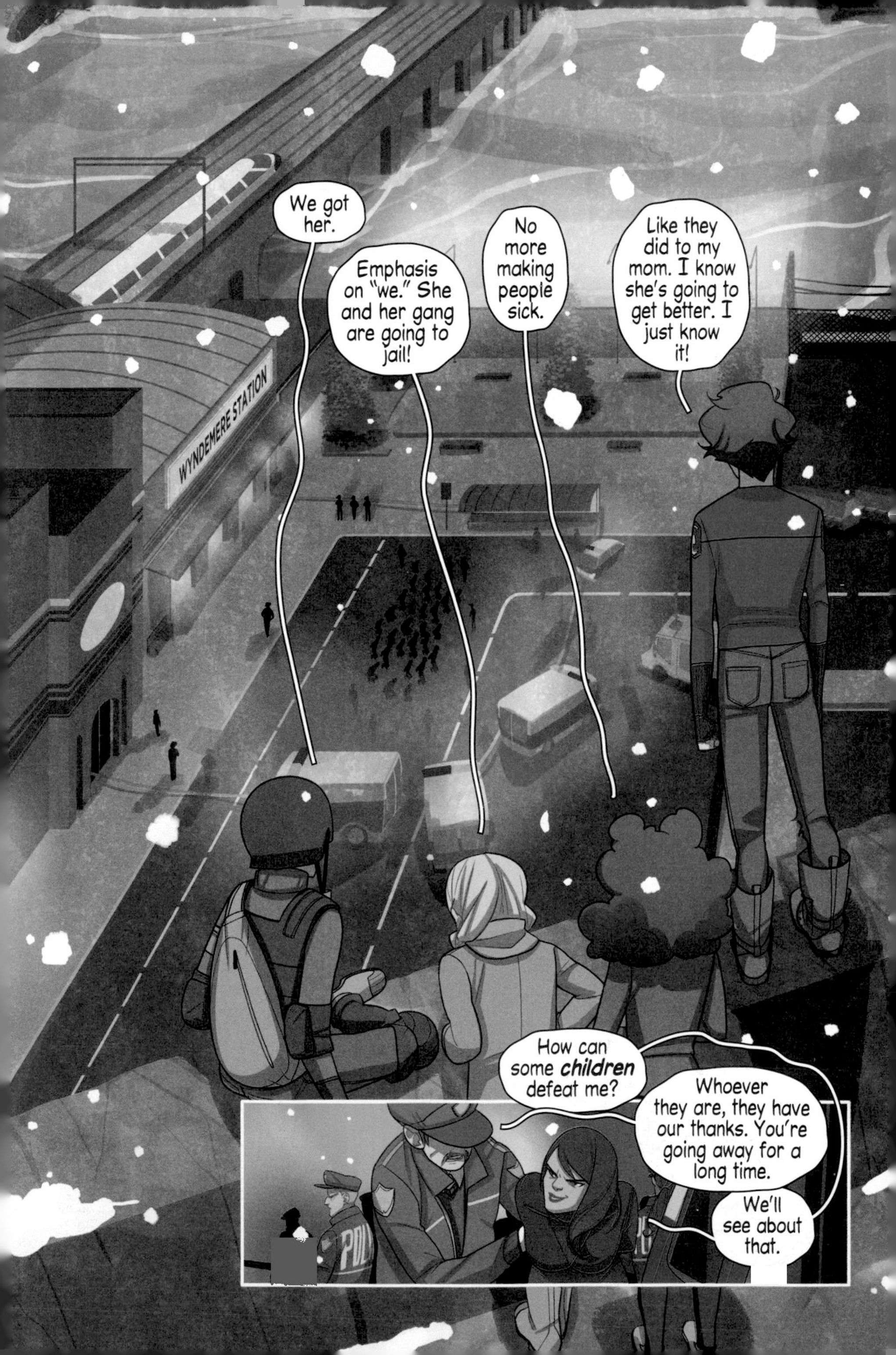
WYNDEMERE STATION
We got her.
Emphasis on "we." She and her gang are going to jail!
No more making people sick.
Like they did to my mom. I know she's going to get better. I just know it!
How can some ***children*** defeat me?
Whoever they are, they have our thanks. You're going away for a long time.
We'll see about that.

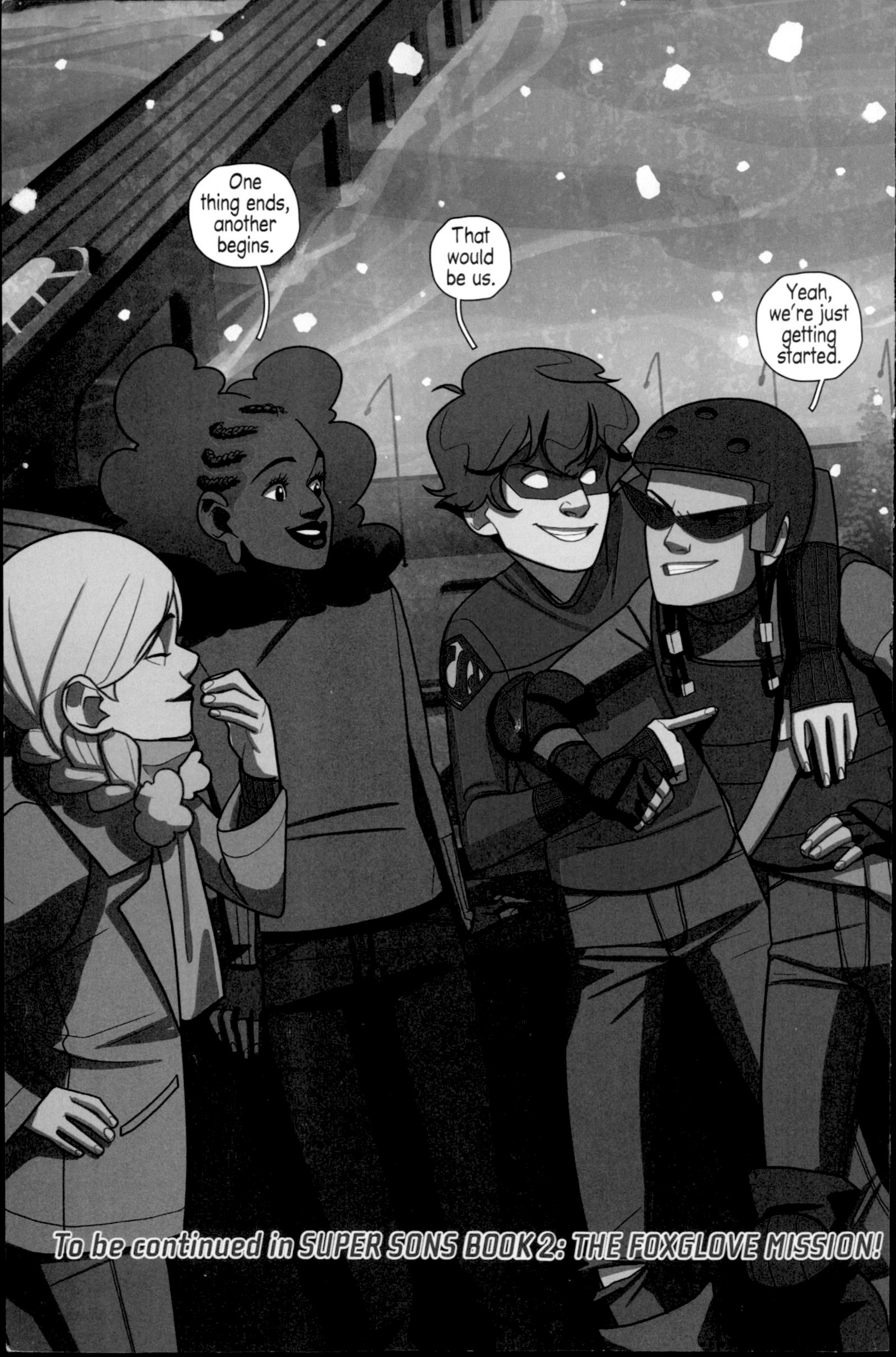
One thing ends, another begins.
That would be us.
Yeah, we're just getting started.
To be continued in SUPER SONS BOOK 2: THE FOXGLOVE MISSION!

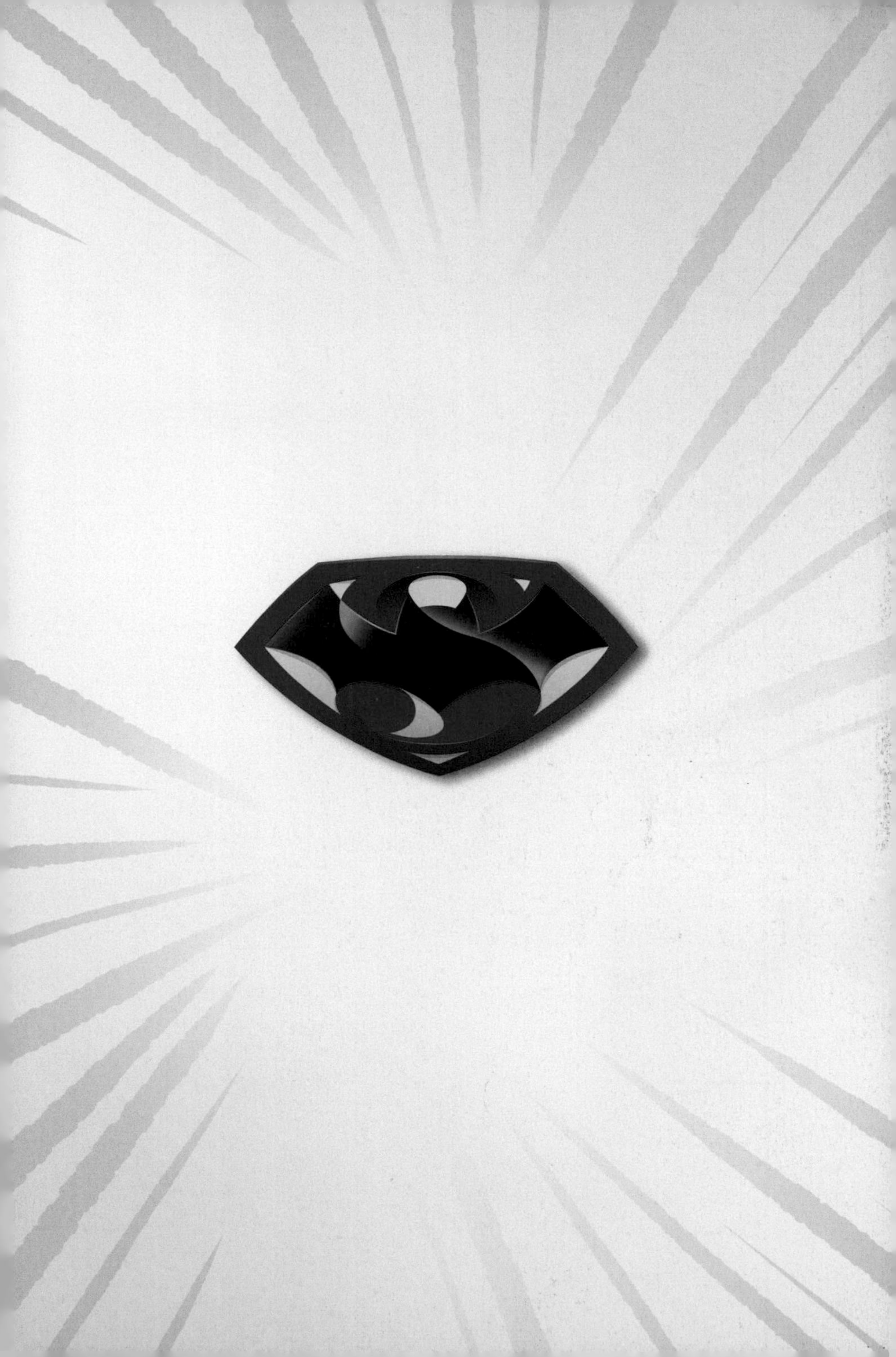

DAMIAN "IAN" WAYNE

Ian doesn't know his mother. He wants to fight by the side of his father, Batman. He has no powers, but lots of gadgets. He is a bit conceited and critical of others. At thirteen years old he is quite independent, and seems older.

BRUCE WAYNE/BATMAN

Billionaire head of Wayne Enterprises (W.E.). His company builds the walls holding back the flood waters. As Batman, he secretly knows Superman. Like Lois Lane, he is worried about the spreading illness.

THE FOUR FINGERS

Four young women representing various districts in Landis. Their mission is to either stop Candace from being crowned empress, or to convince her to be different. Candace treats others as friends. The Four Fingers do not.

PATIENCE

Bruce Wayne's assistant. She also looks after Ian Wayne when Bruce travels.

TACO

Ian Wayne's small but lovable dog. Ian considers Taco his best friend.

CANDACE

Candace was born in Landis, a continent far from the nation of Coleumbria. Her mother was an empress before she died. Candace is thirteen and has been living with an aunt in Wyndemere for the past several years. She will soon have to return to Landis to be named empress, but only if she brings a special oil with her. Others want that oil as well.

LOIS LANE

Mother of Jon Kent. Wife of Clark Kent. An important reporter for the *Daily Planet*. She is currently working on a big story about a spreading illness. She knows Bruce Wayne.

CLARK KENT/SUPERMAN

Father of Jon Kent. Husband of Lois Lane. As Superman he is using his strength to hold back the rising flood waters. He is trying to protect the residents of Metropolis.

JON KENT

Twelve-year-old Jon is the son of Clark Kent (Superman) and Lois Lane (reporter for the *Daily Planet* newspaper). While he can't fly, he can jump high and run fast, and his skin is pretty tough. He's optimistic, full of energy, and a team player.

PERRY WHITE

Lois and Clark's boss and the publisher of the *Daily Planet*.

JILL OLSEN

Lois Lane's assistant at the *Daily Planet*.

TILLY

Tilly spends much of her time reading. She's good with computers and all things mechanical. She goes to school with Jon Kent. She is a loyal friend.

A Guide to the
Characters and World of

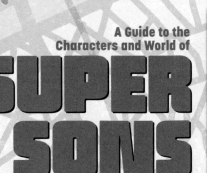

SUPER SONS

MRS. KIACK

Neighbor of the Kent family. She sometimes looks after Jon Kent when his parents are too busy, or are away on business.

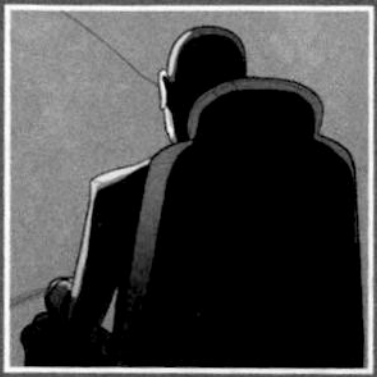

SIR REALE

A politician/businessman who works for G. Reed. When something illegal needs to be done, he makes it happen so that it appears G. Reed isn't involved.

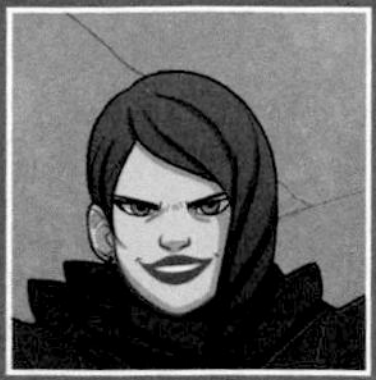

AVRYC

A powerful woman who controls gang members in Coleumbria. Bad people pay her and her gangs to do criminal things.

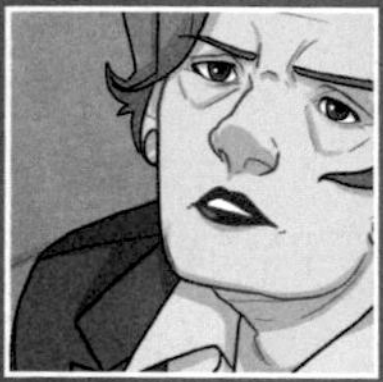

GOVERNOR GENERAL

Currently, a politician who serves as leader of Coleumbria.

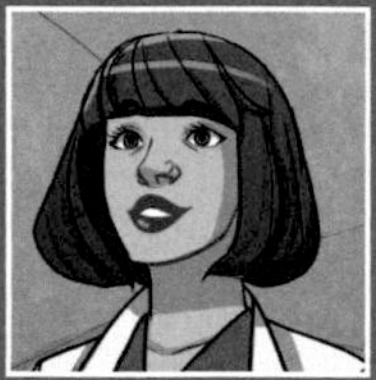

PARA SOL

Para Sol is a good person who runs the government's PolarShield Project. She works closely with Dr. Cray Ving (who's not so good!).

COLEUMBRIA

The world's most free democracy. A country with cities like Metropolis and Gotham and Wyndemere, as well as the capital city, the Coleumbrian Quarter. Climate disruption is flooding the country. Its citizens are moving inland to higher ground.

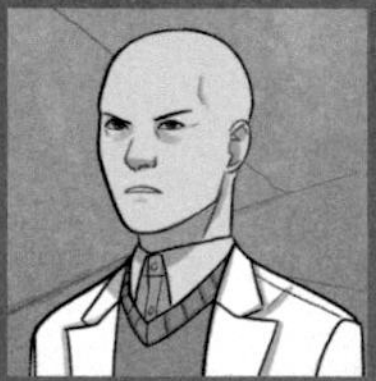

DR. CRAY VING

A scientist working for G. Reed. He is involved with the government's PolarShield Project to stop global warming.

WYNDEMERE

A large city in the north of Coleumbria on the shores of an enormous inland lake. Many residents of coastal cities are moving to Wyndemere.

LANDIS

A vast continent across the ocean that's controlled by an evil general.

ridley pearson is an Edgar nominee, a Fulbright Fellow, and a #1 *New York Times* bestselling author of more than 50 award-winning suspense and young adult adventure novels. His novels have been published in two dozen languages and have been adapted for both network television and the Broadway stage. Ridley's middle-grade series include *Kingdom Keepers, Steel Trapp,* and *Lock and Key.* Ridley plays bass guitar in an all-author rock band with other bestselling writers (Dave Barry, Amy Tan, Mitch Albom, Scott Turow, Greg Iles, and occasionally Stephen King). He lives and writes in the Northern Rockies along with his wife, Marcelle.

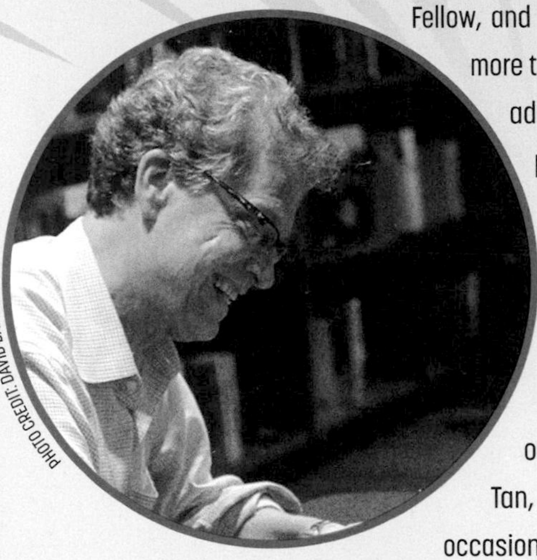

PHOTO CREDIT: DAVID BARRY

ile gonzalez illustrated her first comic strip while in kindergarten and she grew up to study fashion design in college. Deciding graphic storytelling was her first true love, she refocused her creative efforts and landed her first paid work at the digital storytelling company Madefire, working exclusively for them and co-creating their popular middle-grade series *The Heroes Club.*

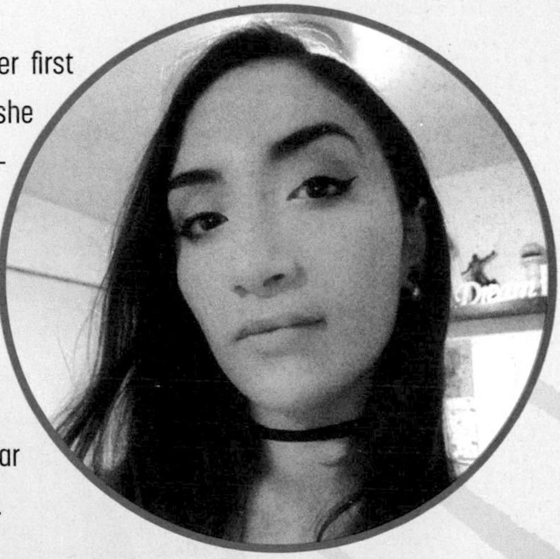

The adventure is far from over!

Check out a sneak peek of
Super Sons Book 2: The Foxglove Mission,
coming soon from DC Zoom!

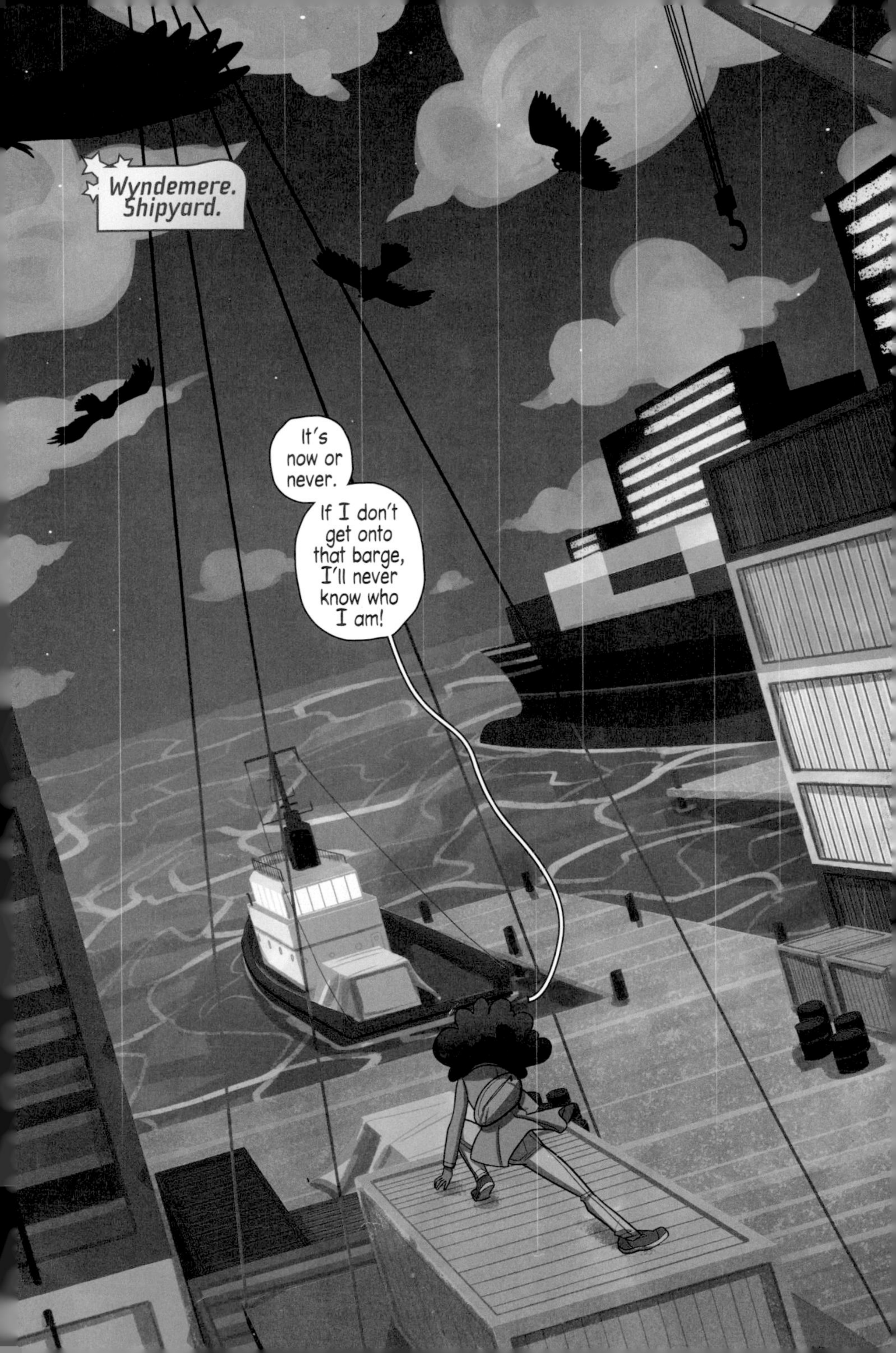
Wyndemere. Shipyard.
It's now or never.
If I don't get onto that barge, I'll never know who I am!

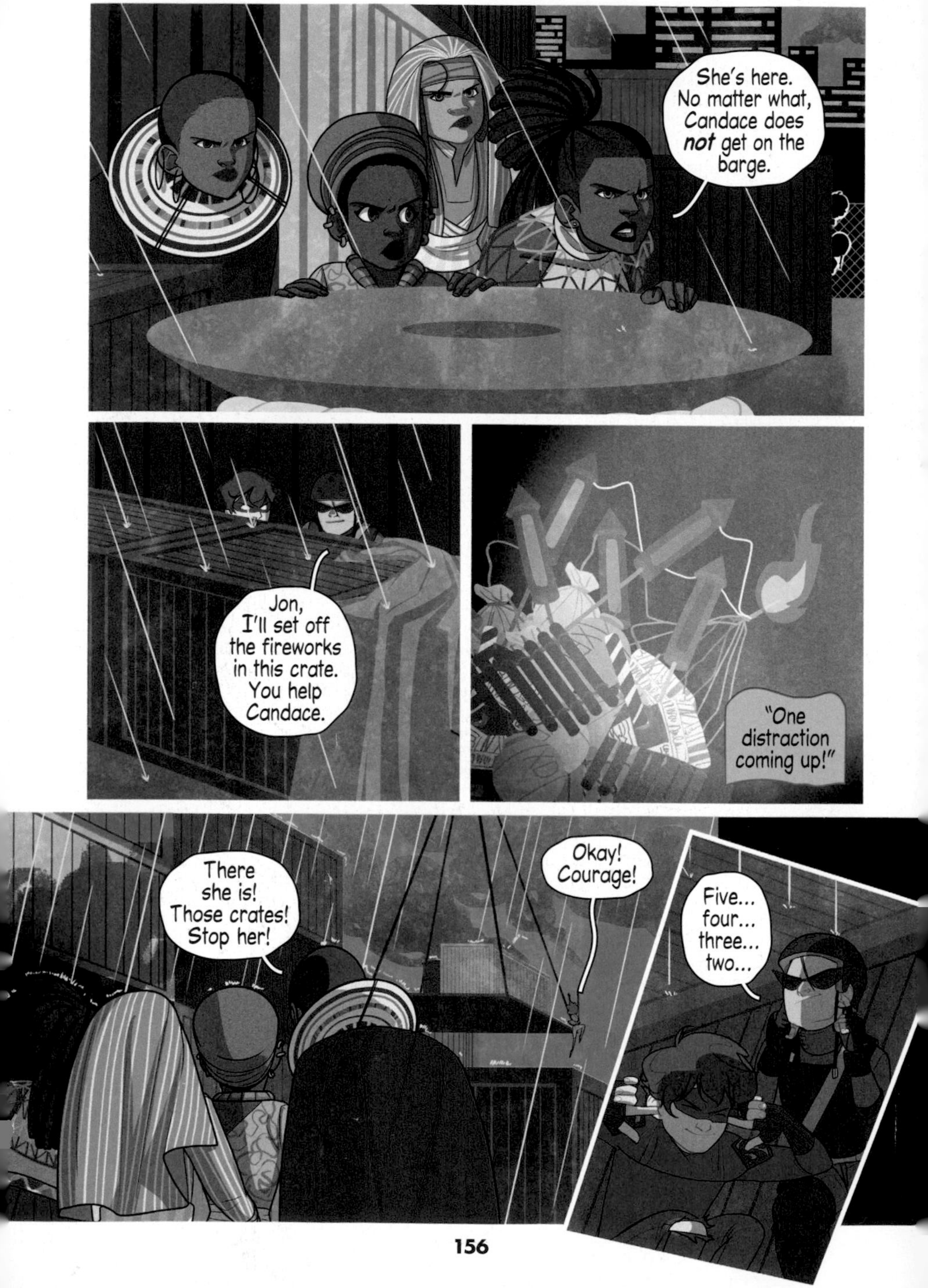
She's here. No matter what, Candace does ***not*** get on the barge.
Jon, I'll set off the fireworks in this crate. You help Candace.
"One distraction coming up!"
There she is! Those crates! Stop her!
Okay! Courage!
Five... four... three... two...

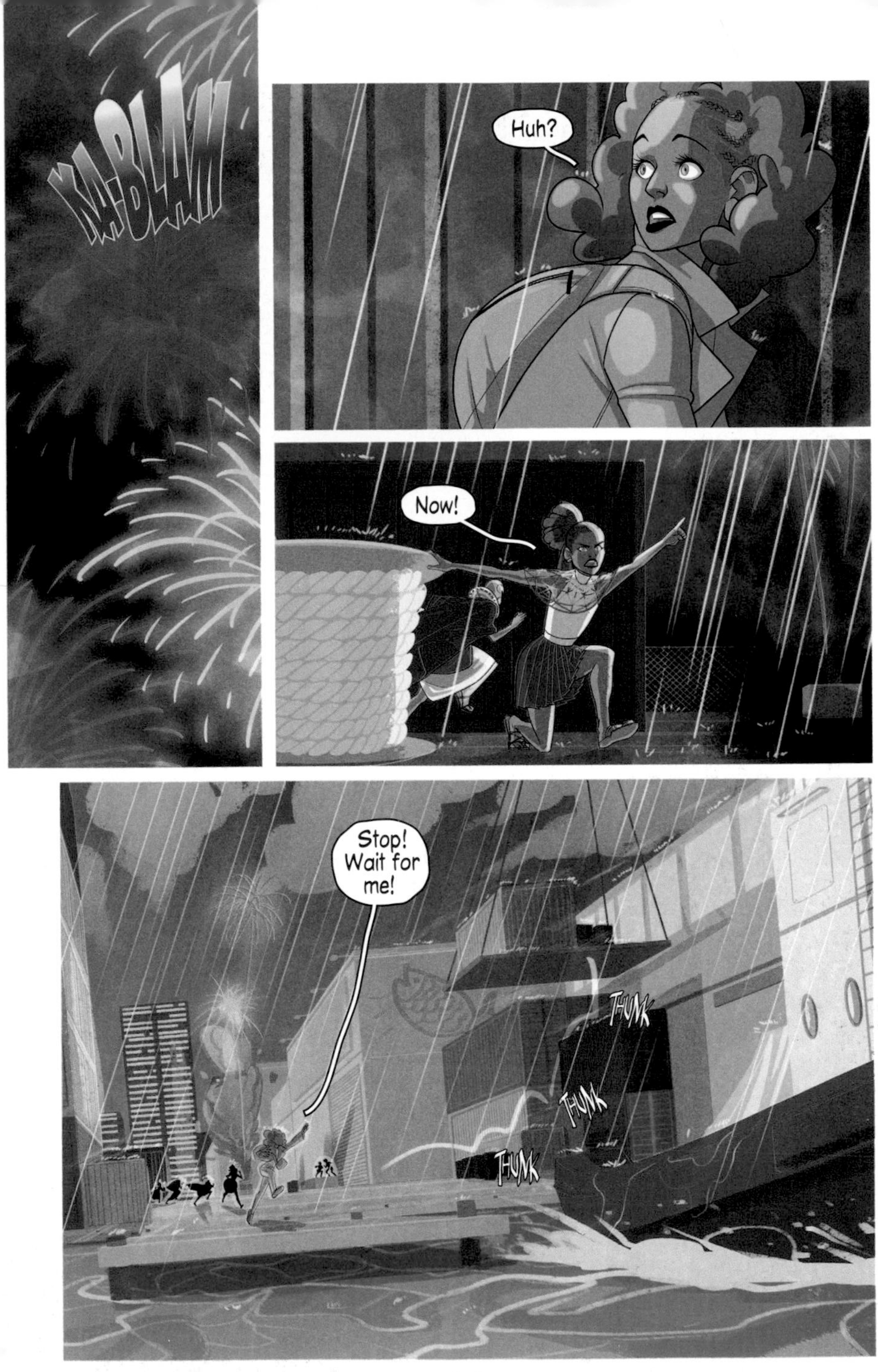
KA-BLAM
Huh?
Now!
Stop! Wait for me!
THUNK
THUNK
THUNK

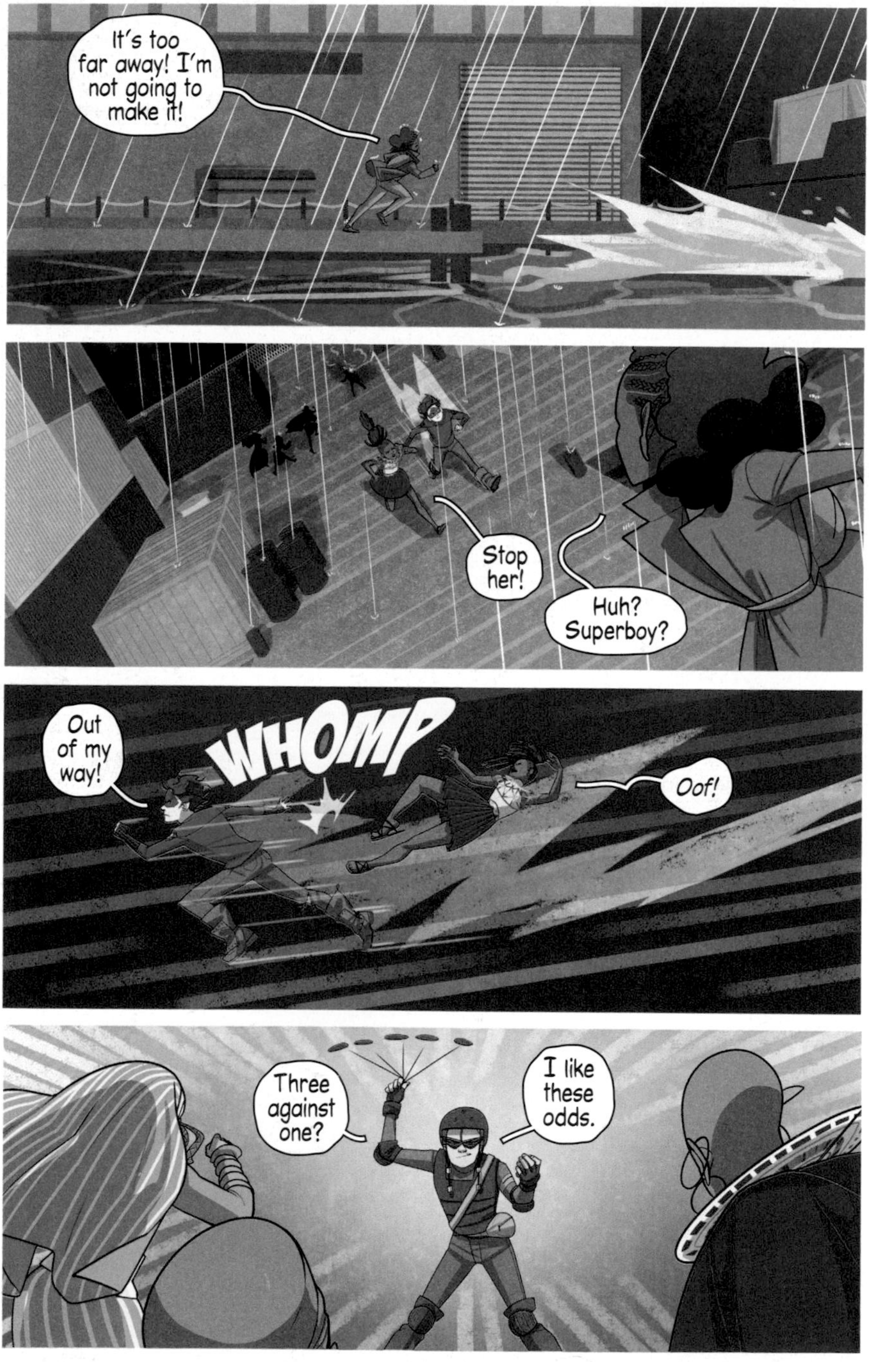
It's too far away! I'm not going to make it!
Stop her!
Huh? Superboy?
Out of my way!
WHOMP
Oof!
Three against one?
I like these odds.

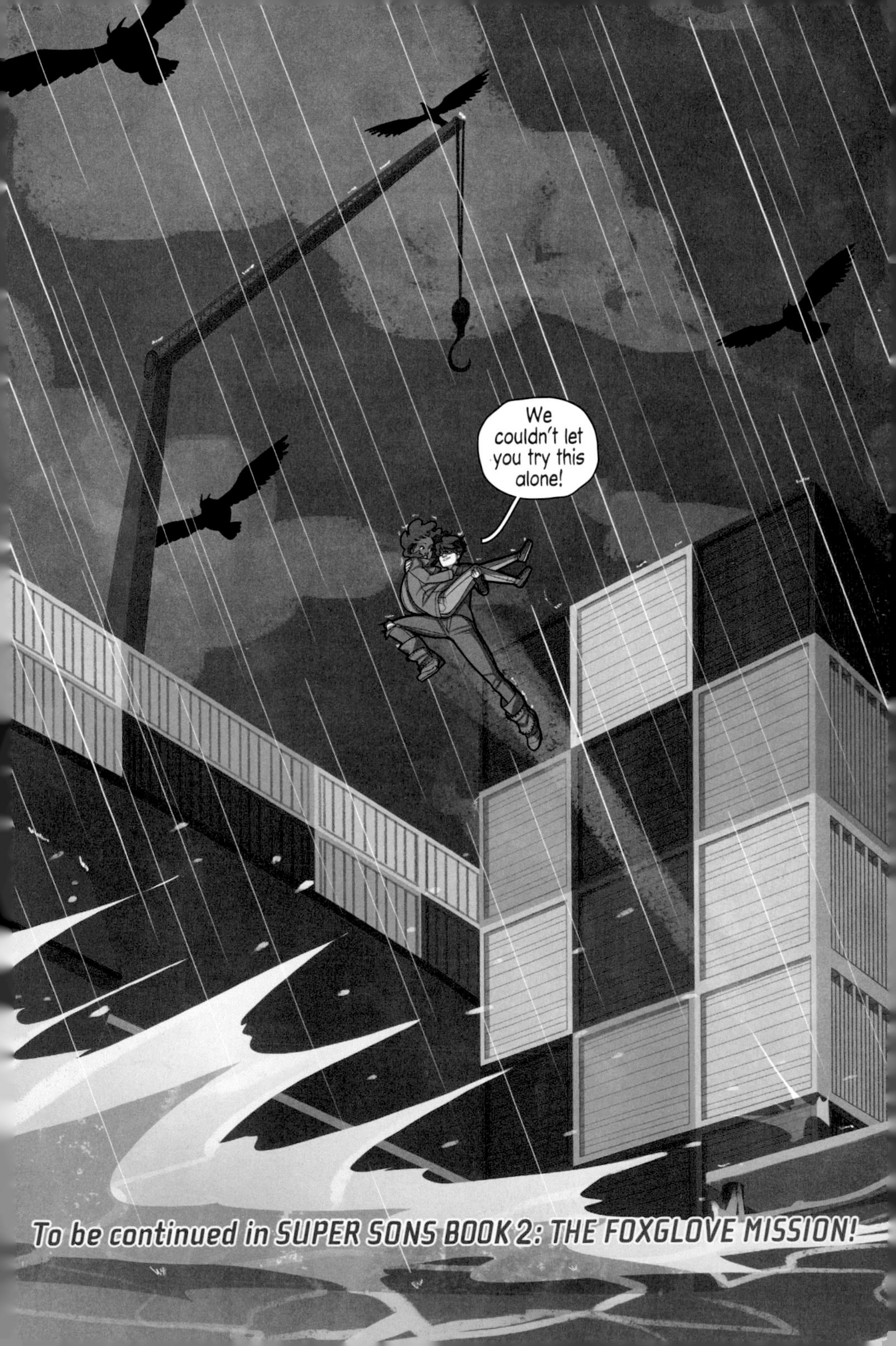
We couldn't let you try this alone!
To be continued in SUPER SONS BOOK 2: THE FOXGLOVE MISSION!

Join your favorite Justice League heroes as they face their greatest challenge yet... answering fan mail?

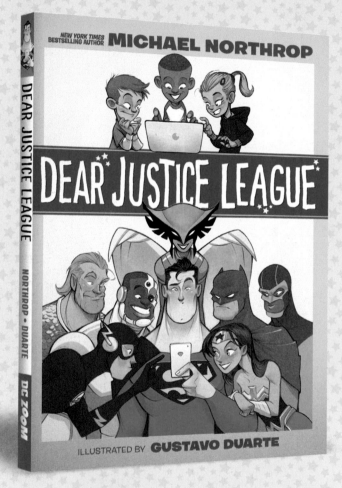

New York Times bestselling author **Michael Northrop** and illustrator **Gustavo Duarte** present this special chapter from *Dear Justice League,* on sale 8/6/2019!

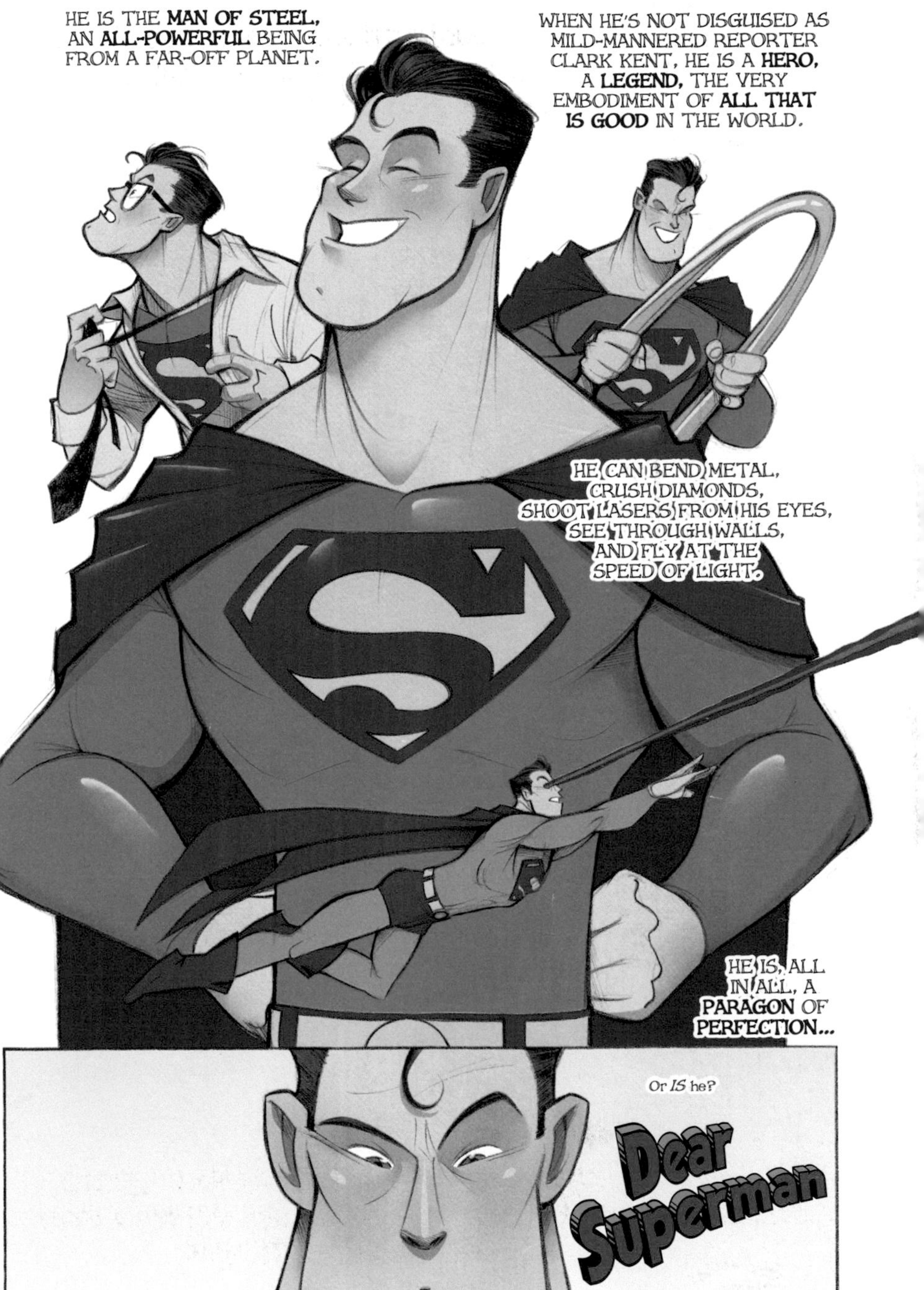
HE IS THE MAN OF STEEL, AN ALL-POWERFUL BEING FROM A FAR-OFF PLANET.
WHEN HE'S NOT DISGUISED AS MILD-MANNERED REPORTER CLARK KENT, HE IS A HERO, A LEGEND, THE VERY EMBODIMENT OF ALL THAT IS GOOD IN THE WORLD.
HE CAN BEND METAL, CRUSH DIAMONDS, SHOOT LASERS FROM HIS EYES, SEE THROUGH WALLS, AND FLY AT THE SPEED OF LIGHT.
HE IS, ALL IN ALL, A PARAGON OF PERFECTION...
Or IS he?
Dear Superman

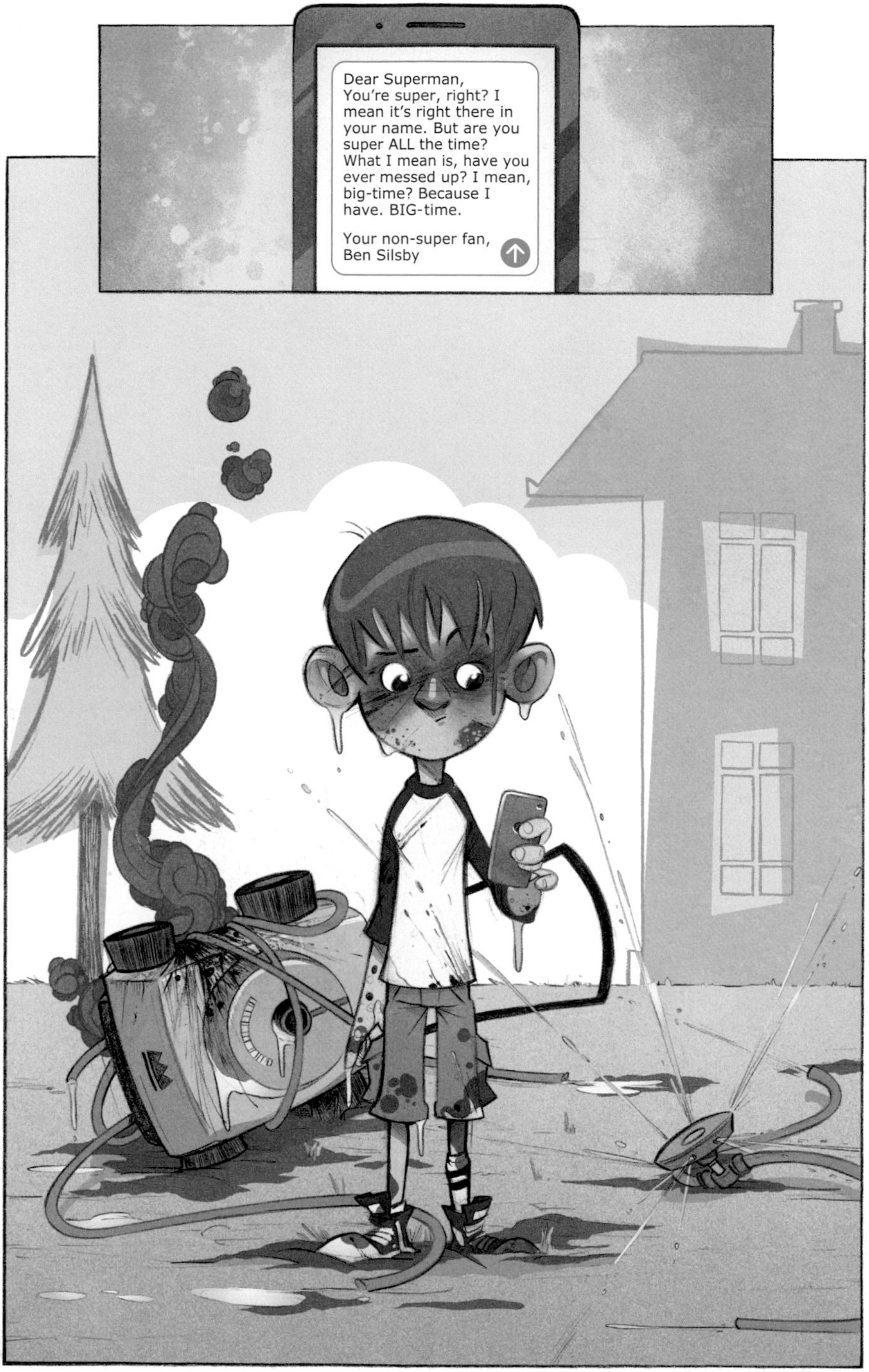
Dear Superman,
You're super, right? I mean it's right there in your name. But are you super ALL the time? What I mean is, have you ever messed up? I mean, big-time? Because I have. BIG-time.
Your non-super fan,
Ben Silsby

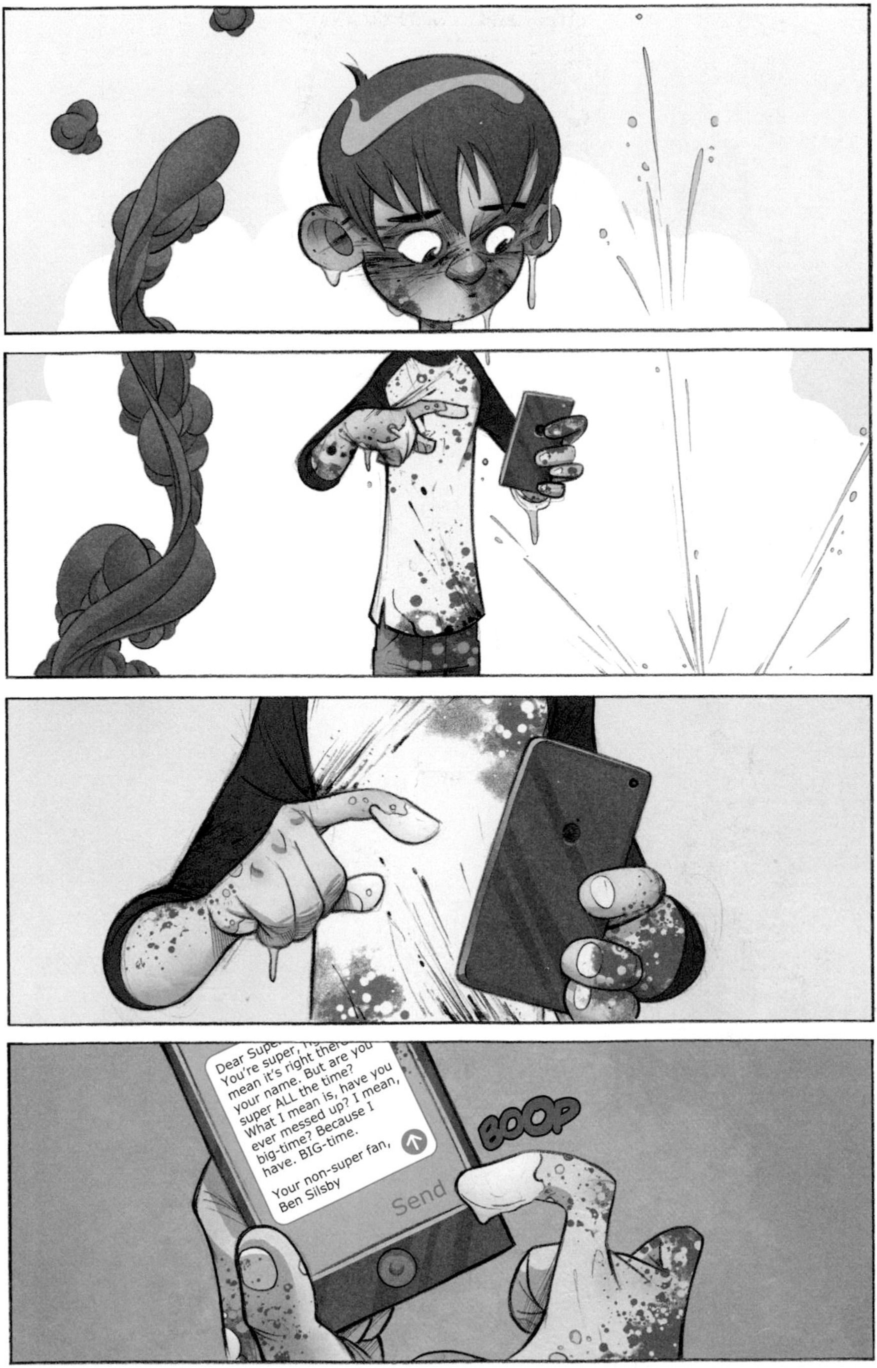

Dear
You're super,
mean it's right
your name. But are you
super ALL the time?
What I mean is, have you
ever messed up? I mean,
big-time? Because I
have. BIG-time.
Your non-super fan,
Ben Silsby
Send
BOOP

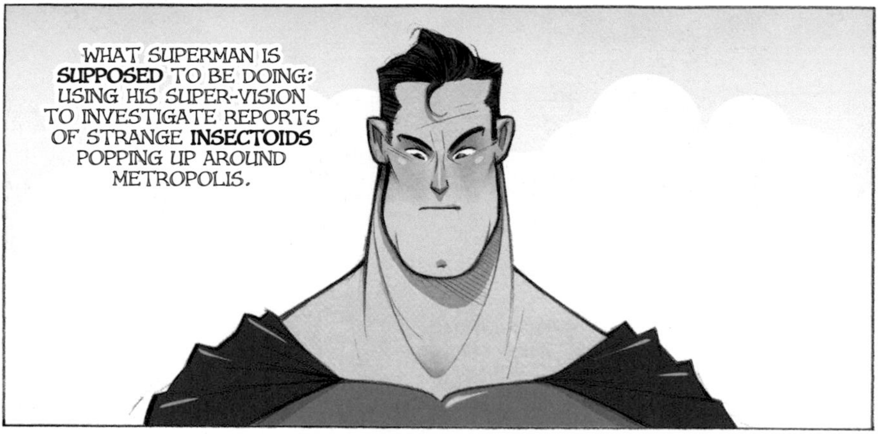
WHAT SUPERMAN IS **SUPPOSED** TO BE DOING: USING HIS SUPER-VISION TO INVESTIGATE REPORTS OF STRANGE **INSECTOIDS** POPPING UP AROUND METROPOLIS.

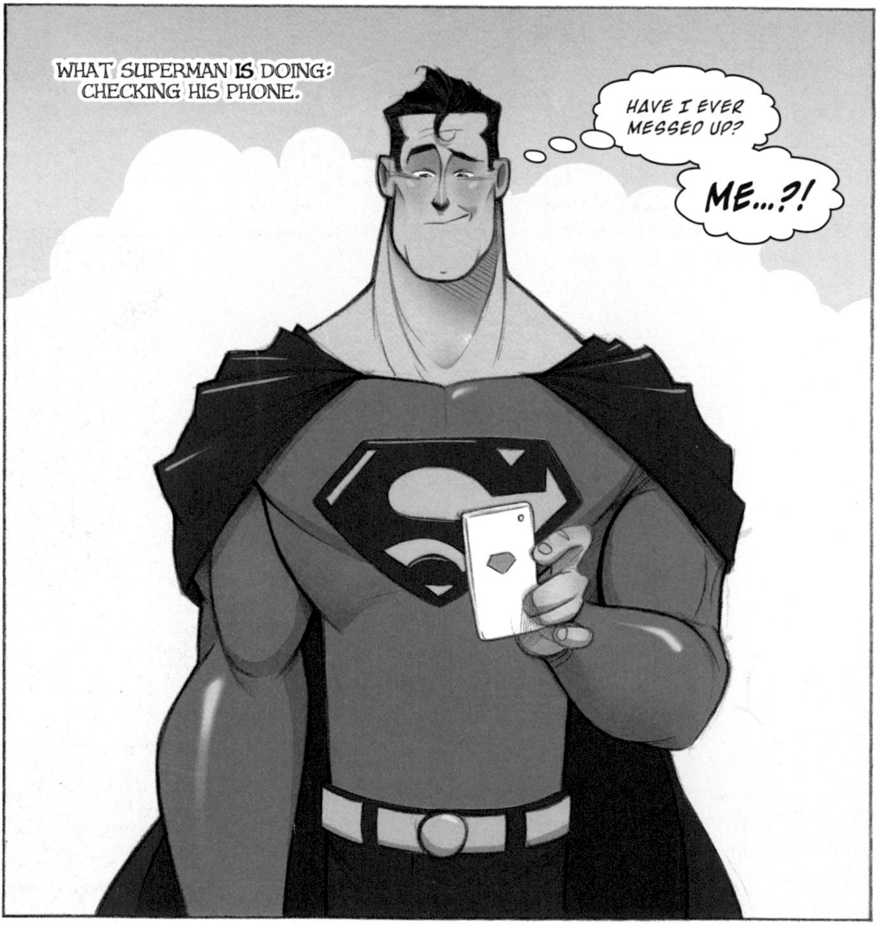
WHAT SUPERMAN **IS** DOING: CHECKING HIS PHONE.
HAVE I EVER MESSED UP?
ME...?!

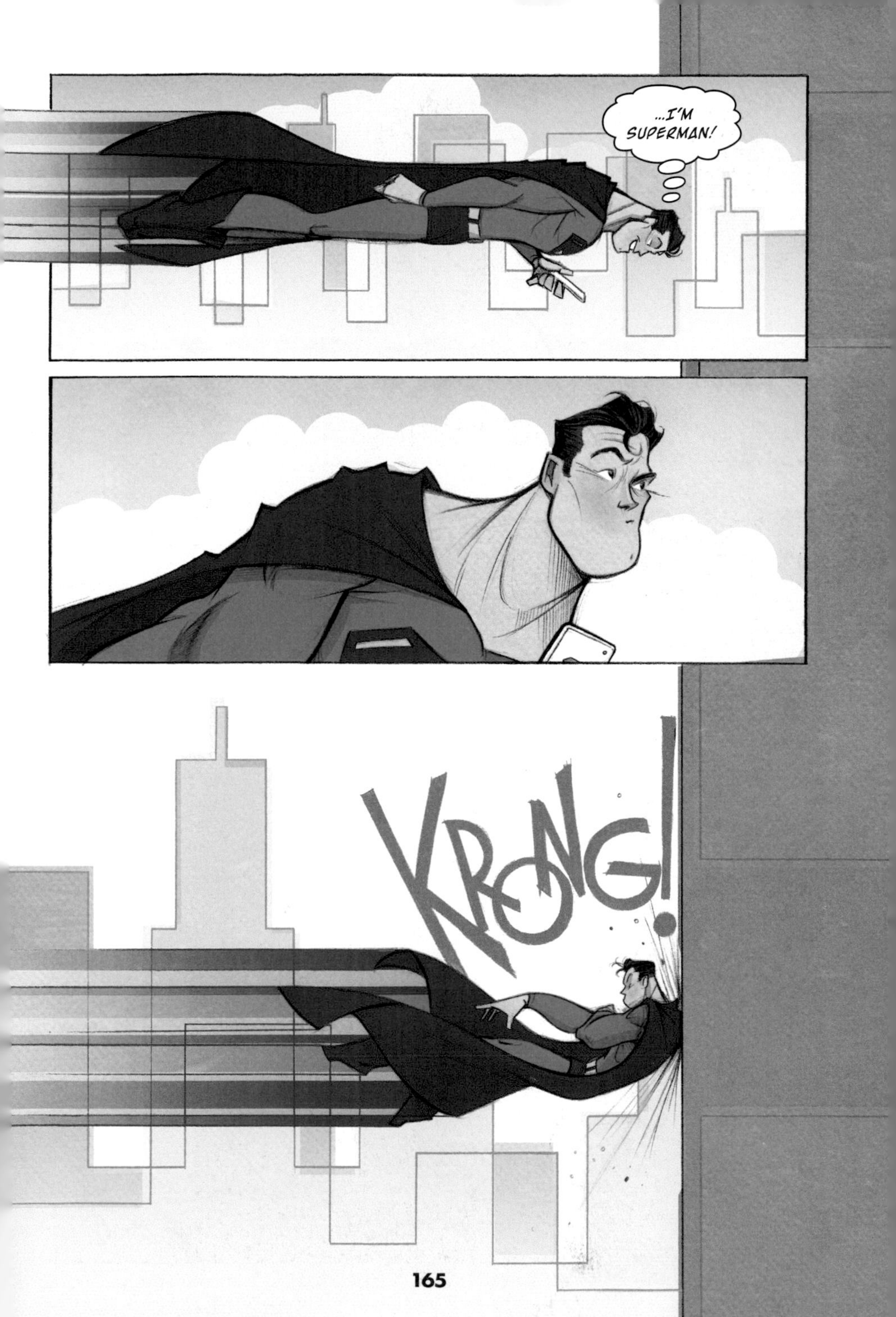
...I'M SUPERMAN!
KRONG!

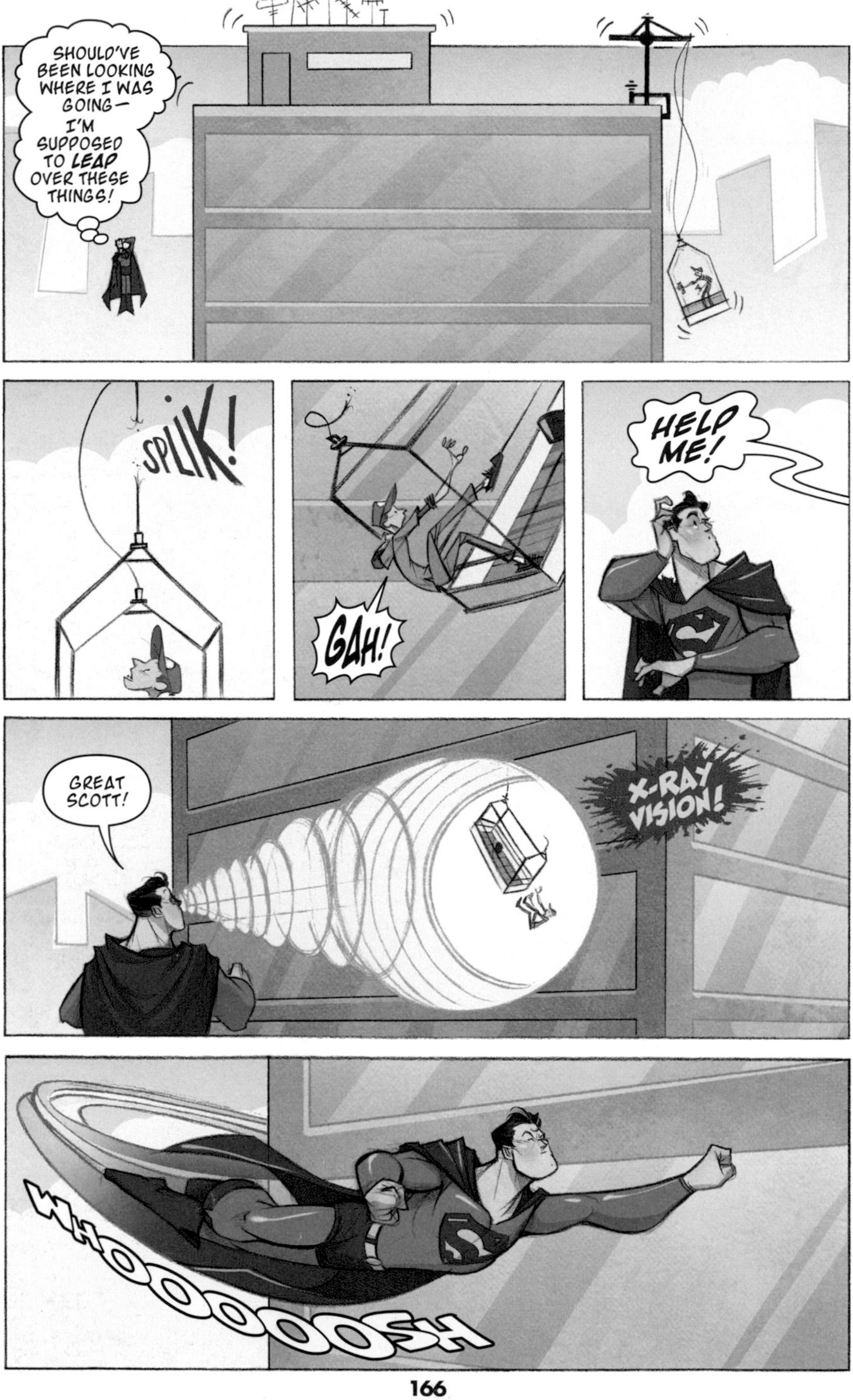
SHOULD'VE BEEN LOOKING WHERE I WAS GOING— I'M SUPPOSED TO LEAP OVER THESE THINGS!
SPLIK!
GAH!
HELP ME!
GREAT SCOTT!
X-RAY VISION!
WHOOOOOOSH

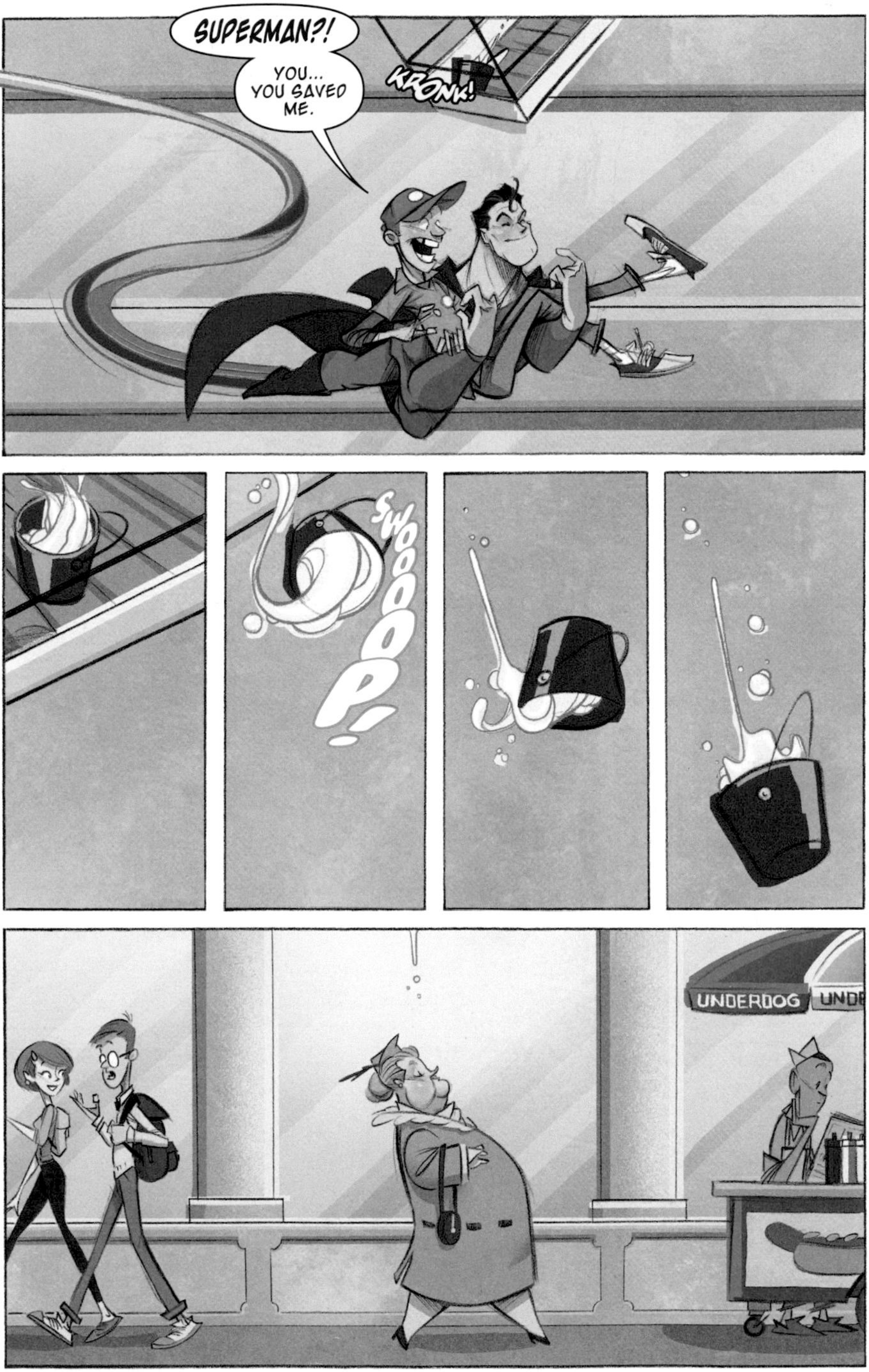
SUPERMAN?!
YOU... YOU SAVED ME.
KRONK!
SWOOOOOP!
UNDERDOG
UND

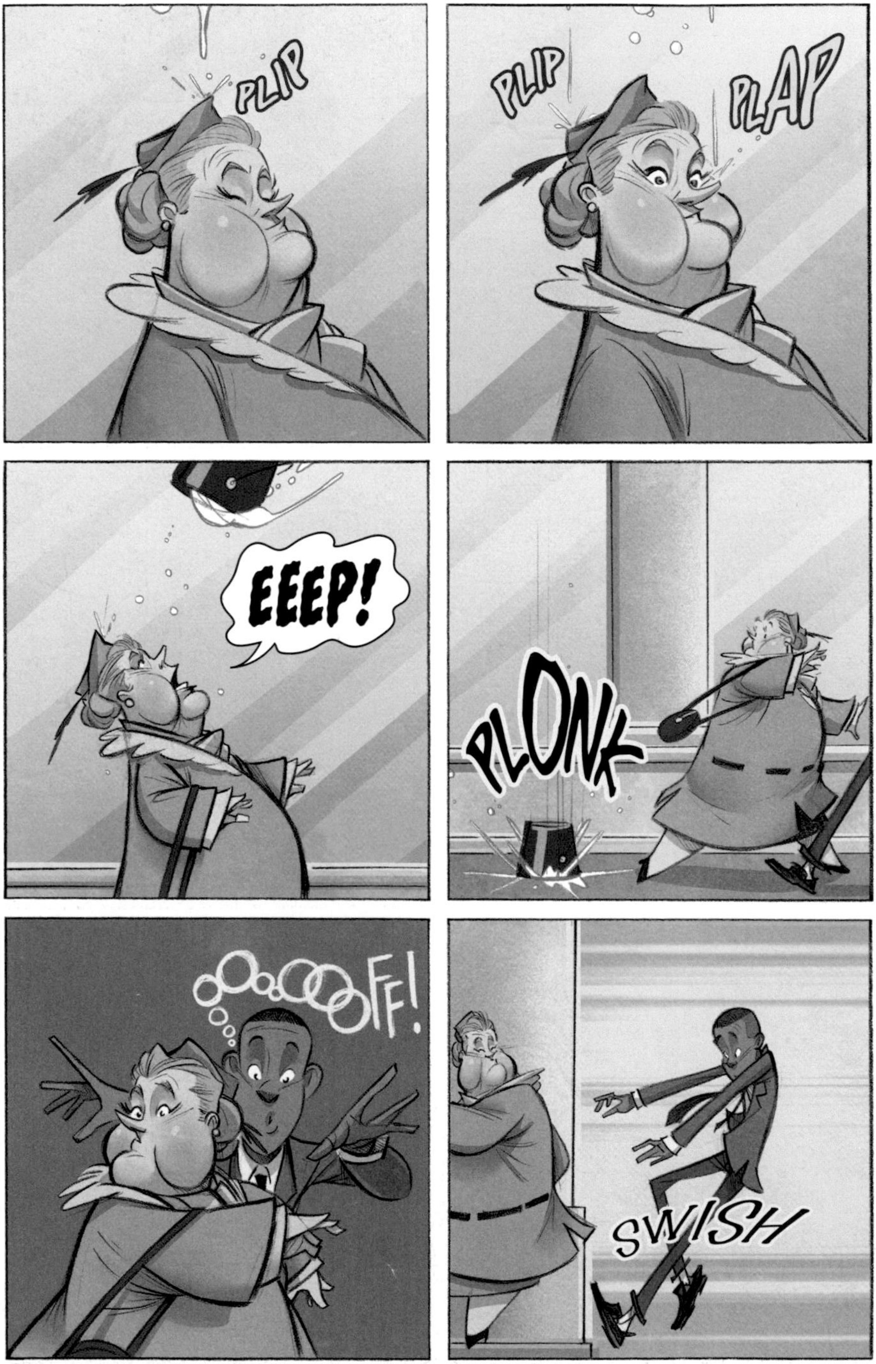
PLIP
PLIP
PLAP
EEEP!
PLONK
OOOOOOOFF!
SWISH

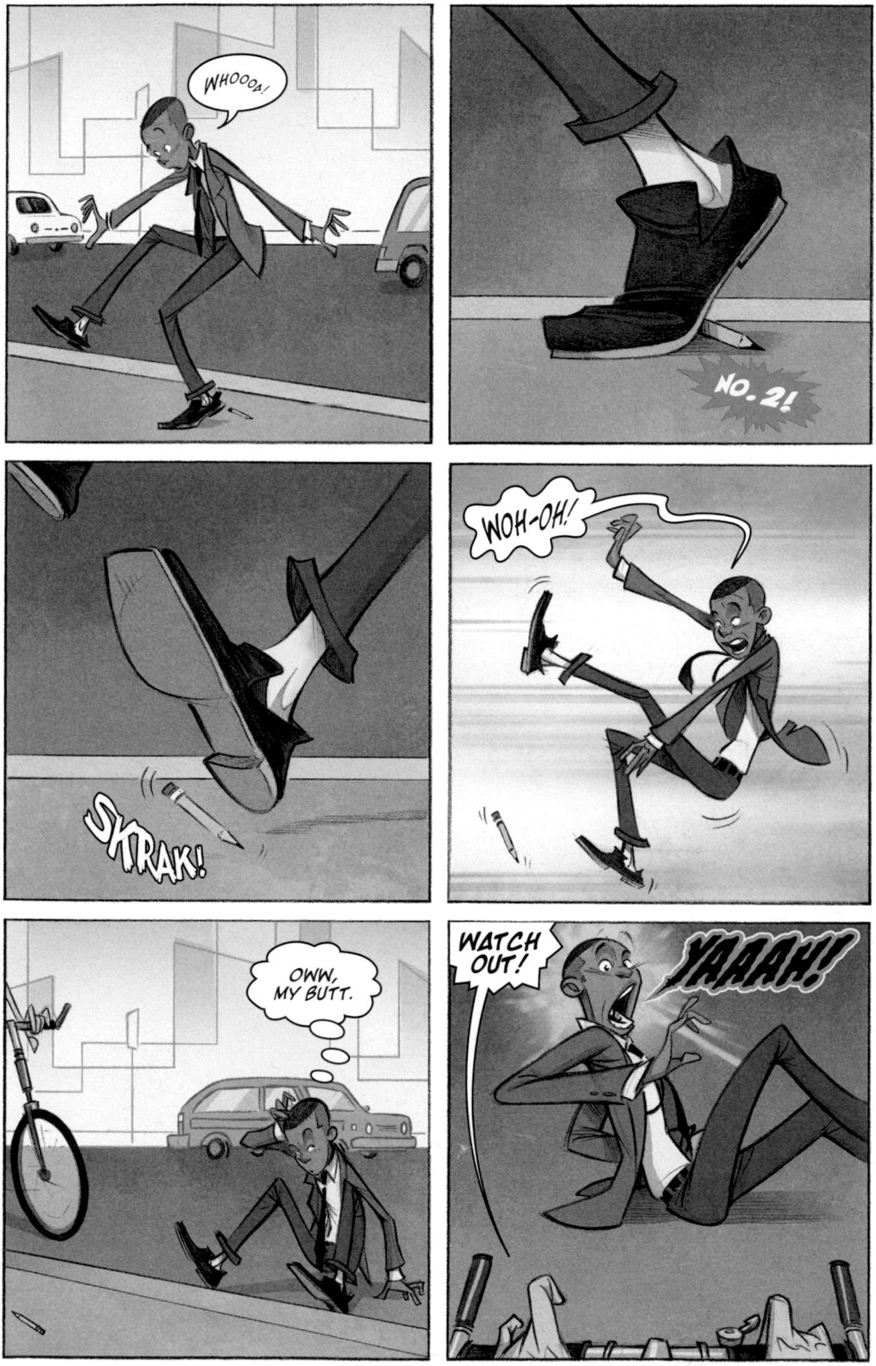
WHOOOA!
NO. 2!
SKRAK!
WOH-OH!
OWW, MY BUTT.
WATCH OUT!
YAAAH!

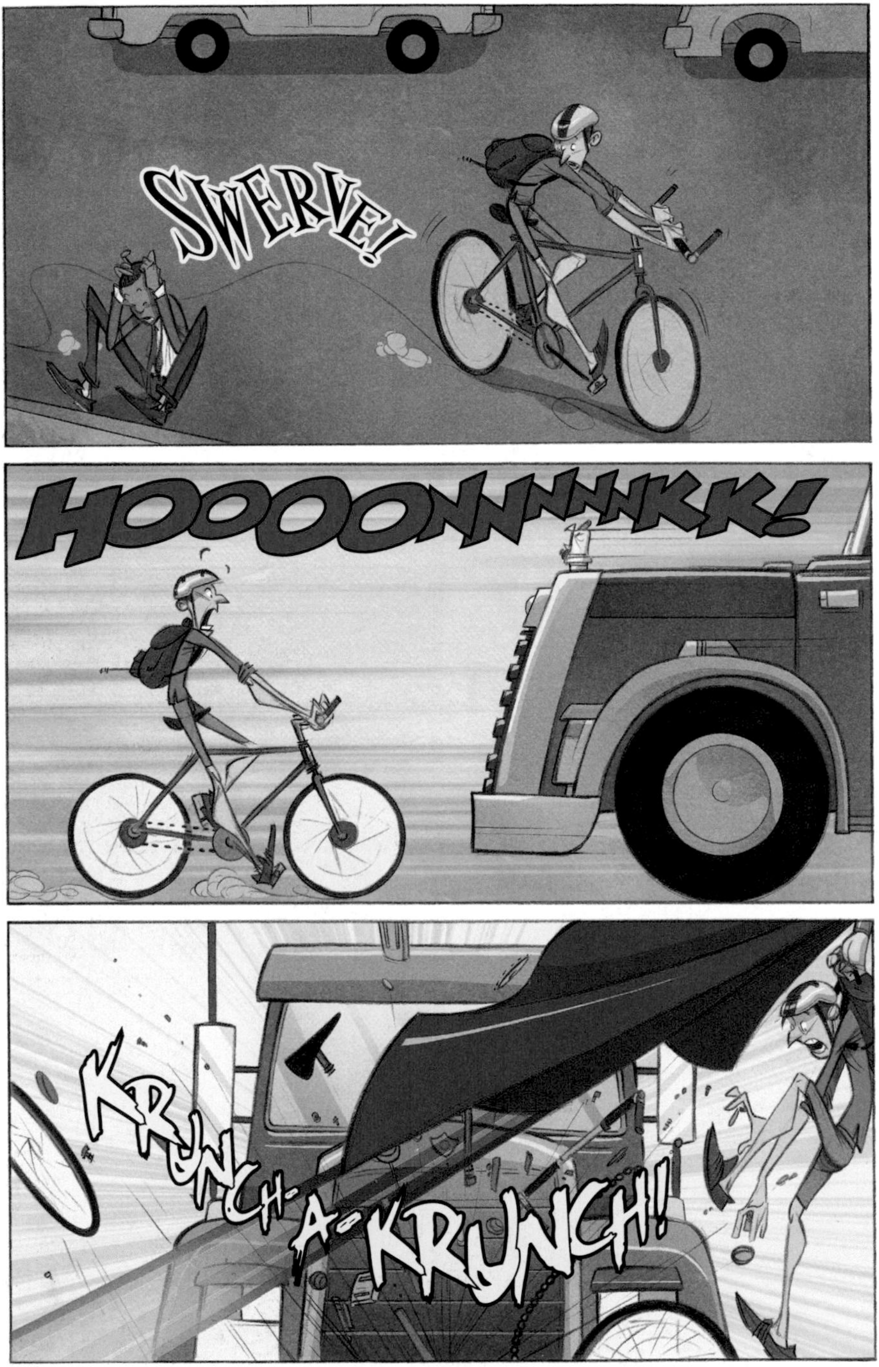
SWERVE!
HOOOONNNNKK!
KRUNCH-A-KRUNCH!

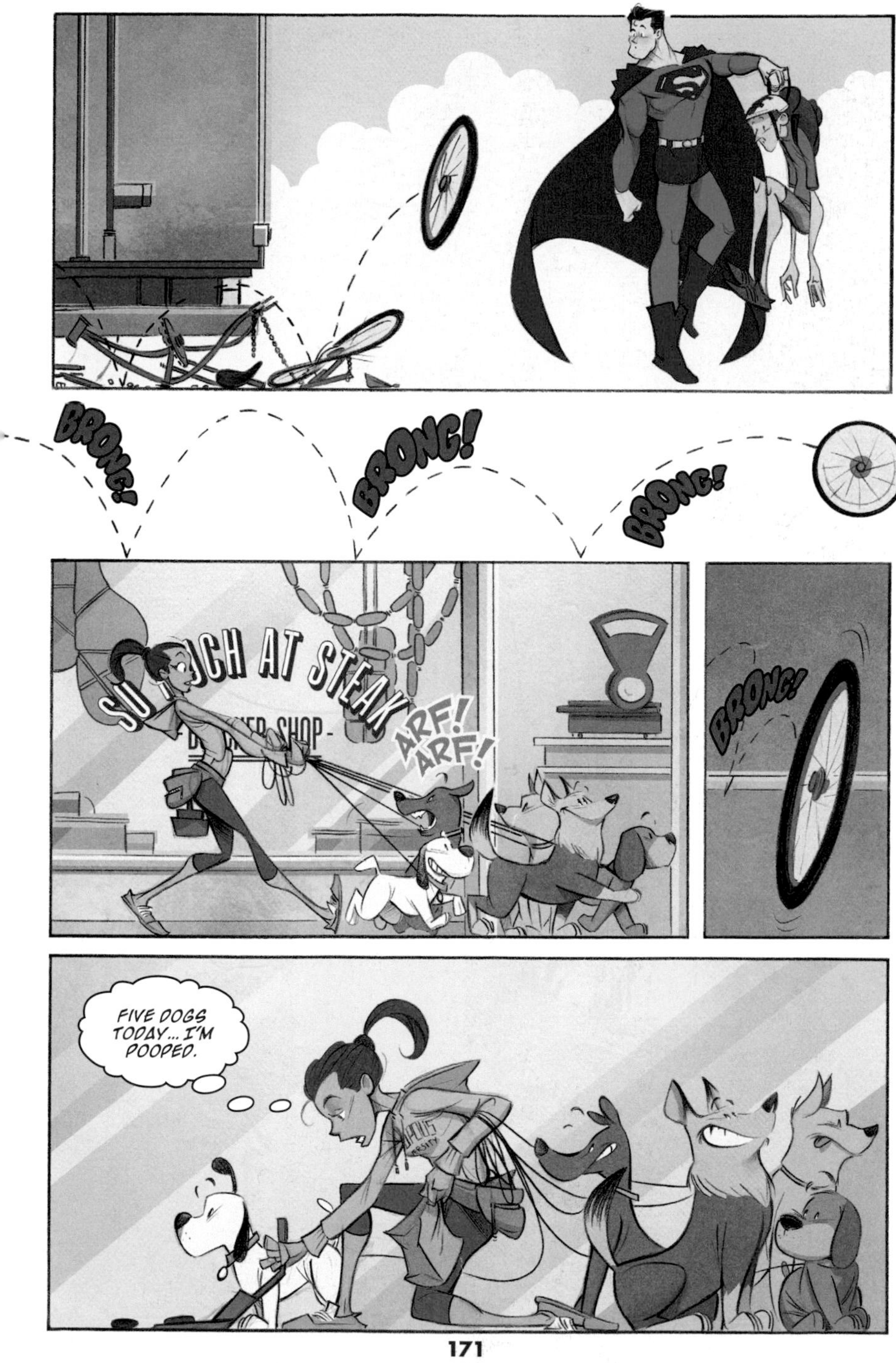
BRONG!
BRONG!
BRONG!
ARF! ARF!
BRONG!
FIVE DOGS TODAY... I'M POOPED.

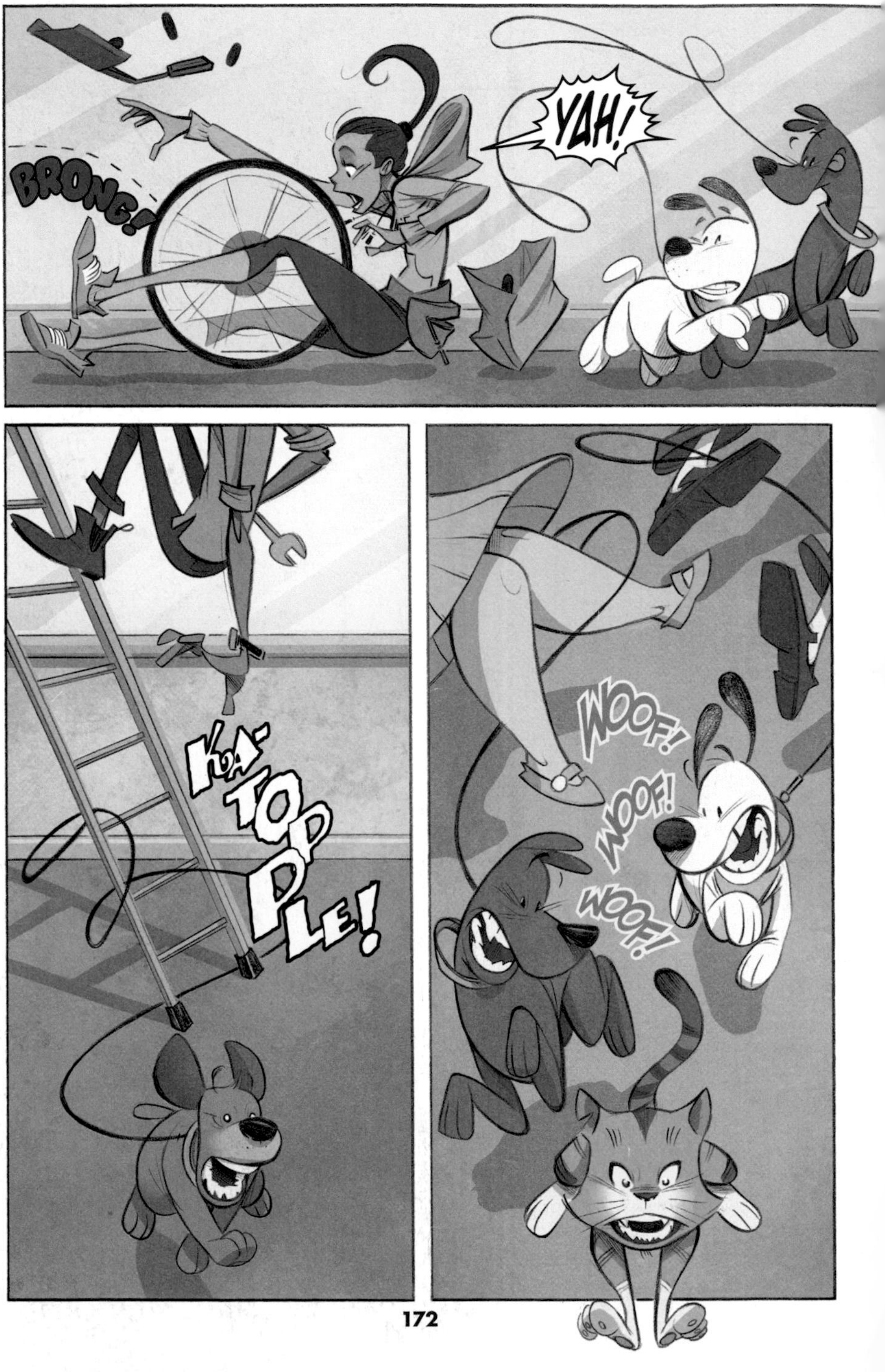
BRONG!
YAH!
KA-TOPPLE!
WOOF!
WOOF!
WOOF!

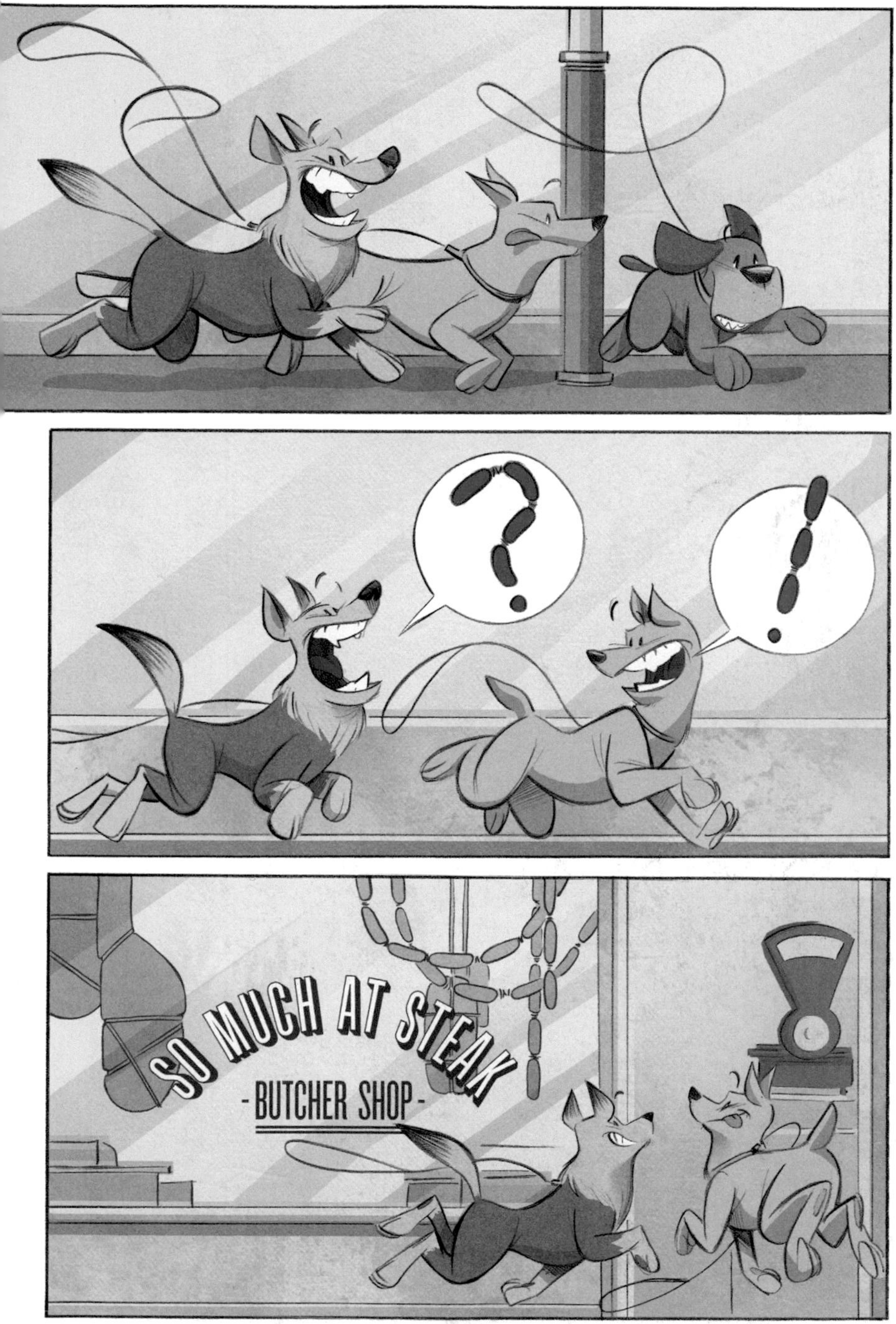
?
!
SO MUCH AT STEAK
-BUTCHER SHOP-

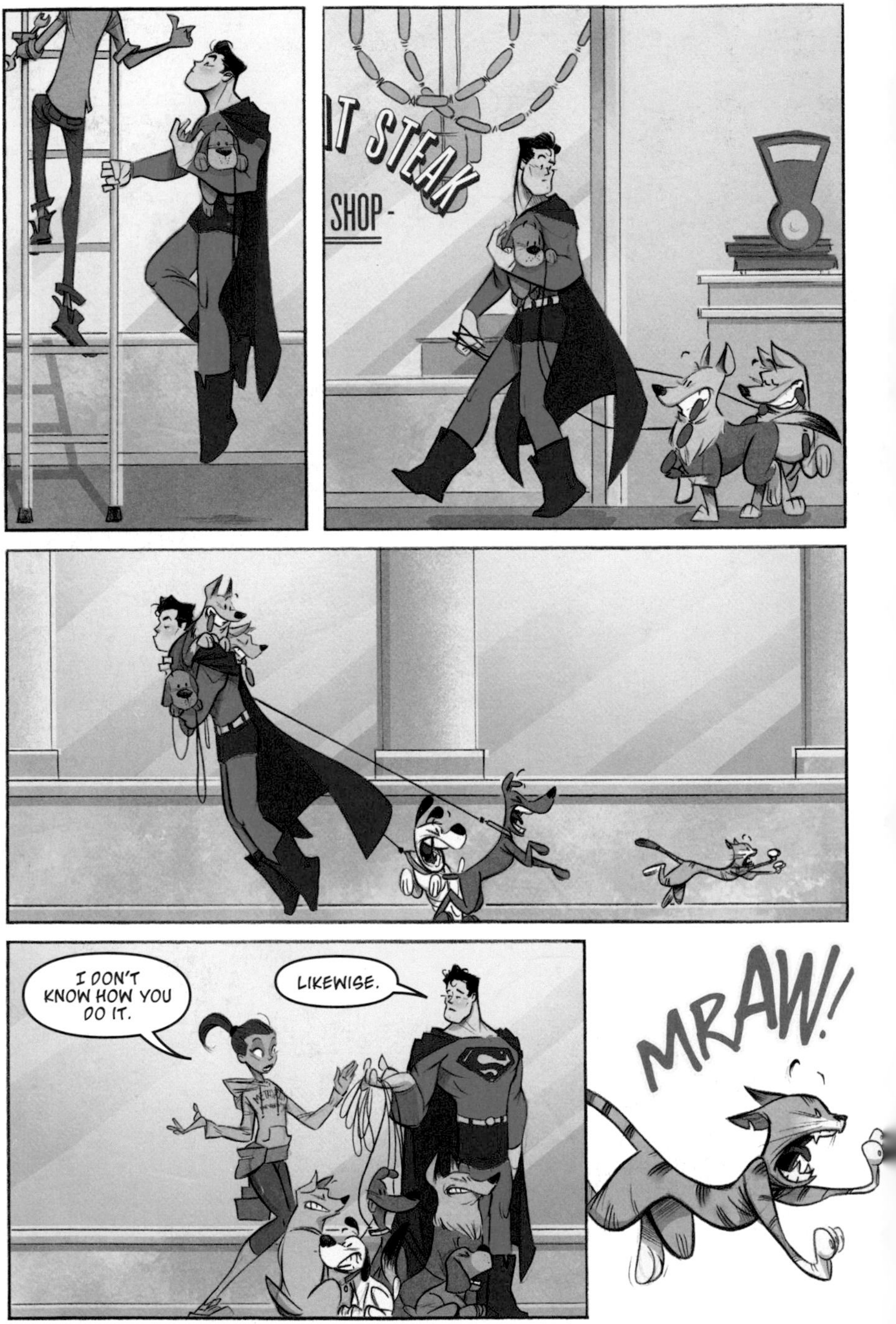
AT STEAK
SHOP -
I DON'T KNOW HOW YOU DO IT.
LIKEWISE.
MRAW!!

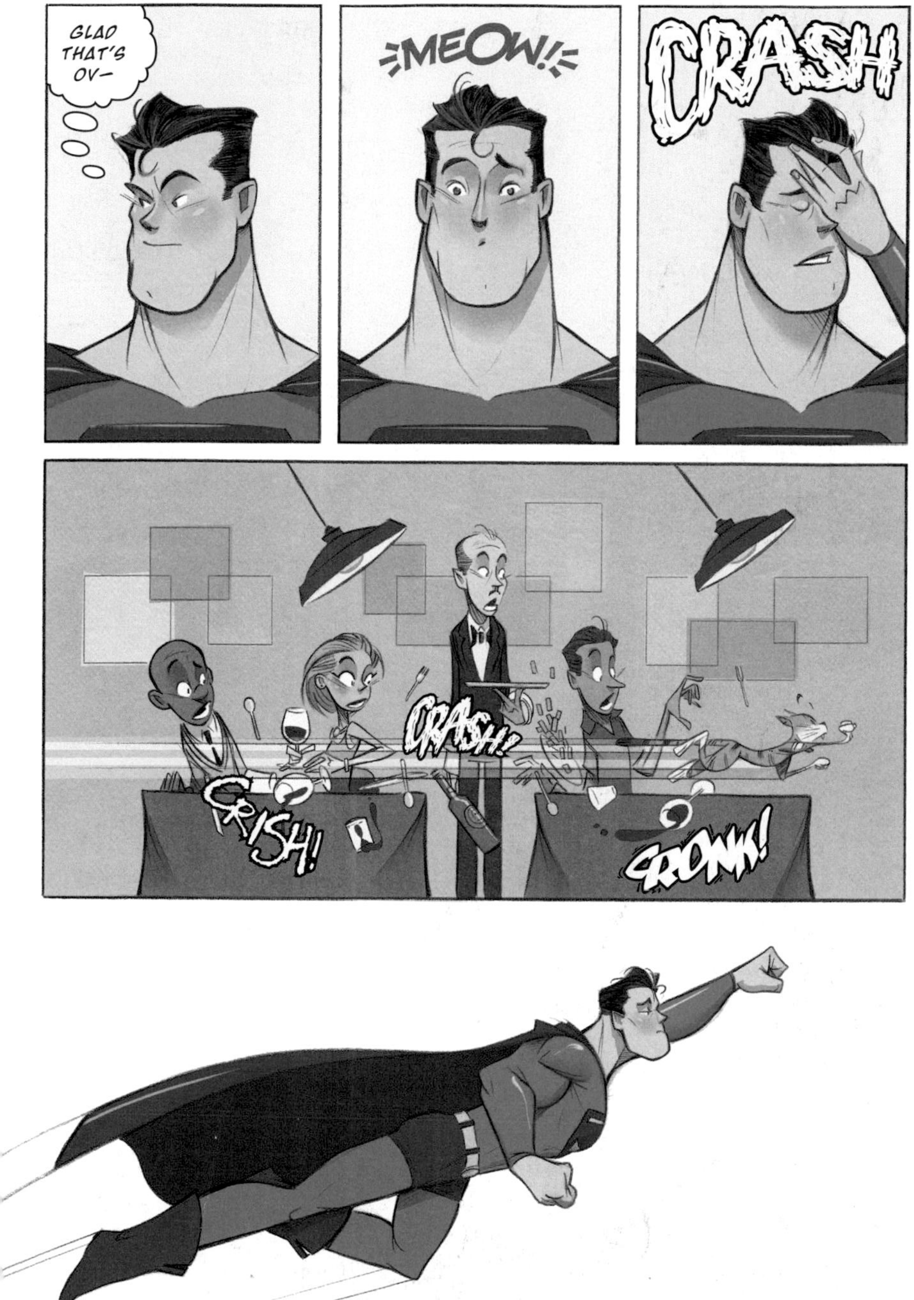
GLAD THAT'S OV—
MEOW!
CRASH
CRASH!
CRISH!
CRONK!

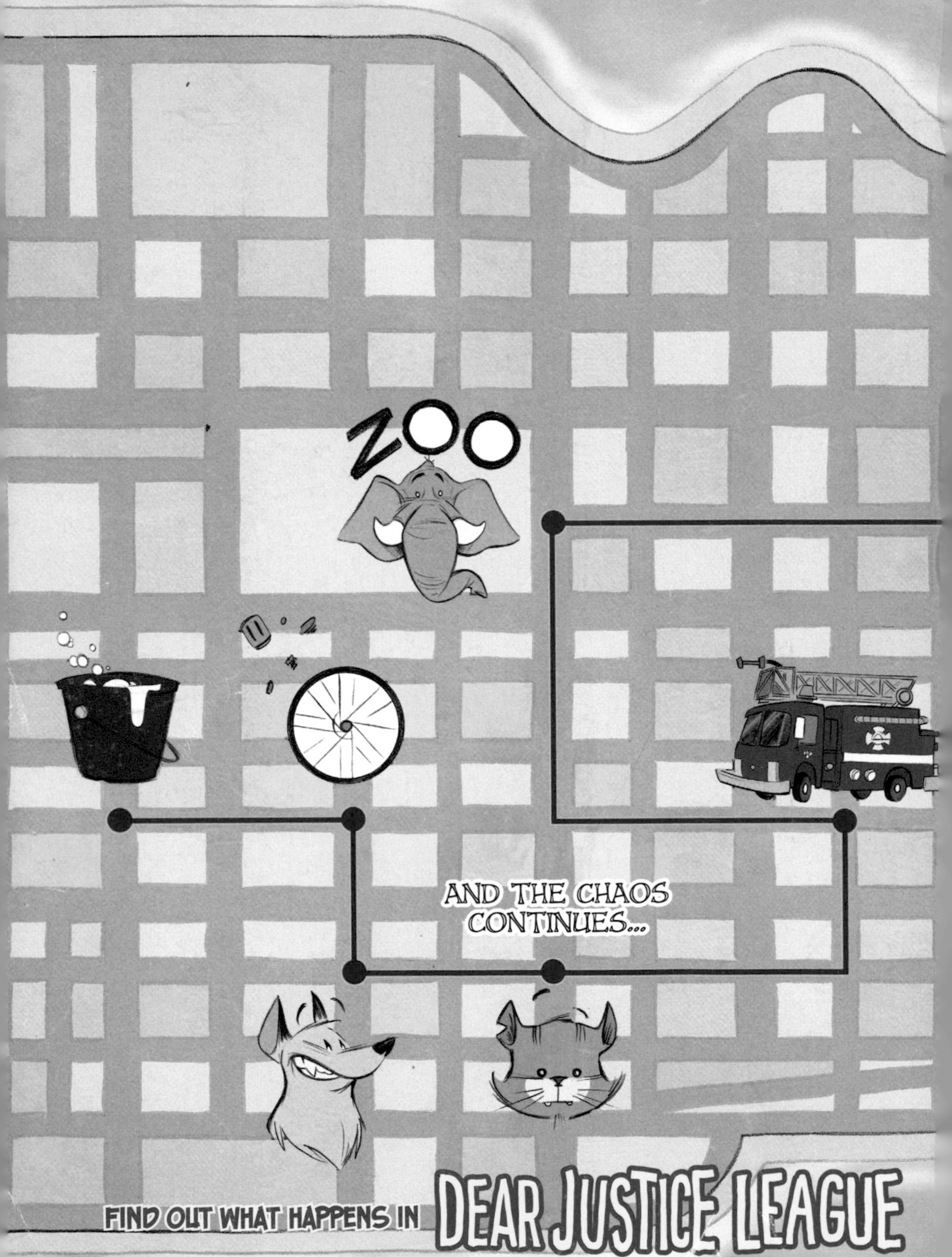
ZOO
AND THE CHAOS CONTINUES...
FIND OUT WHAT HAPPENS IN DEAR JUSTICE LEAGUE